Sherri Schoenborn Murray

The *Piano* Girl

Counterfeit Princess Series

Book One

Sherri Schoenborn
MURRAY

Visit Sherri's website:
www.christianromances.com

The Piano Girl
Christian Romances LLC

Cover photo of Alia by Clari Noel Photography
Edited by: Cori Murray, Kristi Weber and Carolyn Rose Editing

To my daughters—
Eilee and Cori
I promise to never serve you chalky milk.

ΦΦΦ

Tune your ears to wisdom, and
incline your heart to understanding.
PROVERBS 2:2.

Prologue
Blue Sky Kingdom · 1869

To listen well can be a gift.

My father distinctly remembered the first time that I discovered the keys of our grand piano. I had just turned three and happened upon them by chance. The sound the keys made under my fingertips startled me, and I cried. Father scooped me into his arms and comforted me while Mother laughed softly.

I soon wiggled out of his embrace and bravely plodded back to the huge black beast. On tiptoe, I pressed down on one of its ivory teeth and, turning one ear to the sound, stared wide-eyed at Father. He watched in amazement as *I listened*. One by one, I played each key, turned my ear, and listened to the beast.

"You've heard of my great-aunt Victoria?" Father addressed Mother.

"Yes, of course, but you can't possibly think? Why, Alia's a toddler. She's simply curious."

Father strode to the piano and picked me up. I whimpered, holding my arms out toward the beast. Yet, instead of sweeping me away, he sat down in the middle of the bench, providing me a view of the beast's teeth. I stopped crying.

Using the forefinger of my right hand, I pressed down on the center white key. It made a pleasant sound. Turning my head, I smiled up at him. I leaned my ear and listened until the sound faded.

I proceeded to play each key and listen to each sound. Father said I reminded him of our piano tuner, who was blind. I listened deeper than the normal person can, and I relished the unique tone of each key.

"She is being unusually patient," Mother said.

"She is entranced. Call in Louise," he addressed one of our servants.

"Francis!" Mother giggled at my father's enthusiasm.

Louise was our royal pianist. She had tar-black hair, which she wore spiraled on the top of her head. She played whenever my parents desired—during meals, banquets, my mother's coffee parties . . .

"Play something simple for Alia," Father told Louise, and then he carried me away from the piano. "Now, do not fuss, Princess. I want you to listen." He ran a hand through my auburn curls. "Something simple," he repeated to Louise.

Something simple to Louise was six notes, three on each hand. She played "The Ballad of Blue Sky," our national anthem, and I stiffened in Father's arms. I listened so intently that when Louise finally stopped, I lay exhausted against him.

I was supposedly asleep on the settee when my parents took supper in the dining room that same evening. Father heard the music first. Someone was playing a two- and three-note tune, something familiar, but half of the melody was missing. Father chewed slowly and listened intently. Mother said that his face paled a bit as he strained to hear, and then he pushed back his chair.

In the Great Hall, he saw that I had climbed up on the bench. Kneeling, I was able to see the keys as I stretched out my wee fingers. It was a simple version of Louise's song, "The Ballad of Blue Sky."

Mother joined Father in the doorway, leaning her head against his shoulder.

"You were right, Francis. She has a remarkable gift."

When I was growing up, this was my favorite story about Father and me. The war started the following year, shortly before I turned four, and lasted until two weeks before my sixteenth birthday. Much is required of a king during war; and my father, a strategist at heart, thrived on it.

Chapter One

Thirteen years later . . .

In Blue Sky, it is tradition for a maiden, on her sixteenth birthday, to choose the recipient of her first kiss. I, Princess Alia Dory Vankern Wells, intended to follow tradition.

Over four hundred distinguished guests gathered in the ballroom for my party. I knew only a handful by name. While many discussed the conclusion of the Twelve-Year War or enjoyed fine hors d'oeuvres or one of the sixteen different layer cakes, I danced with my father.

"If the war is over, Father, why are you still studying maps?" I smiled up into his hazel eyes. "I saw you today in your study."

"It's very important, Alia, to focus on the moment. Right now, I am dancing with my lovely daughter." He waltzed me about the ballroom. The layered hems of my sky-blue dress teased the floor, and auburn curls spilled out of my high bun.

He'd evaded my question, but he'd given me a rare compliment, a gift. *Lovely*. Though I was known throughout the land for my creamy complexion and for never having a blemish, such a compliment from Father was more precious than the jade ring he'd surprised me with that morning.

Next, I danced with an elderly man, the king of Nearton. In his frail arms, I scanned the ballroom. Decorated war generals and latent kings, but no man under the age of fifty appeared to be at my party. And I looked so beautiful. Not even Pierre was anywhere to be seen. Not only was he my French tutor, he'd taught me the krassant. After dancing with others, I'd known that he was gifted.

As I scanned the periphery of the room, a red braid caught my eye. The tail of my younger sister's hair stuck out from the edge of the floor-to-ceiling drapes. The little spy! At this hour, she was supposed to be in bed.

"Happy birthday, Princess Alia." Without turning my head, I knew it was King Lorenzo's oldest son. Dell bowed before me, hiding his liverish complexion. If he was under fifty, it was just barely. "The first rose of summer is in bloom. May I show you?"

"Ohh!" I was delighted. For the first rose to open on my birthday was a very good sign. "Where did you see it?"

"Allow me." Dell escorted me toward the French doors. I was only too happy to accompany him. If a rose had indeed opened on my birthday, it meant a year of blessings. In the courtyard, I searched Mother's rosebushes, which bordered the bronze statue of my grandfather, King Francis I. There were only tightly closed buds.

"Here," he said, his attention on a section I had not yet inspected. I neared, craning my neck to see, and then with the swoop of a hawk, Dell grabbed me by the shoulders and clamped his clammy mouth on mine.

My kiss! I slapped my hand across his cheek and screamed—one of those heart-wrenching, blood-curdling screams telling everyone a maiden's first kiss has been stolen.

"You are a vixen." Dell smiled with two large rows of teeth.

"You are revolting!"

Three guards rushed into the courtyard, accompanied by my father. I ran to him, and pressing my cheek against his chest, I sobbed. "He stole my kiss!"

"Dell, you are to leave immediately." Father turned to our guards. "Escort him to his carriage, and be certain he leaves the grounds." Patting my arm, Father led me back inside the ballroom, with its marble floors and infirmary of well-dressed guests.

"My *first* kiss," I mumbled.

"There will be other first kisses, Alia."

Though I was shaking, he led me toward the piano. With a clap of his hands, he drew the attention of our guests. "My daughter Alia will now play."

"No." I grimaced. I played piano purely from emotion, and our guests did not want to hear of a stolen kiss, lies, and broken dreams.

"My daughter will now play." With a sweep of his hand, Father motioned for me to take a seat at the Great Beast.

I smoothed the layers of chiffon behind me, sat down, and stared straight ahead. At the far end of the room, my sister's red braid poked out from the left side of the curtain, within feet of where Mother stood speaking with the queen of Nearton.

I inhaled deeply and focused on one truth: never let a warmonger plan your birthday party. Sobs bottled in my throat, but still I was to play, to bare my soul in front of all our guests.

I sighed and began at the right side of the piano, where the octaves are high, and recalled my innocence, turning sixteen, kissing Mother, looking in the mirror as the servants dressed me, fashioned my hair, and added my jewels. The melody went from simple to layers of beauty. I added searching notes for when I'd waltzed with Father and elderly kings, while I looked for Pierre. There was a gentle bliss. And then without restraint, I remembered Dell and plunged my fingers deep into the beast's darkest tones.

Our guests stepped back in alarm, as they often did when I immersed myself.

The memory would not scar me, because I would expose the lie before my soul believed. The kiss was stolen, not given; therefore, it was not my first. Dark notes took on monstrous intonations. Dell's kiss was now a distant memory and, due to the catharsis of the beast, one I prayed I would never relive.

While the crowd clapped around me, I glimpsed my parents at the far side of the room. Tears glistened in their eyes. They loved me. Of this, I was certain.

ΦΦΦ

I slowly made my way across the room to where I'd earlier seen my little sister hiding. As I strolled, greeting guests and exchanging pleasantries, I spotted no sign of Wren anywhere in the blue velvet drapery. But I knew she was there. She was sly, clever, and very keen of hearing.

Near the punch bowl and behind Mother, who was deep in conversation, an elderly woman dropped her serviette. I bent to retrieve it, and I spotted three toes in the ebb of the curtain where the hem met the floor. Who knew all Wren had overheard from her station.

"Ducky, I know you're there," I whispered. "Meet me in the hallway, and I won't tell."

The toes disappeared, and she made her exit without a ripple in the velvet. A flash of light green silk pajamas and red braids slipped from the end of the drapery into the corridor.

I hurried after her. "You sneaky little duck. Come along." Taking her hand in mine, I marched her up the back stairwell.

"I have something to tell you. I wasn't just spying."

Wren was always spying. "Don't worry, you won't miss a thing. In the morning, I'll tell you all about tonight."

"Father is up to something," she breathed.

"He is *always* up to something."

With her hands on her wide hips, Maid Kimberlee waited for us at the top of the stairs.

"I overheard him in the study talking to someone," Wren whispered.

Wren had already made a career of eavesdropping and profiting from vital information. Her ears were perhaps even more sensitive than mine, though we both had the gift of listening.

"We'll talk about it in the morning," I said.

"Father said, 'Nothing is to happen to her . . . nothing.'"

Prior to tonight, *nothing* had ever happened to me.

"And why do you think they were talking about me?" Setting a hand to the polished balustrade, I paused beside her on the stairwell.

"Father said, 'She is the future of Blue Sky.' I'm not old enough to be the future." Even as she said it, Wren had the posture of a queen.

"Anything else?" I asked as we continued up the stairs.

"Oh, so much! Tonight when Maid Kimberlee's not watching, I'll slip into your bed." Wren's eyes widened. "After the party, you'll tell me about everything and I'll tell you."

"No, Ducky." I laughed. "You are to stay in your *own* bed. Tomorrow morning, after a good night's sleep, we'll talk."

I kissed the top of her head, and she sighed as I transferred her hand to Maid Kimberlee's.

Determined that my father would not spoil my party, I returned downstairs.

ΦΦΦ

After the party, Father and Mother kissed me good night while Dr. Krawl stood near my bedside holding a glass of milk. "It's warm, Alia. It will help you sleep."

I yawned. "I will have no trouble sleeping."

"After what happened with Prince Dell, Alia, you are to drink this." Father took the glass from Dr. Krawl's hand.

I sat up and studied my father's eyes. There was only tenderness and love, no signs of plotting or deception. I took a large gulp of the warm milk. Something tasted chalky. Wrinkling my nose, I set the half-empty glass down on the side table.

"Finish it, Alia." Father used his stern commander-of-war voice.

I tried to sit up, but my canopy bed floated about my chamber like a ship in gentle waves. I relaxed deeper into my feather pillow and never wanted to wake up.

Chapter Two

I awoke to slits of light directly above and around me, and something smelled like a barn. My body ached from being in a prolonged fetal position. I tried to straighten, but found myself confined in a wooden box. In the narrow space between the slats, I saw birds stacked in wooden cages on both sides of me. We were in the back of a wagon being jostled over a rutted road. A reddish-brown chicken clucked and grunted as if she were in great pain. With her bottom positioned toward me, she squeezed out a large brown egg.

I gagged.

"Helllp!" I cried. "Helllp! I've been kidnapped! Help! It's Princess Alia and I've been kidnapped! Help, I'm claustro-phobic." The louder I cried, the louder the chickens clucked around me.

The wagon rolled to a stop. The bench seat creaked loudly. Footsteps crunched in the pebbly road as my captor walked around the side of the wagon to my crate.

Please let him be handsome, young, and strong, with nice teeth and dark hair. I whispered my ideals to God and held my breath as reality approached.

Overhead, large fingers slid back the metal bolts and then lifted the lid.

I sat up, straightened my legs, and breathed in the bright sunlight. My captor was not young and handsome, but Father's age. He was balding and, from the rags he wore, a poor chicken farmer. His clothes did not properly fit his large bones. His pants were inches too short, and so were the arms of his shirt. He should have fired his tailor, if he had one.

There was no hope for him.

Standing behind the wagon, he swished his hand. "You may get up and walk for a while, if you desire, Dory."

"My name is Alia. Princess Alia."

"I am to refer to you as Dory—your middle name." He simply nodded instead of bowing.

I disliked frowning. Mother said it made any face ugly, even my beautiful one. I roused myself to my feet and bunched my arms by my sides. I was wearing the most hideous common clothes. They were even soiled. And my shoes were ugly, brown, square-toed plain Janes!

The worst part about the dream was that I wasn't waking up. I pinched my arms and my cheeks and blinked my eyes. I was still in the back of a foul-smelling wagon. I didn't care what the farmer thought of me—I screamed as far as my lungs would take me.

Other than short stubbles of green, the land lay barren. Not a rooftop or even a tree.

"Who are you? Why have you kidnapped me?"

Without showing teeth, my captor smiled. "I am Felix," he said slowly and deliberately, like I was dim-witted. "I was hired by your father because I know the way to the kingdom of Yonder like the back of my hand. For your safety, we are disguised as commoners, as father and daughter, until Yonder."

Nothing made sense.

"Your father wrote you a letter." From the pocket of his soiled shirt, he handed me an envelope. "You are to read it twice, and then tonight I must burn it for our safety."

My father was a brilliant strategist, and now with the end of the war, he was bored and creating one between us. I stared at the royal paper in my hand.

"You may read it up front or remain here." He nodded toward the box.

"Here." I sank down in my box beside the stinky birds, wanting to be alone.

As a slap of the reins set us in motion over the rutted dirt road, I slid the white linen stationery out of the envelope. With a deep sense of dismay, I recognized Father's formal cursive. What was he thinking? Taking a deep breath, I inhaled the chicken-permeated air.

Alia,

I have often thought, while away at war, that I would enjoy having you beside me to awaken your spoiled mind-set to what life is like for others. Your mother has taken you on many outings with that purpose in mind. As you know, you have often proved to be an ugly ambassador, someone who at times I have been embarrassed to claim as my daughter.

And then you redeem yourself at the piano.

And I want to believe that this young woman with so much passion would have a passion for others.

What? What in the world? This was more like Mother's voice than Father's. I rubbed my forehead.

In three months' time, when Prince Wron turns nineteen, you will be married and become the future queen of Yonder.

My hands dropped to my lap, and I stared at the rutted road behind us. "This is all wrong." I grimaced. "Who is Prince Wrong?"

*His father and I used to be dear friends. King Ulrich held
you in his arms when you were only a few weeks old. It was
then that the arrangement was made. Wron is aware of your
birthmark, and it will help prove who you are.*

My hand touched the heart-shaped mark tucked well
beneath my chin.

*Due to the war and the great distance of Yonder, we have
not been in contact as we would have liked. But I know
Walter is a man of his word, as am I. Whether or not there is
love between you, you will marry Prince Wron for your
country.*

This was Father's half of the letter.

"Never let a warmonger plan your wedding!" I stared at
the faces of the nearest hens. "He's exporting me. Exporting
me like . . . like a chicken for his own gain."

There was no clucking this time. Wide-eyed, they took it
all in.

*With the union, we'll be very strong allies with Yonder. A
new road will be built between our countries. Trade and
commerce will increase and benefit both. As our oldest child,
you and your children will be future heirs to this dynasty.
Stop looking in the mirror, Alia. Become a woman of purpose
and passion. You have been greatly blessed, and because of
this, much is expected of you.*

I didn't look in the mirror all that often. Did I?

*You are to obey Felix. He is brilliant and equal to fifty
men.*

I love you. Mother sends her love, too.

Father.

I stared at my father's royal seal—a crown with one blue
gem. The seal of doom.

Lying down in the box, I pulled the lid back in place,
curled into the fetal position, and wept.

ΦΦΦ

I stayed in the back of the wagon most of the day, until I was too famished to be proud. "Felix," I said, loudly. "Felix."

The wagon lurched to a slow, uncomfortable stop. "Yes, Dory. What is it?" he asked, without turning around.

"I'm hungry."

"I have buttered bread for you to eat." Instead of delivering it to me, he remained seated.

I tiptoed around a dozen chicken cages before climbing out of the back of the wagon. After acres of flat green stubble, we appeared to be on the fringe of a small town.

"It's a good time for you to come up front." He reached behind him and brought forth a red-haired wig to which a dreadfully common straw hat was attached. "Wear this. We are too close to Blue Sky, and Princess Alia is known for her auburn hair."

He had to be kidding. I was not going to wear that dreadful combination. What if someone saw me?

"You have to play the part of a commoner or you will put us in danger." Felix held out the wig.

If I saw anyone I knew, I'd die. I tucked my long hair down the back of the cambric shirt and adjusted the ugly wig on my head. I rounded my shoulders and sulked.

"You are still questionable." He glanced at me. "The princess is also known for her clear complexion." From his pocket, he produced a small bottle of brown liquid, and handed it to me. "Wipe this walnut oil on your face, hands, and arms."

Walnut oil. A woman desiring a clear complexion would do no such things. Didn't people bake with it, or use it on furniture?

Felix flicked the reins and stared straight ahead at the minuscule village in the distance. "If recognized, you could easily be ransomed for large sums, or killed to prevent the union of Blue Sky and Yonder."

I was dressed like a peasant, wearing a ridiculous wig. No one would recognize me.

"I myself have only just found out about the union," I said.

"Rumor of your betrothal has circulated for years."

"I knew Father was up to something." I sighed. "The Twelve-Year War was his midlife crisis, don't you think?" To pacify the farmer, and to earn a piece of the thick sliced buttered bread, I wiped the walnut oil on my face, hands, and arms.

"You are not well informed. The Twelve-Year War was a peasant's revolt flamed by grievances amongst townships."

"That's right, I heard a lot about revolting peasants."

My captor regarded me sternly with a lifted brow.

"When I was growing up . . ." My voice faded.

"We are now entering the town of Fhar. For our safety, I think it best that you not speak. If for some reason you must speak, the only word you are to say is *dur*. And hide the ring."

"D-ur?" I asked, and slipped the jade ring that Father had given me only yesterday morning into my pocket.

"*Yes*, just like that, like you are mute and dumb." The corner of Felix's mouth twitched; otherwise, there were no redeeming qualities in the farmer's pudgy face. Yet, for some reason, my father trusted him.

"French is my second language," I said, with a lift of my chin. "I shall speak French."

"On this side of the mountains, it is common knowledge that Princess Alia's second language is French."

Dur was too far beneath me. I would not say it.

The rambling little hamlet bore signs of prosperity—three stores in a row were brightly painted—and then signs of abandonment—half a dozen buildings lay in crumbled piles. I wondered if any store in town carried shoes. I would have loved to buy a new pair. Ones with a little more heel and a lot more style.

"Will we stop?" I whispered.

"At one store. You are not to leave my side."

When Felix parked the wagon in front of Landry's Dry Goods, a crowd gathered on the sidewalk. The people were shabbily dressed in shades of gray and stared almost as much as when my entourage of fifty soldiers shopped with me in Blue Sky.

"Why are they staring?" I whispered.

"Shh!" Felix hushed me and hopped out of the wagon. "Come, Dory." He raised his arms, waiting to lift me out.

It was all a bad dream. Their complexions matched their clothes, a sullen shade of gray. The emptiness in their eyes appeared too real.

I rose stiffly and held on to my hat as my captor swung me to the ground beside him. I followed him to the rear of the wagon, where he stacked three chicken crates together before carrying them. "Come, Dory."

Holding on to my hat, I followed him through a throng of people.

"She is odd," said an old woman wearing an equally odd outfit.

I agreed with her: I was odd. I followed Felix inside the feed store and to the counter. "I have chickens to trade for a pig," he told the clerk.

"All is well?" The dark-haired, middle-aged man behind the counter glanced at me.

"Yes." Felix slid an envelope across the counter. "All is well."

"Drive around back, and we will load it."

Somehow, the man behind the counter knew. The letter was probably an update on my condition, but to whom? Father?

A crowd had gathered outside. As we walked to the wagon, another elderly woman stared unmercifully at me. "Where are you from?" she demanded. Though she was wearing a dress, she reminded me of one of Father's head guards.

I recalled that Felix was as capable as fifty men. I began to count the gathering townspeople. Perhaps it was best that we not take them on.

"Dur," I said.

"The dumb are not welcome in Fhar." She looked at Felix.

"We are only here for supplies, and then my daughter and I will be on our way." He nodded and tipped his straw hat.

"After the merger, the dumb will be taxed the same as the sharp of mind. It will become impossible for you to keep her."

"Pray that Prince Wron governs with heart," Felix said. "My daughter may be dumb, but she is not immune to suffering."

My face warmed beneath the walnut stain. I was in the most bizarre dream. Or perhaps it was my unblemished childhood that was the dream?

The crowd parted, and Felix boosted me up onto the bench seat. I ignored all of the years of etiquette my mother had instilled in me and simply sat down, crumpling the back of my dress beneath me.

At the rear of the feed store, a bale of hay and feed for the horses were loaded into the wagon. Lastly, a loud, squealing white pig with brown spots was carried to and contained in my old cage.

"You did well." Felix shook the reins. "Thank you, Dory."

I clasped my hands in my lap and realized that I was trembling. I'd feel much better when the town of Fhar was far behind us.

"Why were they so unfriendly?" I glanced behind us as we turned left at the last fork on our way out of town.

"After twelve years of war, devastation, and starvation, there is much healing needed in your future kingdom."

Yesterday, I had been dreaming of my first kiss. Why did today have to be such a contrast? Scrunching my face up tightly, I tried to contain my misery, but it still crept all the way down to my fingertips. The next song I played would be frightful. Hopefully, I'd be wearing a different dress. How I longed for my blue chiffon dress and my periwinkle dancing shoes with their silver tips and light-as-air heels.

"Why did I have to pretend to be dumb?"

"You didn't have to pretend." A faint smile teased the corner of his mouth.

Did he think he was funny? The large, stocky man was rude.

"You pretended to be dumb on account of your Blue Sky accent. Unlike other provinces, Blue Sky does not pronounce its *er*s. Dinn-a, supp-a."

My accent had never been commented on before, and I'd danced with plenty of countries.

"What else is there to eat?" I'd only had a slice of bread. Maybe he was starving me so that I'd obey.

"We will stop in a few hours for the night." Felix slapped the reins.

"A few hours?" I huffed. I'd never make it.

"Yes, a few hours. Do not wear your hat tonight."

"Will I be Princess Alia tonight?"

"No. During our journey, you will always be Dory."

My stomach knotted and began to ache. Was this what hunger felt like, or was it something else? If Felix was so brilliant, why hadn't he packed more food? In one day, I'd gone from being the daughter of a king to becoming the dumb, hungry daughter of a chicken farmer.

I wanted my old life back.

ΦΦΦ

The wagon came to an abrupt stop, jolting me awake. I'd fallen asleep against my captor's shoulder. Night had fallen. We were in the country, beneath a huge old tree, parked next to what appeared to be an outhouse.

"Stay here." Felix jumped down from the wagon and disappeared around the corner of the small building. He obviously had to use the privy. In his absence, I thought about escaping. The problems were: I didn't have any money or food; I didn't know where I was or where I could go; I was entirely dependent on the chicken farmer.

Felix soon returned and opened the pig's cage. He lifted out the squealing animal and carried it to the rear of the outhouse. On his next trip to the wagon, he picked up two chicken cages.

"Take off your hat, put it in the burlap sack, and follow me."

I did as he said and followed him to the front of the outhouse. We entered without knocking. It was not an outhouse; it was a home.

I had visited the less fortunate with Mother on many occasions. We'd deliver clothes and food, and sometimes I would read stories to the children, but never had I seen poverty until now. I bit my lower lip.

In this one-room home, there was a fireplace built with mortar and rock, a makeshift table in the middle of the room, a cooking stove, a bed, and a couch made of a hollowed tree. The floor wasn't marble, granite, or brick; it was simply dirt. A little girl sat on the couch cuddled in a drab blanket. The home was so humble, there wasn't even a mirror. There didn't appear to be one anywhere. I sat down in a creaky chair on the same side of the table as Felix. Two tallow candles provided the only light in the room.

A lean, middle-aged woman hovered near the stove. She glanced nervously over her shoulder at me, like she knew who I really was.

"Greda, this is Dory."

Greda nodded. "Dank you for dee pig and dee chickens."

I nodded and tried to hide my surprise at her odd accent.

"Greda is twenty-two years old. Sadie, her daughter, is six," Felix whispered.

I glanced back at the woman. She looked twice as old as she was. Could today's circumstances possibly be real?

I acknowledged Sadie, who was seated ten feet away. With the face of an angel, the dark-haired little girl smiled at me. Like my sister Wren, she was precious and beautiful. *Wren*, I could not think about Wren. Would I ever see her again?

"Momma, do I sdill need do be quied?"

"Yes, Sadie."

"Greda's husband joined Blue Sky's army shortly after they were married. He was killed a year later," Felix whispered. "Except for her daughter, Greda only has one relative; and, due to the war, she has not seen him for many years."

This was all a wild charade. Maybe they were all actors: the outhouse was staged, and the villagers in Fhar and these people were also my father's puppets.

Felix pulled my letter from Father out of his pocket and held a corner of the envelope over the candle's light. My childhood, Father's royal seal, and what might possibly be my only link to my identity grew to a large flame. He carried the letter to the stove, lifted a burner lid, and disposed of it.

Though my heart stopped, I didn't scream. I just stared.

"Soup is ready. Sadie, dime do come do dee dable."

Turning to her tummy, Sadie slid off the couch and began to limp toward me. With her right foot angled toward her left, she walked sideways on it. Maybe it was due to the last twenty-four hours and my extreme hunger, but the largest knot I'd ever had to swallow formed in my throat.

Sadie climbed up in the chair across from me. Dark, shoulder-length curls framed her heart-shaped face. Freckles danced across her pug nose. When a bowl of soup was placed in front of her, glee crossed her face.

"Lendils." Her eyes twinkled. "Lendils!"

I stared at the soup delivered to me. Lentils must be the small, grayish-green disks in the clear broth. I wondered where the potatoes and chunks of chicken and dill—

"Dank you, Fadder, for dhis meal, for bringing Felix and Dory safely do our home, for dee pig and chickens. Amen," Greda said.

"Lendils!" Sadie smiled across the table at me.

My, the little girl was fond of lentils. I took a sip of the broth. It reminded me of the gray-clothed townspeople in Fhar. Ten colors and flavors were missing.

"Do you have salt?" I asked, looking at Greda.

Felix cleared his throat and, with a slight shake of his head, informed me that I was being impolite.

"We haven'd had sald for years," Greda said.

Today was all an act. Somehow Father and Felix orchestrated everything and everyone, the thespians, the props. I smiled. Did they really think I was so gullible?

"Momma," Sadie said, "dee soup is very good widhoud sald."

"You have never acquired a dasde for sald," said her mother. "Someday you will, Sadie, and you will undersdand."

Across the table, the little girl glared at me.

I scooped another spoonful of the flat, flavorless broth.

"You are nod a very nice guesd," Sadie said under her breath.

I lifted my gaze from my spoon; the little girl was looking at me.

"Sadie! You need do apologize," said her mother.

Red stained the child's cheeks. Her eyes blazed and she shook her head. The little thespian had been trained to duel in defense of her mama's lentil soup.

"Sadie, if you dab salt on the tongue alone . . ." I bunched my face up, grimacing. "It tastes overwhelmingly strong, but if you add just the right amount of salt to food—like your mama's lentil soup—it will bring out the flavor. Like your mother said, someday you will understand."

The child stared at me and crossed her arms. "I did nod hear you say you are sorry."

They had picked a talented little actress. A heavy silence settled between my opponent and me.

"You are right, Sadie; I did not say I was sorry, but I explained my circumstances so you will understand why I asked for salt."

Sadie's gaze shifted to her mother. Out of the corner of my eye, I saw Greda shake her head. Sadie shrugged and sipped another spoonful of the warm liquid.

After finishing her soup, Greda turned to me. "Dory, can you sid widh Sadie while I do dee dishes?"

Were there no other courses? My gaze scoured the stove. Nothing else had been prepared. I would surely die of hunger by morning.

"Yes, I will sit with her." I followed the little girl as she limped her way to the log couch.

"I will sleep outside near the wagon tonight," Felix informed us.

He was leaving me in here all alone with them. Where would I sleep?

I sat down first. Sadie wrestled the drab blanket over our laps and wiggled herself against my side, probably for warmth, or perhaps she had forgiven me.

"You can dell me you're sorry now." She glanced up at me and then toward her mother at the sink.

Oh, how I longed to tell her the kind of day I'd had and how she was lucky that I'd only asked for salt.

"Very well." Though the apology was not warranted, I supposed I could humble myself enough to tell the poor child what she needed to hear. "I'm sorry that I asked for salt."

"I forgive you. Now"—she folded her hands very adult-like in front of her—"can you dell me a sdor-ee?"

"Let me see . . ." I looked at the bare walls. What would be appropriate?

"Do you know 'Dee Smiling Princess sdor-ee?"

I shook my head and glanced at Greda. The story was the oldest of fairy tales and inappropriate to tell a little girl.

"Puh-lease." Her perfect little teeth formed an enchanting smile.

"She is familiar widh dee sdory, Dory," Greda said.

"Ohhh." I was surprised. "Hmmm . . ." And against my better judgment, I began. "There was once a young princess who was raised to smile. Good news or bad news, blue sky or rain showers, she was told to smile. As she rode atop her fine, white horse through the streets, she would wave to her countrymen and smile."

Sadie leaned against me and sighed contentedly.

"When other children made fun of her, she was told to smile."

The little girl nudged me. "You are delling id doo quick. Why did dhey make fun of her?"

"Well . . . she was overly protective. Everyone's little mama." I nudged her back. "Now, you make something up."

Sadie's eyes grew wide. "She only had one nosdril."

I waited for her giggling to subside before I continued.

"Once, when the princess heard that war was only a few hours away, she was told to smile. And once when their cook was beheaded, she was ordered to smile." I nudged Sadie. "Your turn."

"Once"—Sadie's gaze lingered on the table—"when her modher said dhere was no more food or money to buy food, dee princess was ordered do smile."

Hot tears bottled in my throat like lava.

"Your durn. Puh-lease add one more *once*." Holding her hands prayer-like, she gazed up at me.

Sometimes Wren would add her version of atrocities here as Sadie had done. Mine felt even closer than the kitchen. "Once . . . when the princess was shipped away from her home to marry a man she'd never met, without saying good-bye to anyone she loved . . ." My voice trailed off. "The princess was ordered to smile."

Sadie hugged my arm and sighed in the contented bliss of a good story.

"So tiresome was her smile that whenever she passed a mirror, she would frown and make the most atrocious faces, simply to relieve her facial muscles."

Sadie melted more against me.

"On one occasion, when she passed a royal mirror, she frowned horridly and her reflection was observed by a handsome prince who'd been invited to dine with her family that evening. It was his first impression of her, and though she smiled beautifully the remainder of the evening, he could not forget the face he'd seen first in the mirror."

Sadie sighed. "I love dhad sdoree."

"What is the moral of the story?" I asked.

"Moral?" She yawned and blinked her eyes several times.

"Yes, a moral is a lesson."

"Oh." She nodded. "Dee lesson of dhis sdoree is . . . even if you are a cripple in dhis life"—Sadie smiled—"you are do . . . smile."

The soup pot clattered in the sink.

A chill crept through my body.

"I am very, very sorry," Greda said. "Sadie, you know you are do say *lame*."

Sadie's mouth bunched as she peered up at me. A fierce determination shone in her lucent green eyes.

"How would you like to word it, Sadie?" I whispered.

Her chest inflated as she gazed across the room at her mother. "I am designed differend."

I waited for the child to explain further, but she didn't.

"When I was growing up, my mother's version of the ending was"—I took Sadie's hand in mine—"that, whatever life throws at you, Little Princess, you are to smile."

She sighed, pressing her shoulder into mine. "Your momma called you Liddle Princess, doo?"

"Yes." I forced a smile. "She called me Little Princess, too."

ΦΦΦ

Despite my exhaustion, I lay awake in the dark on the dirt floor of Greda's home with a blanket that Felix had brought in for me from the wagon.

I recalled the details of Father's letter. What was Prince Wrong like? Was he handsome, or was he like Prince Dell—repulsive? I found myself troubled by all of the what-ifs. Instead, I focused on Sadie.

The little girl's plight nabbed at my heart. What parting gift could I leave her? Except for the clothes upon my back, I had nothing. I had no way to improve her life, and then I remembered the ring that Father had given me for my birthday, the previous morning. I felt the smooth, solid piece of jade on my left hand. I had no notion of its worth, except that it might prove invaluable to Greda.

The next morning during breakfast, I pondered how I would leave such a gift. I feared its loss if I did not address its value. Felix finished his bowl of porridge before the rest of us and rose from the table to carry the bedding to the wagon. In his absence, I slid the ring off my finger and set it on the table's rough-hewn surface, halfway between Greda and myself.

"I would like to help Sadie and you. It is all I have to give."

Greda shook her head, and then she peered wide-eyed from me to Sadie, seated beside her, before picking it up. She cradled the ring in the palm of her hand and marveled at its beauty. When Father had given it to me, there had been rare emotion in his eyes, which I told myself was worth more to me than the gift itself. If I ever had to tell Father that I'd given it to a peasant, I prayed he'd understand.

"I have no idea of its value. But I know it's real. Don't sell it to the tinker; take it to a good shop."

As Greda gazed at me, an amber color emerged in her deep brown eyes. I knew without a doubt that their situation was not merely a manifestation to teach me—a spoiled princess—empathy. A hope beyond acting glistened in the young mother's eyes.

"God bless you, and may your kindness be redurned do you."

Felix emerged in the doorway. "It is time to go, Dory."

I nodded.

"Sadie, id is dime do say good-bye," Greda said.

"I won'd!" Sadie dropped her spoon in the watery porridge and slid out from her chair.

"You musd." As her daughter hobbled across the room, Greda followed her.

"I won'd say good-bye." Sadie flailed in her mother's arms.

"I don'd know whad's godden indo her," Greda said.

I knew. As a young child, I'd watched my father head off to war far too many times. I'd hated good-byes. Maid Kimberlee, who was much older and wiser than me, once told me that when you say good-bye, it's an important time to tell people that you love them and that you'll keep them in your prayers.

"Good-bye, Greda; thank you for your hospitality. You and Sadie will be in my prayers."

I paused in the open doorway and looked back. Sadie leaned her head away from the folds of her mother's skirt to watch me. I walked very slowly toward the wagon. Though Felix was already seated upon the bench, he appeared patient.

Behind me, I heard bare feet patter across the threshold. "Dory," Sadie's voice rang out. As the child approached, I bent down. "Do you have do leave?" she asked.

"A long journey is ahead of me. Someday I will tell you all about it." And as I said it, I prayed I would.

A whimper escaped her as she rubbed at her face with both hands.

I gently took one of her hands in mine. "When I was a child, I hated good-byes so much that I would hide," I admitted.

"You did?" Her wide eyes told me that I had seen her soul.

"But now that I am older, I realize they must be said." I thought of all the people I might never see again back home. Even my own parents had not said good-bye.

"Someday when I dasde sald, I will dhink of you," she whispered.

"You will be in my prayers." I touched the child's cheek with my fingertips and climbed up into the wagon to sit beside Felix.

I waved at Greda and then her daughter.

"Dor-ee," Sadie called. As I turned, the child's eyes widened. "Once . . ." she said, and in the silence that followed, the little girl pasted on a smile and waved as we pulled away.

Chapter Three

When we were well out of Greda and Sadie's sight, I returned the wig and hat to my head. Upon Felix's request, I reapplied the walnut oil to my face and hands.

"I hope that not all of our stops will be as emotional," I said.

He flicked the reins. "Because of her child, Greda has not given up on living. But there are many who have."

"I hope we're not going to visit them next." I felt weary at the thought. I needed time to reflect, perhaps grieve. The child had touched me deeply.

Felix said nothing, nor did he provide any clues to the evening ahead. I disliked this about him. Why hadn't my father chosen a better communicator to be my guide?

Midday, Felix brought the horses to a halt. "Get out." He nodded to the middle of the country road.

For a moment, I questioned if he was going to abandon me, but surely not. His mission and sole purpose were to deliver me safely to Prince Wrong. I climbed out of the wagon and walked to the center of the dirt road.

"Walk like you think Sadie will walk when she is your age."

It was Sadie's right leg that impeded her. I dangled my right foot toward my left and walked sideways on it, as Sadie had done. It did not take many steps for my ankle to ache, and probably in time so would my hip. By the time Sadie was my age, she would most likely be more crippled.

"You are to walk like that in Sherman. We'll be there soon."

"Can I talk this time?"

"It's best you don't."

Situated on a grassy knoll, Sherman appeared to be a thriving metropolis. Felix parked the wagon in front of Sherman Feed Store, a large, barn-like building. He helped me out of the wagon, and I remembered to limp on my first step. My gait drew attention, and a crowd quickly gathered as we walked inside.

"I have chickens to trade for a horse," Felix told the young man behind the counter.

I began to question if we would trade the horse for shelter, as we'd traded the pig the night before.

"All is well?" The young man glanced at me.

"Yes." Felix slid an envelope across the counter.

"Drive your wagon around back."

When we returned outside, the crowd remained.

"Are you new in down?" a gentleman asked, taking off his straw hat.

"No, we are passing through," Felix said. He was good about staying by my side, like a father would protect his lame daughter.

"Good," a few breathed.

A dark-haired woman spoke up: "Dhey will dake her from you when dee new law is passed and insdidutionalize her. Is she dumb also?"

Felix glanced at me. "Only sometimes."

I lowered my eyes to the wood-planked walkway. It must all be a game to humiliate me. I'd get back at him . . . somehow.

"What kind of law would separate a handicapped child from her family?" Felix loudly addressed the crowd. "I cannot trust that kind of government with my daughter's well-being."

I remembered Sadie.

"A handicapped child dakes a good working cidizen oud of sociedy because dhey musd sday ad home widh her. Dee governmend loses in dee end," the dark-haired woman said.

My father had always crammed politics down my throat, but he was getting very creative. Without smoothing the back of my skirt, I sat down in the front of the wagon next to Felix.

"Pray for us." As he flicked the reins, Felix's thick neck appeared to disappear into his large shoulders.

At the rear of the feed store, a gray workhorse was tethered to the back of our wagon.

"Are the letters for my father?"

"Yes, they are written in code. In one month's time, he'll take this route on his way to your wedding."

"One month? Why so long?"

"It will take us almost a month to reach Yonder. You will arrive several weeks before the wedding."

"Before?" It was the first positive thing I'd heard about my wedding.

"Yes. Though you've been promised to each other since birth, his parents want their son to approve of the marriage."

"And if he doesn't *approve* of me?" My mind wandered to the gallows.

"It is greatly in his country's favor that he approve. Yonder does not have the wealth or infrastructure that Blue Sky does. But . . ." Felix shrugged. "If the merger were to be annulled, you'd return to Blue Sky to marry Prince Dell of Nearton."

I shuddered. Dell repulsed me. I was simply a pawn in my father's hand, a commodity.

"Will my mother be coming to the wedding?"

"No, the journey would prove too difficult."

I thought of Sadie. It had already been too difficult.

ΦΦΦ

On our way out of Sherman, we passed a bakery. I elbowed Felix and pointed at the large, curved letters on the storefront glass. CHERRY FRITTERS.

"Do we have any money?" My stomach already felt empty.

"What money I have is not for danishes." He flicked the reins harder.

I crossed my eyes in agony. I would trade my shoes for a jelly-filled croissant. Of course, I would not admit that to Felix. I watched over my shoulder until my view of Sherman was the size of a postcard. I could not dismiss Sadie's fate from my thoughts.

"Is Sadie's future really an institution?" I sat up taller.

"Yes, unless Prince Wron employs a wider rule of his land."

"And you are trying to educate me about my future kingdom?"

"Yes." He nodded.

"What is Prince Wron like?"

"He is not as spoiled as you." A smile softened Felix's unshaven face.

Given the circumstances, I thought I'd behaved quite well.

"Is he handsome?"

"You will meet him in Yonder."

"Is he unpleasant looking?"

"Dory, what did I just tell you?"

Felix was the most obstinate of men.

"Why you? Out of all the men my father knows, why you?"

Hunched, he flicked the reins. "I know the routes to Yonder like the back of my hand, and"—he cleared his throat—"your father trusts me."

"What have you done to earn his trust?" He must have worked for Father during the war.

His barrel chest inflated. "I was one of his informants."

I knew I'd seen him before. "You were a spy."

"No, a runner."

"You were a running spy."

He didn't argue with me.

After endless miles of flat prairie, I fell asleep. When I awoke, the sky was a dark angora blue and my head was against Felix's shoulder. I stiffened and sat up.

"Do they know who I am tonight?" I yawned.

"No, you are always Dory. We arranged tonight as a request from the king, under the guise that you are to play piano for the royal wedding. They know nothing more, except that they will receive a horse in return."

A horse in exchange for one night's room and board? "It must be a very old horse." I glanced at the workhorse hitched to the back of the wagon. The large creature appeared gentle and strong.

"There is a price for safety and secrecy. Reapply the walnut oil to your face and hands. You do not need to wear the wig tonight."

I was relieved.

The sky deepened to navy blue before we entered a small hamlet named Ma's Cow. By moonlight, the town's cobblestone streets and church steeples and the outline of the modest, but sizable, homes enticed the heart.

Felix knocked on the door of a single-level brick home. A plump woman with short, dark hair opened it and invited us inside. She led us down a narrow hallway to a spare room.

"Dhere's a vashbasin in your room. Dinner is ready."

The woman did not correctly pronounce her *T*s or *W*s. Perhaps she had a speech impediment. I eyed the two single beds. Though the lodging was an improvement over last night, I felt uncomfortable about sleeping in the same room as Felix.

"Do not worry; I will sleep outside in the wagon."

"Thank you." Across the room, a washbasin sat on top of a low dresser. I washed my hands and glanced up to see my reflection in a round mirror.

A teetered gasp escaped me.

It was the first time I'd seen myself since the night of my party. The layers of walnut oil made my face appear muddy, stained... older. My hair was matted, and the rags I wore were pitiful. Prior to the mirror, I could only guess at my appearance; now, I knew. I looked like the lowliest of beggars.

"I need a brush, a bath, new clothes . . . I can't be seen looking like this."

"You've already been seen looking like that. You forget, Dory, the reasons you are disguised."

I slumped down on the side of the mattress. "Do I have to be dumb again?"

"No . . ." Felix inhaled. "They know you are a royal pianist, but don't get smart."

"If I am a royal pianist, why am I dressed in rags? Why am I not with the wedding party? None of this makes sense."

"We are traveling ahead of the party, so I will have time to visit Evland—my homeland. Practice that on your tongue, Dory."

"Before *the* royal wedding, my father wants to visit Evland first." Though I was confused, I tried to believe the lie.

I followed Felix down a narrow hallway to a blue-painted kitchen. Our hostess was seated at a long, dark table with the man of the house and several young women about my own age. Though they were already seated, they had waited for us before dishing up. Felix pulled a chair out for me, and I remembered my manners and training as I sat down and he pushed in my seat.

"I am Nora. Dhis is my husband, Gaden," the woman of the household said. She nodded to the gray-haired man seated kitty-corner to her at the far end of the table. "Dhese are our daughders: Ida . . ."

A frizzy-haired brunette shrugged.

"Marda."

Marda, who had the neck of a swan, smiled without blinking.

"And . . . Hild-a."

The prettiest of the three, Hilda's long, raven-black hair rippled below her side of the table.

Nora turned back to me. "I've forgodden your name."

"Dora. I mean . . . Dory."

"Felix and Dory." Nora nodded.

No prayer was said. Three covered dishes sat in the middle of the table, and everyone waited expectantly while Gaden lifted the first lid. Mashed potatoes with a pat of butter were unveiled. I swallowed. He plopped a large scoop onto Nora's plate and his own before passing the dish left, to Ida. She took a scoopful and then passed it to Marda. Wide-eyed, I watched the bowl. I hadn't had *real* food since the night of my birthday party. Felix carefully took one-third of the remaining mashed potatoes. I swallowed hungrily. Hilda took three-quarters of the remaining one-half cup of mashed potatoes.

When I received the bowl, only a smidgen remained. I dumped the bowl upside down over my plate. The remnant fell out with a plop.

Gaden passed the bowl of steamed green peas. Again, our hosts took far too large of servings. The bowl of peas was greatly reduced before it was passed to Felix. He regarded me across the table and divided it as fairly as he could before passing the bowl to his left. Hilda looked at me, took a large spoonful, and ladled it onto her plate before passing me the remaining dish.

"I dhoughd Mudder said do vash up for dinner." Tilting her head, Hilda stared at me.

"I did." I peered into the bowl and counted eight green peas. Again, I turned the bowl over and dumped the peas onto my plate. One rolled off, and I promptly grabbed it and popped it into my mouth. I glanced up to see the hint of a smile on Felix's face.

I felt embarrassed by my action. Mother would have scolded me. Felix's cheeks appeared inverted as if he was biting the inside of his mouth.

"Vhad beaudiful hair you have." Marda smiled at me.

"Dhank you." I met her kind gaze.

"Did you vash?" Hilda glared at me.

I glared back. Never had a commoner dared to speak to me in such a belittling manner. Hilda had pretty skin and large brown eyes. She was wearing a very nice shirt for a commoner, and I strongly disliked her.

"Yes, I vashed," I said. "Go look in your mudder's vashbasin and you'll see nice brown vater, proving I vashed." I huffed and glanced at Felix.

He slightly shook his head. What did he expect? I was hungry, kidnapped, a foreigner in my own future country, and my future subjects were selfish and disrespectful. More than I had ever been.

Gaden lifted the last lid. Meat and gravy. Oh, my mouth watered. I swallowed several times as the silver bowl made its way around the table. When it reached Felix, he glanced at the meager portion on my plate, and I knew he thought about reaching across the table to ladle a spoonful onto my plate. But he was a gentleman, and he knew that reaching was impolite. He took one-third of the meager portion and passed it to Hilda.

Hilda.

Leaning forward, I wondered what huge hips she hid beneath the table. Her selfish appetite would make her a very large woman someday . . . I prayed. She ladled two heaping spoonfuls onto her plate and passed the remainder to me. Her eyes remained locked on mine throughout the exchange, and her mouth twisted into a smile.

When I peered into the bowl, I saw only my reflection. My lungs filled with air.

"Horse." My voice was hoarse as I addressed Felix. "Vee don'd have do sday here, Fauder." I spoke slowly. "Vee can dake *dee* horse vid us and go."

"Dee horse is in *my* shed, and you are ad *my* dable," Gaden, the man of the house, said.

"Led me undersdand someding." I again spoke slowly so they could understand my odd accent. "Vee draded you a horse for food and bed." I waited.

Gaden nodded.

I showed him my plate. "Eighd peas, one bide of podado, and a spod of gravy." I put down my plate and reached for Hilda's. "Vee drade, or vee leave vid dee horse."

"Hilda!" Rising to his feet, Gaden pointed for her to pass me her plate.

ΦΦΦ

Heaven was a full tummy, I mused. The full moon peeked through the parted curtains into my room. After the scene with Hilda, I was afraid to sleep in the house by myself and asked Felix to stand guard in the hallway outside my room.

He lifted one brow. "They will think it odd. If I sleep in the wagon, they will not know that I am not in our room."

"Hilda does not like me." Instead of empathy in his pale gray eyes, I saw humor. Maybe due to Hilda, Felix was beginning to like me. Maybe he was even able to get past his first impression of me and how I'd behaved in the back of the wagon. Not that it mattered.

"Do you think she will try to get revenge on me tonight?" I whispered, and noted that there was no lock on the door.

"I would think if Hilda is hungry, she will know which cupboards to raid."

His answer did not comfort me.

"I will watch your window tonight," Felix said. "If you become afraid, set your candle on the sill, and I suppose"—he yawned—"I can sleep in the hall."

As I lay in bed, I reminded myself that Felix was equal to fifty men. If I did have a problem with Hilda, he would come to my rescue. In the meantime, I glanced at the unlocked door. I would slide the highboy dresser in front of it.

In my nightgown, I scurried across the room, and using all my might, I shimmied the dresser directly in front of the door. If Hilda had any odd ideas of revenge, this would stop her. Then I set the unlit candle on the windowsill and parted the curtains wider. There, I already felt better.

I relaxed deep into the comfortable straw mattress and gave in to sleep.

A soft rapping on the door woke me. I sat up. My heart pounded in my chest as I stared across the room.

"Yes." Enough yellow moonlight shone through the window that I was able to see the door open slightly before it bumped against the dresser.

"Dory?" a female voice whispered. I could not positively identify if it was Hilda. "Vhy is dee dresser in frond of dee door?"

It was Hilda.

"Felix," she said, "I vas vondering if your daughder vould care do have desserd vidh me?"

Flipping back the covers, I tiptoed across the room to where Felix should have been sleeping if he were there. "It is late, Hilda. Go back to bed," I said in a deep, gruff voice. I peered out the window in the direction of the wagon, but in the moonlit gray surroundings, I could not make out what was wagon and what were the outbuildings.

"Dory, I vould like do apologize. I made us some vunderful cake."

I flitted across the room to my bed. "I'm sorry, Hilda, I'm very dired. Perhaps we could share some in dee morning."

"If you vould open dee door a liddle vays, I have made a liddle plade for you. Mudder said dhad you are leaving early, and I vould like do apologize."

Should I believe her? Could she hear the loud pounding of my heart as it echoed in the room, bouncing off the dresser to the window? I had never been so scared in all my life.

I crept closer to the door and, listening closely, sensed that there was more than just Hilda waiting on the other side.

"Dank you, Hilda, for your kind offer, but I am nod hungry righd now. If you vould leave id on the hallvay dable, I vill enjoy id in dee morning."

"Does your fadher vand id, Dory?"

I was certain the last voice was not Hilda's. It was either Ida's or Marda's. Perhaps both sisters had joined her. I tiptoed to the window. I struck a match and was trembling so much that I had to hold my wrist steady with my other hand as I lit the candle. I returned to Felix's side of the room and deeply cleared my throat.

"No, thank you. Go to bed, girls."

I sat on Felix's bed, pulling my knees to my chest. By the flicker of candlelight, I watched as the door thudded repeatedly against the dresser. A rapping sound behind me on the window alarmed me even more. *They've surrounded me* was my first thought, and then I peered closer. Through the glass, I saw Felix.

He was here to rescue me! I reminded myself that he was equal to fifty men, and my heart leaped. I rushed to the window, released the latch, and attempted to slide it open, but it had been painted in place and would not budge. Behind me, the dresser scraped across the floor. I blew out the candle right before the trio of sisters burst into the room. And, in the light from the hallway, I saw the sheen of scissors.

Chapter Four

They were going to either stab me or cut off my hair.

Frantic, I threw myself on Felix's bed and rolled myself up in the quilt, covering my head. Like a blind mummy, I ran about the room. In the dark, they chased after me, cursing. One of them wrapped her arms about my knees and tackled me. Like a roll of carpet, I fell to the floor with a loud thud. I felt three bodies on top of me as they tried to unroll me from the quilt.

"Ged her oud!"

"Ged her hair!"

And then for some reason beyond my comprehension, the room stilled. Beneath the bodies and the quilt, I couldn't see that Felix had arrived, but I heard him.

"Get off my daughter, or it is your hair you will lose tonight."

"Vee can dake him," one of the sisters mumbled.

"Which one of you said that?" Felix demanded.

I knew it was Hilda.

No one spoke, but I felt one body rise from on top of me, and then another. One of the sisters was afraid, like me. She remained seated on my stomach.

"Oh, no," she whimpered. "Oh, no, no, no." And then she rose also.

There was a skirmish, and madness. Groans as bodies were flung about the room. In a wild frenzy, I unrolled myself from the quilt and found my footing.

A kerosene lamp lit the room. I blinked. It took several blinks before I fully comprehended the odd scene before me. The sisters' heads were bunched together like three cherries on one stem. Felix had wound all their hair into one rope, which he held securely in his left hand. With his right, he extended the scissors to me.

I took the long steel scissors, meant more for swaths of fabric than for a woman's hair, and stared at the three sets of eyes glaring at me. Hilda panted, and though she was contorted into a backward C, her hands curved as if to claw me. Though her sisters were her allies, they were not really enemies to me. Yet their hair was entwined with hers.

"Fauder, I desire to cud only Hilda's hair." I dared to voice my thought aloud.

"These girls were *all* willing to cut yours." Felix's eyes were keen in the lantern light.

Ida's and Marda's eyes pleaded with me, while Hilda's dared.

I'd never held the fate of a woman's beauty, maybe a woman's soul.

"Hilda," I whispered. "I desire do forgive you, bud your eyes are haughdy. Almosd daring me do cud off your beaudiful hair."

"Hilda!" Ida pleaded. "For once . . . please."

"She von'd do id." Hilda sounded remarkably calm.

How did she know? My hand that held out the scissors was visibly shaking. I searched Felix's face. With a slight nod, he motioned for me to draw closer. Holding out the scissors, I willed my body to move. I inched them near Felix's grip on the trio's hair.

"Marda," I whispered, peering into her pale face, "vhad do you dhink I should do? Should I redurn a vrong for a vrong?"

Her face bunched up. "Yes," she whimpered and began to cry.

"You mean *no*, you dummy!" Hilda rolled her eyes.

Marda's tears drained the fight out of me. "I only vand do cud Hilda's hair." I looked at Felix.

"On your knees," he ordered and yanked a bit as all three sisters dropped to their knees, facing me. Felix held the rope of hair above their heads, and again I was reminded of three cherries on the same stem.

In my night shift, I wondered if they could see perhaps a little too much of me. I retrieved the quilt from the floor and wrapped it about myself. With a slight lift of my chin, I returned to stand in front of them, the quilt trailing behind.

"Apologize!" Felix ordered.

"I'm very sorry dhad we addacked you," Marda said, and burst forth into another creek of tears.

"I'm sorry doo. You didn'd deserve id," Ida said.

Hilda shook her head, bunching her mouth together.

Felix frowned and let go of their rope of hair. "Marda, go get your father. Ida, stay here." He retained his grip on Hilda's hair.

I sat down on the side of my bed. It all felt too familiar. It reminded me of the time Father had to reprimand one of our cooks for stealing food. Father had threatened the removal of the cook's thumb if he would not tell the truth. When one of the guards brought forth a hatchet, the cook finally told Father everything.

Wearing a dark house robe, Gaden appeared in the doorway. He eyed the dresser near the door and regarded Felix with furrowed brows.

"Your daughters attempted to cut my daughter's hair," Felix said. "Ida and Marda have both apologized, but Hilda has not. Because she has not apologized, I will now cut her hair, unless, of course, you would like us to leave. But if we leave now, I will take the horse."

The gray-haired man sighed heavily. "Cud her hair."

Rising from the side of the bed, I handed Felix the scissors. As he snipped, Hilda's eyes were black as hate. My avenger did not cut kindly. He cut close to her scalp and left no hair longer than two inches. I swallowed and looked at the floor. I had always heard that a woman's hair was her mane of glory, and I'd now witnessed it.

When Hilda beheld herself in the round mirror, she wailed, moaned, and eventually sobbed. Trembling, I hid behind Felix.

Our visitors finally left. Felix set the scissors on the nightstand on his side of the room. He proceeded to slide the dresser in front of the door and turn down the lantern until the wick was snuffed out. "I will sleep on this side of the room tonight, daughter," he said.

"Yes, Father." I curled up into a ball on my bed and stared about the dark room.

"I am sorry, Dory, I underestimated her. I was almost too late." Felix's voice interrupted our silence.

Tears drenched my pillow. A sniffle escaped me, and then another. I smothered my sobs in my pillow. Never had I yearned so much for my mother's soft voice and quiet spirit. I felt abandoned by my parents and alone. The thought silenced my tears, and I stared at the ceiling overhead.

"Everything's going to be all right. I am here now. Sleep, Princess." Felix's voice was kind. "You will like Prince Wron; he is a good man. All this will not be for naught."

ΦΦΦ

We rose early the next morning. After Nora served us porridge with currants, we departed without seeing anyone else in the household. We rode through the picturesque little hamlet in silence. Now that Hilda was behind me, I found the memory of sitting at the table while she had three bites of dinner upon her plate an amusing lesson. I hoped she'd learned something.

"What did you learn from last night?" Felix asked.

I questioned if he would reprimand me. At the table, I'd been smart in a dumb sort of way.

"Um . . . I was not a good guest. And Hilda, well, Gaden and Nora served themselves first, and it's been my upbringing that guests should always be served first."

"Yes, but . . ." Felix gave me time to think.

"But was I rude? That's what you are asking." I frowned. "Trading a horse for a scant amount of food and lodging for one night is not a fair trade."

"Did you learn anything from last night?" Felix flicked the reins.

"Which part—dinner or later?"

"Dinner."

"Obviously, not what you wanted me to." I rubbed my forehead with both hands.

"I believe that learning the language of your people and being able to stand up and speak out when things aren't fair are important qualities for a future queen," Felix said.

My heart warmed. His compliment was so dear to me that I told myself I could live on it for the rest of the journey if I had to.

"You are bright, Dory, just as your father said. When you are queen, choose your battles carefully."

His praise softened me. He was not responsible for the situation. Someday I would speak with my father, and I would tell him all of the things he should have done differently. But number one, he should have told me I was leaving and to whom I was betrothed. My parents should have told me. How I longed for that good-bye and all the endearments that should have been said.

ΦΦΦ

For the next five days, we traveled and camped alongside the road. While I slept in the bed of the wagon with the chickens, Felix slept on the ground beneath us. For breakfast each morning and dinner each night, Felix cooked scrambled eggs in a cast-iron pan over a fire. Though I longed for the pleasures of home, I tried not to complain. I hadn't bathed in over a week. I wanted to see a mirror, yet at the same time I was afraid of what I'd see . . . probably a blemish.

"Tonight will be the last home we stay at before the road ends. Tomorrow, we'll ride horseback. Your father will not travel through Merner. It would prove too dangerous with a large group."

"Tonight, we'll stay in Merner?"

"Yes."

"Does tonight's family know who I am?"

"Only one person knows that you are a royal pianist traveling in disguise. They know nothing more. I want you to use the accent, exactly like the night at Hilda's. The Merner region is hostile to the merger. It is important that no suspicions are raised by your Blue Sky accent."

Chills ran down my spine. "Why is that?" After Hilda, I didn't like the sound of tonight.

"Merner wants its independence. Due to logging, they have a thriving economy. They are situated near the present border of Yonder and Blue Sky. The people feel ignored and unheard, and due to their location, they probably are."

"We're near the border?" I breathed.

"Yes, the most difficult leg of our journey is before us. Listen closely, Dory." His keen gray eyes demanded my attention. "Merner needs its own magistrate, someone to represent the people to the king."

My head hurt from all the information. I didn't remember my mother ever being involved in Father's politics. Maybe behind the scenes, she'd been. Maybe that's why her lovely red hair had turned gray at an early age.

"What are we trading this time?" I asked.

"A table."

"Oh . . ." The poor people didn't even have a table.

"The table's already been paid for. We're simply picking it up and delivering it to our hosts in Merner in exchange for room and board."

"And they know we're coming tonight?"

"Yes. Months of planning, Dory." Felix flicked the reins.

"Do they have daughters?"

"No."

Good. I smiled.

The table was solid mahogany and handsome. It took several young men from the mercantile to load it into the back of our wagon. In another lifetime, I would have deemed several of the craftsmen cute. But because I wore my wig hat and walnut-stained face, I was too embarrassed to take a second glance.

With shoulders hunched, Felix flicked the reins and sighed heavily. "My informant thinks there has been a leak of information. Of all places." His neck disappeared into his large shoulder muscles as he sat hunched over the reins.

"So, they . . . so they know?" I stuttered. "Someone knows it's me?"

"No, no one knows it's you. In all of our planning, you've only been referred to as the piano girl. The Blue Sky piano girl."

That's why Hilda had treated me with contempt! I'd been referred to as the royal piano girl.

"Maybe we should just keep riding," I said.

"No, we'll continue as planned."

Mossy oak trees lined the road and were lovely in the twilight. Felix slowed the wagon to peer at a handwritten sign. Black lettering on a long wooden shingle spelled: Chavers. We began our descent down a winding dirt road.

"Have you been here before?" I held on to the back of the bench.

"Years ago, I spent a great deal of time in these woods."

"I wouldn't call scattered oak trees woods." A rolling green meadow lined the valley floor.

"There used to be fine timber on this section of land." He flicked the reins. "Remember your accent tonight. We will be dining with an elderly couple."

"And will you also have an accent?"

"I am your fauder."

An uneasiness that didn't resemble hunger settled in the pit of my stomach. "My *T*s will be *D*s and my *W*s will be *V*s."

"We should be consistent." He nodded in agreement. "And you are never to say where you are from or where you are going. Be very cautious. You must never mention Blue Sky or Yonder."

"I'm afraid, Felix; all your talk of tension." I studied his profile.

"As your father said in his letter, I am equal to fifty men. Do not be afraid."

I recalled how easily he'd handled the three sisters. He had not warned me of any tension that night, yet tonight he'd warned me twice.

"Tonight you will take a bath and a sauna."

"Oh, good." For a moment, I pictured myself up to my neck in bubbles.

He laughed softly. "I knew that by this stage of the journey, you'd need a bath."

His sentiments reminded me that he'd helped my father plan each step of the journey. "Remind me why we stayed at the sisters'?"

"Their father is loyal to Blue Sky."

Felix drove the wagon past a quaint white farmhouse into a large barn. The smell of hay and sheep mingled in the air. I climbed down from the wagon and stretched my arms above my head.

Felix lifted the bench seat. "Here." He tossed me a wad of dark green material. Fortunately, I caught it; otherwise, it would have landed on the straw-flecked dirt. I held the material out at arm's length. It was a commoner's dress with a smocked top, a huge improvement over my present attire, but vulgarly simple. I almost threw it back.

"This is another part of your plan? A dress?" Perhaps it was from five days of eating scrambled eggs that I felt anxious, or perhaps it was the knowledge that he'd also planned our stay at the three sisters'.

"Yes, each stop has a purpose, Dory. Your parents confided that you've been spoiled, and that I had only one month to reform you. I do not think it will take that long; do you?"

Within a month, I would be Princess Alia again. Wouldn't I? When I married Prince Wron, I would return to the lifestyle I'd known all my life. Wouldn't I?

I followed Felix out of the barn. "So everything's been orchestrated? Sadie, Hilda . . . tonight?"

His neck disappeared into his hunched shoulders as it often did when he was annoyed. "*Outlined* is a better word than *orchestrated*. Where we will stay, what we will trade..." His voice was barely above a whisper. "But I cannot control your response. Glean from it what you will."

"Were Sadie's circumstances real?" The little girl haunted me day and night.

"Yes, everything has been *real*." He lumbered in the direction of the farmhouse.

"Vee are nod pronouncing our *T*s donighd, Fauder." I hurried after him.

He waited for me to catch up. "I was told you are strong willed." His eyes studied mine. "With the right motives and values, that quality will make you a better queen."

"Better queen." I tasted the words and flung the dress over my shoulder. It was all too clear to me now. "My father wanted me to have the adventure. And you're the one who's added the concept of *a better queen*."

Felix's profile was stoic as he strode toward the farmhouse.

I was right. I knew I was!

From the porch, an elderly woman waved at us. She wore a faded apron over a long, drab dress. Her gray hair was pulled into a low bun. "Welcome," she said, smiling. One of her eyeteeth was missing. "The sow-na is ready."

"Dhank you." I looked at Felix and questioned if I should feel anxious about leaving him.

"Go now with Liisa." He nodded.

I followed Liisa through a galley kitchen with white-painted cabinets to a stone-floored laundry area, and then to the back porch. Here, she paused for a moment before resting her hand on a wooden post. "The sow-na is that little house back there." She pointed toward a rustic building about the size of Greda and Sadie's home. "Cleans the pores. If you sit on the lower bench, it will be cooler than the top bench. If you want more heat, pour some water on the rocks. Cleans your pores."

"Dhank you." I waved over my shoulder at her as I strolled toward the sauna house. Though Liisa appeared to be watching me, she didn't wave back.

Like the elderly woman had said, the top bench was hotter. Walnut-colored sweat dripped off me. I sweated in the dry, steamy air until I almost fell asleep. Feeling overheated, I took a cold shower.

In the changing room, I discovered a small round mirror hung on a peg. Turning side to side, I surveyed my face. Though it was red, I was pleased to see that my complexion was no longer walnut. I stepped closer to the mirror. What was that? A hard, raised bump had formed on my chin.

Wide-eyed, I stared at my first pimple.

I wanted to scream! But because I had only the towel wrapped around me, I thought it best I get dressed first. I hurriedly changed into the dark green peasant dress. Below the smocked top, the material flowed loosely past my knees. While it was a huge improvement, it was without question the second-worst thing I'd ever worn. I felt so embarrassed by my pimple and the dress that I would immediately go to bed after dinner. Mother always said that sleep was very good for the complexion.

I wondered what caused the pimple. Perhaps it had been one of the following: walnut oil, lack of sleep, not bathing for a week, or the scrambled egg diet. All maladies were new to me.

I returned to the farmhouse, where I found Felix, freshly showered, wearing clean overalls. I sat down across from him at the new table.

"It feels so smooth." Liisa ran her hand over the mahogany surface.

"It's a beautiful table, Liisa." Felix looked at me and frowned. "You must reapply the walnut oil."

He'd said it right in front of our hostess. She must be the one who knew I was the Blue Sky piano girl.

"Liisa is nearly blind, and she's not who I'm worried about tonight," Felix said.

My stomach knotted. Who was he worried about, Liisa's husband?

"Because of your walnut oil, I have my first pimple." I felt embarrassingly close to tears. "I've never had a pimple in my whole life."

"Remember your accend," Felix said.

"Oh, dear." Liisa shook her head. "Don't tell me she's going to cry because of a pimple."

"I think it is the hardships of the journey," he said on my behalf. "The pimple is ever so slight," Felix whispered to me. "See what little pleasure a mirror brings? You'd been content enough without it."

How little he knew. For weeks, I'd longed to see my reflection. I swallowed tears.

"Liisa, can you do Dory's hair? It is not safe for her to wear it down tonight."

I furrowed my brows, frowning at Felix. I'd never had a blind woman do my hair before, and I didn't find the thought appealing.

"I wish my eyes were still keen." The elderly woman rose from her chair. "Felix said your auburn hair is beautiful— thick and curly."

"It is a pain to brush," I admitted.

"Stay seated, Dory." Felix rose from his chair. "I will apply the oil while Liisa fixes your hair." The elderly woman ambled to the kitchen and opened a drawer.

At least I was not going to a ball tonight.

Liisa worked through my curls with nimble fingers. Though she tried to be gentle, her combing hit a knot. I winced.

"Sorry, Dory. Your hair is the thickest I've ever worked with. Felix, do I have it all in my hands?"

"Yes." Leaning from side to side, he studied me.

After braiding it, Liisa tied it off with a ribbon. I thought we were done, but then she began pinning, and if I was not mistaken, she pinned my hair in the shape of a box on the top of my head. She began working higher and higher, bobby pinning each row.

"My arms ache," she moaned.

"Here, stand on this chair." Felix pulled a chair out from beneath the table and centered it behind me. The blind, elderly woman stood on top of the chair and fashioned the last inches of the braid on top of my head.

My skin was stained a walnut color, I was dressed as a peasant, and now my hair was fashioned like a box on top of my head. Thank goodness we were only dining with the elderly.

"Can I see a mirror?" I asked.

Felix bit the insides of his cheeks and shook his head. In the past, someone denying my request would have proven enough to throw me into a royal tantrum. But I was too tired and hungry to complain.

"I will go to bed immediately after dinner," I whispered while Liisa puttered in the kitchen.

"On account of the pimple or your hair?" Felix whispered.

"If you will let me see a mirror, I will tell you."

His cheek muscles bunched. "Ask Liisa if there's anything you can help her with. And use your accent."

I found the elderly woman in the corner of the kitchen at the cookstove. She opened the oven door and pulled out a baking sheet of warm, golden-brown yeast rolls. They looked and smelled delicious. She flipped the pan over a basket lined with a yellow-and-white checked tea towel.

"Dory, can you carry this to the table?"

"Yes. Hov did you knov id is me?" Hmmm . . . the *W*s would be tricky.

"I can see your outline. Like a willowy gray shadow."

After placing the basket on the table beside Felix, I returned to Liisa's side. "Hoh may I help?" I hated the accent.

"I'm so pleased that you asked. Please set my new table for ten guests."

"Den?"

"Yes. The silverware is beneath the window."

An open wood box hosted butter knives, forks, and spoons. I carried it to the table and ignored Felix's secretive smile. I'd sat at a table all my life, so of course I was aware of how to set one. I set a salad fork, a dinner fork, and the butter knife to the right, blade facing toward the plate, followed by a spoon, followed by a soup spoon, and lastly, a dessert fork and spoon paired together above the plate. After setting six place servings, I ran out of silverware.

"Liisa, vhere is your udder silver?"

"I have all the silver in the box."

"Yes, bud id is nod enough."

The elderly woman huffed softly under her breath as she made her way to the table. With her long, wrinkled fingers, she felt a place setting with her left hand. "Why are there so many forks?" she asked.

"For da salad, da main dish, and desserd."

Liisa felt the dessert fork above the plate area and shook her head. "And why so many spoons?"

"For da soup, da entrée, and desserd."

"Do you think we are royalty?" Facing me, Liisa lifted her sparse gray brows. Her dark gray eyes peered at the pimple on my chin. "Set one spoon, one knife, and one fork at each plate."

That made my job a lot easier.

While I finished aligning the last place setting, there was a commotion in the entryway. Guests had arrived. Several young men and women strolled into the kitchen, laughing and conversing. A young and pretty dark-haired woman hugged Liisa. "Thank you, Grandma."

I wanted to die. Liisa was hosting young adults tonight, and I looked ridiculous with my box bun and a pimple on my chin. With a wry smile, Felix met my gaze. He'd known! With my fists by my sides, I fumed as Liisa's guests seated themselves around the table.

"Uh, Dory." Liisa stood in the middle of the kitchen like she could no longer make out where I was. Didn't she see the silhouette of the box on my head? I walked toward her, and she appeared to look right through me as if she didn't see my gray shadow. I stopped a few feet in front of her, and she looked around me.

"Dory," she said. "I need your help, dear."

"I'm righd here in frond of you."

"Where?" Liisa reached out and with anguish in her dull eyes said, "Everything is dark. It happens when I am tired. Please tell my husband. Ramsey is on the porch."

I left the kitchen in search of an elderly man and found one on the front porch smoking a pipe, seated in a rocker. "Liisa vanded me do dell you dat she is dired and can'd see."

"Huh?" Wrinkling his nose, the plump, white-haired man didn't understand my accent in the slightest.

I knew Ramsey was an ally. "Liisa wanted me to tell you that she is tired and can't see."

"Oh . . ." He rose from his chair. "Why didn't you say so the first time?"

I should have.

When we returned to the kitchen, Liisa was seated in a rocking chair a few feet from the table. Ramsey sat down across from Felix, which left me alone in the kitchen looking at everyone. Perhaps I should sit down also, so I wouldn't feel like a performer.

"Does Dory have on her apron, Ramsey?" Liisa asked.

"Nope. I don't see one."

"Wear your apron, Dory." Liisa pointed to a column of cupboards.

I opened the top drawer. Bottles of spices greeted me. For some reason, the young people had stopped conversing to watch me. I slid open the second drawer to the noisy clatter of pans. In the third drawer, there was a horrid sage-green apron, which I pulled out. The only thing nice about it was that it would almost completely cover my horrid dress. I slid the apron opening above my head and pulled it down in front. It came to my knees. When I went to tie it in back, it was too wide, so I wrapped the long ties around me and tied it in front.

"Dory, the chickens are in the oven. They need basting." The old woman was bossy. Her granddaughter was seated at the table. Why was I, a guest, preparing the meal? Felix! He was behind all of this.

I walked around to the oven that Liisa had earlier pulled the yeast rolls from, but there was nothing inside.

"The other oven," Liisa said.

I returned to the main kitchen area and realized there was another white stove. Two knit hot pads sat on top. Holding a pot holder in each hand, I opened the oven door. Steam leaped at my face. I stepped back, alarmed.

A giggle escaped the red-haired woman at the table; she must have seen me. Conversation resumed as I pulled the large, heavy pan from the oven and set it on top of the stove. Three lightly browned chickens baked in bubbly drippings. If I hadn't had an audience, I could have eaten all three, right there. I wondered if they were our birds. I glanced at Felix. He averted his gaze.

"Are you basting them, Dory?"

I looked around the kitchen. I had no idea what basting meant. "Fe—" My eyes widened. "Fauder," I said. "Fauder."

"Yes, daughder."

"May I speak vidh you on da porch?" I strode out the front door and stood in front of the shingled siding where there were no windows. Felix soon joined me and closed the door behind him.

"I'm not going back in there unless you help me. I don't know how to baste. Everyone's watching, and I've never been alone in a kitchen before, and you know it."

The top of his balding head turned a little red. "I will help you."

"Is my humiliation planned?"

"No, not at all. To baste"—his hand felt heavy on my shoulder—"get a spoon and scoop the drippings from the pan and pour them over the chickens and then put the roasting pan back into the oven."

We returned to the kitchen, and I did as he'd said. The juices and drippings shimmered with fat and crispy dark nuggets. I opened the oven door and, using the pot holders, slid the pan inside. I closed the door, triumphant.

"Dory, you need to start the potatoes," Liisa said.

Felix rose from the table, opened a pantry door, and brought twelve large potatoes to the counter for me.

"Is Liisa your mother?" I whispered.

"No." He handed me what looked like a small musical instrument with a pointed tip.

I picked up a potato in my left hand and thought about my course of action.

"Dory, bring butter to the table." Liisa rocked in her chair. "Our guests can enjoy the warm rolls while they wait."

I looked about the counters. Sometimes cooks left the butter in a covered dish. Felix rose from the table, crossed the kitchen, and opened a cupboard. He handed me a covered butter dish.

"Are you and Liisa related?" I whispered.

"Only by marriage. No more questions."

I carried the butter to the table, no longer caring about our audience. "Fauder," I said, "are vee relded do Hilda?"

"Daughder, nod now." Felix's muscles rose and his neck disappeared.

I nodded.

The young people at the table thought this was particularly funny. I smiled and noted there were two young, nice-looking gentlemen who I had not had the opportunity to admire. And then I reminded myself that I was not my own. I was given away to Prince Wrong when I was an infant, and I had a box for a bun and a pimple on my chin, and . . .

"Dory, are the potatoes boiling yet?" Liisa asked.

My eyes widened.

"Dory, where are you from?" asked one of the young women. Her red hair was stylishly fashioned in a high bun.

"Vhy?" I asked, glancing at Felix. I was not to say where I was going or where I was from.

"Vhy," the woman said. "I haven't heard of Vhy."

"I think she said, 'Why,'" Liisa's granddaughter said. She was lovely. Her clothes were lovely. Her dark hair and her complexion were lovely.

"Well," the red-haired woman began, "because of the way you wear your hair, I was wondering where you're from."

"Boxden. I'm from Boxden." I returned to my potatoes.

They laughed, of course. They thought I was hilarious.

At the sink, I peeled a potato with the odd instrument. I whittled the once-large potato to the size of a slim pickle. Now what was I supposed to do with it?

At the table, Ramsey cleared his throat. "Liisa, if we want potatoes for dinner, you best help Dory in there. You can peel blind better than she can with sight."

"Stay seated, Grandma, I will help," said the granddaughter. She strode gracefully toward me. Perhaps she was of royal birth, but if she knew how to peel potatoes, she definitely wasn't.

She opened the same drawer that Felix had, and found another potato instrument. Shoulder to shoulder, we stood at the sink. "Just take a little bit of skin, and grip the potato firmly with your left hand, like this."

"Oh, I see." Her grip was similar to that of holding a tennis racket. Mother always said to shake hands with the racket. Starting at the top of the potato, I pulled the peeler toward me. This technique helped a lot.

"You'll cut yourself if you keep peeling like that, and we'll have bloody potatoes." She nudged me, and the potato slipped out of my hand onto the floor. Bending to retrieve it, I hit my box bun on the counter.

To my embarrassment, several at the table chuckled. While I tried to regain my composure, the young woman beside me smiled sweetly.

"I'm Eliza."

"I'm Dory, and I've never peeled podados before."

She giggled and put the potatoes in a pan, covered them with water, added salt, and lit a fire in the stove. I watched with keen interest. At a young age, I'd wanted to participate in the kitchen, but Mother never let me. She said it was beneath me.

My children would learn to cook.

"Dory, take the chicken out." It was Liisa again. "You'll need to start the gravy and the peas."

"Do you want me to stay and help?" Eliza asked me.

"If you ever vand do ead."

Eliza's cheeks puffed out before she giggled.

I stirred the drippings while she added cornstarch, cream, and seasonings. Adding ingredients was like playing and creating something edible. I enjoyed helping, being useful, not sitting like the dolts at the table.

"You need to start cutting the chicken," Eliza whispered. "I'll take care of the gravy."

I had never cut a chicken. I'd slept with plenty of them, but I'd never sliced into one of them before, and I knew there was an art. I sighed nervously.

Felix rose from the table. "I'll carve the chicken."

After all the food dishes were delivered to the table, I was allowed to sit down in the chair on Felix's left. Eliza's gravy was exceptionally delicious, as was the entire meal. I had not eaten to such content in quite a while. For comfort, I untied the front of my apron and leaned back in my chair. Never had a meal tasted so good to me. But then again, I'd never before dined for five straight days on scrambled eggs.

Chapter Five

"**D**ory, it is time to get up." Felix roused me in the middle of the night. "I have prepared our things."

I sat up against my elbows. It was pitch black outside. "It's too early." I flopped back down, exhausted.

"Get up, and be quiet." He squeezed my pinkie toe until I was indeed awake.

I sat up and slid on my shoes. Half-asleep, I followed him down the wooden stairwell. He left an envelope on the table for Liisa. Leading the way, he quietly pulled the front door closed behind us. A full moon hung high in the midnight sky, lighting the way to the barn.

We rode in silence. With a blanket wrapped about me, I huddled next to Felix on the bench seat. The oak trees that earlier appeared laden with green foliage looked like black, gnarly creatures crouched on the silvery hills.

Several hours later, I awoke with my cheek pressed against Felix's shoulder. Heavy gray shadows hung beneath his eyes, like he had not slept all night. The sun was halfway to its usual perch. My empty stomach told me it was well past breakfast time.

"Why did we have to leave so early and not even say good-bye?" I yawned and stretched.

"Some of the young folk there last night were not expected. Liisa is afraid her granddaughter may have slipped about you being a pianist from Blue Sky."

"I thought Liisa was the only one who knew."

"It sounds like Liisa also slipped." Shoulders hunched, he flicked the reins.

"Who could they possibly be?" I mused out loud.

"I don't know, except one of the young men had a hole in his earlobe."

"Huh?"

"Fallon, the dark-haired young man, had an earring scar. A sign of gypsies."

I glanced over my shoulder at the empty road and was relieved that Felix had waited ten hours to tell me this.

The countryside changed from scrub, barren hills to mountainous forest.

"If anyone does follow us, most likely he will head the wrong direction. In my letter to Liisa, I told her that I am delivering chickens to an old friend in Rivers."

"Where is Rivers?"

"West, and we're headed south." He flicked the reins. "What lesson did you learn at Liisa's?"

There were so many lessons from Liisa's. "I want my children to learn to cook, and to baste, and to make mashed potatoes." I glanced over my shoulder at the road behind me.

ΦΦΦ

After endless hours of sitting on the wagon bench, my back began to ache. "How are you related to Liisa?" I asked.

Felix sat hunched with his elbows to his knees. "When my wife and I were first married, we lived with Liisa and

Ramsey. They were her great-aunt and uncle. It was a long time ago."

"Oh, is your wife still alive?"

"No, she died nine years ago."

"I'm so sorry." My heart ached for him.

For lunch, I cooked scrambled eggs over a fire that Felix had built alongside the road. Little sunlight filtered through the trees. The shady, dreary scenery matched my mood.

"At the next town, we'll get fresh horses," Felix said. "You'll need to wear the wig again. For the remainder of our journey, we will camp. This is our last meal of eggs. After Dover, we will only eat what we shoot."

"I could never kill anything, Felix. I don't want to." I had no desire to learn the art of shooting.

"You've eaten meat all your life. Now is not the time to become a vegetarian." He kicked dirt at the fire, smothering it.

In Dover, a pretty town nestled in the foothills, Felix parked the wagon in front of a feed store. This time he would not allow me to remain alone without him.

He informed the clerk, "I have chickens to trade for horses."

The man nodded and glanced at me and then my wig. Today my complexion was not stained walnut color, but my hair was hidden. "All is well?" he asked.

"Yes." Felix slid yet another envelope across the counter.

At the rear of the building, we parted with our wagon in exchange for two fresh horses. We rode side by side through the streets. Felix carried a shotgun openly in his saddle.

"If my father's taking a different route, why are you still leaving letters?"

"If anything were to go wrong, the letters would help him track us."

"Oh." Their planning had included many details.

"The horse you are riding—his name is Waluga. Our animals may look common, but they were raised by the best in Blue Sky." As he rode, Felix stroked the large horse's dark mane.

"Blue Sky?" Waluga, my brown mare, could easily have passed for a farmer's workhorse. Felix's brown, dappled horse was much larger. "What's the name of your horse?"

"Plenty. She is one of the strongest, one of the best."

"All the way from Blue Sky?" Like much of our journey, it did not make sense to me.

"It was your father's idea. In the leather satchel, there are three dresses for Yonder that you may require before your *entourage* arrives."

Just hearing the old French word made me smile. "When will my entourage arrive?"

"A few days prior to your wedding."

"Why didn't I travel with them?"

"You forget, Prince Wron wanted to meet you. And, before you marry and become queen of the vastest empire on our continent, your father wanted you to have these . . . experiences."

"You mean adventures." I patted Waluga's velvet brown neck.

We rode for several hours. Oftentimes, I felt like I was asleep in the saddle. The countryside didn't help any; it was just miles of barren land—not a tree or a bush or even a prairie dog.

"Tell me more about Evland," I said.

Felix rolled a kink out of his thick neck. "Evland is a small town, two days' travel from Yonder. Before the war, my wife and I lived there in a white rock cottage, with a sweeping view of the valley. When you ride through town . . ." He told me exactly the way to get to his old homestead, and because of the emotion in his voice, I listened carefully. "If you ever make it there, Dory, stand at the threshold of our old home and look to the valley."

"Why did you leave?"

"On account of the war, we had to. I hid letters that we'd written to one another in an old canister beneath a large rock south of our home." He appeared thoughtful. "After I deliver Yonder's future queen, I will find the letters."

"Why didn't you just take them with you?"

"My wife and I made a vow to each other that we would return." His chest expanded as he flicked the reins. "I am finally returning."

"Oh." My heart hurt for Felix.

We traveled until sunset, and then we set up our tents and tied the horses to trees. Over the campfire, Felix baked bread on a stick and roasted a handsome bird that he'd flushed on the trail. He cut off a chunk of meat for me.

"Chukar is better than chicken." His gray eyes glistened.

I unashamedly savored each bite. "I can't believe how hungry I am."

He leaned across the fire to hand me a roll that was golden on all sides. "The sourdough is hungry, too." He nodded toward a frothy, cream-colored batter. "I will put you in charge of feeding it some flour every day."

"Where did you get the sourdough?"

"There is a woman in Dover who made the starter—the batter."

I peered at the tinful of the odd, frothy batter before taking a bite of the slightly sour bread. I liked it. The chukar and sourdough was one of our most delicious meals of our trip, second only to the meal we'd enjoyed at Liisa's home.

"Will you teach me to shoot a gun tomorrow?"

Felix glanced up at me, the firelight in his eyes. "You are not as stubborn as your father led me to believe."

"I have never been this hungry before." I grinned.

"It is good to know a little hunger." He wrapped a ball of dough around the end of the stick and handed it to me to hold over the coals.

After supper, I snuggled in my sleeping bag and gazed overhead at the diamond specked sky. A deep sadness contained me. "I wish I could have told my family good-bye."

"Hmmph . . . it was a difficult start for you." Felix added wood to the fire. "Your parents were afraid you would not cooperate."

I remembered my life with them compared to now. "I would not have gone quietly."

"I don't think you would have either."

ΦΦΦ

Over the next few evenings, while we sat near the fire, Felix explained in great detail the parts of a shotgun: the double barrel, the sight, and the butt that I'd hold against my shoulder. And, how if I didn't load it properly—if there was any gap between the black powder and the shot, it could cause the barrel to blow up. Finally, one evening at twilight, he handed me the gun.

"You're ready," he said.

I felt ready. I stood with my feet shoulder width apart, propped my right elbow to my hip, and pressed the butt of the shotgun to my shoulder.

"Sight in that pinecone hanging from the longest branch. Remember to look through the V. There will be a kick that follows; you must brace yourself." He stood up, perhaps to guard me from falling into the fire.

I sighted in the pinecone and pulled the trigger. The gun kicked more than I'd expected, and I fell back a step in alarm and mild pain. When I glanced up, the pinecone hung peacefully in place.

"Try again. Shooting appears to be something that may not come as naturally as your gift for the piano."

Felix knew. We'd never discussed my gift before. Oh, how I longed to play, to pour my heartache into the Great Beast.

"The night of your birthday celebration, you played unlike anyone I've ever heard. With a passion both fierce and gentle."

"Dhank you, Fauder." I pulled the trigger a second time and fell back a step. Again, the large pinecone dangled peacefully from the limb.

"I always play from emotion and memory, and Prince Dell of Nearton"—I glanced over my shoulder at Felix—"had just stolen my first adult kiss. The piano has always been a type of catharsis for me."

"You played with great passion." He nodded.

"Was it too dark?"

"No, not dark, but spellbinding. You have a powerful gift."

His praise made my fingers twitch with a desire to play.

ΦΦΦ

I stopped thinking about home so much and thought more about my betrothed—Prince Wron. I said the first of many prayers: *Lord, if he is ugly, let him be kind. If he is handsome, let him be kind. Someday, let me love my future husband.*

Many days later, the sun was hot; and the dry, flat land disappeared into the horizon. The rolling green velvet hills of Blue Sky were only memories. At dusk, we saw our first tree of the day—a lone, gnarly figure without foliage of any kind. It was here that we camped.

My face felt sunburned as I sat on a rock near the campfire. I was thirsty and famished, and my body ached from eight straight hours on horseback. Enormously exhausted, I gave in to feelings of self-pity. I wanted to be alone under the canopy of stars and took a few steps away.

"Stay close, Dory; the desert is full of night animals," Felix said. "Coyotes will call tonight; we must keep the fire going."

I returned to my sitting rock. I disliked the lowly coyote. I knew enough about them to know that they gathered courage in a pack. As had become routine, dinner was sourdough bread baked on sticks and an odd-shaped bird.

"Is it the blue bird?" I asked.

"Yes, not as tasty as chukar, but the meat is not blue." Felix handed me a chunk of meat.

"You are a good shot, Felix, and a fine cook."

"We'll continue our shooting lessons tomorrow before the land changes to green."

"Grass again?" I asked, hopeful.

"No, marsh."

I lay in my sleeping bag and listened to the coyotes howl at the full moon. Their wails sounded closer and closer.

"As long as the fire burns, they're harmless, a pack of whiners." Felix snapped a branch from a gnarly tree, adding fuel to the fire.

"Good." My eyelids felt heavy.

"Good night, Princess."

ΦΦΦ

Midmorning, we stopped at the crest of a hill to survey our surroundings. A frothy lime-green river about one hundred meters wide stretched as far as the eye could see. Felix cupped his hands over Plenty's ears.

"The horses do not like Swamp Valley."

"Any crocodiles or surprises I should know about?" I felt only slightly anxious. Each day was a new adventure with Felix.

"No crocodiles; it's the mosquitoes and the swamp plants that will eat you alive." He took a small bottle out of his travel bag. "Vinegar. Mosquitoes don't care for the smell." He poured some of the clear liquid into his hand and scrunched his nose as he wiped it on his wide forehead and cheeks, and then he handed me the bottle.

"Horses don't like the swamp. There are stinging plants. Whatever you do, Dory, don't get off your horse."

"Is there no other way?" Beginning with my forehead, I wiped the vinegar on my face.

"There is, but it would take a week longer." Clicking the sides of Plenty's belly, Felix started down the hillside. I wanted to follow precisely in his steps and prodded Waluga to keep up. Skunk cabbage—pretty from afar—sent out a strong sour odor as we edged closer to the basin.

Knee-deep in the frothy green water, our horses slowly made their way over decaying logs and through thick, sinewy fronds. I swatted at mosquitoes as they dipped for blood. Up ahead, Felix's horse whinnied, high stepping forward and then back. My own horse plodded into reverse; I didn't resist her. In the fronds below, a creature the size of a muskrat darted toward us.

Then, all I saw was sky, as my horse went back on her hind legs. Waluga rocked down and bucked, and I was catapulted over her head into the muck below.

"Get up, Dory!" Felix yelled.

A noxious green slime burned my skin and blurred my vision.

"Get back on your horse!" On foot, Felix appeared through the gray-winged fog. He grabbed Waluga's reins and lifted me back onto her. I held tight to the saddle horn as sanity and delirium struggled for position. I was no longer in charge of the reins as Felix on horseback towed us up the hillside. Everything about me stung as if I'd taken a bath in poison oak and ivy. With no assistance from me, we crested the summit.

"There's fresh water in a couple of miles," Felix yelled back at me, and then he rode the horses hard. A burning itchiness enveloped my being, and my vision narrowed to a slit as thin as paper. "Fifty more . . ." Felix's voice carried in the wind.

I held on to the saddle horn for dear life, as if I were hanging on to a root at the edge of a cliff. Finally, the animals halted. Felix carried me like a rag doll over one shoulder, and when he was knee-high in the water, he tossed me into the deep.

I plummeted deep and bobbed up gasping. Everything about me itched. Sputtering, I went down again, and then Felix pulled me out by the back of my collar.

"The swamp plant's bite is bad. I'm sorry, Dory," he said, towing me to shore.

"I itch! I itch!" Everything itched so fiercely that I wanted my life to end.

"You can't scratch! It makes it worse." Felix hoisted me onto his horse. "You're going to be all right. You're going to be all right."

Chapter Six

"**F**elix! Felix!" Yelling his name, I awoke from a terrible dream. My skin pulsed with an itchy fire. Everything about me tingled and throbbed.

"He's in the garden," said an unfamiliar voice beside me. We were in a cluttered one-room cottage, and a wizened old woman sat in a chair beside my bed. Bundled herbs hung overhead in the open rafters.

"Is he alive?" I whispered. Was he buried in the garden?

"Yes, of course he's alive. Lie down, you're delirious."

I lay back against the straw ticking and studied the woman's sage-green eyes. Her bony face was a cross-stitch of wrinkles.

"I'm Dixie, the herbalist." She dabbed at my forehead with a warm muslin bag.

"We were entering a heavenly meadow." Trembling and chilled, I felt extremely fatigued, and every inch of my skin itched.

"Shepherd's Field." Dixie closed her eyes and nodded.

"Very large women—giants—appeared from the shadows."

The herbalist clicked her tongue against the roof of her mouth. "After hibernation, the giants are always starving."

"They were." My memory traveled from the dream of terror to the terrible swamp. I lifted my tingling hands and stared. My long, piano-playing fingers felt swollen . . . tight, and were covered in a red, bubbly rash with bright pink centers.

"My hands. My piano-playing hands." They belonged to a strange creature, not to me.

"Shhh!" The old woman hushed me. "Anxiety only makes the symptoms worse."

"Do you have a mirror?" My lower lip felt numb, yet plump.

"I have never owned one," the old woman lied.

"Then bring me one of your shiniest kettles."

"I only have copper, and its reflection is blurry."

"Bring me that kettle you have on the stove." Lifting my arm, I pointed across the room. The hunched little woman ambled to the stove before I lay back, exhausted. She held the kettle out in front of me. With great effort, I propped myself up on my elbows. I had never seen such tarnished copper. My reflection was a mottled blob.

Felix appeared in the doorway with an armload of herbs. He was truly alive! It had only been a terrible dream.

"You're back." Dixie rose from the chair. "I'll make tea."

"She's awake." Felix set what smelled like fresh mint on the table.

"I had the most awful dream." I peered up at him. "At the entrance to Shepherd's Field, there were these giants."

"Don't tell him!" the old woman snapped.

"Tell me." Felix swiveled a chair from the table and sat down.

"There were these huge women with stringy brown hair, and the whites of their eyes were the size of . . . teacups!"

"Teacups?"

"The tea I'm making will take away the dreams." Dixie puttered near a potbellied stove.

With a slight nod, Felix encouraged me to continue.

"It was so real." I stared at him. "They lumbered out of the shadows."

"Now is not the time to tell him. You are weak. You must rest."

"I'm so glad you're alive." I gazed up at Felix, my lifeline. He was the only one who knew where we were going. Up until the terrible nightmare, I had no idea how important he was to me or how much I'd come to care about him.

"You need your rest, Dory." He patted the gray wool quilt in place about me.

"Does my face"—I touched it with my swollen fingertips—"look like my hands?" I searched the mirror of Felix's eyes.

He closed his eyes and nodded.

"Is it another lesson?" I recalled the muskrat, and the way Waluga had reacted. If it was, Felix was ever so clever.

"No." He shook his head.

"The final straw to teach me humility?"

"We must get you well." His Adam's apple bobbed up and then down.

"It may be months, even years. But what's done is done," the old woman muttered. Carrying a chipped mug, she neared my bedside.

Chopped leaves floated in a strange green brew. "I'm too tired." I slumped back into the straw-ticked mattress.

"Three sips." As thin as a fence post, Dixie hovered over me.

"No, I'm tired. I won't have bad dreams."

The old woman needled my shoulder with her bony finger for several minutes before I finally sat up to sip the hot tea.

"No more dreams," she whispered, removing the mug from my hand.

As I drifted to sleep, I remembered the faces of Dr. Krawl and Father looming over me, and my mother's, as she clutched her hands to her heart on the other side of the bed. No more nightmares, only memories.

Then, I was dancing, swishing back and forth in my sky-blue gown and light-as-air dancing slippers. A young man bowed before me. "Princess Alia, is your father really Felix?" He waltzed me onto the floor. It was a riddle. How could my father be Felix, if I was Princess Alia?

"You do not dance like a chicken farmer's daughter." He waltzed me about the room and spun me until I was dizzy, and then he spun me again, like he was trying to unravel the truth.

When I awoke, Felix sat oddly slumped with his cheek to the table.

"I'm writing down remedies for you, my dear." Seated across the table from Felix, Dixie held a writing quill. "The herbal recommendations for swamp pox are: Parsley. Cut small and add to a cup of boiling water. My most common recommendation is queen of the meadow." She lifted her gaze. "It grows in meadows, but only where the soil is very rich. It's a tall plant, five to six feet high, with tubular-shaped purple flowers. It's the root that's medicinal. You'll see it when you ride through Shepherd's Field, but you are not to get off your horse. People, horses . . . shoes . . . disappear in Shepherd's Field. Be careful or you'll want to lie in the meadow and stare at the clouds."

"Do you believe my dream?"

Her mouth bunched tight. "In the first few hours after the swamp pox bite, you see the fate of someone you love."

I glanced at Felix. "I love my father very much."

"Many have tried to bottle the swamp plant's bite as a truth serum." Dixie rose from the table and dabbed my forehead with the moist muslin bag. "When Felix was gathering herbs, Princess Alia, you told me your real name."

I stared overhead at the bundles of dried, crunchy plants suspended from the rafters. Were we safe? Had she drugged Felix, too?

"Yonder kingdom awaits Princess Alia's arrival, yet you will arrive common. Be careful that you are not deemed a counterfeit. They will take you to the hills to never find your way out."

Counterfeit?

"What do you mean?" My skin felt stingy and stretched.

"You'll arrive filthy and in rags. Your beauty guised." She glanced over her shoulder at Felix. "Tell no one. No one will believe you."

Unknowingly, Felix had brought me to a witch. Or with Felix, maybe knowingly. This lesson was simply to teach me discernment.

I suppressed a smile. "How long will my spots last?"

"It could be days or years. The problem with swamp pox is that remedies vary; everyone responds differently. One Yonder guard's spots improved when he ate garlic, while another had to eat chicory on everything."

"Years?" I managed a weak laugh. If my future husband was anything like Prince Dell, it served him right.

Dixie sat down again at the table. Perhaps Felix was indeed asleep; it was difficult to tell. With her back to me, Dixie continued with her writing. "Duron is the guard who ate garlic. He is a very robust man. He told me if there was anything he could do to repay me, he would. I will ask him in this letter to help my friend Dory."

Had the witch given Felix some strange kind of tea?

"What did Felix tell you under your spell?"

She laughed softly under her breath. "He is very torn about something. Very."

Could I believe her? "Did you know I would stop here?"

"Yes, I saw that your sickness would bring you here."

"Then surely you know how much I dislike my shoes." I smiled. "If you were a true servant of Yonder, you would have seen that those boats"—I pointed toward my ugly, square-toed plain Janes near the door—"are not fitting of a queen. And you would have provided me with a beautiful new pair."

Dixie returned to her writing and with her back to me said, "You will arrive to Yonder . . . barefoot. To provide you with a new pair would only have been squander."

I didn't find her comments very comforting, except for the fact that she had not mentioned *alone*. Perhaps Felix would survive my dream.

ΦΦΦ

After we left Dixie's, we spent a long day on horseback. We set up camp near a small stream. I found kindling and started a fire, while Felix skinned a rabbit for our supper.

"If we are separated, there are tricks in the forest," he said.

"In the Forest Maze?" On several occasions, he'd mentioned the odd maze.

"Yes, the fir trees, not the cedars, are the secret. When in doubt, look up. Fir trees are not as lacy or as pretty. When I've been near the end of the forest, there have always been talking ferns. There are little people in the ferns who try to confuse you." A smile stretched across his broad features. "They think it's funny to see big people lost in the woods."

Please, Lord, keep Felix safe.

"If you stay too long in the forest, there are red berries under the shiny plants. They taste like licorice, but you can't eat too many." He placed the skewer of meat over the fire.

Please, Lord, I don't want to go through this alone.

"If for some reason Father doesn't make the wedding on time, Felix, I want you to walk me down the aisle."

"Your father would not miss your wedding for the world." He molded the sourdough onto a stick.

Though it was not a lie, I found Felix's last statement comparable to his sentiments of *better queen*. His own take on the subject.

"Felix, though you've been like a father to me, you are not *like* my father." Sadly, I inhaled the truth. "My father shipped me off without even a good-bye." One salty tear escaped, stinging my pox on its way down. "A father like that could very well miss his own daughter's wedding, Felix."

"He has every intention of making your wedding. Never question your father's love."

I'd spent my childhood questioning my father's love. How he could be away from us for years at a time? One year I'd asked Mother, *Why couldn't he just stop the war for Christmas and be home with us? Wasn't he the one in charge?*

Mother often said that I asked for too much. Perhaps it was a royal trait.

ΦΦΦ

The next morning, while Felix made oatmeal over the campfire, I set a hand to his shoulder. "How did you sleep?"

"If the giants are not hibernating, I will slide off of my horse. I want you to take Plenty's reins, or the giants will eat them. You are to ride as fast and as hard as you can through

Shepherd's Field. You must not look back, and whatever you do, do not get off your horse."

"We'll go back to Merner and take the other route."

"No, we are only a few days from Yonder, and you need rest to get well. We won't be able to prove who you are until you're healed." He pointed beneath his chin. "In my saddlebag are three dresses for you to wear in Yonder."

"Is that all? Did Father provide a letter?" I voiced my frustration. "Something with his royal seal?"

Felix shook his head. "We didn't foresee the pox. If the giants are awake, I'll catch up to you. Do you understand?" He waited for me to meet his gaze. "Do not wait for me. I'll catch up to you."

In the first few hours after the swamp pox bite, you see the fate of someone you love. I recalled Dixie's words.

"Are you listening to me, Dory, or to the witch?"

I'd known she was a witch!

"If the giants are awake, I will serve as a distraction and catch up to you. If they are still asleep, we will ride together."

Despite my dream, his words gave me hope.

"Listen to *my* voice."

For several miles, Felix rode behind me, and then he rallied to within only a few strides. A hundred yards ahead, the gray-cast sky changed to a brilliant, ethereal blue.

I turned to look at him, this gentle man with his soft features and bag-ridden eyes. "Thank you for all . . . everything—"

"Something isn't right." His gaze locked on the foliage-laden trees ahead of us. He slid off his horse. "Take Plenty's reins and ride hard. Do not look back." As he spoke, the enormous, long-haired women from my dream emerged from the shadows.

"Go!" Felix slapped the rears of both horses. "Go!"

Unlike the dream in which I'd frozen in terror, I dug my heels into Waluga's sides. Leaning close against her neck, I focused on the open trail ahead, and clutched onto Plenty's reins behind me.

Barefoot, the giants lumbered out of the brush and trees. The ground shook with their strides. Up ahead, one edged dangerously close to my path, and then another, and another.

"Breakfast!" they yelled. "Breakfast!" The Goliath-sized creatures bounding toward me yelled similar chants, and then within strides of me, they veered off in the direction of something or someone behind me. I relived my nightmare as, head down, I kicked Waluga's flanks. I did not look back, all the while knowing that Felix served as a distraction.

I rode hard through brush and open plain for what felt like miles before I dared to glance over my shoulder. I was now in the heart of Shepherd's Field. Off in the distance, a grove of maple trees appeared to mark the edge of the meadow. Where to look in the meanwhile, as everything was curiously beautiful.

Underfoot, large, yellow clematis-like flowers blanketed the ground. The sky had never appeared as brilliantly blue or the clouds more picturesque. I recalled Dixie's words: *Be careful, or you'll want to lie in the meadow and stare at the clouds.* A floral fragrance nipped with honey permeated the air.

Behind me, Plenty snorted. Perhaps the horses were also affected. Birds sang sweetly back and forth to one another. My mind wanted to drift, relax, and drink in the serene surroundings.

"I am not to get off my horse." Even my voice sounded happy.

I glanced down at my hands. The spots were gone. I was healed! Turning them over, I marveled at how my skin had changed back to a healthy pink hue.

"The meadow has made me well," I said, brightly. Over my shoulder, I noted tall, hardy green foliage with purple flowers. I could get my own herb—queen of the meadow. I slid off Waluga, touching my feet to the ground.

What am I thinking? I am well; I don't need the plant. I need to ride out of here. Holding on to the saddle horn, I tried to lift my knee, but I couldn't budge my feet. Clematis vines had climbed over my shoes, weaving my feet to the ground.

I giggled. The meadow had affected my state of reason.

"Get back on your horse!" I yelled at myself.

My tone shocked me, yet I could not budge my feet. The vines climbed up my calves. I slipped out of my shoes and, shaking off the clingy, tentacle-like plant, climbed onto Waluga's back.

From the direction of the giants, screams of anguish reached my ears. I buried my face in Waluga's mane and dug my heels into her sides. "Ride out of here. Ride out . . ." The vines had wrapped around the horses' legs. After a few tugs, they were able to uproot them, and like a bride's train, the yellow flowers trailed behind us.

Chapter Seven

Overcome by grief, I no longer saw the beauty around me. I didn't hear the birds' sweet song, or note the lovely fragrance in the air, or notice that the sky could easily tempt me to recline in a meadow and make wishes on clouds. The cries of battle behind me kept my focus on the path ahead.

I rode until the gray of night. At a mossy hollow, an uprooted tree would serve as my roof for the night. I laid a sleeping bag under the log, made a campfire, fed the sourdough, and baked bread on a stick.

In the light of the fire, my pox had reappeared on my hands, raised and red. The meadow was merely an illusion. I lay on my bag and gave in to my overwhelming grief. My sobs echoed in the fog-ridden air. I sniffled and listened to every swoop and creak of the forest as night owls foraged through the trees. At last, I found the fortress of sleep.

I dreamed in vivid colors. I was at Blue Sky wearing my periwinkle-blue gown, not a blemish on my face. I strode beside Prince Dell out the French doors and to my mother's rose garden. I was reliving the theft of my first kiss. *Wake up. Wake up.* Dell grabbed my face.

My screams silenced the forest floor. I bolted straight up. The fog crept like a hunched old man between the dark trees.

I gripped the barrel of the shotgun beside me in my bag and, somewhat reassured, lay down and closed my eyes.

In the morning, I made parsley tea over the fire. Back home, the tinkle of a bell in the dining room meant breakfast was ready. Would I ever return to the luxuries of my childhood? I held a stick wrapped with sourdough over the fire. Though it was delicious and warm, it did not fill me. I needed protein for sustenance. I dropped the black powder into the gun and compressed it with the ramrod. After loading the gun per Felix's instructions, I held the gun to my shoulder and prayed I'd done everything right.

Out of the brush, a bird flew through the trees. Sighting the bird in the V of the barrel, I pulled the trigger. I missed. I must have not kept the gun steady enough. I reloaded and waited. A second bird took flight. I shot, and a bluebird fell. The protein would calm my hunger and ward off impending discouragement.

Over the course of the next few days, my accuracy with the gun increased. I enjoyed pheasant and partridge, and then I went three days without seeing a bird. I only had sourdough bread to eat and an occasional cup of green parsley tea. Felix should have caught up to me by now. I feared I knew the fate of my dear friend.

By the time I reached the Forest Maze, I no longer cared about living. My soul was numb, and I could tell from my hands that the parsley tea wasn't working. I recalled a Bible verse that Maid Kimberlee had taught me: "That suffering bringeth about character and . . ." At the edge of the forest, I slid off my horse and peered overhead at the pale sky and wondered if God would listen.

"I've made it this far, through Swamp Valley and Shepherd's Field; therefore I think you want me to live."

Head tilted back, I studied the clouds. A peace hard to describe filled me. And I realized that I did want to live.

I no longer felt alone; I felt guarded and loved. I recalled Felix's words: *Follow the firs; they're not as pretty as the cedars.* The cedars were lacy. I looked overhead and saw the distinction between the tall, towering trees. "Follow the firs," I whispered.

Paths meandered through the trees in every direction, but I knew the secret was to look up. After several hours, my neck ached. I slid off my mare, and holding on to the horses' reins, I spotted shiny, low-growing foliage. I lifted the leaves to find little clusters of red berries, the berries that Felix had mentioned. I plucked them and popped them in my mouth. They tasted like black licorice.

"I needed a sweet," I said, popping more berries into my mouth.

Little voices giggled. Their murmurs sounded no more than six inches off the ground. The voices surprised me; they meant I was near the edge of the forest. My heart leaped.

"She said she needs a sweet."

"See her swamp pox."

"What a sight."

"What a fright."

The voices were tinier than I'd expected. It was as if little people were talking into tin cans trying to make their voices sound large.

"No one told her that the berries make one berry sleepy," one voice giggled.

I needed to follow the voices. It took a great amount of energy for me to mount Waluga. I was indeed tired. Yawning, I gripped the reins in one hand and the mane of my mare in the other and tried to hold on. When I awoke, it was evening. The trees and ferns around me all appeared the same. I no longer recognized from which direction I'd come and which direction I was headed. I pitched my tent and hoped a good night's sleep would bring clarity.

With the shotgun by my side, I lay in my sleeping bag and listened to the sounds of the night—the crackle of my campfire, the wind in the trees, and the dew's wispy fingers as it knit blankets of fog.

ΦΦΦ

In the morning, I took down camp, prepared the horses, and mounted Waluga. Around me the trees looked like identical twins in uniform; even the groupings of ferns appeared the same. Worn dirt paths rambled off in several directions. I tried not to let my mind dwell on the fact that many had lost their lives here. If I was close, if I was in the same spot as the night before, why weren't the little people talking? Perhaps they were sleeping.

With only sourdough for breakfast, I felt a nip of discouragement. I thought on King David's prayer, taught to me when I was a child. "The Lord is my shepherd, I shall not want." I was hungry, and I did *want* something to eat. I did want, but I was not supposed to want. Without my prompting, Waluga pressed forward.

Moving was better than being idle. "He makes me lie down in green pastures, He leads me beside still waters, He restores my soul. He leads me in the path of righteousness." A salty tear trickled down my cheek, stinging my pox.

Waluga halted, and I patted the mare's smooth neck.

"Lord . . . I am afraid. I am hungry. I am broken. Help me. You haven't brought me this far to let me die in the forest."

Little voices began to giggle. Hope breathed in me. *Follow the voices.*

"Stop it!" I said in my nastiest of tones. I hoped the voices would become louder if I appeared crazy. "Stop it!" I pretended to cover my ears.

"Stop it!" one jousted in return.

"Swamp Pox is hungry and afraid," a small voice sang solo.

"Help me!" the voices said in harmony.

"Green pastures," giggled another.

Where there was no semblance of a path, the voices wove through the ferns. I followed after them. In unison, the voices stopped. I stared straight ahead. Huge trees and shadows surrounded me.

"Though I walk through the valley of the shadow of death, I will fear no evil, for you are with me; your rod and your staff, they comfort me."

"This is a forest, not a valley," one voice whispered.

"Sh! I think she knows."

Should I look for firs or cedars once I heard the voices? Despite the fact that I held the reins firmly, Waluga pressed forward. I decided to trust the animal's instinct and loosened my grip.

"She's a goner."

"Sh! She might hear you."

I continued the prayer. "You prepare a table before me in the presence of my enemies. You anoint my head with oil; my cup overflows." Waluga trotted now. My shoulder burned from the strain of holding on to Plenty's reins behind me. Finally, Waluga slowed, snorted heavily, and stepped out of the forest into sunlight.

Off in the distance sat Yonder. A river with lush green banks meandered along the south side of the kingdom. The castle's stone colonnades—purely military in scope and design—were a sharp contrast to Blue Sky, with its brick walls and red-roofed turrets. A long moat spanned the river.

The village sat immediately outside the gates, and farms and vineyards dotted the landscape beyond.

"Surely goodness and mercy will follow me all the days of my life, and I will dwell in the house of the Lord forever."

Chapter Eight

A large, navigable river flowed from the mountains toward Yonder. A deep moat lined one side of the castle, a ravine the other. Under enemy attack, the dam could be opened to fill the ravine and drown impending armies. I'd often overheard my father discuss such military design; it was ingenious.

As I approached the gatehouse, the guards on duty were obviously aware of me—a lone rider with two horses. Their dull, gray-and-black uniforms were a bleak contrast to the crisp blue and white of my countrymen.

I slid off Waluga. Barefoot, pox ridden, and in rags, I approached the gatehouse. "I wish to speak with a guard named Duron." I addressed a middle-aged guard stationed out front. He had a large belly and a tuft of white hair atop his head.

"Disease is not welcome in Yonder," the guard bellowed, though I was standing right beside him.

"I have swamp pox. I am not contagious. I was told Duron might find work for me."

"You've been misinformed. You best be on your way." He spit something toward the ground.

I struggled with disappointment. "Is there an area that an outsider may hunt and set up camp?"

The guard pointed south. "Go over the bridge; you will see a campfire pit. No one may hunt near the river. You must go south of the aspen trees to hunt."

I was surprised by how heavily they pronounced their *er*s.

"Disease is not welcome in the kingdom," said another guard from atop the walls.

"The spots on my face are not disease. I have swamp pox."

Men on horseback crossed the moat, nearing the gatehouse. The guards stood rigid, looking straight ahead. I knew the look: royalty approached. I pulled the horses closer to me and backed against the thick stone wall.

A group of ten men rode slowly through the gatehouse. A dark-haired man rode in the middle. Standing on tiptoe, I could barely see him. His dark cape streamed behind him as he rode with his men over the stone bridge toward the hills.

"Off with you," one of the guards shouted at me, waving his hand. "Disease is not welcome."

Struggling with disappointment, I mounted Waluga and rode over the south bridge and the dark green river below. Far off in the distance, aspen trees lined the hillside. The group on horseback was no longer in sight.

I was weak from hunger and needed energy to set up camp. I rode past the trees, slid off Waluga, and tied the horses to a sturdy limb. Walking tentatively through the cheat grass, I cocked my shotgun. A squirrel scurried down a nearby limb and jumped to another. A chukar ran through the grass before taking flight. With a steady aim, I pulled the trigger, and the small bird fell to the ground. I dropped to my knees and looked heavenward.

"Thank you, Lord." The bird would provide a delicious meal. "Thank you that I made it here. Please heal me soon, before my wedding."

A shot reverberated in the distance. On a hill on the horizon, the men on horseback trailed a white-tailed deer before its front legs buckled to the ground.

I returned to the campground area and tethered the horses near the river, pitched my tent, and started a fire before night fell. I knew that the knot in my belly would not let me sleep. I would eat first and then close my eyes.

Holding two green sticks over the flames, I slowly turned and roasted the chukar in one hand and the sourdough in the other. I felt extremely weepy. If Father had known what would happen, he never would have allowed us to leave.

In the darkness, horses' hooves pounded the earth as the hunting party returned. A large deer lay over the flanks of one of the horses. How had the group ever managed to get it up there? My pulse quickened; for some reason three riders separated from the group and rode toward my camp. One of the guards slid off his horse and approached my fire, while the man wearing the cape remained on horseback in the shadows. As he drew closer, the guard's wavy blond hair became visible in the fire's light.

I rose to my feet, holding the skewers.

"You are a stranger to Yonder?" the guard asked. My future countrymen heavily pronounced their *er*s. I suppressed a smile.

"Yes." I glanced past him. Was the man on horseback my betrothed? The night was too dark to see anything but shadows.

"Is it swamp pox on your face?"

"Yes," I said, pleased that he was familiar with it.

"Do you wish to settle here, or are you traveling through?"

"I . . ." I cleared my throat. "I desire to heal here before traveling to Evland."

"What business do you have in Evland?"

His tone surprised me; I hadn't thought that far ahead.

"Cragdon, we must leave," said the man on horseback.

I waited for them to tell me that I must leave Yonder, or that I must pay some kind of tax. Instead, the guard mounted his horse, and the men rode off together.

Trembling and overwhelmed, I did not get even a glimpse of my betrothed's face.

ΦΦΦ

I feared their return. I feared interrogation. I feared my identity would be detected, and I was too tired to be tactful. I stuffed a chunk of chukar in my mouth and ate as I gathered my things. I packed my belongings, slid a sourdough roll in my pocket, and doused the fire with the water from my teakettle. With an adrenaline that made me feel shaky, I rode toward town.

A hint of candlelight flickered through the closed shutters of the thatched-roof homes. I slid off Waluga and led the horses through the cobblestone streets on foot. A man whistled as he walked outside to close the large swing doors of his shop.

"Is there a place I may stay the night and rest my horses?" I called out.

"There is a smithy 'round the corner to the right." The man pointed east. "You will have to knock."

"Thank you."

In Blue Sky, the brick streets were lit by gas lamps, while in Yonder the streets were lit only by the moon. My heart could not help but compare.

Yonder Smithy. A rustic, hand-painted sign hung crooked from the rafters. The odor of animals lay heavy in the air. I slid from my horse and knocked on the rough-hewn door.

The door creaked open, revealing a bent-over, little old woman who peered at my bare feet. "You are dirdy and have draveled far."

"Yes." I spoke to the woman's gray bun, gathered at the back of her head. "I need a place to rest my horses and myself."

A lean, elderly man with a small tuft of white hair above both ears joined the woman in the doorway. "How many horses?" he asked.

"Two. I cannot pay you until I sell one of them."

"The village auction is tomorrow. You can sell one there." The old man hobbled out and took the reins from my hands. I followed him and removed the saddlebags. When his back was to me, I slid my gun amidst the woodpile.

Their home was one small room lit only by the embers from the fire. The woman prepared a bed by spreading a worn quilt over a straw-ticked mattress.

"Wash your face, hands, and feed," she said, handing me a tin basin filled with water. Hmm . . . her accent was a simple one—her *T*s were *D*s.

I sat down on the side of the bed, washed, and slid the saddlebags between the mattress and the wall.

"She is not a talkative one," said the husband.

"She is dired."

ΦΦΦ

There was no campfire to tend. No coyotes to keep away. The ground was not hard beneath me. I gave in to my fatigue and slept soundly.

In the morning, the elderly couple quietly ate their porridge. The man eyed me while I drifted in and out of sleep.

"She looks like she has been picking gooseberries and not washed."

"She washed."

"We need to wake her soon for auction," he said. "She will sell a horse for money to pay us."

The hunched old woman rose from her chair and stopped at my bedside to nudge me. It was then she saw my swamp pox for the first time. Certain that I, their guest, had brought disease into their home, she wailed, "She is sick! She is sick!"

"Sh!" Her husband rose from his chair. "You will scare her."

The elderly couple peered down at me.

I blinked myself further awake.

"Are you sick?"

"I have swamp pox. I am not contagious."

"Swamp pox?" the old woman echoed as she puttered about the room. "Swamp pox," she said as if she had never heard of the ailment before. She set a bowl of porridge on the table. "You musd ead. Aucshun is soon. You musd sell a horse so we can buy coffee."

The porridge was salted, but unsweetened. It tasted like wet chicken feed, but I did not complain. Wearing the same clothes that I had worn every day for the last fortnight, I followed the elderly man out the side door to the stable area.

"We must hurry; the auction is under way," he said.

I quickly determined that I would sell Waluga, as I had already unstrapped all my belongings. Then I thought about selling Plenty instead. The elderly man waved at me; I didn't have time. I grabbed Waluga's reins, and on foot, we led the large workhorse to the center of the village.

"I am Dory." I pulled my hood up to cover my dirty hair.

"I am Leeson. My wife is Elza."

"How long have you been without coffee?"

"Longer than we have been without tea. When Prince Wron marries, Yonder trade will improve."

"Why is that?" I was keenly aware of everything: the gray-uniformed guards who rode on horseback through the streets; the drab colors of the women's clothing; the simple, rudimentary storefronts.

"A new road will be built." Leeson's voice was filled with hope.

"It will take years."

"Years are better than today."

"Is there a road to Evland?" I asked.

"Evland is poor. Blue Sky is rich."

I thought of the red-tiled rooftops of the homes in Blue Sky in contrast to the thatched-roof homes of Yonder. Yes, Blue Sky was rich.

In the center of the village square, people brought animals, furniture, and other items of trade for auction. Bids were yelled until the final price was reached. A huge, muddy sow stood in the middle of the square.

The people yelled, "Dirty pork." The pig sold for nineteen dixels.

It was my turn next. I led Waluga to the center of the square while Leeson, clutching his hands, waited on the perimeter. I kept my head covered and my face low, but still there were murmurings among the crowd.

"She is an outsider," one said.

"Her face is odd."

"She is trying to hide."

I was not trying to hide. I was trying to sell a horse. No one knew me here. Though I was presently a stranger, I would someday be a part of their history. I flung back my hood.

The villagers nearest me stepped back, alarmed. Murmurs rippled through the crowd, informing those who couldn't see of my greasy hair and pox-riddled face.

"I am not selling myself. It is this fine mare and leather saddle that are for sale."

A hush fell over the crowd, followed by more murmurings.

I looked for Leeson's lean face amongst the crowd. The elderly man rolled a hand beneath his chin for me to continue.

"What is on your face?" yelled a teenage boy.

"I have swamp pox. It is not contagious. I fell face-first into the muck at Swamp Valley. Now . . ." I waited for the crowd noise to dim. "Waluga is a good horse. He is gentle and strong. He does not complain. With some hand-fed oats or hay, he will be your good friend."

The women, children, and even the men appeared mesmerized. Not by the horse, but perhaps by my speech and accent.

"Ten dixels. Who will part with ten dixels?" asked the mediator.

"I will." A guard raised his hand.

"Eleven," said another.

"Twenty," a voice boomed. I hoped twenty was enough to pay for lodging and food. Remorse about getting rid of such a fine animal gripped me, but I had no choice.

The bidding stopped at forty-four. I patted Waluga's neck and whispered a sweet farewell. The final bidder—a shabbily dressed middle-aged man—came forward and handed me a selection of tarnished copper coins.

"The Swamp Woman at forty-four." The next item was rolled to the center of the square—a large wagon wheel.

Leeson took the back of my elbow and guided me through the crowd. Men, women, and children alike stared at me, while maintaining their distance.

"Your swamp pox are keeping you from being pick-pocketed. Forty-four dixels!" he mumbled. "Half a year's wages!"

"It is?" Most likely it had been the fine leather saddle that had increased Waluga's value. "How much do I owe you?"

"Half a dixel." Leeson stopped on the steps of a shingled mercantile building and turned to face me. "Why do you have a gun?"

He must have found it when he brought wood in for the morning fire. I met his faint gray eyes. "On the way here, my companion died in Shepherd's Field. It was his gun. I would not have survived without it. I often shot pheasant, quail, sometimes even chukar for my meals."

Leeson's shoulders lifted as he swallowed.

"If you will allow me to stay one more night, I will try and shoot a chukar for dinner."

He exposed a toothless grin. "If you buy some grain for your horse, you may stay for free."

His kindness sparked unexpected tears. Lodging at Leeson's would give me time to heal and plan. I followed him inside the store and set a five-pound sack of coffee beans upon the counter.

"You must not buy the coffee," Leeson said.

"A proper guest always brings a gift to the host."

His sparse white brows gathered. "Then I have never been a proper guest."

ΦΦΦ

In a kettle hung high above the fire, dark coffee brewed. The smell filled Leeson and Elza's home with memories. At their rough-hewn table, we enjoyed freshly brewed coffee in chipped earthenware mugs.

"Where are you from, Dory?" Elza asked. Hunched forward, she peered into her mug.

"It is best that I not tell you, Elza." I looked across the length of the table at Leeson. "I can tell you that it is from far away and that I will not bring any harm to you or your home."

"Dhen why nod dell?"

"After I heal, I will tell you."

Shaking her head, Elza disagreed.

Leeson cleared his throat. "Is good coffee, Elza," he said to silence his wife, and I was grateful.

Chapter Nine

In the aspen area where I'd shot the chukar two days before, I tethered Plenty to a tree. Shotgun in hand, I walked quietly through the cheat grass. I wanted to be quick about my hunt, as I feared running into Prince Wron and his guards. I was certain of one thing: I could not meet Prince Wron, face-to-face, until I was well.

In the open meadow area, three quail took flight. I shot once, bringing down two, and felt my luck was providential. *Thank you, Lord.* I quickly found the first bird, but the second bird took more time. After circling around the area thrice, I gave up and started back to my horse. Near Plenty, at the edge of the aspen trees, I was surprised to find the bird's small, lifeless form in the grass. I put both birds in my saddlebag and rode back toward the village.

As I rode past the gatehouse, one of the guards waved at me. I pretended not to notice and kept Plenty at a steady, natural pace. At Leeson's smithy, I dismounted and quickly pulled the horse into the stable and barred the door. Through the solitary window, I watched as two uniformed guards on horseback rode through the streets.

They couldn't be after me. I'd done nothing wrong.

ΦΦΦ

Elza fried the quail in suet. I patted the sourdough into biscuits and hung the cast-iron pot over the fire. Leeson brewed the pot of coffee on a warm brick. The three of us turned our chairs to face the hearth, and firelight danced in our eyes.

"Dory has broughd delicious smells do our home," Elza said. "All dhad is missing is music."

Off a cleft in the bricks, Leeson picked up a hand-carved flute. As he placed it to his lips, an earthy melody filled the toasty warm room. It was rare for me to simply relax and enjoy someone else's music. The poignant melody transported me to the beauty, and also the memory, of Shepherd's Field. Closing my eyes, I tried not to remember my dear friend's fate.

Elza held a thick cloth to lift the pot's lid and peered inside. Using both arms, she carried it to the table and set it down on two cold bricks. We moved slowly about the room until dinner was ready.

"Like a Chrisdmas meal; all dhad is missing is an onion."

After our fine meal and coffee, I asked for permission to go to the mercantile.

Elza nodded. "You remember dee way and you will redurn?"

"Yes."

At the mercantile, I purchased a bag of onions and a crock of honey. I had often thought on the trail how much sweeter my circumstances would have been with honey to slather on my sourdough. When I returned and set the honey and onions on the table, Elza could not stop mumbling.

"You will spoil us. You will run oud of money. God has send us an angel in our old age."

I rested on my bed in the warm little room. With my back against the wall, I studied my dirty bare feet. On my next trip to the mercantile, I would see what Yonder sold in the way of shoes. Perhaps my next set of shoes should not have heels, as they would not be very practical for hunting.

Elza set a spindle of yarn by my side, and I began rolling it into a ball for her. Their home was the perfect environment for my healing. I would stay here, gather herbs, and follow the medicinal instructions that Dixie had written down for me. I leaned back against the wall, content with my decision.

The front door swung open. Leeson's shoulders hung low, as if he carried bad news. Two uniformed guards walked in behind him. The fair-haired guard I recognized as Cragdon from the night before. I remained seated on the bed while a hundred questions raced through my head.

"These men have come to talk with Dory," Leeson said.

Elza looked at the men's dusty leather boots. "Would you care for coffee?" she asked.

"No, thank you." Cragdon looked over at me. "Leeson and Elza are good citizens of Yonder," he said. "But you, Swamp Woman, were seen hunting on the king's land today."

"I was told to hunt south of the aspens," I said.

"Two of our men, who were hunting in the hills, saw you pick up game off the king's land."

I thought of the bird that had fallen on the edge of the cheat grass. "One of my birds fell close to the aspen. Closer than I foresaw. But I was not on the king's land when I shot."

Behind him, Elza clasped her hands below her chest in silent, but visible, prayer.

"I am sorry, Swamp Woman, that you are not more familiar with Yonder's laws. You owe the crown one month's time for your crime."

"Crime?" The fire crackled in the hearth.

"Yes, thirty days." Cragdon nodded.

"What do you mean?"

"You will be imprisoned. After your crime is reviewed, you will labor for the crown for one month."

"She was only trying to please us with a special meal," Leeson informed them.

"I am sorry," Cragdon said. "But the law is the law."

My hands were tied in front of me, and while Elza began to weep, I was ushered outside. From the cinching and the rope's frayed edges, the dry, scaly spots on my hands cracked and oozed. Adults and children alike paused from what they'd been doing to watch as I was led through the streets.

When we reached the gatehouse, the guards blindfolded me.

"Is this to add to my torture?" I didn't understand.

"No. It is so you will not know the way, should you try to escape," Cragdon said.

As they led me through the gates, I imagined a courtyard on my right, as there was a floral scent in the air, perhaps of lilacs. To my left was the braying of stabled horses, and the smell of hay. *Do not be afraid.* I relied on the comforting voice that sometimes whispered inside my head. *You have been through worse.* Despite what I had already been through, I was terrified. I'd never toured my father's prison at Blue Sky, but stories had reached me. Stories that often kept me up when I was young, and made me scared enough that I would encamp outside my parents' room to eventually sleep at the foot of their bed.

Father . . . Tears ebbed at the corners of my eyes. A door groaned open, and I was led down a rocky, uneven path. As we descended toward the underground, the air dampened and cooled. Absent was the light that had earlier teased through the blindfold. *Father* . . . I thought on his loving eyes. *If only you knew how wrong your plans have gone. You'd be here now to save me. You'd be here.*

The two guards who guided me down into the bowels of death were my future countrymen. They would remember my bravery and my fear.

Father in heaven, help me to be brave.

ΦΦΦ

My blindfold was removed, and my heart gonged loudly in my chest. I peered down a cavern-like corridor with torches between each of the cells, which appeared to have been excavated out of the rock. A guard pulled open the first barred door on our left and then pushed me inside. I stumbled to my knees and waited there. A key turned in the lock. Footsteps retreated. I was alone. Or was I?

I listened.

"Who is she?" a muffled voice asked.

"Silence," a hoarse voice whispered.

Fingers of daylight seeped through the gaps in the upper masonry of my cell. It did not make sense to me how we could descend into this pit, yet still have daylight. I stayed several feet back from the door—afraid of what I'd see, and of being seen.

My gaze shifted. Directly across the corridor, my nearest companion, a gaunt, wiry man, waved a hand. "Hello." Wild gray hair plumed about his ears.

"Hello. I'm Dory." I waved slightly in return.

"I'm Knot."

"Oh." Knot was an odd name. I wondered if he meant he was *not* Dory?

"Why are you here?" Knot asked loud enough for the other prisoners to hear.

"Disobedience. Why are you here?" Leaning my head, ever so slightly, I counted two more prisoners on Knot's side—a massive human and a lean, elderly man.

"The same."

"How long have you been here?" My mouth grew dry.

"Three years and . . ." He gestured to tally marks on the stone behind him. "Well, to be exact, today is my 1,151st day."

From the looks of Knot, he had not eaten in those three years.

I sank down on the wood plank cot that spanned the back wall of my cell, and tried to think of something humorous. Maybe someday Prince Wron would find out that I was Princess Alia, and he'd feel bad that I died of hunger and discomfort in his prison. Maybe my father would regret that he'd sent me on this grand adventure with only one chaperone. Instead of humor, I found that I had many memories to repress and no piano.

Had anyone ever died in my father's prison? Had anyone died here?

"Up, you." A robust man stood on the other side of my cage, holding a long wooden stick. "It's time to earn your bread."

The gaoler called over another guard, and one by one the cell doors were opened. I joined the other prisoners, and we shuffled down a narrow, mold-ridden stairwell, toward what appeared to be a wide paddle wheel. With the gaoler barking orders and batting the stick in his hand, we took positions on a blade of the paddle and held on to a bar that was shoulder high. One of the prisoners, a tall, thin man named Long, was blind. Everyone waited for him to step into place on the end of the paddle wheel.

The large wheel loomed above the roar of the river. I didn't understand in the slightest what was happening. Knot stood on my right, his face skeleton-lean.

"We're going to walk for miles," he said. The foul odor that hung in the air between us made me question when he'd last brushed his teeth, or taken a bath.

"Silence!" the gaoler yelled.

"Then explain to the Swamp Woman," Knot demanded.

He knew my title.

"Silence!" the gaoler yelled. "You are to earn your room and board. You are to walk the treadmill until I tell you to stop. You walk together, or the paddle will not turn to grind the grain for Yonder."

"We walk together so no one gets hurt," Knot whispered. "Do not let go of the bar."

On the count of three, the six of us began walking. Each step was similar to climbing a steep hillside. The water from the blades splashed the bottom of my long skirt. My legs quickly grew heavy, and my lungs burned. If I fell, my body would be crushed by the blades and plummet to the river below.

"It is monotonous work that breaks a prisoner's soul," Knot said. "In prison, you will find that your mind is your greatest enemy."

"The same holds true outside of prison," I said.

"What is our new friend's name?" asked Long, the blind man.

"Dory," I said.

"Silence!" the gaoler yelled.

"Duron is harmless," Knot whispered.

Duron, the *robust* man who Dixie had recommended, was the gaoler! I had not imagined meeting him under such circumstances.

The bread we'd earned for walking the treadmill was a stale piece of rye with no butter and a main course of watery porridge. I looked at the crude bowl and could not eat.

"You must eat the gruel, Swamp Woman," Knot said. "You will need the energy. We will walk again soon."

I took a bite of the dribbly meal. "How did you know that I am the Swamp Woman?"

"The guards talk, and your face is proof of who you are."

Shortly after our meal, we again worked the treadmill. The second time was not as interesting as the first. Not being able to converse made the work feel endless. To endure, I escaped inside my mind and thought of Leeson and Elza.

"Duron is not looking. What is your favorite pie?" Knot asked.

What an odd topic. "I prefer the tartness of gooseberry. And yours?"

He smiled. "Rhoda's peach pie."

"What is your favorite entrée?" I asked.

"Rhoda's pork tenderloin with apricot glaze. And you?"

"Oh . . ." My mouth watered at the mere thought of where I was headed. "Coq au vin."

"Rooster with wine?" Knot chuckled.

He'd obviously not had it. "Yes, chicken slowly cooked in red wine with sautéed onions, mushrooms, and bacon."

"You know how to make a prisoner weep. And, I must say, you are well educated for a commoner," Knot said.

"You are well educated for a prisoner." Already, my lungs had begun to burn, and I felt short of breath.

"I was adviser to the king." His face was jaundiced and the whites of his eyes yellow.

"What happened?" My smile faded.

"I gave the wrong advice."

ΦΦΦ

After we worked the treadmill for a second time, Duron locked my cell behind me. I gathered courage. "Do you recall Dixie, the herbalist, and her awful parsley tea?"

"Aye." He scowled.

"What remedy healed you?"

"Garlic, but you won't be getting any here." He walked away. Duron was not as kindhearted as I'd hoped.

I was going to shrivel away to nothing like Knot and die here in the dungeon of Yonder. Instead of *Our Beloved Queen*, my grave marker would simply read: *Swamp Woman.* Or would they even bury me, a prisoner? They might just drop my body through the slats of the treadmill to the river below.

If only Felix were here. If only he'd made it. My breath caught in my lungs, and though I covered my mouth, pitiful sounds escaped me.

Between sobs, I heard someone yelling.

"Stop crying. Stop your blubbering or we'll all go insane!" Knot's voice echoed in the low-ceilinged pit.

Somehow I managed to halt my near hysteria.

"It gets easier," Knot said.

How could it get easier without a piano? I needed to play. "I'm a prisoner to my soul." I gripped the edge of my cot. "A prisoner to my own memories."

"Enough!" With his hands over his ears, Knot paced.

I'd been a difficult child. Stubborn. My parents knew I would not go easily. I would have challenged their authority, made a scene. How could I ever have said good-bye to Wren? The thought made me ache. Yet I was not even given the chance. My parents knew the good-bye was too big for me to bear. They had to drug me. I never would have left willingly.

My memories might haunt me for the rest of my short existence.

"I'm sorry, Dory." Knot's voice faltered. "I spoke harshly. You are not used to deprivation; I am numb."

On the cold, hard cot, I wrapped my arms about myself.

"In the prisons of our mind"—Knot gripped the bars—"we must learn to live with our mistakes and to forgive ourselves."

"Thank you, Knot." I inhaled deeply, picked up a small, thin rock off the floor, and like my first friend in prison, scratched one tally mark into the white stone above my cot.

"Write your name, too," Knot said. "I think the next prisoner to have my cell will feel honored when he reads: *Knot, adviser to the King.*"

I suppressed my first giggle since I'd arrived. Thanks to Knot, I'd found something humorous about being a prisoner in Yonder.

Behind me on the wall, I engraved into the stone one word: **DORY.**

ΦΦΦ

"Swamp Woman . . ." Duron rung his stick back and forth across the bars.

Too scared to whimper or complain, I slowly rose and crossed the cell. I was exhausted, but must walk the treadmill or be flogged. When I reached the door, he did not unlock it. "A blanket . . ." Through the bars, he handed me a folded brown blanket.

"In my hand," he whispered, turning his back to me. In his large, open palm, he held forth a head of garlic.

"Thank you, Duron." I dropped it into the pocket of my skirt. "Is it time to walk?"

"No, it is time to sleep and peel."

I lay on my side, with my back to Knot. I'd never worked with garlic before, and slowly peeled off the fragile, paper-like skin. I popped a raw clove into my mouth and crunched. It was like a pungent firecracker going off. Garlic permeated my nostrils and my brain. I forced myself to eat three more before I spread the blanket over me. Hopefully by morning, no one would recognize me.

Chapter Ten

Three days passed, and I could not rid my hands or my breath of the stench of garlic.

"Do not speak, Dory," Knot and Long both complained as we walked the treadmill.

"The smell is manageable if you don't speak." Despite his words, there was a twinkle in Knot's jaundiced eyes.

"Has my complexion improved?" I asked, gripping the bar.

"Are you asking me or Knot?" Long asked. "If you are asking me, your complexion has always been lovely in my eyes."

"Thank you, Long."

"No, Dory, I am sorry to say your complexion has not improved," Knot said.

"Stop talking," yelled Duron.

"Though Dory smells like garlic . . ." Long's aged voice hummed a tune as he often did. "Hmm . . . what rhymes with *garlic*?" He usually sang tunes about his wife. "Sick, lick, trick, tick." He cleared his throat. "Though my Dory smells like garlic, it doesn't bother me a brick that she is sick."

"Stop singing!" yelled Duron.

As the exhausting work continued, I retreated inside my mind to happier times—waltzing in the ballroom with Pierre, gooseberry tarts, the comfort of Felix's shoulder when we traveled—but still my mind struggled. Finally, the treadmill slowed, and we staggered back to our cells.

Later that morning, a new prisoner was escorted in by Cragdon and two other guards. He was both blindfolded and chained. When the cloth was removed from his eyes, my heart lurched in my being. It was the dark-haired young man from Liisa's—Fallon, with the earring scar. His clothes were soiled and his hair disheveled. What was he doing here?

As he neared, I waited with bated breath. Could he possibly recognize me? What crime had he committed to end up here?

"Swamp Woman," he jeered as he walked past.

ΦΦΦ

I stared at the scuffed stone floor and recalled Liisa's. Felix had been so right to leave in the middle of the night. "Why is he here?" I whispered across the way to Knot.

"He is a newcomer." Knot chiseled today's events on the wall behind him.

"Who is talking about me?" Fallon gripped the bars of his cell.

"I was telling Dory that this is your first time here," Knot said.

I closed my eyes. Knot had mentioned my name. I didn't want the gypsy to know I was—

"Dory . . . Dory of Boxden?" His voice echoed in the cavernous pit.

Shoulders stiff, I remained seated on the edge of my cot. An uncomfortable silence passed.

"Boxden?" Knot said.

"Where is your chicken farmer father?" Fallon laughed.

I remained silent, willing myself only to breathe.

"Where is your father?" Fallon now demanded. His voice echoed through the cavern.

"At the entrance to Shepherd's Field . . ." I paused, collecting myself. "He used himself as a decoy to save me from the giants." I looked across the way at Knot. "They weren't supposed to be awake."

"Do you mean hibernation?" Knot asked.

I shook my head. I wasn't ready to remember.

"The giants' hibernation always ends in May, when the ground thaws," Knot said.

"What happened to your odd accent?" Fallon's voice rose above my ability to reason.

"It's too bad your father did not know," Knot said.

"Know what?" I breathed.

"What happened to your accent?" Fallon gripped the bars of his cell.

"Leave the Swamp Woman alone!" From the front of his cell, Fjord, the massive human, glared at him.

Fallon eventually sat down upon his cot, lowering his head.

I would tell him nothing. How in the world had a gypsy been invited to Liisa's home that evening?

"Dory . . . what happened to your odd accent?" Fallon's voice was now a whisper.

If Felix knew his way to Yonder like the back of his hand, he should have known. *I am familiar with the giants.* If he was familiar with the giants, he should have known they weren't hibernating. I tried to make sense of it all.

"What happened to your accent, Dory?" Fallon asked, loudly.

My mind knotted with questions. Liisa's was in Merner—the most politically dangerous section of our journey. And now this gypsy was here. Had he followed me? Did he know who I really was? He was not to be trusted.

"Are you absolutely positive that the giants' hibernation is over in May?" I stared across the corridor at Knot.

"Yes, May has always been the spring thaw."

I stared at the stone wall of my cell. *I was hired by your father because I know the way to Yonder like the back of my hand.* How could Felix have missed such a huge detail?

"Is it possible"—my chest expanded as I peered at Knot—"for one man to fight the giants and win? A large, very strong man?"

Knot smiled. "That is a question for Rhoda."

ΦΦΦ

Overhead, the sunrise cast long, slender fingerlings of light through the gaps in the masonry. We had not had our porridge yet or walked the treadmill, as Duron had the morning off, and a young guard was on duty.

My stomach threatened to turn itself inside out in hunger. For a long, punitive moment, I let myself dwell on the things of home: my soft, light blue slippers, the thick, down-filled coverlet upon my bed, Cook's apple pan dowdy, my mother brushing my hair . . . How I longed to pour my mourning and despair into the Great Beast. I missed the catharsis of self-expression.

"Knot," I called across the way to him.

"What is it, Dory?"

"I was told that I may work a month for my freedom?"

"Yes, that is correct." He stretched his skeleton-lean arms to grab the highest rung of the bars. "One of the king's men, sometimes the Queen, will decide if you are fit for castle work or for the farms. Usually it is on Tuesdays that new prisoners are positioned."

"What about you, Knot?"

"I will continue to walk the paddle. King Ulrich knows that I would be too set on freedom, and that I am keen enough to escape."

"Do you think he is correct?" I wondered how much longer Knot could live; he was skin and bones.

"It has been his conviction for over three years, and the man knew me well. When you are working in the castle, Dory, sneak me a piece of Rhoda's peach pie."

Fallon's snide laughter echoed through the prison. "The Swamp Woman does not know how to cook or clean. They will make her return to walk the paddle."

"Is serving prisoners pie a punishable crime?" I asked, ignoring Fallon for the blemish that he was.

"Undoubtedly." Knot smiled. "But it would mean so much to me."

There was boisterous banter; it was Fallon again. Singing loudly, he'd taken off one shoe, and, walking back and forth, he strummed it against the bars of his cell.

"He could be tricky," Knot informed Jorgensen, the young guard, who walked past. "Do not underestimate him. I would not get too—"

"Now, that's enough. Stop being a nuisance. You're to be orderly during my watch." Rapping his stick into his open palm, the guard stopped near Fallon's cell, and then he turned to walk away.

With hands as fleet as dove's wings, Fallon reached through the bars and, snatching the stick, struck the guard on the back of the head.

"Duron! Where is Duron?" I gripped the bars.

"He is not here," Knot said.

I couldn't bear to watch, yet I could not pull my eyes away as Fallon pulled the body of the guard close to his cell and rummaged through his pockets. He found the gaoler's keys, unlocked his cell, and dragged the body of the guard inside.

"Help," I yelled toward the gaps of light, hoping someone, anyone in the outside world might hear me. "Help, we need help!" Only leftover stars littered the morning sky.

No one answered.

"Is the guard dead?" I whispered. Was Fallon a murderer? Was that why he was here?

"No." Knot shook his head. "If it had been to the side of the head, it might have been different."

Fallon locked his cell door behind him. Would he come for me? Did he know who I was? I sat down and gripped the edge of the cot, afraid.

The wiry young man stopped in front of my cell. "I've heard swamp pox can last several years. That is a long time to wait for even a woman of your beauty and . . . position."

I kept my head bowed, not meeting his gaze.

"You see, not everyone at Liisa's could keep a secret."

Fallon knew! My eyes flashed open to stare at my hands. What would he do with the truth?

"A royal pianist traveling with her father under the guise of chicken farmers," he whispered and then laughed. "Never for a moment did I believe you."

So many parts of the plan had been good.

"It is not too late, Fallon, for you to have a good life. Stay here. Apologize for what you have done and work for your redemption. There is both evil and good in all of us. Fight for what is good."

"Says Dory of Boxden." He bowed, keeping an eye on me.

"It is not too late." I met his dark gaze.

From his bowed position, he dropped the keys to the ground, several feet in front of my cell. Swift of foot, he disappeared up the quarried path.

Chapter Eleven

If I had had shoes, I would have taken them off and used them for extra leverage in reaching the keys.

"Are you trying to escape?" Knot asked.

"No." I pressed tightly against the bars, stretching my arm, my wrist, my fingers, but still the keys were a hand's breadth beyond my grasp. "I'd like to help the guard."

"Then employ your blanket."

When rolled, the dark brown blanket made itself into a snakelike instrument thin enough to flick through the bars. Slowly, I batted the keys toward me, sometimes away from me. My fellow inmates clutched at the bars of their cells. In pensive cries and moans, they agonized over my progress. At last, the keys to freedom were in my grasp.

Cheers of "Onderyay!" erupted.

When I reached my hand through the bars to unlock my cell, the prison was as quiet as a sleeping babe. My door creaked open, and I walked toward Fallon's old cell.

"Dory, unlock mine!" Stapleton ran back and forth in front of his cell.

"I haven't seen my wife in years," Long, the blind man, cried.

"Dory, my brother will take us in, feed us. Chicken, eggs, bread . . ." Fjord gripped the bars.

"Dory, don't listen to them." Knot's voice reminded me of Felix's—low and firm.

His was the voice I would listen to.

The red-haired guard sat propped in the corner against the wall. I touched his forehead. He was not cold; blood still pulsed steady through his veins. I praised God that he was alive.

I returned the keys to his side and left the cell door propped open.

My fellow inmates moaned, pulling at their hair. I blocked out their bleatings and stopped in front of Knot's cell. At one time he'd been one of the king's most trusted men.

"The guard is alive. Should I seek help or . . . ?"

"There are two stairwells. One is more secret than the other." He motioned toward the quarried path. "When you reach the second bend, there is a notch knee-high on the wall," he whispered. "You must push it firmly for the route to the kitchen to be revealed. When you reach the top of the stairwell, you will arrive in a breezeway. A door is straight ahead; it is the back entrance to the kitchen. Inside, you will find a... large woman. Her name is Rhoda. Tell her that you are the Swamp Woman, and that Knot has sent you. Tell her that there has been a disturbance in the prison, and help is needed. She will tell Prince Wron. After you tell her, you are to immediately return here. Promise me you will return."

"I promise." I took a step away.

"What do you promise, Dory?"

"I promise I will return here, Knot."

He nodded. "When you return, you must hit a notch knee-high on your left side to release the door. Do not be afraid. Rhoda is sensitive."

Torches lit the rock walls of my ascent. At the second bend, I looked behind me. I could see nothing of the prison below. I feared running into Fallon more than speaking with the woman. Only because Knot had told me to look knee-high did I find the notch in the stone. A short wall in the rock rolled back a few feet, wide enough for a tray of food to be transported through. This passageway was dimly lit by only one overhead torch. Instead of a sloped path, there were twenty stone steps to the top. Fallon was not here.

I forced a heavy door forward to find daylight and an empty breezeway. I remembered my vow to Knot and strode into the back room of a white brick kitchen. A band of large kettles hung from the ceiling. Heaped baskets full of breads, apples, onions, and yellow pears lined the countertops. A live chicken perched on the windowsill. There was a powdered round cake on the counter, and the incredible smell of bacon frying.

"Who are you and what are you doing in my kitchen?" In the center of the room stood a giant of a woman with massive shoulders and dark hair pulled into a strict bun. In her hand she gripped a wide-bladed cleaver.

My mind returned to the entrance to Shepherd's Field. With her hair down, this woman would look like the giants who now haunted my nightmares, the weight of their steps pounding the earth. Panic surged through my being, and my limbs began to shake. Perhaps it was due to my deprived state that I remembered my mother's words at such a time: *A daughter of the king does not shake. Our country looks to us for assurance. Even when fear is at our doorstep, we can never quake.*

Though my knees felt like I was standing on the saddle of a galloping horse, I forced my shoulders back. "Knot sent me. I am the Swamp Woman. There's been a disturbance in the prison, and we need help."

With eyes as wide as teacups, the giant woman nodded, and then she waved the meat cleaver toward the door. "Leave my kitchen, and then I will tell them."

I understood. I was a prisoner, and because we were being starved, and food was the ultimate of our longings, I was not to be trusted in the king's kitchen. I swallowed and, despite the rackish feeling of my emptiness, forced myself to turn and retrace my steps. Without being seen, I crossed the breezeway, hurried down the stairwell, and found the notch on the wall. The stone rolled back a few feet. Once I was home to my cell, I pulled the door closed behind me.

"I told Rhoda." I felt trembly and out of breath.

"Good girl. What did she say?" Knot watched the stone walkway.

"She insisted that I leave her kitchen before she would tell them."

He laughed, and began to cough.

"I like how you told me that she is large rather than the truth—she is a giant."

"Since you are familiar with the giants, I should have told you: Rhoda will not be a worry for you—she is a vegetarian."

ΦΦΦ

The hem of my sky-blue dress teased the floor as I danced with Father. His slim hazel eyes sparkled with love as he gazed down at me.

Loud voices interrupted the affirmations of my heart; it had only been a dream. The hard wooden cot beneath me and rock ceiling overhead reminded me that I was in the pit of Yonder.

The loud voices continued. With their backs to me, two guards and a man of royal cloth gathered in front of Knot's cell. I recognized one of the guards as Cragdon. With my luck, his companion was Prince Wron.

The pink spots with scaly dry centers remained on my hands. When I met my betrothed, I would not be healed. I peered up toward the gaps of light and prayed: *Heal me. Please heal me.* As the men approached my cell, I continued the prayer. *Please heal me. Heal me.*

"Swamp Woman," Cragdon said.

I was not healed.

"Knot informed us of your role after our prisoner's escape." He extended a piece of buttered bread through the bars.

Wide-eyed, I took it, and though I did not forget my manners, I began to eat in front of them.

"It appears that Jorgensen is fine, and the prisoner did not get far." He nodded toward the far side of the prison.

Fallon was back, lying on his bunk. I had slept through more than I'd realized. My gaze shifted to the dark-haired man beside Cragdon. He was of solid stature with broad shoulders. Though he was handsome, it was not love at first sight for either of us.

"Knot said that you knew Fallon prior to prison." My betrothed's voice was clear and pleasant, as was his face.

He was nothing like Prince Dell.

I swallowed a bite of bread. "I met Fallon in Merner. We happened to be at the same home for supper."

"Knot said that your name is Dory." My betrothed flicked a leather glove into his open palm.

"Yes."

"And that you are from Blue Sky?"

My stomach curled into a tight fist. I glanced toward Knot's cell. Had he overheard Fallon, or had he somehow figured it out on his own? Did he think me a counterfeit, with the ultimate of all ploys?

"I believe he is correct. I have only heard the Blue Sky accent twice, but it is very distinct." Prince Wron glanced at the fair-haired guard beside him. "Cragdon, that is one thing we must tell the counterfeits to improve upon. They are still rolling their *er*s like they are from Yond-er."

Heat climbed up into my pox-riddled cheeks. He was indeed Prince Wron.

"Is Knot correct? Are you from Blue Sky?"

"Yes." My mouth felt dry. I glanced toward Fallon's cell. Could he hear us?

"Don't worry about him. He will be here for a very long time," my future beloved said. "How long did you live in Blue Sky?"

"All my life."

His gaze narrowed. "What did your father do there?"

"He worked for the king." It was not a lie.

He suppressed a smile. "What skills do you have, Dory?"

I lifted my gaze to his icy blue eyes. What he was really asking was how Yonder might enslave me. I had to be careful. In my hideous state, I could easily be assigned to work the fields or stables.

"What are your skills?" he repeated.

"Tomorrow your skills will be bartered for your freedom, Dory." Knot's voice climbed the rock walls. "It is the only way out of this pit."

"Her pox will limit her from public service?" Cragdon said.

Wron held up a hand to silence him.

I became all too aware of my greasy, matted hair, my soiled dark green dress that I'd worn since the night at Liisa's several weeks ago.

"Though I am sorry to hear about your father"—Wron gripped the glove in his hand—"the fact that you are familiar with Fallon—a liar and a cheat—is not in your favor."

I sat down on my cot and, wide-eyed, gripped the edge.

"I play piano."

"And . . ." Wron shook his head. "Do you mend, cook, teach . . . ?"

My skills were very limited, except I could teach ballroom dancing, French, lessons in etiquette, how to sight in a gun, clean small birds . . .

"I play piano." I lifted my gaze from the cold stone floor to his eyes.

"That is all." He nodded.

"No one will employ her," Cragdon said as they walked away.

I wanted to shout after them: *I am Alia*, but all it took was a glance at my spot-riddled hands to silence me.

ΦΦΦ

"Who are you, Dory of Blue Sky?" Knot paced his cell. "Dory who plays piano and speaks French. Dory who doesn't know how to cook or clean." The cunning old man's gaze narrowed, and then he shook his head. "But your father died in the Giants' Snare."

Felix had never given name to the entrance to Shepherd's Field, and now I understood why. Using my fingers, I combed through my matted hair, halting on a knot.

"A pianist who arrives from Blue Sky only weeks before Princess Alia is expected." Knot paced.

I had almost deemed Knot a friend, yet now he thought me a counterfeit.

With his back to me, he studied the numerous inscriptions etched behind him on the wall. "Dory, from Blue Sky . . .

you've been imprisoned in the wrong kingdom." He chuckled, shaking his head. "There is no piano here."

ΦΦΦ

"No piano?" I echoed.

No piano. My mind tried to wrap around the impossible.

"There is no piano in Yonder." Knot etched the tally mark for that day into the rock. "Thirteen years ago, someone made the mistake of playing the piano the night Queen Eunice's infant died in her arms. Prince Wally was only two."

"What happened?"

"His fever would not break. Though the bells were rung, and all the people of Yonder prayed—night and day—Prince Wally's soul was taken."

My heart broke for the Queen and for myself. My knees buckled beneath me to the hard stone floor.

No piano.

Overhead, the gaps of light felt like my only view of God. Tears streamed down my cheeks as I told Him the petitions of my heart.

Perhaps my tears were audible; Long's tenor voice reached its way through the bars as the dear man tried to console me.

I sniffled.

"My missus will be sorry she sent me for bread.

Not a dixel in my pocket, just a song in my head."

His crackly old voice carried a tender tune.

"A loaf in my coat, I tried to escape,

but the bowels of this hell

were to be my fate.

A slathering of jam, a rim of butter,

Does my wife of fifty years

remember me at supper?"

Though his lyrics were melancholy, everyone listened, for in his melody there was hope.

"In the pit of hell, Father," I whispered to the rays of light, "I learned that there is nothing like a chunk of bread for the hungry, a blanket for the cold, and the gift of music for the wounded soul." Tears dripped down my cheeks. "Nothing.

"Please, Lord, if it's not asking too much, find me a piano."

I found the small stone that I'd used for my seven tally marks. To my earlier inscription of DORY, I knew what I would add. Though *The Swamp Woman* was fitting, each time I heard it, it caused me pain. Instead, I etched into the rock two words, a nickname from my childhood.

If I survived and someday became queen, I would return and scribe *Princess Alia* into the rock. I stepped back to review my work and was pleased with:

DORY—Piano Girl.

Chapter Twelve

On Tuesday, only three of the prisoners were released to be interviewed for castle work: Long, Fjord, and me. Duron, with the assistance of another guard, blindfolded us with dark strips of itchy cloth. Our hands were tied behind us with the same.

The comrades we were leaving behind strummed their water tins against the bars. "It is a weekly ritual, Dory," Knot's hoarse voice said. "Remember to bring me a slice of pie."

Fallon added a snide laugh.

"I hope I am so lucky," I managed, before a guard grabbed my elbow and pushed me forward into the darkness. I soon joined the others to climb the rocky path.

"Let it be this time, God, that they find work for an old blind man like me," Long whispered. "Let it be this time that I am set free. How I long to see my grandbabies and my wife, if she has not deserted me."

To block out Long's constant mumbling, I prayed silently to God. I asked that He'd show favor on me; find me a job in the castle, not the fields; and, of course, heal me.

In the bottom fringe of my blindfold, I detected a threshold of light and then even ground. Still we stumbled along, shoulder to shoulder, with Duron barking orders. There were the sounds of horses whinnying and the smell of crisp morning air. The guard behind me tugged on my shoulder, motioning for me to stop.

Duron removed my blindfold. Even though the sky was gray, I blinked repeatedly at the brightness of daylight. We stood in an inner courtyard across from stables which were, judging from the mountains, on the south side of the castle. A woman several years older in appearance than my mother called Duron over to where she stood beside an umbrella-shaped mulberry bush.

"Do you get to walk up here very often?" I asked Long.

"Each Tuesday they bring me up here to break my heart all over again."

I hoped today would be different for him. Duron and the queen conversed for a few minutes before he beckoned us over.

With Fjord on my right, and Long bobbing into my left shoulder, we awkwardly made our approach. My future mother-in-law was of medium stature, slightly plump, and her hairstyle resembled three snowballs, one on top of the other.

"How are you today, Long?" she asked. Her striped dress had balloon-like sleeves and a white, lace-trimmed collar high up the neck.

"I am well, Your Majesty," he said, as we stopped in front of her. "Even though I am blind, I am not useless. I can thresh wheat, knead dough, sing songs to my grandchildren upon my knee . . ." My heart ached for Long and his apparent suffering.

"You are good at song, Long." I nudged him. "Sing something for the Queen."

She wrinkled her nose, but gave him a moment all the same.

He swallowed. "Uh . . . uh, uh . . ." His voice sounded like a warted toad crept up his throat. "Give an old chance, give an old chance, on meeee, old man."

"Grossly unremarkable." The queen stepped past him and lifted her wire spectacles to peer at me.

Poor Long. My future mother-in-law's lack of empathy greatly disappointed me.

"Pick an old man like me.

Give me a try.

Pick an old man like me

Before I die."

Long's tune was too late.

"I have never seen them up close before." The Queen's voice softened as she studied me. "They're like unsightly canker sores, except for the pink-and-white dots . . . everywhere. They are hideous. Do they hurt?"

For a moment I wondered if falling through the treadmill's blades to the water below would have hurt as much as her honesty. "In the beginning, they itched unbearably. I believe they are now more unsightly than they are irritating."

"Very unsightly. We are in need of a female server, but you can't be seen. Do you have any strengths?"

"Yes." I inhaled. "I play piano."

"And Long sings." Lifting her spectacles, she studied my spots. "Do you play anything else?"

"No." I never imagined my future kingdom without a piano or my future mother-in-law without empathy.

"That is too bad. I am quite fond of"—she glanced at Long—"good music. I hear you are from Blue Sky. What color is Princess Alia's hair?"

"Auburn."

A line deepened in her forehead. "What color are her eyes?"

"Hazel." I prayed that I would someday love this woman.

"Are your eyes not hazel?" Behind the round spectacles, her swamp-green eyes appeared enormous.

"They are a greenish brown."

"My husband is against having you pay penance in our home. I am not to mention it. He thinks you are a part of some grand plot—a pianist with swamp pox from Blue Sky." She clicked her tongue against the roof of her mouth. "I must say you have a very bad case, one that might last years."

"How do you know?"

"I don't. It's just so, so . . . disagreeable." Her eyes locked on mine. "Are you really from Blue Sky?"

"Yes, I am." My heart ached at the mention of my beloved homeland.

"When Princess Alia and her father arrive, they will be the judge. If your words do not match the truth, you will be abandoned deep in the hills to never find your way out." Her voice held dramatic flair.

"I understand, Your Grace." The thought of her reading fairy tales aloud to my future children buoyed my heavy spirits.

She eyed me thoughtfully. "Word came to me late last night that there is *one* piano in the village."

Darest I breathe?

"Roger . . ." The Queen waved her fingers for a middle-aged guard's attention. He had a generous belly and a tuft of white hair on top of his head. "What is the name of the shop woman with the piano?"

"Peg," he said.

There was indeed a piano! Though my hands were tied behind me, my fingers began to twitch.

"If she has a piano, why is the odd little woman not in prison?" the queen asked.

The guard shrugged. "No one knows how to play it."

"If Peg does not approve of the Swamp Woman, she may work the fields."

"Peg?" Roger asked.

"No, you ninny, the Swamp Woman may work the fields." She turned to address me. "You will work for thirty days. Then the wages you've earned will be paid to the crown."

"Might I ask where I will live?"

"Details are not my specialty." She stepped past me to Fjord.

"Queen Ulrich, I petition," I said, without thinking. To petition was the way Blue Sky citizens often addressed my father. "Might I stay at the Smithy—Leeson and Elza's home—while I work for the shop?"

"I don't see why not." She tilted her head back to peer up at Fjord's face, taking in his mass. "My husband needs to see you. What are your strengths, young man?"

He smiled.

ΦΦΦ

The shop with a piano was not a shop at all. The stand-alone stone building on the edge of town had its own belfry tower and must have been a church at one time. The sign that hung from two brass chains read: The Bell Tower. In smaller print beneath it: Home of Hope and the Mutton Burger. Inside, torch sconces lit the smoky stone walls, and on the left, a boar's head hung above a rock fireplace.

My hands were finally untied, and Roger, the middle-aged guard short on conversation, introduced me to Peg.

"I'd shake yer hand, but you look contagious." Peg topped out near my shoulder, and I was only of average height. Her front teeth slightly overlapped each other, and she wore her tight curly red hair in two fluffy piles atop her head.

"I can assure you that swamp pox are not contagious, unless we fell in the muck togeth-er." I didn't mean to grab her accent, yet I heard it slip out.

"Ah, you're a sight, but I heard ya plaaay."

"I do, though I haven't played in months." I scanned the dimly lit room, the crude wooden tables, and the captain-style chairs. A few patrons sat at a table near the fire.

"Where is your piano?" I asked.

"On the stage. Over dere." Peg waved a hand toward the raised stage at the back of the room.

I saw no Great Beast, only a squatty, blockish thing.

"Where is it?" My eyes scanned the raised platform.

"Right there." She pointed to the blockish thing. It looked like a grand piano that had been used as a battering ram. Only the front portion was intact.

"They didn't tell me you were blind, toooooo. It cost me twenty dixels a year ago at auction. I want to hear you plaaay before I keep you."

I tried to manage my disappointment while I walked up several steps to the wooden stage. A thick layer of dust coated the little beast's scarred wood. I lifted back the front lid. So worn were the ivory keys that I could see the imprints of the prior owner.

I pressed my forefinger down on middle C, closed my eyes, and listened. The tone was favorable, and the key lifted with ease. Then, I smoothed the back of my soiled dress and sat down on the round bar stool. I don't remember if Peg spoke to me or not after that.

Back straight, shoulders down and relaxed, I reflected briefly on where to begin. I thought of Mother brushing my hair, of all the sweet pleasantries of Blue Sky that I might never know again. I started with the outer keys and played toward center. From my childhood, I moved to the potion-tainted milk that Father and Dr. Krawl had given me the night of my birthday celebration. I'd gone to sleep a princess and woken up a pauper.

The keys were worn because the piano had been well loved. Only one key stuck for my pinkie, two octaves over on my right hand, and only for two counts. Tears slid down my cheeks at the emotion I was finally able to expel.

"She'll do," Peg told the guard behind me. "And as long as she doesn't turn around, the fellas will think she's right pretty."

ΦΦΦ

After my first full day of work at The Bell Tower, I walked the dirt road home to Leeson and Elza's. The children along the roadside already knew my name.

"Swamp Woman," some of the boys sneered. The young girls simply avoided eye contact with me, while younger children hid in their mothers' long skirts. There was a long stretch where, finally alone, I picked a bouquet of wildflowers for Elza. I paused to admire the sky at twilight—pinks and violet-orange hues.

I was free and felt older for it.

I told Elza and Leeson of my trials in prison and wept in the folds of the elderly woman's skirts. She made me a late meal of stewed beans, sourdough bread, and honey. Following dinner, she prepared a bath for me in the center of their small, one-roomed home. She ushered Leeson out, and he groomed the horses while I bathed for the first time since Merner.

That evening while Leeson played his flute by the fire, I thanked God for keeping me safe, for not having me work the fields, and for the comfort and companionship of this dear couple. In my thankfulness, I thought on Felix. If my dear friend were still alive, I'd tell him the lessons I'd learned in prison that would someday make me a better queen.

Chapter Thirteen

The morning of my sixth straight workday at The Bell Tower started out routine. Peg studied my face and gave her little speech. "Yer plaaayin' is good for business, but yer pox are bad. I want my customers to have an appetite. Make sure they don't see yer face."

I went about grinding the mutton burger for the day and then shaping the seasoned meat into patties. Midmorning, I assisted the cook in grilling the burgers. I kept reminding myself to ask Peg for a favor, but each time she stepped into the kitchen, there were interruptions.

"Peg." I finally grabbed her attention. "I have a favor to ask."

Her gaze darted to the cook, who might overhear.

"There is a kind, elderly man in prison named Long. He has been there for years for stealing a loaf of bread for his starving family. He makes up little songs, and he sings."

"What's the favor?" A deep line creased in the center of her forehead.

"He hasn't seen his wife or his children for years."

"Everyone knows Long is blind." She was familiar with him.

"Would you give him a chance, like you did me?"

"You've brought in a ditty of dixels." She bunched her mouth together, thoughtful. "What will he do when he's not making up songs?"

"Sit there at the table." I motioned to the back of the room. "He can dry dishes."

"Aye, we'll have him dry the knives." Peg broke into a chuckle, and Lefty, the cook, laughed too.

Gerdie's high, nasal voice interrupted our discussion. The waitress's singing was cue that it was time for me to play. I passed the long-handled spatula off to Lefty and then made my way through the swing doors.

"Keep your appetites, folks, and watch Gerdie," Peg bellowed to the patrons.

Near the entry, Gerdie sang as she served hope—the amber-colored beverage made of rye—while I tiptoed through the back of the room toward the dimly lit stage.

All the tables were filled, which was the norm, but the number of uniformed guards seated near the base of the stage was unusual. Was royalty here? I could not survey the room without turning too much to look. Was it Prince Wron? Had he heard about my playing?

"To hear the Swamp Woman play, you must order from the menu," Peg bellowed. The menu consisted of mutton burgers, fried mussels, chips, and hope.

Barefoot, I smoothed my cotton skirt beneath me and sat down on the stool, my back to the dimly lit room. My pile of curly hair hung loose, nearly to my waist.

Because I played solely from memory, it always took a little while for me to settle on which memory I would follow.

"Swamp Woman, play," a man bellowed from the far side of the room.

"Play, wretched creature." Sadly, I recognized the voice of one of our regular customers.

"Be kind," ordered another of our regulars.

Somehow, I tuned out the voices, and the melody began with longings of the heart. It moved from Long still in prison and how he yearned for his grandchildren, to Knot and how he longed for peach pie, and then to myself and how I longed to be healed and for my father to arrive. Knowing the men at Peg's would appreciate bold emotion, I gave in to a memory I hadn't yet reflected on: Felix and the Giants' Snare.

With fists full of dark chords, I immersed myself in the memory of his struggle and the screams I'd heard from afar. Tears rolled down my cheeks, and I knew I could not stay in this memory too long, so I allowed it to ride to the haunting beauty of Shepherd's Field.

I had grown up among fine-looking things, but never had there been such an infusion of the senses: the birds' sweet song, the floral perfume, even my pox had temporarily been healed in that beautiful meadow. The pinkie key on my right hand stuck and did not resurface. I nudged the key back up and then abruptly clasped my hands in my lap.

There was a distinct sniffle, and then the rowdy table-clapping began.

A man trespassed onto the stage and lifted the back lid of the piano. "Sounds like there's a blooming orchestra in there." He grinned back at the audience.

Chuckles reverberated about the room.

After I finished playing another memory-inspired tune, only one set of hands clapped. The large group of guards had only stayed for one song. A nip of disappointment settled on me.

"Where did you learn to play like that?" a woman's voice asked.

Though Peg didn't want me to, I glanced over my shoulder to scan the room. Only one patron remained, a middle-aged woman in the center of the room. A dark shawl covered her head and shoulders, and two bags of pears were stashed beside her on the table.

We were completely alone.

"I play from ear and from memory—my memories."

"Then play me one of your favorite memories." She sniffled and dabbed a handkerchief to her eyes.

It was a rare request.

Each time Father returned from war, I would run and throw my arms about his neck, and he would just hold me and hold me and tell me *Everything is all right.* Even though he smelled like war, and sometimes tobacco, to me his voice was the sweetest sound in all of the world. It was like God had put a bell in my heart that only my father could ring. Even though he was a warmonger and made me mad at times, I loved him in the deep trenches of my soul.

I began with middle C because it is as close to home on a piano as one can be. From there I moved to memories of beef burgundy, which was Father's favorite homecoming dinner; Mother's happy, tear-streaked laughter; and the smell of his pipe in the study. Happiness bubbled within us, teamed with the awareness that with Father's homecoming loomed his inevitable good-bye.

When I finished my favorite memory, the audience's applause had returned to its normal volume. Was the commoner still seated amongst them? I did not turn to see.

I played for another hour before I took a break to the kitchen to peel potatoes.

"The guards were in and out, in and out. It was like they couldn't make up their minds," Gerdie said.

The heaviness in my bones returned.

"Now, don't look so glum." She lowered a basket of sliced potatoes into a large vat of oil. "You did your best; that's all you can do."

ΦΦΦ

Three days later . . .

"Now's a good time for you to ring the bell, Swampie," Peg said. "Come right back in. I'm sure there's folks waiting to hear you pla-aay."

It was the second time I'd been given the privilege of ringing the bell. I enjoyed walking out front of the shop and getting fresh air. The dinner bell was rung each evening at six o'clock—reminding Yonder citizens that it was a good time to visit The Bell Tower.

I wiped my hands on the front of my apron while I exited the stone belfry. In the distance, three guards walked the dirt road toward me. Cragdon, the fair-haired guard in the middle, carried a large, limp plant.

"Swamp Woman," he called loudly.

"Hello, Cragdon." My hand rested on the pull for the heavy front door.

"This is for you." After several strides, he extended the wilted foliage with its long taproot and draped the plant over his arms onto mine. Small, trumpet-shaped purple flowers hid amongst the fuzzy, dark green leaves.

"Thank you." If I wasn't mistaken, it was the same plant I'd seen in Shepherd's Field.

"It's queen of the meadow, a possible remedy for you. It is a gift from the Queen."

My gaze narrowed. "The Queen?" I smiled, both surprised and pleased. "Please inform the queen that I am touched by her kind and considerate gift."

The door swung open behind me. "What is taaaking you sooo long, Swampie? I told you—" Peg's gaze took in the royal guards.

"A gift from the Queen." Cragdon nodded to the wilted plant in my possession. Stepping toward Peg, he handed her a sealed envelope.

"Tell the Queen she can't have her. The Swamp Woman's mine for another twenty-one daaays." Peg stuffed the envelope down the front of her tunic. "A deal is a deal."

"I'm merely the messenger." Cragdon bowed slightly.

I carried the plant into the kitchen and hung it carefully on a nail, next to other dry herbs. While I peeled potatoes at the sink, a million worries galloped through my mind. What did Peg mean . . . *have her*? After Peg's, I would be a free person again, wouldn't I?

ΦΦΦ

The following day, Peg had still not breathed a word to me regarding the letter. I found myself too curious to remain silent. "Peg, what was in the letter from the Queen?"

Standing in the middle of the kitchen, my employer shrugged. "If ya heal early, the Queen wants you. But if ya don't, you get to staaay here." She smiled, looking at my pox.

Had the Queen heard me play? Or perhaps heard about it from the guards? To my knowledge, Prince Wron had not visited The Bell Tower.

"Who was that woman with the pears?" I asked.

"I dunno. We were all ushered out while you were plaaaying, like I didn't have a saaay in my own place."

ΦΦΦ

Midmorning, Peg yelled for me from the dining area. I wiped my hands on a dishtowel and hurried through the swing doors.

"Swampie, I brought ya a friend." Hands on hips, Peg grinned.

Two guards ushered Long past us toward the stage. Dixels must have been dancing in Peg's head for her to act so quickly on my request.

"Let me hear ya sing, old man," Peg bellowed.

I recalled his awkwardness with the Queen, and tossed the dishtowel at Peg on my way to join him on stage. "Sing for me, Long." I curled my arm in his. "Something simple. Sing the song about your missus that you sang for us in prison."

"Awh . . . Dory, I missed your sweet voice." As he smiled, his Adam's apple bobbed up and down.

"My missus will be sorry she sent me for bread.

No dixels in my pocket, just a song in my head . . ."

Without a tremor, Long finished three stanzas of the tune.

Peg's mouth bunched thoughtfully. "He'll do, but it won't be good for business, Swampie, you standing with him onstage. Keep your pox covered." She shook her head and walked away while I hugged Long.

ΦΦΦ

When Long sang, the audience at The Bell Tower reminded me of prison: the crowd noise hushed to a pensive silence. News of Long's freedom spread throughout the kingdom, and more and more folks gathered at The Bell Tower to hear him sing.

"Do you see my wife?" he asked me for the fourth time that day. We stood together on the stage.

"What does she look like?" This opening had quickly become a part of our act.

"She used to be . . ." His hand outlined a woman with plump curves. "With coarse hair and strong hands." I gripped my hood about my face and peered below us at the dimly lit sea of faces.

"I don't see her, but don't worry. It won't be long."

He cleared his throat, peering into the darkness.

"Little old woman . . . where are you?" His voice trembled as tears clouded his eyes.

"Our children have grown,
I'm here all alone.
Little old woman who shared my bed.
Little old woman who sent me for bread.
Little old woman, where are you?"

He crossed his long, knobby fingers over his chest.

"My heart's on fire waiting for you.
How many years have gone and come?
Our son is a man, our girl a mum.
Little old woman, these words are true,
Tonight, I get to go home with you.
Please be alive, and well with thee.
Please be my Molly who married me.
Little old woman . . ."

With his eyes closed, Long slowly turned his head, listening. I took his hand in mine and assisted him offstage.

"Long, give her time. She'll come." Tears threatened to spill down my cheeks. "She'll hear about you. Give her time."

ΦΦΦ

"Long's depressing songs are surprisingly good for business," Peg whispered while I peeled potatoes. "There's standing room only, and the folks are still coming."

"Long hasn't seen his wife in years; that's why they're here," I said.

Eyes narrowed, Peg stared at me. She truly didn't understand.

"To share in the joys of the day," I said. "Their sweet reunion."

Chapter Fourteen

With several of his men, Prince Wron walked the cobblestone streets of the heart of the village. Under Cragdon's direction, they took the dirt road heading north toward Delfrey. The shutters of the nearby homes were open, which was out of the ordinary for this time of evening. Most often folks wanted privacy around the dinner table. Perhaps they were enjoying the poignant melody that drifted in the air.

"Is this what my mother wanted me to hear?" Wron asked.

"Yes."

"Where is the music coming from?"

"The Bell Tower," Cragdon said. "Your mother wants me to go to Delfrey tomorrow and find the nicest piano I can for the Great Hall. She was very impressed with the Swamp Woman."

"So I've heard. I still can't believe she did what she did." He smiled at the thought of his mother dressed like a commoner, and seated at Peg's, of all places, amongst their guards. But she'd always loved music.

"I believe she found the Swamp Woman's music healing."

"Yes, I think so, too." Last night, she'd appeared pensive while she knit in front of the fire, and perhaps a little lonely.

Up ahead, a surprising number of people picnicked alongside the road.

"If Peg knew the townspeople listened for free, she would not let the music escape," Cragdon said.

"Yes, she would buckle that place up tight. She is all business." Though Wron chuckled, he felt uneasy. The music tugged at him, swirling the deep waters of his soul. He was reminded of the tale of the Pied Piper and how the rats followed the piper, only to drown themselves in the river.

"I have every intention of marrying her," Cragdon said.

"Peg?" Wron suppressed a laugh.

"No, you know I meant the Swamp Woman."

Cragdon's incessant search for a bride continued. "Well, I'm sure your beloved will not take kindly to being called Swamp Woman."

"*Dory*." Cragdon's voice softened.

"There is hope for you. You have not fallen for a woman's beauty first, this time."

"I've reserved a table for us near the front." Cragdon led the way, while several guards accompanied them inside.

Peg greeted them and, with a spring to her step for so late in the day, escorted Wron and Cragdon to a table, several rows from the stage, and then took their order—two glasses of hope and a plate of chips. The fire in the hearth lit the dining area, and torch sconces lit the stage.

With her back to the room, Dory played without sheet music. The mesmerizing piece appeared to be bottled up in her head and in her fingers. Peg delivered their beverages and the plate of chips.

"She is very good." Wron nodded toward the stage.

"If you're here on account of the Queen"—Peg bent low to his ear—"remind yer mother that the Swamp Woman is mine for at least twenty more days."

"Have you read her correspondence yet?" Wron asked.

"Remind her that a deal is a deal."

Wron grinned, returning his gaze to the stage. Dory's long, lean, pox-riddled arms ebbed away from her willowy figure, and then back again with grace and uncanny deftness. Her auburn curls rippled to the curve of her waist. With her back to the audience, the girl was beautiful.

Perhaps it was the music that transformed her appearance. He glanced about the room at the other patrons. Shoulders down and relaxed, softness forged their faces. Her music, if used in the right way, might have reduced the Twelve-Year War to ten. After the entrancing song ended, Dory stepped away from the piano. Barefoot and with her back to the audience, she quietly walked offstage.

"Is that it?" He nudged Cragdon's elbow.

"No, Long, the blind man, will sing."

A young, fair maiden sang loudly near the entrance. She was tone-deaf, and her voice was not altogether pleasing.

"Keep your appetites and watch Gerdie," Peg bellowed. "Do not look toward the stage."

Wron did the opposite and turned to watch as Dory, with a hooded cloak over her head, led an elderly man up the steps and to the front of the stage.

"Has anyone seen Long's wife today?" Dory asked the audience. Her disfigurement was hidden in the shadows of her hooded cloak.

"I saw her with an apronful of corn standing in her garden," said someone near the front.

"I saw Molly hanging clothes on the line," yelled Clarence from the mercantile.

"It appears everyone has heard the good news, except, that is, for Long's wife," Dory said. For a moment, Wron found himself entranced with her accent as much as the rest of the audience appeared to be.

"Can anyone help us find her?" Dory asked the crowd. "It has been three years since Long has seen his wife."

"It's been longer than that." Clarence's bellows were followed by a rowdy round of laughter.

"My home is not far." Long's clothes hung on him like they no longer had stitching. "You take a right at the Mill Road. You'll pass a cherry tree, and then you'll see my Molly . . ." Gesturing with his hands, Long outlined a plump woman's curves.

"I'll go. I know where she lives." Weaver, a young tradesman, stood up near the front. "But save my chair." He downed his glass of hope, ran a forearm across his mouth, and proceeded toward the door.

Long cleared his throat and the mumbling dimmed.

"Home . . ." The elderly man's aged voice filled the room.

"The comforts of home." A sheen filled his eyes, and his Adam's apple bobbed in his lean neck.

"Where we warm our souls by the fire,

A straw-tick bed when we're tired,

A bowl of my Molly's mutton stew . . .

My home . . . little old woman

. . . is you."

Wron grinned and clapped loudly along with the others.

Long turned to his left and held out one hand for Dory. She rose from the piano stool and took his arm in hers.

"Dory, what do you see? Do you see my Molly?"

With a hand cupped over her eyes, Dory scanned the entry area. The audience's gaze followed hers.

"It won't be long, . . . Long." Her voice trembled. Like the audience, she was on the verge of tears.

Wron closed his eyes. Please help Weaver find Molly, he prayed. Please help him find her for the sake of this dear old man.

"Little old woman, where are you?" Long's unseeing eyes roved the room.

With the rest of the audience, Wron glanced over his shoulder toward the door. Weaver, the young man, stepped through the doorway. A hush fell over the group, as a frizzy white-haired woman with windblown cheeks and wearing a soiled apron walked in behind him. Across the room, her gaze found Long.

The fire crackled in the hearth and heads turned as Molly walked the middle aisle.

"Long . . ." Dory said, "a beautiful woman with flowing white hair is walking toward us."

"Does she look like she's forgiven me?" The light flickered in Long's glazed eyes.

Emotion burned hot in Wron's throat.

"Yes. She looks like a bride; there is so much love in her eyes."

"Little old woman . . ." Holding his hands out, Long turned slightly toward the stairs. "I'm so blessed . . ."

Lifting her dress at the knee, his wife slowly climbed the steps.

"Words cannot express . . ."

She pressed her cheek to his chest and wrapped her arms about Long's lean waist.

"Awh . . . my Molly." Sighing, he kissed the top of her hair.

Wron glanced over his shoulder to where Peg stood near the stone fireplace. Tears glistened on her cheeks before she wiped them away.

There was hope for the shopkeeper.

ΦΦΦ

I shared the joys of the day with Leeson and Elza. After supper, Elza applied the steamed leaves of the queen of the meadow plant directly to my pox. Her wrinkled fingertips felt soft against my cheeks. Using her mortar and pestle, she ground the dry root into a powder, which she used to make a discolored broth. She handed me a cupful of it.

"It smells awful." I eyed her above the brim of my cup.

"Does dee Bell Dower have a mirror?"

"No." I looked toward the fire. "I'm afraid that if see a mirror, I will come home and say, *Elza, please make me a potful of that unpalatable tea.*"

She held her tummy, and her body shook, yet no sound escaped her.

"Do I look as bad as my hands?" I held them above the table for her to see.

"If queen of dee meadow does nod work, domorrow we will dry onions."

"We are out of onions," Leeson said.

"Then I will buy more." My money was hidden in Elza's salt jar. "Does my face look like my hands?" I again asked Elza.

Her head bobbed as she nodded. "You have nod improved, dear one."

The weight of my secrets crushed my spirit, and it took all my strength to move from the table to my bed. I lay down, facing the wall, and in silent prayer, I blubbered my worries to God. I stilled my mind, waiting for His whisper. One word tiptoed in so softly that I almost didn't hear it.

Patience.

That couldn't be it. That couldn't be all that God had to tell me. I'd already been patient. For weeks I'd been patient. Couldn't He give me more words than that? Words like you'd find in one of those China Woman's cookies. Words like: *Tomorrow you will be beautiful in your betrothed's eyes.* Or *Your dear friend is not dead.* Or *Tomorrow your father will arrive, and he'll be so proud of you.*

I sniffled and waited for God's whisper. Instead, Elza sat down on the edge of my bed, and in small circular motions, she rubbed my back.

"I don't know if it's just the emotion of the day or . . ." I said.

"Shh!" she hushed me. "Dee h'ard can only hold so much."

I needed to hear her tender words. Not *Swamp Woman* or *Play more, you wretched creature*. Tender words like Elza's.

ΦΦΦ

Before breakfast, I left early to purchase a bag of onions and potatoes at the mercantile. While there, I spotted new women's shoes on the rack. They were so plain; I could not bring myself to try them on. I would rather go barefoot.

When I returned to Leeson and Elza's, a band of soldiers—on horseback and on foot—surrounded the smithy.

Had the Queen decided to take me?

Leeson closed the door behind me. In the center of the small room at our crude table sat Prince Wron and Roger, the middle-aged guard. Soon I would be leaving here to become the Queen's possession.

I set the bag of onions and potatoes near the sink. "Good morning, Prince Wron. You are visiting early." I walked around the side of the table and sat down on the edge of my straw-ticked mattress. Elza had been busy. Both freshly brewed coffee and sourdough biscuits warmed on the hearth.

Elza set chipped mugs of coffee in front of our guests. She clasped her hands below her chest in silent, but visible, prayer, and watched Prince Wron take his first sip.

"The coffee is very good, Elza. Dark and rich." He glanced up at her. His short dark hair bore a cowlick in the middle.

"Dory boughd id for uz."

"Will I be working at Peg's today?" I asked.

"No." Wron lowered his cup to the table. "You will return with me to play for my parents."

I was leaving whether I was healed or not. So, this was what a wilted plant from the Queen meant.

"Tonight, Peg wanted Long and me to repeat last night's performance." I'd seen Wron and his men last night at The Bell Tower.

"You'll need to discuss it with my mother."

Was it because Wron had seen the performance that I was now leaving?

"Earlier, I was told she did not want me in your home until I was healed."

"My mother is concerned that not enough is being done for your healing." His dark brows lifted.

I would not stare or allow myself to dwell on his good looks. I was a wretched creature.

Elza puttered to the hearth. Carrying a wire handle wrapped in cloth, she set a dark cast-iron pan in the center of the table beside a dish of honey. "Dee sourdough is Dory's recipe."

"Thank you, Elza." Wron held a biscuit beneath his nose and inhaled the sourdough aroma before taking a bite. "It is unique and delicious. I would like you to show Rhoda, our cook, how to make these." He glanced at me.

I hurriedly shook my head. The Giant Woman scared me.

"You do not like change, do you?" Wron regarded me.

If he had undergone as much change as I had, he wouldn't either.

"Will I be allowed to stay here?" I loved the simplicity of Leeson and Elza's home, the love and care they showered upon me.

"No. Now that we have physical proof that you are from Blue Sky, it's best that you stay under our protection, at least until Princess Alia and her father arrive."

"What proof?" I asked.

"The Blue Sky insignia is in the shoes of your horse in Leeson's stable."

"Oh . . ." I had not told Leeson and Elza where I was from.

"Dee princess!" Elza gasped, and covered her mouth with both hands.

In the silence that followed, the room felt stuffy and overly warm. Wron looked at Elza and shook his head. Completely at ease, he stretched his long legs my direction and crossed them at his royal boots.

"Dory, tell me your circumstances." His gaze narrowed.

In the gleam of the coffeepot that warmed on the bricks, I saw the small, distorted reflection of an odd, miserable creature. Prince Wron was young, handsome, and waiting for Princess Alia to arrive. If I told him who I really was, would he stare at me in horror? Would they abandon me in the hills to never find my way out?

"At the age of seven," I said, "I became Blue Sky's royal pianist." It was not a lie. After my father lavishly complimented my piano recital, the royal pianist threw a vase. Father fired her, and at age seven, I'd simply replaced her.

"The age of seven?" Incredulity tinged his deep voice.

"Yes. I am well known in Blue Sky, if not famous, which is why my father had me travel in disguise." So far I had not lied.

"Are you here for the wedding?" He shook his head.

"We traveled two weeks ahead of the wedding party so that my father might have time to visit Evland. Yes, I am to play for your wedding."

I had just lied to my future husband, and felt slightly sick to my stomach.

"Two weeks . . . I see. And tell me again why you traveled in disguise?"

"I am quite famous in Blue Sky. My father and King Wells thought it best."

He nodded thoughtfully, taking it all in. "Much of Evland was destroyed during the war."

"I would still like to see my father's homeland," I said. My second lie. I held two fingers out against my knee, trying to keep track.

"I understand." He nodded toward the guard at the table. "Roger is from Evland. Both he and Cragdon speak of it with great emotion. After you've served your time, you may go there."

"During my penance, may I board here with Leeson and Elza? I have found their home to be very comforting," I requested once more.

"No." Wron rose from the table and nodded toward Leeson. "Because Dory is from Blue Sky, she is valuable to us at this time."

Elza's shoulders quivered as she began to weep. Leeson set a hand to her back. At the open cupboard, I took down the crock of sourdough. After stirring in several cups of flour, I divided the dough and set half of it in a chipped earthenware crock. I told myself that it was not good-bye.

"You will redrun do us, Dory?"

"Often, Elza, you are like family to me." I set an arm about her rounded shoulders. "Remember to feed the sourdough. You now have your own to share with others. My other horse is yours to sell. I want you to keep the money," I told Leeson.

"No, it is too much. I will not sell it without you," he mumbled.

As I crossed the threshold, I closed my eyes; I could not look back.

Chapter Fifteen

From the inner courtyards, one would never have known the region had been plagued by over a decade of war. An orchard of fruit trees lined the right side of the cobblestone walkway. Light green baby apples loaded the branches, a welcome I found promising.

"You will bathe and change. By then the piano will be situated in the Great Hall." With a long gait, Prince Wron strode ahead of Roger and me.

"Where was the piano purchased?" I asked.

"There is a fine shop in Delfrey. Cragdon was told to select the best."

I hoped it was not a baby beast like Peg's. "Did Cragdon tell you Peg's response last night when he delivered the letter?" I called after him.

"Yes; if Peg has finally read it, she will know that my mother is willing to share you one afternoon a week until your penance is paid. Roger will accompany you."

"You play beautifully, Swampie." Roger cast me a faint smile.

"Her name is Dory, Roger."

I smiled at Roger. "I don't mind." Peg's nickname had kind of grown on me.

I was thankful that at least once a week, I'd be able to make the evening reenactments with Long, however corny they might be. For now, I would reacquaint myself with my future in-laws and play the piano. If they were unkind, I'd escape to Leeson and Elza's in the middle of the night.

The lead guard held open the postern, a side door of the castle. The wide stone hallways were lit by torch sconces. The floors were slate, not lovely white marble like Blue Sky. This was my future home, and though my heart wanted to, I would not compare.

I glanced over my shoulder, and in a window into another hallway, I locked eyes with an odd-looking creature. I stepped back for a moment and peered again. It was not a window but a large mirror trimmed with slate, reflecting my darkest nightmare.

The creature was me.

Roger stepped back to join the creature in the mirror.

"Please . . ." I touched the puffy, nickel-sized spots. "Please don't be me." Yet I knew my reflection did not lie. My eyes were swollen, mere slits of green. The pox was crusted and unsightly. A heaviness anchored in my being. How could Wron, or anyone, bear to look at me?

"I did not recognize myself." I swallowed tears. "I'm sorry, it's a great shock."

Wron, who'd disappeared around the curved corridor, returned for us. "Come now, my parents are waiting."

Blindly, I followed him. The day she'd assigned me to Peg's, the Queen had seen me up close. Her love for music must be great to allow me in her home.

"I looked bad in the reflection of the coffeepot," I whispered. "No one told me how terrible, terrible . . . I really look. No one."

"What was that?" Wron stopped ahead of us.

"Nothing," I mumbled.

"I heard something."

"She said no one told her how terrible she looks," Roger said.

Wron waved a hand toward a small chamber. "This will be your room." Two plump feather beds sat against one wall, and at the far end of the room, a tall arched window provided daylight.

"You will room with Rhoda, our cook."

"Rhoda?" A giant would be sleeping no more than four feet away from me.

"Yes, you will like Rhoda." He nodded ahead. "Down the hallway, a warm bath has been prepared, and Mother has selected clothes for you."

"Is it true that Rhoda's a vegetarian?" I asked.

"At times, she does not eat meat. Make haste; the piano will arrive soon."

Though my circumstances were not ideal, I was finally here. Despite numerous complications, I'd made it. I was in Yonder's royal family's home. I thought on the one word God had whispered to me, *patience.* He must have an incredible sense of humor to think that one word would pacify me in such a time as this.

But . . . I was home.

Now I just needed to wait for healing, for my betrothed to fall in love with me, for Father to arrive, and for *patience.*

Chapter Sixteen

The attire Queen Eunice had selected for me was a white peasant blouse, a gray checked gingham skirt, and heaven forbid, a pair of plain Jane brown shoes. I'd rather enjoyed my experience of being barefoot in the village. I'd felt so rebellious. Now that I'd bathed, I was at least a *clean* creature with spots. I avoided any mirrors as I entered the slate-lined corridor.

Please let the piano be a concert grand, highly polished ebony black and finely tuned with a matching bench, I whispered my requests to God and followed the voices to the Great Hall.

Prince Wron sat at a long, black granite table with his parents. Silver-and-black banners hung high on the walls. Goatskin chairs and a cattle leather couch were grouped in front of a massive stone fireplace. Off to the left, in an alcove with tall arched windows, sat a baby grand piano with carved legs.

My heart lurched. Though not as magnificent as The Beast back home, the baby beast was grand. I ran my hand along the darkly aged wood and, judging from its heavily waxed patina, estimated that it was at least half a century old.

Yonder had invested a small fortune in me.

"Dory . . ." Queen Eunice cleared her throat. She sat very upright, with the three-snowballs hairdo spiraled upon her head. "Come closer, Dory."

I stopped several feet shy of the table, clasping my hands in front of me.

"Did you try the queen of the meadow?" She lifted her wire spectacles to study me.

"Yes, Your Highness. Elza made a poultice for me, and she also ground the root to make a broth. Thank you for your thoughtful gift."

"Was it pleasant?"

"No, I'm afraid it was, uh . . ." I recalled her earlier description of my pox. "It was very disagreeable."

Her mouth bunched tight, while one brow arched very expressively. "The plant does not appear to have worked the magic we hoped it would."

"Father, this is Dory," Wron said, "the piano girl that Mother's been telling you about."

King Ulrich lowered the newspaper to peer at me. His thick white hair was parted on one side, and his face gleamed a shiny pink. Even before he spoke, I knew I would like him.

"I've heard you're from Blue Sky." His voice was raspy, but charming all the same.

"Yes, I know Princess Alia well."

Silence followed, and then King Ulrich rustled the paper open and lifted it until only an inch of his white hair was visible. "Wron, the timing is too coincidental."

"I know. But the Blue Sky emblem is engraved both in the hooves of her horse and in her saddle, and also in the horse and saddle that she sold at auction," Wron said.

Wron's research both surprised and pleased me.

"Now is a time to be on your guard," his father said.

"Wait till you hear her play, Walter." The Queen patted the table between them.

"Dory, my father is concerned that you will prove to be a counterfeit princess." Wron glanced up at me.

Given my reflection in the mirror a short while ago, such an accusation surprised me. I gave in to a giggle.

"Are you another counterfeit?" Walter lowered his paper to regard me.

"No, Your Highness, I am not a counterfeit."

"We shall see."

A wee smile escaped me from the irony of it all.

ΦΦΦ

The piano at Peg's had helped me purge much of my heartache, yet due to its size, it did not have the auditory potential of the baby beast. I sat with perfect posture upon the sweeping bench. The alcove windows overlooked a large herb garden and manicured beds of lavender, and in the distance, purple hills embraced the sky. I recalled the sweet little tune that Felix had often hummed while we'd ridden in the wagon. Leaning my ear low, I recited the simple melody.

Though oftentimes difficult, remembering was always part of my healing.

After my one-finger recital, I added six- and seven-note chords, merging the memory and the melody into one. While I played, I recalled Felix and our talks by the fire, the camaraderie and laughter that we'd shared. And now carrying that memory forward, I reached for high notes to express my longing to be healed, to appear beautiful in my betrothed's eyes, to have at least one evening of courtship with Prince Wron before our vows.

For weeks, I had longed to hear the moving melody in its entirety.

I set my hands in my lap and recalled what my first piano instructor had told my parents years ago: Princess Alia has a rare gift. She has a remarkable ear and can recite anything I play. She will never need to read music; she will only need to listen.

I was still learning to listen. In the small gasp and heavy sigh behind me, I heard that the melody had reached the Queen's heart.

Wron's parents clapped and then requested that I play another.

"Does anyone know the name of that piece?" I asked, my back to the room.

"I believe you played a familiar tune called 'Waiting,'" Wron said. "Though there were parts I did not recognize."

"What would you like me to play, Your Majesty?" I asked.

"Call me Queen Eunice. What pieces do you know?"

"Have you heard 'The Ballad of Blue Sky'?"

In the reflection in the window, I saw her shake her head, and her snowball hairdo stayed perfectly in place.

"Have you heard 'Pray, My Child'?" I asked.

Again, she shook her head.

"Our songs are different, I believe."

"Do you know 'Tomorrow, Today'?" Her voice held a tender note of longing.

"No, but if you will come and sing it for me, I will play it by ear." I patted the bench beside me.

Eunice hesitated for a moment before rising from her chair. Her love for music dismissed any remaining reservation, and she sat down beside me. In a sweetly aged soprano voice, she sang:

"Tomorrow you say you'll love me, but I want today.

Tomorrow you'll say you'll leave me, but I want you to stay.

Your eyes are full of joy, but your words are filled with pain.

Tomorrow, my love, tomorrow, today."

"Is a sad song," I murmured. Leaning my right ear to the piano so Eunice could not see my troubled eyes, I let the tune run through my head until it was down to my fingertips. She sang softly, and note for note, I matched the slow and moving melody. At last, the poignant song ended.

"Music is such simple joy." She sighed.

I was finally here in my future home. I'd made it. There was no need to fear anymore. It was just a period of waiting for me now, for healing, for Father's arrival, and for him to claim me as his own.

ΦΦΦ

I played piano throughout the day, gulped down a servant's dinner, and played late, past an orange-tinged sunset. Eunice finally began to yawn. She either had gone too long without music or had an endless appetite for it.

"I'm exhausted," she finally crooned.

"Mother, I'm sure Dory is more exhausted than you." Wron chuckled. "I will escort her to her room."

His offer surprised me.

"Oh, Wron, I'm quite sure Dory can find her way back." The skein of lavender yarn Eunice had been knitting with was now a blanket, covering her lap and spilling onto the floor.

"It is her first night here, Mother, and the hallways are often not all that well lit," Wron said.

"If it is important to you," she sighed.

"I will escort you to your room." He strode ahead of me.

I quickly said my good nights to his parents and followed Wron into the corridor. What was he up to, or did he think *me* up to something? I found that I was no longer the naïve, trusting young woman I'd once been. Perhaps it was due to losing my first kiss to Prince Dell, being drugged by my own father, or almost losing my hair to Hilda.

In between the torch sconces, giant shadows loomed in the hallway.

"I've known for the past six years that I am betrothed to Princess Alia," Wron said, cupping the candle's flame with his free hand. "Yet you are the first person I have met who can tell me anything about her."

"Since you were twelve," I said, thoughtfully. It had also taken his parents a surprising number of years to break the news.

"You told my mother that Alia's hair is auburn, and that her eyes are hazel."

"It's true."

"What else can you tell me about her?" His pace slowed.

"Your question is so vast." I laughed.

"I know that she is a firstborn. Does she have siblings?"

I inhaled deeply. "Yes, she has a seven-year-old sister, Wren." With a small gasp, I realized Wron's and Wren's names differed by only one vowel. "Are you an only child?" I countered.

"No. I have a younger sister, who has already married. Despite my parents' approval, she fell in love. They live in the resort town of Delfrey, an hour from here. So . . . to have been an only child for so long, is she very spoiled?"

"Yes, she had an idyllic childhood. Except for her father being away at war a great deal of the time."

"So she has not wanted for much." Pursing his lips, he nodded.

I stopped outside my bedroom chamber. He paused and for a moment appeared thoughtful. "Rhoda snores.

Sometimes her snoring is unbearably loud. If you cannot sleep, I will help you turn her to her side."

I didn't understand. "Where is your room?"

"Right there." He pointed to a doorway across the hall from mine.

"You are so close to the servants."

"It is Rhoda who is so close to us. She is like family, and she has bad knees. The rest of the servants are on the upper level. When Rhoda falls asleep on her back, she is very loud.

"Is Alia musically inclined?" He looked directly in my eyes now. It was kind of him, considering my condition.

"Yes, she is." I did not want him to ask any more questions, so I gave in to a yawn. "Good night, Prince Wron. Thank you for your escort." I closed my chamber door behind me and pressed against it. *Please, Lord, make me well. How can he even look at me?*

ΦΦΦ

A sliver of moon shone shyly into our room. Rhoda must have still been in the kitchen, as I was alone. Usually, I was a fairly sound sleeper, so the trick was simply to fall asleep before she came to bed. I stilled my mind and my breathing as I'd done so many nights alone in the Forest Maze.

I was home at last, and not only was my future husband handsome, he was also kind. He could be far worse. *Stop thinking. Picture black.* Yet a large portion of my mind wanted to be awake when my roommate arrived.

I awakened from a light slumber to the creak of the door opening. Light from the hallway sconces spilled inside before the door closed. Outlined by moonlight, Rhoda's giant silhouette moved to the opposite side of the room. I clutched the covers beneath my chin and prepped my voice, ready to scream.

Rhoda wore a long white sleeping gown and a droopy white hat. Her knees crunched as she knelt beside her bed. Bowing her head, she mumbled her prayers. Something about food, pies . . . dinner. When I'd said my prayers, I had not bent my knees. I peered at the ceiling in penance.

The giant woman had difficulty rising. She set a hand on both the bedside table and the bed as she pushed herself out of her kneeling position.

"Dory, if I snore, simply roll me to my side." Rhoda flipped back the covers and lowered herself into bed. "Your piano playing is almost as lovely as my pie." Her compliment was followed by a yawn, which seemed to suck some of the air out of the room. "I heard your music while I washed dishes. I am famous for my pie."

"Oh." I suppressed a yawn. "What kind do you make?"

"Peach."

I waited for her to say *apple, gooseberry, human...* but she did not elaborate. "Knot talked highly of your peach pie," I said.

"I miss Knot."

"I do, too," I mumbled, and then I forced my mind to picture black, so I might fall asleep first. Within minutes, Rhoda's snoring echoed off the stone walls. Wide-eyed, I lay awake. I likened sharing a room with this giant woman to being in the bottom of a canyon with a full moon and a coyote.

Throwing back the covers, I routed my feet to the floor and tapped lightly on her arm. She did not move. Despite my fear of her, I wrapped both my hands about the curve of her ham-sized shoulder, and gently shook. Her snoring did not lapse.

I waited for a pause between snores. "Rhoda . . ."

She was dead to the world.

"Rhoda." I was afraid to yell as I might wake the entire castle. Sliding a hand beneath her shoulder and her hip, I attempted to roll her to her side, but I could not lift my hands up from the mattress. She was solid—all muscle, and heavy. Seeking more leverage, I knelt and pushed up. It did not make a difference. I would have to wake Wron.

I wrapped a robe about me, crossed the dimly lit hallway, and rapped softly on the heavy wooden door. The door swung inward. Chuckling to himself, Wron shrugged on his robe.

"Why is Rhoda my roommate? Is it penance?"

"No." He strolled past me into the hall, a pewter candlestick in his possession. "Your only other option for roommates is Needa, and her home is too small."

"But I value my sleep. Perhaps I can stay at Leeson and Elza's."

"Once King Wells and Alia arrive, you may return to Leeson's." He hastily set the candle on the nightstand, and the wick dimmed and smoked. "In the meantime"—he paused, waiting for Rhoda's snore to end—"you will stay here. Counterfeits could use you to find out more about Blue Sky."

What an awful thought.

In the sliver of moonlight that seeped into our room, he bent low and pushed on Rhoda's shoulder and hip, much as I'd attempted, except he was successful in rolling the mammoth woman to her side.

"Good night, Dory," my future beloved said.

I waited for a snore to pass. "Good night, Prince—"

Rhoda's snoring interrupted our pleasantries, and the door creaked closed behind him.

"Good night, Prince." I smiled.

Chapter Seventeen

The next morning, I played piano while Eunice knitted. Afterward, she invited me to accompany her to Rhoda's herb garden. While I snipped primroses, she read aloud the herbal remedies from Dixie's writings.

"Wron loves to hunt. He spoke endlessly about the Swamp Woman who carried a gun," Eunice said. "He is no longer allowed to go on his lengthy hunting trips, not with Alia expected any day." She sighed. "You know how men are—you keep them home too long, and they begin to feel caged." She lifted her eyeglasses, studying the page. "She also penned *Parsley*. Heaven knows we have heaps of it."

"Perhaps a hunt will do him good." I looked up from my snipping.

"Not with all of the counterfeits lurking about. We need him here." She shook her head. "Did you hear much about the Wells's travel plans?"

"King Wells? Oh, it was all very hush-hush."

"That sounds like Francis." She sighed. "Your hair is beautiful. It is definitely your best feature. What color is Princess Alia's hair?"

"Auburn," I reminded her.

"So you said. The last batch of counterfeits said that Alia's hair is gold and luxurious."

"Her hair is long and auburn." I rose to my feet to peer over her shoulder at Dixie's scribblings.

She appeared only slightly uncomfortable at my nearness. "You are remarkable, Dory. I have really only known you for two days, but I am quite certain that I want you to stay in Yonder, indefinitely."

"As a servant or a free person?"

Her chest inflated and her chin tipped up. "As my royal pianist, of course." She turned to head back toward the kitchen.

"I should inform you that I am betrothed."

"To whom?"

"The son of one of my father's friends. I plan to meet him when I'm well."

"Well . . ." She glanced back at me as she crossed the threshold into Rhoda's white brick kitchen. "Royal pianists are often allowed to marry."

I carried the basketful of herbs, and followed her inside. Pots and pans hung from an oval rack suspended from the high ceiling.

The giant woman chopped turnips with a large knife. It was only my second time seeing Rhoda in the daylight, and my pulse quickened.

"Rhoda, you've met your new roommate?" Eunice asked.

"We have not been properly introduced," I interrupted. "Rhoda was up earlier than I this morning."

"Oh, well then, Rhoda, this is Dory. She has swamp pox. She is a new addition to our staff and, as you know, plays the piano beautifully."

"Are they painful?" Rhoda held a hand to her own mottled cheek.

"Awful, and they are beginning to itch again, but I am not contagious."

"Where is Needa?" Eunice asked, searching the countertops for something.

A gnomelike creature no more than six inches tall stepped out from behind an earthenware crock. She was adorable, like a child's small doll.

"Here is Needa," the gnome said. Frowning, she crossed her arms behind her. Blonde plaited pigtails poked out from beneath her green pointed hat.

I tried not to stare. I'd heard of gnomes but had never seen one before. They were rarely seen, rarely captured, but stories flourished in Blue Sky that they were real.

"I'm sorry; I'm staring," I whispered.

"Needa Gnome," Needa said, tapping one foot. "Long-term prisoner of Yonder. I'm one hundred years old now, Queen Eunice. I should be courting and marrying, and instead . . . I am seasoning."

"Needa is of great help to Rhoda. She is in charge of all of the herbs and spices for our dishes. Now, Needa, politely greet Dory, our pianist."

With a half-hidden scowl, Needa curtsied.

"I'll return to my knitting." On her way out of the kitchen, the Queen added a regal wave.

"You're one hundred years old?" I had no idea gnomes lived so long.

"Yes. My great-grandmother lived to be three hundred and sixty-eight, and she would have lived longer had she not been trampled by a horse. My great-grandfather is well over four hundred. He may or may not be alive. I haven't been home for eleven years."

"You're a prisoner?"

"Yes, of the Twelve-Year War. So is Rhoda." Needa held out her hand toward the large woman.

"I am not a prisoner; I am like family," Rhoda said, chopping a turnip.

I walked around the extensive brick island, trying to familiarize myself with the room. "I do not know much about cooking; I know more about serving, but I will help in any way I can."

"Serving is good; I will let you serve," Rhoda bellowed.

"Where are you from, Needa?" I asked.

Carrying her shoulders low and her knees high, Needa raced across the top of the island toward me. "I'm from Evland." She panted. "I heard Yonder soldiers in the forest, and I hid in a hollowed round of wood. One of the soldiers picked up the wood for the fire, found me, and put me in his pocket. And, of course . . ." She flung her forearm across her forehead, with dramatic flare. "Queen Eunice fell in love with me."

I bent down at eye level with her. "When I was in the Forest Maze, there were little people hiding in the ferns."

"They are not gnomes. They are forest fatties." Needa tapped her toe, crossing her arms in front of her. "Gnomes are not as round or as rowdy."

"After I heal here, I will visit Evland," I decided out loud. I would find Felix's white brick cottage with its sweeping view of the valley.

"We will escape together." Needa squealed and jumped up and down.

Rhoda clicked her tongue against the roof of her mouth.

"I am not a prisoner of Yonder," I whispered. "I'm a visitor. I will help in exchange for room and board. When I am healed, I will *visit* Evland."

Needa slowly smiled. "You are a prisoner of Yonder; you just don't know it yet."

"I am paying my month's time. That was the agreement." I held my ground.

"Everyone in Yonder serves the king." Needa twirled the tail of one of her braids. "You will see."

There was much clatter as Rhoda took a large soup pot down from the band of hanging kettles. "Queen Eunice said you will take your meals with us."

"See." Needa smiled. "You are just like us—prisoners of Yonder."

"I will make you cabbage soup." Rhoda slid the turnips into a large iron pot. "My mother said cabbage cures all. We will see."

"Thank you," I said. "Rhoda, has Duron always been in charge of cooking the prisoners' food?"

"I make them a very nice meal each Christmas. They are always excited."

"Knot wanted me to ask if you'd make him peach pie."

"I will not make peach pie until Prince Wron's wedding."

Rhoda's peach pie must be very special. I was glad that I liked peach.

"But I will make Knot gooseberry." Rhoda smiled and began to hum.

ΦΦΦ

Rhoda, Needa, and I took our lunch in a dining alcove off the kitchen. The arched window above the table had a lovely view of the herb garden. Like a centerpiece, Needa sat at a gnome-sized toile-painted table in the middle of our table. While their plates were heaped with slivered partridge, mashed turnips and gravy, and petite peas, my lunch was a bowl of cabbage soup. The shimmering gravy on their plates made my mouth water. Everything is better with gravy. Life is better with gravy.

Rhoda bowed her head. "Good Lord above, thank you for the delicious meal that I made and for Dory, our new friend. Help my cabbage soup to heal her pox, and for Needa to stop talking about Evland. Yonder is home. Help her to be happy. Amen."

Needa frowned, picking up her fork. "When you're one hundred years old, we'll see if you're still happy here."

Rhoda shrugged and took her first bite of mashed turnips and gravy. "Oh my"—her large round eyes fluttered open and closed—"this is the best gravy that I have ever made." She carved her first bite of partridge.

Wait! Partridge was meat!

Wide-eyed, I stared as memories of the giant women with their long, stringy hair thundered out of the woods. "Waaaait! . . ." I exclaimed before the forkful entered the gallows of her mouth.

With her dark brows gathered, Rhoda stared at me.

"I thought you were a vegetarian."

"Lent is over." Rhoda's eyes rolled back in her head as she savored her first bite.

Had Knot lied? My roommate—a female giant—was a meat eater, and a meat lover. Oh, if it had only been Lent when we'd traveled through Shepherd's Field!

I peered down at the gray cabbage broth. It reminded me of the soup at Greda and Sadie's home, except there were no lentils or carrots floating in it. I swallowed and summoned the courage to take a sip from the pewter spoon. The broth needed salt, meat, potatoes, lentils, carrots . . . A strong bitter taste followed my first sip.

Behind us, someone cleared their throat in the doorway. Over my shoulder, I saw that it was Prince Wron. I hoped he needed me for something, so I might escape the cabbage soup.

"Sorry to interrupt, ladies." He smiled and bowed slightly, a sweet gesture on his part. "I saw Leeson in the village, Dory, and he requested your presence today in auctioning off one of your horses."

"I would love to." I rose and set my napkin on my chair.

"Eat your soup." Rhoda pointed a drumstick-sized finger to my bowl.

I remained standing and glanced at Wron.

"Dory, as you will soon learn, Rhoda is queen of the kitchen." His cheeks bunched, but he did not break a smile.

Rhoda pointed to my chair. "My cabbage broth will heal you. Sit down."

Though I tried to think pleasant thoughts, each spoonful of Rhoda's cabbage soup that traveled down my throat threatened to crawl its way back up.

"We must hurry, Dory," Wron said from the doorway.

I inhaled deeply and glanced at him. It's easy to hurry through sourdough bread slathered with honey, or mashed potatoes and gravy—I eyed the remaining portion on Rhoda's plate. But not this. I glanced down at the gray broth. Never had my body been so offended by food.

"Hurry, Dory." Wron's voice was firm.

I gulped a large spoonful. My throat gurgled. My body heaved like a human wave to the point that when I gripped the sides of the table, it shook. And then there was calm.

I peered at my swampy reflection in the bowl. I was almost done. I spooned the last bite. Onderyay! I was done.

"Every drop." Rhoda pointed her drumstick-sized finger in my bowl.

The apples of Wron's cheeks bunched. Was he suppressing a laugh or simply impatient?

I downed the remaining *drop*, rose from the table, and set my napkin on my chair.

"Collect your dishes. I am not your mother," Rhoda said.

"Thank you for the soup, Rhoda." I collected my dishes and set them near the sink.

"Why does she get to go to the auction?" Needa asked. "You have never taken me to the auction."

"You know I spoil you, Needa," Wron said. "We need to hurry; Leeson is waiting for us."

I followed him out of the kitchen and through the Great Hall.

"Where are you going with my pianist?" Eunice asked.

"I am accompanying Dory to auction, where she will sell one of her horses."

"Don't take too long. I . . ."

Her voice did not reach the hallway. Wron chuckled as I grabbed my cloak from my room. To keep pace with Wron's strides, I had to lift my long skirt and jog after him.

"I pray I heal tonight, because I cannot down another bowl of Rhoda's cabbage soup," I said, trying to stay up with him.

"No one looks forward to Rhoda's cabbage soup, but her heart is right." When we exited the gatehouse, a legion of guards followed us, both on horseback and on foot.

"Well, I won't eat it again. I cannot stomach it."

"You must. For Rhoda."

"I won't. Her soup is torture." Simply the thought of tasting the soup again triggered my gag reflex.

"In Yonder, it is not good etiquette for a woman to have the last word."

"Even if she is right?" I asked.

He halted in the middle of the cobblestone street to look at me.

I lowered my head. In the bright sunlight, I did not want him to see my pox.

"What is wrong?" he asked.

"Don't look at me. It is difficult enough for me to leave my room, much less be viewed in broad daylight."

"You were absolutely fine until you saw the mirror." A lock of dark hair fell forward into his eyes.

His words unraveled some of my memories of Felix. "Yes, but now I know what I *really* look like." It was difficult for me to admit it.

"Now that my mother and Rhoda are intent on your healing, you won't need to worry for long." He continued his hurried pace, and I had to work to keep up with him. At the end of the main village street, the auction was in sight.

Friday's auction had a larger turnout than Wednesday's. While I waited in line with Leeson and Plenty, I soon lost sight of Prince Wron. I did not see him among the uniformed soldiers on horseback who lined the periphery of the village square.

"The Swamp Woman is here," someone murmured in the crowd.

"The Swamp Woman's here."

A nearby woman patted her teenage daughter's shoulder. "Even though she is sick, she still has good posture." The mother glanced at me.

Her daughter pulled her shoulders back and lifted her chin.

"Will she ever play again at The Bell Tower, now that she is the Queen's?" Such murmurings rippled near me in the crowd.

Ahead of us, a dirty hog on a leash squealed. The hog brought in seventeen dixels. Next, a handsome pair of white doves brought in three dixels. Then it was my turn. Leeson stayed behind me in the crowd while I led Plenty to the center of the square. I flipped back my hood, but this time my hair was not greasy and thick with dust; it was clean and rippled down my back. The murmurings hushed.

"This is the last of my horses that are for sale," I spoke loudly. "Her name is Plenty, and she also has a fine leather saddle. Her late owner often said that she is 'a horse of plenty.'" To show the crowd Plenty's gentle and obedient nature, I took hold of the reins and led her about the circle. "She will still have *plenty* of energy left after a long, hard day. She will eat more than *plenty* of grain, as you can see from her stomach of plenty, and she will help you harvest your fields to abound with *plenty*. Who will give me fourteen for Plenty?"

A uniformed guard opened the bidding with ten dixels, and then it continued until it reached thirty. I searched individual faces in the crowd, and for a moment thought the bidding was complete.

"Tell us about Plenty's owner," a farmer said, as he gripped the bibs of his overalls.

I looked to the mediator, a tall man with a sharp nose and a dark beard. He nodded for me to continue.

"Tell us about Plenty's owner," someone else yelled.

The crowd's curiosity surprised me. I had to be careful. These were my future countrymen. If I called Felix my father, they would always remember. The audience waited with keen interest.

I cleared my throat. "Plenty's owner fell victim to the giants before Shepherd's Field, also known as the Giants' Snare."

Gasps rippled through the crowd.

"The giants were awakened from their winter slumber earlier than we'd expected. When I rode through the Giants' Snare, Plenty's owner served as a distraction." I raised my chin. "He was a stocky man, as robust as Duron, Yonder's gaoler. Plenty never complained of the weight she carried in life, as must neither you nor I." My gaze scanned the crowd. "Is thirty the final bid for Plenty?"

"Thirty-two," said one of the royal guards.

"Thank you." I nodded.

"Thirty-three," said the inquisitive farmer. The bidding continued until it was in the mid-forties, which I now understood was very high.

"Fifty," someone said from amidst the royal guards.

The crowd awed and then hushed.

"Thank you." Nodding, I looked around me at the citizens of Yonder. "Surely fifty is plenty for Plenty."

I walked across the square to hand the reins of Plenty to the highest bidder. Amidst the regiment, the man who slid off the horse was not a guard, but Prince Wron without his royal cloak. The crowd dispersed as his people bowed. I bowed as well, hiding my surprise.

Wron walked over to where I knelt and motioned for me to rise, and then for everyone else to rise as well. Taking my free hand in his, he raised it high into the air. "I am touched by the bravery of this woman that you have named the Swamp Woman."

Surprised by his words and actions, I shook my head.

"Now, Dory . . ." he murmured under his breath as, holding my hand high, he turned with me about the circle to face the crowd. "Be as brave tomorrow, should you need to eat another bowl of Rhoda's soup."

My future countrymen clapped.

Chapter Eighteen

I handed Leeson the fistful of dixels that I'd received for Plenty. He slid them into his coat pocket and, with a shake of his head, clutched the lump of coins tightly to him.

From a distance, I watched Wron speak with the farmer who had also bid on Plenty. Wron removed the horse's leather saddle, and then handed the farmer the reins. My heart swelled from the generosity of his offer.

With the saddle strewn over his shoulder, Wron strode toward us. I realized that a host of guards stood round about me—Yonder's royal pianist.

"Elza, my wife, would like you to visit for coffee," Leeson informed us.

Surely Wron wouldn't accept Elza's offer, not when his mother wanted me home to play piano.

Wron glanced at me and then up to the clock tower before nodding. "We can stay for a short time, Leeson. One cup."

With my arm hooked in Leeson's, we walked home. I couldn't help but admire my future husband for his kindness with the farmer, with Leeson, and with me.

ΦΦΦ

Wron, Cragdon, and I sat in Leeson and Elza's warm little home while twenty or more guards surrounded the smithy for our protection. We drank coffee from chipped earthenware mugs while Elza hummed and baked a batch of sourdough rolls over the fire.

"Their cook made me eat cabbage soup for lunch," I told Elza while she puttered about the room. "It is her mother's belief that cabbage cures everything."

"It is also her own belief." Wron wrapped his arm around the top knob of his chair and stretched his boots toward the fire.

Leeson sorted his pocketful of dixels in tidy rows on the table. "Prince Wron . . ." He cleared his throat. "Elza and I, we would, uh . . . we would like to . . . to buy Dory's freedom." The lean, elderly man rubbed at his eyes. "She is like our own child."

Their cupboards were almost bare, and they were willing to give away so much for my freedom. Bottled tears burned my throat.

"I'm sorry, Leeson, but Dory's penance cannot be bought." Wron tilted his head and looked softly at the dear man. "She is very important to Yonder, especially at this time."

Brows gathered, Leeson looked at me, and the corner of his mouth twitched.

"Thank you for trying." I reached to pat his trembling hand.

"May Dory visid once a week, for dinner, dhen?" Elza asked.

"Yes, once a week." Wron nodded.

"Can she sday donighd for supper?" Elza asked. "I will bake an onion."

Wron smiled and glanced to my eyes. "I do not want you walking home alone."

"I will walk her to the gate," Leeson said.

"And I will play for Queen Eunice this evening."

"Yes, let's hope that pacifies her." Wron rose from his seat. "Leeson and Elza, Dory's beautiful piano music has captured my mother's heart. Pray she is not too disappointed this afternoon."

His words were like honey to my soul. If happiness could heal swamp pox, my complexion would have been radiant.

"Leeson, if you could hear her play"—it was Cragdon who spoke—"you would understand why her music has won the people's hearts."

That was very kind of Cragdon. I thanked him with a smile.

Wron cleared his throat. "Thank you for coffee, Elza and Leeson." The men rose from the table and said their good-byes. After the door was bolted behind them, Leeson bolted the side door as well.

"Whad will we do widh dee money?" Elza's voice trembled.

"You will grow fat and sleepy in front of the fire." I beamed, hugging Elza's rounded shoulders. "You will have coffee, cream, and honey. You will want for nothing."

She sniffled into my shoulder. "We and our neighbors have wanded for so long."

"We will buy onions and coffee for our neighbors," Leeson said. He set his arms about our shoulders and kissed the top of Elza's head.

"Dhad is whad we will do, my husband."

I listened to the ways of Yonder. Elza had just had the last word, but it was in agreement with her husband. When in accord, perhaps it was acceptable in Yonder for a woman to have the last word.

ΦΦΦ

Elza's onions were baked whole over the fire in a seasoned broth. Right before serving, they were doused with more liquid. A large onion in a shallow broth with sourdough bread was our meal. Thankfully, I was also fond of onion and found it sweet and baked to the perfect crunch.

"Dell me id is good."

"It is very good." I patted the dear elderly woman's hand. In the reflection of Elza's spoon, I glimpsed her smile.

After dinner, we sat in front of the fire and drank coffee. Leeson fell asleep. I nearly fell asleep also, but remembered Eunice. "Elza, I must go. The Queen is waiting for me."

Elza patted her lap. "Kneel before me. I wand do see your face."

"Oh, Elza." I cringed. "I cannot bear to even glance in the mirror. I am so awful to look at."

"Come here." She patted her knees.

Remembering the creature in the mirror, I knelt down in front of her and searched Elza's slim brown eyes. Her chest rose slightly as she scanned my forehead, my cheeks, and lastly my chin.

"If id is all righd widh dee Queen, you will come on Mondays. We will have onion soup each dime. Id will make you beaudiful again. You wand do be well for Prince Wron, don'd you?"

"How did you know?" I breathed.

"Your words are sdrong." She kissed her fingertips and flung the kiss into the air. "Bud your body drembles."

"I don't know why," I sighed.

"He may be a prince, bud he is only a man."

I laid my cheek to Elza's knee and closed my eyes.

"In dee old coundry, my grandmodher said, 'Onion cures everything.' We will see."

ΦΦΦ

With my hood over my head, I walked through the cobbled streets of the village. At first I walked with my head down, and then I remembered the auction and the mother's comment to her daughter about my posture. Instead of slouching, I walked with the perfect posture that my mother had instilled in me.

Passersby nodded or greeted me with a surprised "Hello."

"Good day," I said.

"It is a lovely day," an elderly man said, looking to the sky.

Never in Blue Sky had I been allowed to walk the streets alone. I found the experience exhilarating. The people were kind and unexpectedly friendly.

I veered off the main road and jogged across the street to peer in the mercantile window at their shoes. The same two pairs sat on display. My future kingdom needed lessons in fashion.

In the reflection of the glass, a group gathered behind me.

I turned into a thick barricade of coats. Hands grabbed at me, covered my eyes, pulled at my clothes, reached down into my pockets. I tried to scream. I twisted and kicked in an effort to escape. Finally, my voice escaped in a mangled cry, and my attackers were gone.

I lay below the mercantile window, trampled and alone.

One of the shop assistants joined me and then two men who had witnessed the scene from across the street. "Are you all right?" they asked.

"Yes." I sat up and slowly moved my fingers and then my toes. "Nothing is broken."

"Did they steal your money?" one man asked. "From the auction?"

"No." I patted at my clothes. All my pockets were pulled inside out.

I did not make eye contact with anyone until I reached the gatehouse. There, I acknowledged one of the guards by name. "Hello, Plano. It is I, the Swamp Woman, returning to piano duty." My voice sounded forced, shaky, but I managed a smile.

Once I was allowed inside the gates, I felt reassured by the ten-foot-thick walls of the fortress. Fifty paces ahead, Prince Wron strode toward me. I would not tell him what had happened. He'd been right; I'd needed an escort. I felt my pockets to make sure they'd been pushed back in.

He stopped abruptly in front of me. "You told me Leeson would accompany you!"

"He was asleep."

"You are not to walk alone. Yonder is a good place, but it is not perfect."

I wondered if my hair or my pockets showed his country's imperfection.

"I will never walk home alone again, My Lord." Perhaps it was my meekness, for he rolled a kink out of his neck and did not lecture me further.

ΦΦΦ

In the doorway to the Great Hall, Rhoda was seated on the leather couch. Eunice stood over her swinging a pendulum-like instrument back and forth. I paused in the wide-arched doorway, entranced.

"Now repeat it again, Rhoda, what do you say?"

The giant woman's teacup-sized eyes watched the pendulum, back and forth. Back and forth. "I will ignore my cravings. I will not give in to temptation. I will not think about—"

I retreated to the corridor and, leaning back against the stone wall, stilled myself to breathe. They were hypnotizing the giant to behave. My roommate did indeed crave human flesh. She was a people eater!

I waited a few minutes, and then, steeling myself, strode into the Great Hall.

Rhoda was nowhere to be seen. Eunice had returned to her knitting. She pointed the tips of her long needles toward The Beast. "According to Wron, you've had a busy day. Tomorrow we'll do our herbs while the men are away."

"Thank you, Queen Eunice," I said as I sat down upon the bench.

"Wron said that since he will not sell you, he arranged with Leeson for you to visit once a week. I'm so glad you're not for sale."

The setting sun shone directly in my eyes. I bowed my head. "One cannot sell what one does not own."

"You are so full of wit, Dory." Eunice laughed. "Today, when you were not here, I realized that our home is quite dreary without your music. Please play."

I sat down upon the bench. Tonight when I hoped to sleep, I did not want to dwell on the mobbing or Rhoda. Determined to get them both out of my system, I drove my hands deep into the keys, six and eight notes at a time. I purged myself of the mobbing, the chaos, the shock and my distress, and lastly, the proof that my roommate indeed had a serious problem of the flesh.

"Dory, your playing is so akin to my day," Eunice said with awe. "It has been a very disturbing one, and you have brought closure to it."

"What's happened?" I turned from the piano to regard her.

Pale cheeked, she peered up from her handiwork. "Each year, I try to knit the same color blanket for the new babies in the kingdom. Last year's new mothers received a lovely pastel green, and this year's color is lavender. I've just been informed that the shopkeeper can no longer purchase this lovely lavender." She lifted the skein off her lap. "Of course, I bought all he had. But it may not be enough. Last year, thirty-nine babies were born in Yonder."

"I'm certain the mothers treasure your gift and thoughtfulness, Your Highness."

"Thank you, Dory." She smiled. "How was your day?"

"Eventful." I was thankful for the catharsis of The Beast.

"I know. Wron said that the craftsmanship of the saddle he bought at auction is unmatched, and that it is indeed the Blue Sky insignia." She paused from her knitting to regard me. "And that you told him Alia is musically inclined. What does she play?"

Oh, the webs we weave.

"Alia plays piano, Queen Eunice."

Her needles dropped to her lap. "Are you a counterfeit?" Her voice was barely above a whisper.

"No, I am not."

Waving a hand, she'd surely dropped a stitch. "No, of course you aren't, child. Your father died in Shepherd's Field." She bit her lower lip, considering me. "I'm sorry, Dory." Her chest inflated at her tactlessness. "Please end on something lovely." She flitted a hand toward The Beast.

I agreed with her; now that I had the trampling out of my system, I wanted to reflect on something lovely, and I knew just the one: the auction when Wron had raised my hand to the crowd. From there, my memory traveled to coffee at Leeson and Elza's. His kindness to the elderly couple and to me—the Swamp Woman—was a quality beyond what I'd dared to imagine in my future husband. As I often did when I played something new, I began one note at a time. It sounded rather sweet, almost poetic. Then I added a handful of chords, and the melody moved gently along.

Wron's kind ways made me want to get well. I finished with a sweet refrain.

Eunice left her knitting to stand beside me. "You must tell me the name of this piece, so I may request it again." She set a soft, smooth hand upon my shoulder.

"The piece is new. You may name it."

"Ohh . . ." She sounded pleased. "We will call it 'Lavender,' because it's lovely and there's not enough of it."

Chapter Nineteen

That night, I was still awake when Rhoda's knees crunched to the cold, hard floor. She bowed her head to pray. "Thank you for the wonderful dinner; it was the best. Thank you for Needa. Help her to not complain. Thank you for Dory. Help her to heal. Though she is already beautiful, help her to be beautiful on the outside, too." She mumbled a few indecipherable prayers, but I was touched by what I'd heard.

Dear Rhoda. Even though she might someday eat me as dinner, my roommate had a kind heart. She worked from sunrise until moonlight, and never complained. "If I were ever queen, Rhoda," I said, "I would get you more help in the kitchen, so you could have at least one day off each week."

"Queen Eunice would not be happy to hear you talk like that, Dory. So do not talk like that."

Surprised by the force of emotion in her voice, I paused to weigh my words. "I was just trying to say that you are so good to all of us that you deserve a day off."

"Do not talk that way, ever again." Rhoda inhaled deeply and sighed. If there had been a lit candle in the room, it would have been extinguished in the gush of air.

"Why, Rhoda?" I did not understand her vehemence.

"I do not want you to be abandoned in the hills."

"That *is* an awful thought," I whispered. Would Father ever come?

Rhoda turned to her side facing me, and tucked her hands beneath her round cheek. "Dory, are you still itchy?"

"This morning I was not as itchy, so I felt brave enough to look in the mirror. Oh, Rhoda, it was such a disappointment."

"Tomorrow, I will be your mirror." She yawned.

"Rhoda . . ." I told myself to be brave. "I have a question to ask about giants."

In the moonlight, she nodded.

"If a man were to get off his horse in the middle of the Giants' Snare when the giants were *not* in hibernation . . ." Adrenaline pulsed through my limbs. "Is there any chance, any way that he could possibly survive?"

A pensive silence followed. "Was your father a very, very fast runner?"

"Not that I'm aware of."

"That is too bad." She yawned.

As I feared, Rhoda fell asleep first, and on her back. Using the same lifting stance as Wron, I leaned over and tried to leverage her to her side. Though I tried, I could not budge her. I wrapped a blanket around me and passed Wron in the hallway on his way to my room, a hand cupped around a tallow candle.

We paused to acknowledge each other.

"Why did you wait so long?" he asked. "I can't sleep through Rhoda's snoring either."

"In the future, you have my permission to knock on *our* door."

"Thank you, Queen Dory."

Someday he would remember tonight and smile.

He set the candle on the nightstand and bent to one knee near Rhoda's side. "Tell me more about Alia. How spoiled is she?"

I waited for a snore to pass. "Um, well . . ." I sat down near the foot of my bed, the blanket wrapped about me. He was going to make me think. "At her sixteenth birthday party, there were sixteen different cakes." I paused. "At her fifteenth, there were fifteen."

"It is unheard of. She must be fat."

"No, the cakes were for the guests, not just for her." I laughed.

"And her personality?" With his back to me, he took his time in turning Rhoda. "What do you dislike about her?"

I thought about how vain I used to be. How I could not pass a mirror without admiring myself. I now dreaded my reflection.

"She's never known hunger or any true discomfort." At least it used to be true.

"She does sound spoiled."

"She is." It was easy to be honest in third person.

"Yet you feel there is hope for her?" Using his legs, he rolled Rhoda onto her side. "I hear it in your tone."

"I suppose I do."

"Did she confide in you?" He slowly moved to retrieve the candle.

"Yes."

"Tell me this, then . . . has she ever been kissed?"

I deliberately waited for a snore to begin and pass. "Not of her own free will. At a ball, there was a horrid man, Dell—King Lorenzo's son." I paused, timing myself with Rhoda. "He told her that he had just seen the first open rose of summer out in the courtyard. And, because it was her birthday, she deemed it a very good sign and followed him outside to see it," I said quickly.

"What happened?"

I glanced at Rhoda to make sure she was indeed sleeping, and not pretending, as my sister Wren would have done at a time like this.

"There was no open rose. Dell grabbed Alia and . . ." I found myself feeling nauseous at the memory. "Her first kiss was not by choice."

"Then she cannot consider it a first kiss."

"Thank God!" I smiled.

"To be considered a first kiss, it should have been a mutual decision." He briefly chuckled. "Good night, Dory."

"Good night, Prince . . ." I sighed.

ΦΦΦ

Rhoda nudged me awake. The early morning sky was twilight blue. "Do not look in the mirror today, Dory." Stretching, she lumbered about the room.

It was not what my heart wanted to hear.

While Rhoda cooked breakfast, I made toast and set the table. Holding three platters, I served Eunice, then Walter, and lastly, I slid the white, oval-shaped plate with sliced ham and poached eggs in front of Wron.

"Several spots are gone." Wron pointed to his cheek.

"Oh, did you hear that, Rhoda?" Queen Eunice said loudly toward the kitchen. "Several of Dory's spots are gone."

I hurried to the gilded mirror above the dark walnut buffet and turned my face from side to side. On my right cheek lay a clear patch of skin, the size of a dixel. It was the cheek I'd been lying on in our dimly lit room. Rhoda had not clearly seen my complexion. I recalled every specific meal of the prior day . . . porridge, Elza's baked onion, Rhoda's—

"Is my cabbage soup!" Rhoda joined me at the mirror.

"Heat up some more for her, Rhoda," Eunice said.

The disappearance of one spot gave me hope. I sat down in front of The Beast and played "Sunrise," an old, familiar tune. The beautiful melody reminded me of the sun rising on a new day. I put my heart and fingers into the chords and added some of my own imagination as to what "hope" should sound like. I simply lost myself.

After the piece ended, I sat for a moment, embarrassed by my departure. Setting my hands in my lap, I glanced over my shoulder. Above the table, Walter held Eunice's hand.

"Breakfast, Dory," Rhoda bellowed from the kitchen.

Reality turned my stomach. I rose from the bench to face my awful fate.

"You look as if you are trudging off to war." Wron laughed. "Did you see her, Mother?"

"Eating Rhoda's soup is not intended to be the spectator sport that you like to make it, and poor Dory is already so self-conscious."

Despite his mother's admonition, Wron sat across from me at the breakfast table. My future husband enjoyed a good laugh.

"I look forward to when you are sick, and we get to watch you eat a bowlful," I said.

"You look forward to when I am sick?" Grinning, he shook his head. "Those are not kind sentiments." Elbows on the table, he watched me force each spoonful down. Several times, when I gripped the table to swallow, he threw his head back and laughed. Needa laughed with him, clutching onto his ear as she sat on his shoulder. Even Rhoda would stop her chopping to stand beside the table and watch me.

"I haven't laughed this hard in months." Wron patted the table.

"You are cruel," I said.

He smiled, and I could tell that he liked that I held my ground with him.

I scooped up every last drop of the torturous soup and set my dish near the sink. "There is something I need to speak with your father about. It's very pressing."

Wron's brows lifted. "He is in the Great Hall."

ΦΦΦ

Wron followed me into the Great Hall, where I found his father seated in one of the goatskin chairs by the fire. I bowed low before the king. "Your Highness . . . I petition thee."

"Stand up, girl." He closed the book he'd been reading and laid it on the side table. "What is it?"

I rose to my feet, clutching my hands in front of me. "On behalf of the men in prison, I would—"

"Do you mean *prisoners*?" Walter's white brows gathered.

"Yes, it is regarding the prisoners' meals." I pressed forward. "They are forced to work beyond what they are receiving in nourishment. They are weak and susceptible to sickness. During the week that I was in prison, we ate dribbly porridge and stale bread. The men are being starved."

With his head slightly tilted, Walter stared at me.

"Someday, Your Highness, they will be Yonder citizens again, and when they are released they will be full of contempt for you—Food is a great mediator."

"Are you full of contempt for me, Dory?" Walter eyed me curiously.

"No." I shook my head. "Though there was great deprivation, I found the experience beneficial to my soul."

"Father, may I interrupt?" Wron stood near the table.

Walter held a hand up toward Wron and then, lowering his chin, addressed me. "What do you propose I do?"

I took my time, weighing my answer. "If the men could have a noon meal that contained protein and fruits or vegetables with color—a decent meal, King Walter, it would boost prison morale."

"Is that not an oxymoron?" he asked.

"They are still your countrymen, past, present, and future," I said.

Walter smiled. "While I appreciate your passion for what is right, I also need to inform you that Wron has already brought the dire situation to my attention."

"After my visit"—Wron edged closer—"and seeing Knot's condition, the men are now receiving two hot meals a day."

Not fully grasping the enormity of what he'd said, I stared at him.

"I did not recognize Knot, and for most of my childhood, he'd been like a father to me. Unfortunately, we put too much trust in one man."

"Duron is now serving time in prison," Walter said. "For a week, he is only receiving dribbly porridge and stale bread."

Retribution.

"I cannot tell you how relieved I am." Hearing that Knot and the rest of the men were receiving proper nourishment was salve to my soul.

"After dinner this evening," Walter voiced, "I want you and Rhoda to personally deliver our men a protein-packed meal. Wron"—he looked up at his son—"inform the woman who is presently in charge that she has the evening off." Walter turned to address me. "Any future ideas either of you have, I would like you to first speak with me. I do not want them to become spoiled, but reformed."

"Thank you, Your Highness." I rose to my feet and returned to the kitchen to tell Rhoda.

ΦΦΦ

That evening, Rhoda and I dished out five meals; each included sliced mutton, steamed baby carrots, a buttermilk biscuit, a square of crumb cake, and a glass of goat's milk. Rhoda assisted me by carrying down one of the large trays.

I passed Knot's meal through the narrow rectangular opening in the bars.

"It's not Christmas for five months," he murmured. Taking the plate, he proceeded to the corner of his cell.

"King Ulrich has passed a new addendum. Each day there will be a protein-rich meal."

"God bless you, Dory and Rhoda." A pale light gleamed in Knot's eyes.

"And Prince Wron and King Walter," I added.

He nodded, stuffing a slice of mutton into his mouth.

And so it was with each meal that we passed between the bars: the prisoners said, "God bless you."

When Rhoda and I ascended the stairs, I did not worry about why the men in prison were there or what their crime was. I cared only that my fellowmen were fed, for I knew that hunger brought about discouragement and discouragement a defeated mind.

ΦΦΦ

I felt melancholy as I sat at the Great Beast that evening. Eunice joined me on the bench, as she did from time to time. She requested "The Ballad of Blue Sky," and after I played my country's national anthem, Eunice touched my arm.

"You have made the waiting easier. Each day feels like a year for Wron right now." She glanced over her shoulder at the men seated near the fire. "As soon as my husband saw baby Alia, he wanted her for Wron. He said she was the most beautiful little thing. Not to mention the deal that he and King Wells made," she whispered, shaking her head. "It was a big deal."

Rhoda brought Needa to sit in the Queen's lap. In between songs, Needa jumped from Eunice's lap to mine and ran sure-footedly up my arm, clutching onto the material of my cambric shirt along the way. She plopped down on my shoulder and, without a word, set her hand behind my neck to steady herself.

"The thought never occurred to me before that we could have a live-in pianist," Eunice said. "We should have done it years ago. Imagine waiting only for parties to have music."

I recalled the metal-on-metal sound as the cell door swung closed behind me. Duron had simply turned the key in the lock and walked away. If for some reason I didn't marry Wron, I might easily become a slave of the household, as Needa, for life.

"Do you know the 'Troll's Tune'?" Needa whispered in my ear.

"No, can you sing it?"

"Yes." She cleared her teeny throat. "Hidden in the bracken, hidden underfoot, a gnome is known to whistle as he goes about the woods." Needa's wee voice cracked. "A troll's foot is set before thee, wider than a tree, in one step you've lost your freedom, now another's dainty." The light tune had quickly turned dark. "Can you play that?"

"I will try."

I started with one finger before adding chords. The little tune became lovely under my fingertips. Needa sat very still on my shoulder before she sniffled, brushing tears onto my neck.

"I used to have a music box that played that tune. I listened to it every day before I was taken away from my"— Needa looked at Eunice—"beloved Evland."

Chapter Twenty

For lunch the following day, another bowl of cabbage soup waited for me on the table in the alcove. Wron did not join us this time. I was relieved. Healing was not always a delicious process.

"Tomorrow your spots will be half-gone, because you will have had twice as much soup," Rhoda said.

"I fear that I will die of hunger. Pretend to look out the window long enough that I might steal some mutton off your plate."

"Cabbage and water alone will cleanse you." Rhoda stuffed the last morsel of mutton into her mouth.

"Cabbage and water alone will make me want to steal my gun from Prince Wron's cabinet to shoot chukar in the field."

"I love chukar." Rhoda sighed and set her large elbows on the table. "My brother used to hunt in the fields when I was a child. Chukar is fit for a king."

"Sometime when Prince Wron is gone, I will shoot chukar for our dinner." I beamed. "I need to find his gun cabinet first."

"When you get your gun, get me. We will escape to Evland together," Needa said, swinging her feet back and forth beneath her gnome-sized table.

Rhoda waved a finger at me. "You will soon feel like family here. But you must obey."

"Sometime when Prince Wron is seated, I will slide the keys to his gun cabinet out of his pocket." Needa kept her voice low. "When you are ready to escape to Evland with me, I will do my part."

"Remember prison, Dory." Rhoda's enormous eyes pleaded. "Next time, you will stay longer."

Wide-eyed, I watched the verbal tennis match between the two.

"Aren't I the cleverest centerpiece, ladies?" Needa lifted her mini pink teapot and glanced toward the doorway.

"What is this talk of Evland?" Beneath her morning powder, Eunice's face was a deep pink.

Needa poured herself a cup of mint tea and daintily bent her pinkie finger as she lifted the cup from its saucer. "Prince Wron has given me many treasures that I will not be able to replace." Needa laid her hand to one side of her nose. "When we escape to Evland, Dory, you must give me time to pack."

Was she trying to get me in trouble?

"Neither of you must talk of escaping or Evland ever again," Eunice said.

"I have my own little place; all that's missing is a husband." Needa slid off her chair and crossed the wooden table to stand in front of my glass of pear juice. "I want to show you my house." The gnome tilted her head slightly. The apples of her cheeks bunched as she suppressed a smile.

"You have never shown me your house," Rhoda said.

"You are too big. With a little budging, Dory will be able to squeeze inside."

"I am not hurt. I would be claustrophobic."

In the kitchen, there was a small blue door that Needa often went in and out of. "Don't eat another thing." Needa set a finger in front of her lips. "We'll go now before Queen Eunice requests music."

"I am right here, Needa. I can hear everything you say." Eunice rolled her eyes.

I picked Needa up, carried her into the kitchen, and set her down in front of the knee-high door. For a better view, I crouched down on my hands and knees.

"You're really going to do it?" Eunice said, behind me.

"I would get stuck," Rhoda said.

Needa stood inside waving at me. With a twist of my shoulders, I was able to pop inside. The problem was my hips. I had a small waist, but ample hips. I floundered like a fish on the floor before I flopped my way through the doorway.

Once I was inside, Needa closed the door. "You are my first visitor. See all of my beautiful things." She hurried to a miniature kitchen hutch and lifted down a blue-and-white platter. "Bone china." She held an exquisite platter in front of my eyes.

"Very beautiful," I said. On my side, my hip was flush with the ceiling. The room was too crowded for me to turn around in. I thought of Rhoda's word, *claustrophobic*.

"Prince Wron found this for me on one of his travels." Needa held up a gnome-sized copper teakettle. "It is just like one my grandmother had. And have you ever seen such a beautiful settee?" She pointed to a Needa-sized red velvet sofa.

"You do have Prince Wron's affection." Was there enough oxygen in the room for me?

"Yes, but I need a man my own size." Needa twisted the tail of her blonde braid. "When we escape to Evland, I will find a man and bring him back here. Or are you coming back?"

To hush her, I held my forefinger in front of my lips. "We are not to talk about Evland."

"At least not very loud." She pointed up. "When he designed this room, Prince Wron put in a fresh air vent. If the ladies are still near this end of the kitchen, they may hear our voices."

I looked up through the vent and could only see the kitchen's stone ceiling.

"We are not to talk about Evland, but we can whisper." Needa set her forefinger in front of her lips. "We will soon be needed with Prince Wron's wedding—you at the piano and me at the wedding cake table. I am always in charge of the mints. We should leave today or tomorrow."

"It feels too quiet," I whispered.

"Tonight, before you play piano, set me in Prince Wron's lap. I will slide the keys from his pocket. Hide your gun in your room, and I'll return his keys before he realizes they are missing."

I shook my head. Someone in the kitchen coughed. "Your home is lovely, Needa," I said in my normal tone. "I need to return to the kitchen now. Can you open the door for me? I'm afraid I must leave feetfirst."

"Next time you will stay for tea." Needa started for the door.

Making sure my skirt stayed in a ladylike manner, I slowly wiggled my feet out first. For a moment, I thought I was stuck before I was able to maneuver my hips out the small door. After this major accomplishment, someone took a firm hold of my feet and pulled me out the rest of the way. Thank heaven, it was only Rhoda.

The Queen was still in the kitchen, her face beet red. "I heard everything you talked about. Neither of you are going to Evland!"

Needa stood in the doorway of her very small house. Bunching her mouth, she stuck out her tongue at Eunice before pulling the door closed behind her.

Eunice sighed. "What do I do, Rhoda? She is behaving like an insolent little brat."

Rhoda pulled down a large pot from the overhead supply and loudly set it on the stove. Next, she took a large butcher knife and a head of cabbage and began chopping. "I am making cabbage stew. Both Needa and Dory need to eat my soup for dinner."

"Needa's lonely," I said. "And she longs for a husband. She worries that soon she will be too old to have children." I sighed deeply for emphasis.

"Dory, if you don't stop looking from other people's perspectives so much, you'll easily become one of those grossly unremarkable do-gooders," Eunice said.

Rhoda stopped chopping, and her massive shoulders sagged. "Dory is right. For eleven years, all Needa has talked about is finding a man her own size."

Despite her cabbage soup, I loved Rhoda. Would Eunice never listen?

ΦΦΦ

After a lovely gooseberry triffle that evening, a loud marching noise echoed down the corridor toward the Great Hall, where royalty were gathered.

"Dory, stay at the piano." Eunice rose from the bench.

Roger, accompanied by three other guards, entered the room. "A caravan has arrived," Roger announced. "A large crowd has gathered near the gates for the princess of Blue Sky."

"Escort only the princess and her royal family. Have at least ten guards in attendance," Prince Wron said from where he was seated by the fire. "And have our men surround her remaining entourage."

Wron, accompanied by his mother and father, strolled out onto the terrace. I followed and paused near Eunice's side. In the distance, near the gatehouse, half a dozen men in gray uniforms lowered a carriage to the ground.

"What do you think?" Wron glanced over at me.

"The Blue Sky uniforms are a dark blue for battle and royal blue with white for home. I do not know the color they'll wear. But to have carried her for such a long journey is . . . very ambitious." I suppressed a smile.

"Why?" Eunice lifted up her eyeglasses.

"Swamp Valley, for one, unless, that is, they took the other route."

"What do you think, Wron?" his mother asked.

"You know what I think, Mother." He chuckled under his breath.

"He likes to interview them, to see how devious they are." Eunice turned and with very large eyes peered through the eyeglasses at my pox. "Play 'Blue Sky' when they enter, Dory. See if they recognize it."

"Everyone, take your places." Wron headed back inside to take his seat by the fire. "When you are done playing, Dory, you may turn around. You will ask pertinent questions. At some point this evening, you will tell us whether or not she is Princess Alia."

"I will know upon seeing her."

"Yes, but if it is not Alia, it will be interesting to see how devious they are." Wron glanced at his mother.

"As you know, Wron, I can also identify the princess," Walter said.

"Such close examination may not be needed, Father."

They were referring to the birthmark tucked well beneath my chin. Due to my pox, I could not presently reveal the mark, even if my life depended on it.

I played "The Ballad of Blue Sky," my country's national anthem, while the counterfeits arrived. Though I longed to turn around, observe, and eavesdrop on their conversation, I focused on the last refrain.

At last I rose and bowed slightly to my audience before lifting my eyes.

A middle-aged couple were seated on the couch. They appeared quite dignified in appearance and wore the finest of clothes. An exquisite young woman sat in the chair near the fire. Her red hair, styled in a high bun, reminded me very much of my mother's before she'd turned gray. Something about her was very familiar.

Seated across from the counterfeit princess in a wingback goatskin chair, Wron appeared remarkably calm.

"Dhad piece was beaudiful, vhad is ids name?" The middle-aged woman flicked open a fan.

I tried not to stare, but her odd accent was strangely familiar as well.

"Dory, this is Princess Alia, and her great-aunt and uncle." Eunice waved a hand toward those in attendance.

I bowed politely. "Where is King Wells?"

"Queen Vells is quide ill. He is by her side," said the uncle. His features were lean, and his pointed beard looked like it had been dipped in dark ink.

"Oh, the poor dear." Eunice sighed. "Irene, like me, never did like to travel."

"Vhad happened do your face, child?" the counterfeit aunt addressed me.

"She has swamp pox," Eunice said, before I could.

"Did you just arrive today?" I looked from the well-polished matron and her husband to the lovely young maiden, who wore a light blue silk dress very much like one I had back home. My gaze lifted to her face, and with an intake of air, I remembered quite clearly where I knew her from.

Merner.

She'd sat at the table with the youth—with Fallon—when I'd mashed potatoes and basted chicken in Liisa's home.

"Yes, we jusd arrived doday," the aunt said.

I almost needed to sit down. Still in prison, Fallon hadn't been able to warn them of my change in accent. They were basing their Blue Sky accents off mine from Merner. Heat flushed my face. I was ready to send them all to prison, but for Wron's sake, I would ask questions first.

I drew closer to the fire and, hands clasped in front of me, addressed the counterfeit princess. "What leg of the journey did you find most fascinating?"

"Shepherd's Field," she replied.

"Tell us your experiences." Biting my lower lip, I tried to steady my emotion.

"Ve vere . . . in dee carriage, of course, and oudside dee world vas more magical than I'd ever seen . . . id," she said with a theatrical air.

"Please, in more detail." I gazed at the fire, smiling at her slip. *V*s and *W*s were the hardest.

"Dee field vas golden." She glanced at her aunt. "Golden like id had been kissed by dee sun and dee sky vas a wiolet blue and—"

"A hypnodic dream qualidy came over all of us," the aunt interrupted. "Bud ve'd been varned do nod ged oud of dee carriage."

"How many are in your entourage?"

"Dvendy in all," the aunt said.

"And there were no casualties?" I asked.

"No." The uncle appeared bored. "I ordered dhem all to sday on the padh and do look sdraighd ahead."

Wron flicked a hand for me to continue.

"Tell me about Swamp Valley," I again addressed the princess.

"Is dhad vhere ve sav dee alligador?" She looked at her aunt.

"Such imagina-shun, Alia." The uncle chuckled, shifting in his chair. "Ve draveled dhrough many moisdure-rich valleys, bud none bore such a name."

"If you traveled the route of Shepherd's Field, you'd remember Swamp Valley," I said. "There is a strange plant in the water that bites the horses."

Narrowing his eyes, the uncle glared at me.

Had anyone else seen his menancing look? I sat down on the nearest ottoman and averted my attention to Wron.

"Dee valleys vere nod marked vidh signage," the aunt said. "Our animals vere ofden candankerous. Dhere are many legs of dee journey dhad vere enjoyable, and a few dhad vere not. But ve are nod here do dalk aboud our dravels. Ve are here do celebrade dee upcoming marriage of our niece Princess Alia do Prince Vron."

Eunice smiled and nodded my direction.

It was purely entertainment for them.

"Growing up in Blue Sky and being raised in the castle . . ." I watched the aunt's eyes widen at my remarks, and her features froze. "I was in attendance at Princess Alia's sixteenth birthday party." My gaze moved to the counterfeit princess. "At the time, her hair was auburn, similar to my own. Her complexion is fair, though her eyes are hazel like yours. Tell me, Princess Alia, about your fabulous party?"

"Are you insinuading dhad ve are lying?" The aunt's neck rose out of her gown.

"You jump do conclusions, my dear." Her husband set his hand upon her knee. "Dhis creadure is merely insinuading dee obvious: Alia dyed her hair for dhis occasion, and dee color is capdivading."

"I do nod remember ever seeing you before." The aunt's face reddened as her voice rose. "And do insinuade dhad you addended my niece's birdhday pardy!"

Walter yawned. "Dory, is she or is she not Princess Alia?"

"No, Your Highness." I peered down at my hands.

"Arrest them!" Walter's voice resonated through the Great Hall. "And arrest the other gypsies that were with them."

"She's the chicken farmer's daughter!" The counterfeit pointed at me. "From Boxden."

"Shud up," snapped the uncle, as guards appeared in every plausible exit.

I took pity on the counterfeit princess. I'd had a hard time with the accent too.

"Gypsies . . ." I whispered, shaking my head. Felix had been right.

Only Eunice remained seated. "We've foreseen them spinning such a web. We're so glad you're here, Dory. You're improving, dear. Whatever did you have for dinner?"

I crossed the room to examine myself in the gilded mirror above the buffet. The pox were still there, but much of the swelling had receded. My cheekbones were now visible. Yet it was my eye area that pleased me most. My lids were no longer puffy.

Had it been Rhoda's soup, teamed with prayer?

Prince Wron returned to the Great Hall and stood with his back to the fire.

"What will happen to the gypsies now?" I asked.

"They will spend one night in prison. In the morning, they will be escorted to the southern hills. They will be left without horses or food to make their way home. It will take them at least a week, if they survive."

"Did you see the uncle try to silence me with an evil look?"

"He is a fool to think it is only you who spoiled their plans." Wron looked to his mother. "Did you not think last week's counterfeits the most convincing?"

"Yes, I worry." Eunice sighed. "What was the harm in looking for the mark?"

Wron glanced to where I stood behind Walter's vacant chair. "We don't even want the mark to be mentioned, Mother."

"Yes, I suppose you're right. The real Alia will remember to tell us about it." Eunice glanced uneasily at me.

"The counterfeit was lovely." I did my best to change the subject.

"My country cannot afford for me to find counterfeit princesses lovely." Wron tossed a small chunk of wood into the fire.

Eunice pulled at her skein of yarn. "This marriage has been sixteen years in the making; it's not like we didn't give our enemies time to plan."

Needing to be alone with my fears, I strolled out onto the terrace and stared toward the end of the wooden bridge as it stretched across the river's ravine. Had Father given our enemies *too much* time?

Father in heaven, please watch out for my father and my fellow countrymen who accompany him. Keep them safe. Amen.

ΦΦΦ

Sleep evaded me for a long stretch, and then I sank deep into it. The counterfeit uncle stood near The Beast while I played. With a piercing look, he tried to silence me. I awakened to the sound of chains being dragged across slate. I sat straight up, staring into the darkness. The dragging-chains sounds continued.

I sighed. It was only Rhoda's snoring.

Someone rapped softly upon our chamber door. *The uncle!* I scooted back against the headboard. "Who is it?" My voice cracked. The door creaked open, and I prepped myself to scream, hoping it would be loud enough to wake Rhoda.

"It's me." The voice sounded almost like Wron's. I pulled the covers snug under my armpits and held my breath.

Candlestick in hand, Wron stopped near the foot of my bed. "Dory, I believe you were having a nightmare."

"I was. Did you see him give me an evil look?" I mumbled.

"Who?"

"The uncle," I breathed.

"Yes, I did. But he's a fool to think that only you saw through them."

I nodded. "I thought Rhoda's snoring sounded like chains being dragged across slate, and then I awoke." Wide-eyed, I stared at him.

"You were indeed having a nightmare." He crouched near Rhoda's bed and, using good lifting form, turned the giant to her side. "Do not worry about the uncle, Dory." He returned to the foot of my bed. "Tomorrow they will be escorted to the hills, and you will never see him again."

His words soothed my tattered soul.

"Now, go back to sleep."

I sank down and pulled the covers beneath my chin.

"Good night, Dory."

"Good night, Prince—" The door closed firmly behind him.

I crossed my arms behind my head and found myself smiling. "Good night, Prince."

Chapter Twenty-One

Rhoda nudged me awake. "Do not look in the mirror today, Dory." Stretching, she lumbered about the room.

I laid in my soft comfy bed, and let Rhoda's greeting stew in my heart. I said a two word prayer: *Please Lord.*

I remained in bed determined to hear from him. I closed my eyes, waiting.

Dor-ee . . . A child's voice called me back to the memory of Sadie as our wagon pulled away from their home. "Once . . ." the child had said. Then she'd pasted on a smile.

Warm tears began my day.

I pasted on a smile and went about my morning routine as I set the butter, maple syrup, and sliced fresh peaches on the dining table. Wron and his parents were already seated. "It'll be just a moment; Rhoda's baking her special pancakes," I informed them.

"They are now called Queen Cakes," Eunice said, fluttering her fingers. "I've renamed them, as they are my favorites."

"They are Giant Oven Baked Pancakes," Rhoda bellowed from the kitchen.

"That is much too long of a name, Rhoda." Eunice frowned.

"Giant Cakes," Rhoda said, carrying two plates into the dining area. "Be careful, they are hot."

I strode to the kitchen for the third cake. Gripping it by the hot pad, I returned and slid the billowy, giant oven cake in front of Wron.

"It's official, Mother, they've been renamed to Giant Cakes." He glanced up at me. "Thank you, Dory."

"Play, Dory." Eunice flitted a hand.

I sat down at the piano. At first only Wron's visit to my room last night came to mind. For a moment, the melody was beautiful beneath my fingers. Then the counterfeit uncle's evil look crept into my memory and demanded escape.

"Dory, are you well?" Eunice asked.

"Yes, Your Highness." I continued playing.

"Your playing is quite moody this morning."

Eunice was not an easy woman to explain things to. "You know how you occasionally drop stitches, and have to unravel to make things right?" I glanced over my shoulder at her.

"Yes." She nodded.

"I'm unraveling."

"You'll have plenty of time to unravel at The Bell Tower today." Eunice sighed.

"After I work for Peg today," I said, over my shoulder, "may I go to Leeson and Elza's for dinner?"

"Yes," Wron said.

"And spend the night?" I persisted.

"Yes," Wron said.

"Wron!" Eunice gasped. "Why in the world . . . why?"

"You must be home tomorrow morning in time to serve breakfast," Wron said.

I cast a "Thank you" over my shoulder.

"A whole day without music?" Eunice's teacup clattered to her saucer.

"You'll survive," Walter said, thrashing the newspaper closed.

ΦΦΦ

The Bell Tower was not the refuge I was looking for. In the breadth of half an hour, I'd gone from the royal pianist who *must* play for the Queen to the Swamp Woman at Peg's—the creature to whom customers spewed obscenities when they'd drunk too much hope. To offset the humiliation, I remembered someone's kind sentiments: I was also *the pianist enjoyed by the commoners who would sit outside of Peg's to hear me play.*

These were the people I would play for today. My people.

We ended the evening at The Bell Tower with the reenactment of Long and Molly's reunion. At the end, when we all stood onstage, bowing to the audience, Peg turned to me. "We've pert near bled this one dry," she whispered. "Keep your ears open for the next."

"Tomorrow night will be our last reenactment," Peg announced. Despite the audience's nays and boos, Peg shook her head. "Tell your friends, if they want to see it one last time, tomorrow night is the night."

At dusk, when I exited The Bell Tower, Cragdon was there to walk me home.

"Prince Wron did not think it wise for you to walk to Leeson's unattended."

"I appreciate his concern," I said. The memory of the mobbing was one I'd never shared yet with anyone outside of the Great Beast.

"Each time I see you, you look better."

"Oh," I said, surprised by Cragdon's compliment.

"Today your cheeks are more defined than the last time I saw you."

I'd had Rhoda's cabbage soup for breakfast; at work, one of the cooks had cut up an onion, dipped it into batter, and tossed it into the deep fat. It was the most delicious onion that I had ever eaten. I'd also had a mutton burger, which was not new for me.

Halfway home, I stopped to pick wildflowers along the roadside. "Elza doesn't know I'm coming. When I lived with them, I often used to pick her a handful." I apologized for delaying the young guard, but he appeared happy enough to linger and chitchat with me.

As I carried the bouquet, I found myself thinking about my future wedding day. Would Wron and I be married in the church or in the Great Hall? I didn't know Yonder's traditions.

"After supper tonight, some other guards and their girlfriends are meeting at The Bell Tower. Peg allows us to meet there, for a fee of course."

I laughed. "Of course."

"Would you go with me, tonight?"

The uneasy knot that had formed in my tummy had been for good reason. Cragdon was beginning to see past my pox. Or imagining he did.

"I'm betrothed to another, but thank you," I said, relieved that we were within a few strides of Leeson and Elza's home.

"Betrothed? Where is your betrothed from?" Cragdon tried to slow our pace, but I continued on ahead of him.

I knocked on the smithy door, and while I waited, Cragdon stopped beside me in the doorway. "Please reconsider my invitation."

"No, thank you."

When the elderly couple opened the door, Elza could tell by my pigeon-toed stance that my spirits were low. "Come in, Dory." She peered at Cragdon's dusty boots. "Where is Prince Wron?"

"He is hunting today and hopes to shoot a turkey for dinner. In his good graces, I am allowed to spend both dinner and the night with you."

Elza gripped her hands together, pleased.

"Thank you for escorting me home." I nodded to Cragdon and stepped inside the warm room.

"I am to escort you in the morning," Cragdon said as I began to swing the door closed.

"Tell Prince Wron that Leeson will escort me in the morning. Thank you." I firmly closed the door.

"Is everything okay?" Leeson eyed the door.

Elza giggled. "Dory has an admirer."

ΦΦΦ

After eating onion soup and sourdough rolls, Elza and I sat in front of the fire and drank coffee, while Leeson gave in to an early nap.

"You are quied," Elza whispered. "Is id because of Prince Wron?"

"Yes." I nodded with a heavy heart.

"He's waiding for Princess Alia, and you, Dory, dhreaden his heard." Only the plump curve of Elza's cheek was visible as she stared into her lap.

"It's so good to talk about it. I've felt so alone." I reached over and patted her hand.

In the morning, after eating another baked onion for breakfast, Leeson walked me home. I was not as comfortable as I'd once been in town, so I wore my hood to cover my hair and much of my face as we walked together through the streets. When we reached the gatehouse, I pressed my cheek to Leeson's shoulder and hugged the dear man good-bye.

"We will see you soon, dear one," he said. I watched Leeson's lean stature as he crossed the bridge.

Plano, the young guard on duty, stood overhead cracking walnuts with his hands. "The Swamp Woman returns for piano duty," I said, with a slight lift of my chin.

With a perplexed scowl, the guard regarded me. "Let me see that you are the Swamp Woman."

Usually, Plano was not so gruff. I flipped back my hood and peered up at him. His brows gathered. "You do not look like the Swamp Woman." He nudged his nearest companion, and together they laughed.

"Who do I look like, then?" Wide-eyed, I thought to look at my hands. I held them out in front of me. They were spotless. My long, elegant, piano-playing hands were again lovely in appearance. Taking several strides away from Plano, I lifted my hands toward the blue sky and marveled at their restored appearance.

"Thank you, God," I whispered. "Thank you!"

I yelled up at the men of the gatehouse, "It is I, the Swamp Woman. I am healed." Smiling, I showed them my hands, which were spotless in appearance.

They simply stared.

"Cragdon escorted me to Leeson and Elza's home last night, and now, Queen Eunice is waiting for me to play piano."

Plano picked at something between his teeth. "Roger!" he yelled, searching the stone keep high above us. "Roger!"

"What is it?" the middle-aged guard yelled down to us.

"She saz she is the Swamp Woman." Plano pointed at me. "She sounds like the Swamp Woman, but she does not look like her."

Roger took the stairwell down. Surely the middle-aged guard would recognize something about me. He stopped beside Plano, tilted his head to one side, and stared.

"Roger, it's me, Dory. Cragdon escorted me to Leeson and Elza's home last night."

He regarded my clothes and my face, and then his dark brows bunched together as one. "You are dressed like the Swamp Woman, but . . ." He scratched the side of his head. "I will need to escort you."

"Your escort will be unnecessary." Lifting my chin, I saw Wron approach. "Prince Wron has noticed my delay." That or he was just out for a stroll.

Wron was handsome, with his cape flowing behind him. He had not seen me yet, or if he had, he did not recognize me. I lowered my chin, bracing myself for his response. Thirty feet away his stride slowed and, for the briefest of seconds, his eyes widened.

My heart pounded wildly as he stopped within arm's reach. "Prince Wron, I know Queen Eunice is expecting me, and I have been unable to prove to your men that it is I, the Swamp Woman . . ." I swallowed. "Dory, the piano girl."

"You are well," he whispered.

"Yes." I dared to meet his eyes. In his face, not a dimple or a laugh line showed, nor a sparkle, or even a flash of light in his icy-blue eyes. Not even the slight semblance of a warm smile. His response to my recovery, my healed complexion, was merely a cold, blank stare.

I swallowed my disappointment. "Please escort me inside. I will prove who I am at the piano."

In silence, we walked to the postern and from there inside the castle. He'd said nothing. I was healed of my long affliction, and he'd not even congratulated me.

"Did you shoot a turkey?" My voice wavered.

"Yes . . . you missed a feast."

When we neared the hallway mirror, I stopped. "I don't mean to be vain, but I'd like to be certain that I am . . ." My voice trailed off. I paused to look at my reflection in the large gilded mirror, and my heart warmed at the young woman with clear skin and hazel eyes who stared back.

"You are well." Wron waved a hand.

"Yes. Tonight is the final reenactment of Long and Molly's reunion at The Bell Tower. Please help me convince your mother that I should go."

"You must." He laughed softly.

I walked slightly ahead of him down the hallway. In the Great Hall, Walter and Eunice were seated at the long table. I was late. They were mid-breakfast. Eunice glanced up from a bowl of raspberries and cream. Her eyes widened as we approached, and her gaze locked on me. She swallowed a spoonful of raspberries while she regarded my clothing and long hair. Then she set one hand to her heart, and the other she slapped on the table between Walter and herself.

Walter turned to look at what had provoked his wife to act without her usual word flow. His thick brows gathered as he scanned me up and down thrice. My hair was especially familiar to them both, and they continued studying it.

"The piano girl?" Walter said.

"Dor . . . y?" Eunice finally whispered.

"Yes, Mother," Wron said. "Dory is well."

"She is," Eunice murmured. "You are well, indeed, my dear."

I smiled, relieved at her reception.

"Rhoda," Eunice said loudly over her shoulder. "Rhoda, you must come see."

Rhoda emerged from the kitchen with Needa on her shoulder. "Dor-ee, is that you?"

I nodded. There was an uneasy silence while everyone including Wron gazed at me. They had all become accustomed to the strange little creature that I'd been, and now it was as if they looked upon a stranger.

"I ate two baked onions today at Leeson and Elza's. I didn't know that I was well until the guards would not let me in."

"It is Dory." Needa clapped and almost fell backward off Rhoda's shoulder, before clutching the collar of the giant woman's dress.

"It's nice that you are well for the Summer Ball." Eunice patted her snowball hairdo. "Such a beautiful young woman working at the castle. It will not take long to marry her off. Walter, will we allow her to marry?"

The king frowned before clearing his throat to speak.

"I am already betrothed," I reminded Eunice.

"Yes," Eunice smiled, "but that was before Yonder."

Chapter Twenty-Two

From my view in the alcove of the Great Hall, I watched the sun slip behind the distant hills and the sky fade from fuschia to charcoal gray. I had just finished playing a long dinner melody for the royal family when I heard a clinking sound behind me. Using her fork, Eunice tapped the side of her glass.

"That's very annoying, Mother," Wron said.

"Well, I'm trying to get Dory's attention."

"Yes, but there are more polite methods."

"Maybe I need a bell." Eunice sighed. "Would you rather have Dory serve us dessert or one of the guards?"

Hearing their conversation, I rose from The Beast.

"Dory, will you serve dessert?" Eunice waved a hand toward the kitchen. "Rhoda has gone to bed with a giant headache, the poor thing."

"Yes, of course." I collected their dinner plates and set them beside the sink in the kitchen. Then I knocked on the small blue door to Needa's home.

"What is it now?" Needa groaned.

"It's dessert time, and Rhoda has gone to bed with a headache." I carried the grumpy little gnome to the island. A warm pan of kuchen sat on the countertop. Slices of apple peeked through the golden-brown cake.

"Rhoda must have used the canned apples in the pantry; the king apples are still a pale green," Needa said. "Please slice me a smidgen."

I set pieces of cake onto dessert plates and a smidgen in Needa's dish.

"Rhoda already whipped the cream." Needa pointed to the icebox.

I found the chilled bowl and mounded a plop of whipped cream on top of each slice.

"Rhoda makes it look so special." Needa scowled at me, eyeing my blob. "Fly me over the top." I knew what she meant as I'd occasionally seen Rhoda *fly* her over the food like a jay in flight.

Needa pinched her fingers in a bowl of cinnamon, and then I glided her over the top of the plates, over which she twitched a cloud of cinnamon dust. "Whee!" she squealed.

I carried the plates out into the Great Hall. Eunice's eyes widened at the cinnamon-sprinkled blob of whipped cream on her plate. I waited for her to refer to my dessert skills as *grossly unremarkable*.

"Dory, please play something lovely, like 'Lavender.'" Eunice flicked her hand toward The Beast. "Afterward, I would like you to clean the kitchen for Rhoda."

I smoothed my dress behind me and thought about what I'd play. I smiled at the reflection I remembered seeing in the mirror just a few hours earlier that day. There was a lovely melody to be followed, and I did for a spell. Healing had brought peace to my heart. Yet another image crept into my playing, and it was almost as depressing as my pox. The memory of the giant pile of dishes that Rhoda had left for me in the kitchen. What was I to do with the mess? I'd never done dishes before. Yes, I'd rinsed a dish, but I hadn't washed one. Where to begin? And why was I the one to do it?

"Dory . . ." I heard the clicking sound of silverware on glass as Eunice tapped her dessert fork. "Are you unraveling again? That is not 'Lavender.' Let me name that one also. Let me see, I shall call it . . ."

I thought the name "Dirty Dishes" quite fitting.

"I shall name it . . . 'Grossly Unremarkable.'"

"Mother, your manners are grossly unremarkable," Wron said.

I suppressed a smile.

Eunice patted at the corner of her mouth with a cloth serviette. "Never mind, Dory, we're done."

Everyone, including Wron, moved from the table to sit by the fire. I carried the dessert plates into the kitchen and stared at Rhoda's mess. On the island and counters sat pots and pans, piles of plates, and cutting boards with discarded vegetables. Plops of batter were sprayed everywhere, like Rhoda had danced while she whisked.

What was Eunice thinking?

If I were Rhoda, I would have a giant headache, too. I sighed, surveying the mess. If I could make it through the Forest Maze alone, I supposed I could survive this.

First, I scraped everything off the plates into the garbage. I then stacked the plates into one pile. The dirty silverware I put into one cup. The clean-looking silverware I put back inside the drawer. Next, I put all of the dishes inside the roasting pan and carefully fit the dirty glasses around them. I would hide this dirty dish container inside the oven. In the morning, when Rhoda felt better, she'd find it there.

I deemed myself a genius as I carried the roasting pan toward the oven.

"Here," Wron said, entering the kitchen, "let me help you with that."

I made it to the stove and rested the roasting pan on top. "I have it," I breathed. "Thank you, though."

A line deepened in his forehead. "Do you need help, Dory?"

"Well . . ." I flicked my hair over my shoulder. "You could wipe the table off in the other room."

Brows furrowed, Wron studied the dirty dish container. "What are you doing?"

I inhaled, pulled down the oven door, and slid the large pan inside the oven, which was still warm.

"Dory . . ." Wron shook his head, and his wide smile could have sugarcoated the moon. "I've heard that it's much easier to wash them in the sink. Here, let me help you with that." I backed up as he transferred the large pan from the oven to the island.

Maybe I should just go to bed and let him do the dishes.

"You don't want to leave Rhoda this mess." He opened an upper cupboard. "Look"—he waved a hand—"there won't be enough plates for breakfast if you hide them in the oven."

Though he was right, Wron was no longer attractive to me. He was a meddling righty-tidy.

"I'll help. You can wash and I'll put away." He appeared serious.

Frowning, I pumped water into the large sink and rubbed a bar of soap between my hands for lather. I started scrubbing stuff and handed him a sudsy plate.

He handed it back to me. "You must rinse it first." Kneeling, he found a tub beneath the counter. "I'll fill this with rinse water." I scooted to the left as he worked the pump and filled the tub with plain old water. He hummed a delightful little tune that I'd never heard before.

I also hummed the tune, trying to remember it.

He set the tub to the right of the sink, and I handed him the sudsy plate.

"Did you wash both sides?" he asked.

Why did I need to wash both? They'd only eaten off one side.

"You always wash both sides, Dory." His brows gathered.

"You're going to have to give me a better answer than that, if you expect to be a good king someday." I met his gaze.

"Because they're stacked in the cupboard. Bottom, top. Bottom, top."

With a little huff, I took the plate from him and washed the other side.

He plunged the plate into the rinse water, dried it, and slid it inside a cupboard. While the cupboard was open, his profile was hidden from view. Hurrying, I set a couple of dirty glasses in the closest cupboard.

"What are you doing? You should already have another dish washed and waiting for me."

I began to worry about my future. He might be one of those husbands who demanded perfection.

I quickly washed another plate, handed it to him, and repeated my routine of stuffing dirty dishware in the closest cupboard while he slid the clean plates inside the cupboard to his right. Feeling rushed, I handed him a glass to rinse.

"Where is everything? That counter was full."

Wide-eyed, I glanced at the counter and then at him.

"I only put away two plates and one glass." He frowned at me. "You're stuffing them somewhere. And your touch is too soft. You almost act like you've never washed dishes before."

"I haven't." My mouth bunched up. "I am a royal pianist."

"But you worked at The Bell Tower. Surely . . ." Frowning, he shook his head.

"I'm very good at peeling potatoes."

He walked past me and opened the cupboard that I'd hidden them in. "Dory, I pity the poor fool who marries you. You are lazy and show no consideration for Rhoda and the mess she'll find in the morning."

Feeling heat rise in my face, I plunged the pot that Rhoda had used for the potatoes deep into the water.

"Kettles are always washed last, because they're the dirtiest." He continued to nitpick.

"I am a royal pianist!" I threw the rag into the sink and glared at him.

"I am royalty by blood." One brow lifted as he faced me. "And I'm helping you. No more putting dishes in the oven or hiding them in the cupboard. I will help until we're done."

I retrieved the washrag and sighed. Three feet of counter space was still covered with dirty dishes, pots and pans, a gravy boat . . . I wanted to scream! Setting the saucepan to my left, I began with the glasses. I washed the inside and outside of one and handed it to him.

Wron rinsed it and held it up to the light. "See how it sparkles? My parents used to make me wash dishes as penance. They were very good about overseeing my work. 'One cannot be lazy about doing what is right' was one of their favorite mottoes." He paused as he dried. "Tell me more about Blue Sky."

"The sky is blue."

"And Alia, what color are her eyes?"

"Blue."

"And her hair?"

"Blue."

"Hmm . . ." His cheek muscles twitched. "And what is her personality?"

"Blue."

Mr. Righty-Tidy held another one of my glasses up to the light. "If you keep washing like this, Dory, you could someday find work as a scullery maid in a kitchen."

I'd had enough of his mocking. Soapy remnants of potato lay inside the large pot. I scooped up a handful and, turning toward him, smeared it into the side of his unshaven face.

Mouth agape, he stared at me. "That was very uncalled for."

I bit the insides of my cheeks. It was very called for.

He grabbed my shoulder, slid a hand inside the pot, and rubbed sudsy potato into my face.

I stormed. He'd even rubbed it near my eyes, whereas I had been far gentler. At the same time, we both reached for the remaining potatoes in the pot. We fought with one hand as we held onto each other's shoulders with the other. It was exhilaratingly intense. Outside of my mummy roll with the three sisters, I had never had a physical fight of any kind, and I'd so wanted to.

The plods of potato were gone. I reached for the saucepan first and dipped it half-full of water. He tried to block me, but the water splashed down the front of him. Again, his jaw dropped, and I laughed at his stunned expression. Sudsy muck dribbled down the front of his dark cambric tunic. I laughed and refilled the pot. He wrestled with me again. Gripping my forearm, he maneuvered my arm above my head, and there was no stopping him as the whole pot of water cascaded over me.

I remembered that the garbage was full of scraps. I swung the cupboard open and plunged my hands into the scraps, smearing them down the front of his shirt. Laughter roared out of him. He grabbed my arm to keep me from running, and one-handed, he grabbed for the scraps. He dredged my face and neck, and lastly rubbed a handful into the top of my hair.

I wiped food off my face, and then swiped at him. He grinned and backed away. I skated in potato peelings and sudsy water toward him before my feet lifted out from beneath me and my body crashed to the hard stone floor.

Dazed, I looked up at the ceiling. Wron knelt down beside me and peered into my face. "Are you all right, Dory?"

"Yes." I smiled. A clump of mashed potato clung to his cheek. My, he was fine.

"Can you wiggle your toes?"

I paused to wiggle my toes. "Yes," I breathed.

"Wron, what is going on here?" Walter's voice boomed from the doorway, and then he rounded the side of the island. I did not tip back my head to see him; instead, I watched as Wron's face reddened beneath the layer of potato.

"What in the world?" Walter whispered.

"I believe this is called a food fight." Wron's Adam's apple bobbed.

"Hurry and clean up this mess!" his father huffed and then retreated.

Wron assisted me to my feet. In silence, we finished the dishes and cleaned the counters and the floor.

"I'm sorry about your hair. I became overzealous."

For my response, I opened the lower cabinet and pulled out the garbage can. I leaned over it and shook my head. A plop of something fell inside.

Wron laughed.

ΦΦΦ

After a long, hot bath, I tiptoed into my room, and my bed only slightly creaked as I pulled the covers over me and sighed as I recalled the evening. My swamp pox had helped me to see the kindness of my betrothed's heart. If I'd always been blemish-free in Wron's eyes, I knew I would not appreciate him as I did now.

"How did it go without me?" Rhoda's question interrupted my sweet thoughts.

"You're awake." Facing her, I tucked my hands beneath my cheek. "Everyone loved the apple kuchen, even though I made the whipped cream look like a lump on the plate. Are you feeling any better?"

"Yes, so much better." She yawned.

"Do you get headaches very often?"

"Only when I eat choc-o-lot." Rhoda sighed. "I went to the village for cinnamon, and I . . . ended up buying all their choc-o-lot. Once I eat one piece, I cannot stop."

"I'm sorry. Chocolate can be a problem for a lot of—"

"I have tried to give it up, but the craving has never left me."

My breathing slowed. "Is that why you had the headache?"

"Yes. If I eat it, Queen Eunice says I am to get a giant headache. And I do." Rhoda sighed.

Her weakness was not human flesh, but chocolate. Oh, how I loved Rhoda!

"Before the hypnosis, how were you around chocolate?" I asked.

"Awful. God has cursed us with a deep yearning for choc-o-lot."

"Us . . . do you mean all giants?" My toes curled beneath the covers.

"Only the women. The men merely like it." Rhoda sighed. "I should not go to the mercantile anymore."

Rhoda had made a scene. "I'm sure we can . . . *they* can put someone else in charge of groceries. You do so much already for Yonder."

"I smell choc-o-lot, even when it is in a box—all wrapped up." Rhoda sighed her heavy, almost-asleep sigh.

I lay wide awake. A sliver of moonlight streamed through the arched window. *Do not wait for me. I will catch up to you.*

Too bad Felix didn't know the giants wouldn't be hibernating or that the giant women had an insatiable love for chocolate. I lay awake in the darkness thinking about my dear friend.

Chapter Twenty-Three

When I arrived at Leeson and Elza's home for dinner, a letter sat propped up on the table against the saltshaker. My name was scribbled across the front of the light gray envelope.

"Dhis arrived for you doday," Elza said as I studied the slanted cursive.

"Who delivered it?" I knew from being a warmonger's daughter that one should always be mindful of the messenger.

"Not Cragdon, but an older guard with a patch of hair"— Leeson motioned to the top-back of his head—"and a barley belly."

He'd described Roger. I sat down on the edge of my bed and unfolded the note that was tucked inside.

Dory,
I'll pick you up at eight o'clock tonight.
—Prince Wron.

Pick me up for what? I glanced at Elza. "It's from Prince Wron. All it says is he'll pick me up at eight o'clock."

"For whad?"

"I don't know."

Deep in thought, Elza tapped a spoon against the side of her mug. She tilted her head toward me and smiled. "Maybe dhis is a good sign."

While perhaps a good sign for Dory, it was not a very good sign for Alia.

Over the course of the next hour, I bathed in a big tub brought in from outside, changed into a clean cambric top and long gingham skirt, and dried my hair by the fire. Though I told myself I wasn't nervous, my stomach wouldn't listen.

"You look beaudiful, Dory." Elza smiled, her head tilted toward me.

We all listened as a carriage stopped in front of the smithy, and then there was the shuffle of boots outside. I joined Elza at the table, and as the seconds slipped by, she patted my hand.

Someone knocked three times, and Leeson rose to answer the door.

"Hello, Leeson." Wron's clear voice carried inside.

"Please come in. I would like to speak with you," Leeson said.

"Hello, Elza." Wron sat down at the table, across from me. "Dory . . ." He nodded, without really looking at me.

"Hello." I also nodded.

Leeson did not sit down, but paced between the fireplace and the table.

"Is Dory nod beaudiful?" Elza twisted her neck to view Wron.

Without looking at me, he smiled and nodded at Elza. "Yes, she is." He lowered his gaze to the table.

"Why do you not look at her, then?" Leeson asked.

I agreed with Leeson. The evening did not make sense.

We all sat in silence. Wron was soon to be a married man. He was not here for me. The evening was a ploy. In my gut, I knew he was matchmaking me with Cragdon. And in the meantime, these dear people thought the worst of him.

"Dory already knows, Leeson . . . and Elza, that I think she's beautiful." Wron fully met my gaze, and for a moment his chest expanded as he smiled at me.

I wanted to dwell wholeheartedly on his words, but in the back of my mind I knew that he'd only said it so I would leave with him this evening.

"I do not feel good about tonight." Leeson scratched at the back of his head as he paced. "We will talk outside by my horses."

Wron rose and followed the elderly man out the side door into the stable area.

"I don'd know, dear one." Elza patted my hand. "Dhere is nod his usual charm, donighd."

"I sense it, too." Wron was acting very uneasy.

The side door opened soon enough. Wron crossed the room and held the front door open for me. "It's time to go, Dory."

I glanced at Leeson for some sort of sign. The elderly man merely shook his head before Wron closed the door behind me. A footman assisted me inside the carriage. I sat across from Wron in the middle of the bench seat. At a very slow pace, the horses walked the road I usually took to The Bell Tower.

"Why do I feel like you are taking me somewhere to meet Cragdon?" I pretended interest in the sliver of moon perched high in the sky.

"Because imagination is another one of your strong suits."

Imagination was also one of his. "If you are trying to matchmake me with Cragdon, I need to remind you that I am betrothed to another."

"Then, where is this betrothed fellow of yours?"

I stared at him.

I had decided I'd tell him I was Alia the night of the Summer Ball. I would wear one of my Blue Sky gowns, and we would dance. Over the course of the evening, I would gather courage, and I would tell him. And if for some reason, he held me at gunpoint tonight and tried to force me to marry Cragdon, I would have to tell him sooner.

"Remind me of why you are here in Yonder?" he asked.

"At first it was to heal, and now I am paying penance for a petty crime." I added heat to my words. "I shot a bird on common land, but it fell in royal."

"Yes, and I remember talk of your going to Evland, but . . . you've sold both your horses?" Our eyes locked.

My stomach knotted at his observance. "I don't need such a full-time workhorse to get to Evland. With the money that the horses brought in, I can easily hire a carriage."

He seemed content enough with my answer and turned toward the window and the sliver of moon. "My mother does not do well when you are away. She says, 'It is too quiet.' Even when you are only gone for dinner, she misses you."

I was caught off guard, and warmth gathered behind my eyes. I played with a loose thread on my skirt. Had he missed me, too? Did he care for *Dory* too much? I found myself gazing at his profile with questions in my heart.

The carriage came to a gentle stop. Our destination was indeed The Bell Tower. What did they have planned for me here? Perhaps it was his mother who was getting creative again. Perhaps she'd dreamed it all up during their quiet dinner.

Wron pulled the front door open for me, and I stepped inside. Though the stage area was empty, all of the torch sconces around it were lit. I felt emotionally spent, and hoped I was not the one to perform. Wron led the way to a table near the front. Except for the guards stationed at every plausible exit, there appeared to be no one else here. Not even Peg. Just the two of us. Could the evening possibly be for just Wron and me? I suppressed the hope that wanted to take wing, fly, and pirouette.

Hope snapped as, guitar in hand, fair-haired Cragdon walked from the back of the stage into view. He carried the round piano stool, the one I usually sat on, closer to the front of the stage, and then sat down.

Now that I was well, my betrothed was intent on marrying me to another man.

Tuning his guitar, Cragdon glanced at me. "It's good to see you tonight."

I lowered my gaze to the table and felt betrayed. I peered at Wron. He kept his profile to me.

Cragdon strummed a moving melody and then added his rich tenor voice.

"I knew. I knew. I knew . . .

Beneath the veil, I knew

Was a woman, a woman like you."

I felt like Rhoda had sat on my chest. Cragdon's song was proving far too serious to sit through. I knew of one possible exit that most likely was not accounted for.

"Excuse me . . ." I patted Wron's arm. "I'm going to use the ladies' room."

Eyes wide, he stared at me. "Stay here."

"I knew. I knew. I knew . . ."

"I can't," I said. Wide-eyed, I pleaded with him.

Wron leaned toward me. "He's put a lot of time into this. You can." His soft voice tried to tame me.

Shoulders heavy, I sighed.

"On my knee, I'll pledge this very night . . ." Onstage, Cragdon lowered himself from the stool to one knee.

Without permission, I stood up and, looking straight ahead, strode toward the back hallway toward the Wenches' room. The door was locked. I couldn't wait. I turned the knob of the Gents' room and locked the door behind me. In the dark, unlit room, I slid the upper window open and, stepping up on the sink, shimmied my way through into the cool night air. If I walked through backyards on my way home, chickens, cows, and dogs were bound to litter my path. I had to take the road.

But the most obvious place to find me would be the road. I had to get my wits about me. Think. Think. Slowly, I inched around the side of the stone building. The carriage now faced home. On top of the bench seat, the coachman's head bobbed as he slept. The guards who leaned against the front of The Bell Tower were mid-yawn and mid-stretch as I slipped past them to the rear of the carriage. I boosted myself onto the ledge where luggage was usually stored, and hugged my knees, pulling myself into a tight little piece of baggage.

Several minutes passed before the front door was flung open.

"Hey . . . did anyone see Dory leave?" Wron called out.

"What? Huh!" Guards yawned themselves awake. "What?"

"Did anyone see Dory—the woman who was with me—leave?"

"No, we've been here the whole time," one of the guards said.

"For the next five minutes, I want everyone to search, and then return here. She is smart, cunning. Look in every nook and cranny."

Someone approached and opened the carriage door. I didn't move a muscle, didn't breathe. The door creaked closed. Boots crunched on the pebbly dirt road as someone rounded the team of horses, the carriage, and then back toward me.

The Bell Tower door creaked open again. "No sign of her inside. Just the open window in the Gents' room." It was Cragdon's voice.

"She's either hiding somewhere close or walking the road," Wron said, rounding my side of the carriage. "I don't think she would walk through yards this time of night." Though I was tightly packaged and hidden in shadows, he stopped beside me, and his hand brushed the edge of my skirt to rest upon my knee.

I dared not breathe.

"I'll walk the road and see if I can catch up with her." Cragdon sounded weary.

"I'll ride ahead and see if she's returned home," my beloved said.

Wron waited until Cragdon disappeared into the distance. "Get in the carriage, so he doesn't see you when we drive by," he whispered. "I'll wait here for a moment until one of the guards returns."

Uncoiling myself, I dropped to the ground and crept inside the carriage. A few minutes passed before one of the guards returned. "No sign of her," he said.

"Stay here and inform the others that Cragdon and I have gone ahead." Wron gave orders. "Once all of the men have returned, inform them that it is time to head home, as I believe the girl has already done." He sat down inside the carriage, across from me. And then remembering one more thing, he leaned out the window. "Stop at Leeson's on the way home," he addressed the footman. "I want to be certain that the girl is there."

While the carriage jostled over the rutted dirt road, Wron and I smiled at each other. Like a swan seeks its reflection in the water, my heart waltzed under his open gaze.

"Lie low now, as we are nearing Cragdon," he whispered.

I curled up on my side of the seat and waited until Wron motioned that it was all right for me to again sit up.

While the carriage jostled over the rutted dirt road, Wron and I smiled at each other. Like a swan seeks its reflection in the water, my heart waltzed under his open gaze.

"Lie low now, as we are nearing Cragdon," he whispered.

I curled up on my side of the seat and waited until Wron motioned that it was all right for me to sit up.

"You needn't worry again." His mouth twitched. "I am done helping him."

"I'm glad." I sighed, happy.

After the carriage stopped at the smithy, Wron stepped out of the carriage and knocked on Leeson and Elza's door. I stepped quietly out of the carriage, and he blocked the coachman's view of me until Leeson opened the door.

"You are home at an early time," Leeson said, pleased.

"Has Dory arrived home yet?" Wron asked loudly for the coachman's ear. "I am glad to see that you are here and safe and sound."

Leeson's brows knit together. I stood in the doorway, now with the light behind me, and gazed up into Wron's face. "Thank you for tonight," I said.

Leeson stepped away from the door to leave Wron and me alone in its wake.

"Will you be at The Bell Tower all day tomorrow?" he asked.

"Yes." Would he miss me? "Tomorrow night is our final reenactment of Long and Molly's reunion. Peg's afraid we've bled it dry."

He nodded and scratched his neck. "I am going to walk home. Tell me something about Alia. Something that she would want me to know about her, that I might think of her . . . and not"—his chest expanded as he looked away from me—"the moon."

I wanted to close my eyes and waltz, but instead I had to think. What would I want him to know about me in such a time as this?

"Alia is also a good shot."

His brows lifted with surprise.

I nodded. "She enjoys hunting, and its rewards."

"Really?" He was genuinely pleased. "Thank you, Dory. That was unexpected . . ." His voice trailed off. His eyes dulled as he nodded his good night.

I stepped out in front of the smithy as he told the driver to go on ahead. Then I watched as, alone under a sliver of moonlight, Wron strolled home, thinking about me.

ΦΦΦ

"It's our last show, Dory," Long whispered, and feeling the air, he reached for my arm. From the kitchen doorway, we faced the crowded, dimly lit room. For our final reenactment, The Bell Tower was even more packed than our first performance had been.

"Tonight is bittersweet," I whispered, hooking my arm in his.

"Keep your appetites, folks, and watch Gerdie," Peg bellowed from where she stood near the stone fireplace. "Do not look toward the stage."

Near the front entrance, Gerdie broke into song. With the hooded cloak over my head, I led Long up the steps. We stood near the front of the stage, and waited for the ruckus to dim.

"Dory, pull back your hood," yelled a man near the stage.

"She'll do that at the end," Peg bellowed. "Now, everyone be quiet!"

Long patted my hand as we waited for the room to still and then we waited some more for that deep silence when you fully have the audience's attention.

"Do you see my Molly?" Long leaned toward me.

"What does she look like?" I asked.

"She used to be . . ." Long held his hands out in front of him, outlining her plump curves. "With coarse hair and strong hands."

Taking my time, I scanned the sea of faces that were familiar to me now. Near the fireplace, at the right side of the room, sat a giant of a woman. Though her face was cast in shadow, I knew it was Rhoda. Beside her at the table sat a woman whose dark shawl covered her head and shoulders. Perhaps Needa was here, too, hiding in the Queen's bag of pears that were stashed on the table. Though disguised, they were seated amongst their countrymen. My heart wanted to cheer.

I forced my gaze to the other side of the room. "I don't see her, but don't worry. She won't be long."

He cleared his throat, peering into the darkness.

"Little old woman . . . where are you?" His voice trembled with emotion.

"Our children have grown,

I'm here all alone.

Little old woman who shared my bed.

Little old woman who sent me for bread.

Little old woman, where are you?"

I spotted Wron's familiar broad shoulders, one table away from his mother.

"Has anyone seen Long's wife, Molly, today?" I asked. Keeping my face hidden in shadows, I waited for Raul, the liveryman who was seated near the front, to say his part. Instead, he took a sip of hope and popped a chip into his mouth.

"Has anyone seen Long's wife today?" My voice rose for emphasis as I peered down at Raul.

"Yeeeesss." He cleared his throat. "I saw her with a cornful of apron standing in her garden."

Chuckles reverberated throughout the room.

"I saw Molly hanging clothes on the line," yelled Clarence from the mercantile.

"It appears everyone has heard the good news, except, that is, for Long's wife. Can anyone help us find her?" Again, I scanned the sea of faces. "It has been three years since Long has seen her."

"It's been longer than that." Clarence's bellow was followed by the regular round of laughter.

"My home is not far," Long said. "You take a right at the Mill Road. You'll pass a cherry tree." He reached his hand high to his left. "And then you'll see my Molly . . ."

"I know where she lives; I'll go." Weaver stood up near the front. "But save my chair." The young man downed his glass of hope, ran a forearm across his mouth, and proceeded toward the door.

Clearing his throat, Long waited for the whispers to fade.

"Home . . ." His crackly voice was now a part of my fondest memories.

"The comforts of home.
Where we warm our souls by the fire,
A straw-tick bed when we're tired,
A bowl of my Molly's mutton stew . . .
My home . . . little old woman

. . . is you."

Emotion heavy in their eyes, the audience clapped.

We waited so no one would miss a word, and then Long leaned his head toward mine. "Do you see my Molly?"

With a hand cupped over my eyes, I scanned the far side of the room. The audience turned in their chairs to look, also. And like he did during our first performance, Wron also turned to watch.

"It won't be long, Long," I said.

"Little old woman, where are you?" His unseeing eyes roved the room.

Weaver returned. A hush fell over the group as a disheveled, white-haired woman walked in behind him. Her hair was frizzy, her cheeks were windblown, and her apron was soiled. Slowly her gaze found Long across the room.

No fire crackled in the hearth this warm night, but a new melody had begun in my head. In a very short time, I would be walking toward Wron, and my face would be just as radiant.

"Long . . . a beautiful woman with flowing white hair is slowly walking toward us."

"Does she look like she's forgiven me?"

"There is no doubt," I whispered and then in my normal pitch, "Yes, she looks like a bride, there is so much love in her eyes."

"Little old woman . . ." Long held out his hands and turned slightly toward the stairs. "I'm so blessed . . ."

Lifting her skirt at the knee, his wife slowly climbed the steps.

"Words cannot express . . ."

Molly took that final step toward him, and then pressed her cheek to his chest. Her arms wrapped about his long waist.

"Awh . . . my Molly." He kissed the top of her hair.

I glanced toward Eunice and Rhoda. Tears glistened on their cheeks before they were wiped away. And, perhaps tempting fate, I stole a glance toward my future beloved. Wron's gaze made my heart flutter, and then I saw seated beside him at the table a tall, lean form, and someone of much shorter stature, her head bowed and tilted to the side. Leeson and Elza.

Tears sprang to my eyes. They were finally here to witness the scene I'd told them about a handful of times. My betrothed was a kind and thoughtful man. Tomorrow night at the Summer Ball, I would wear one of my gowns from Blue Sky, and at the close of the evening, I would tell Wron and his parents who I really was.

Long, Molly, and I remained onstage together and bowed. Under Peg's direction, I flipped back my hood. Murmurs and gasps rippled through the audience, as there were still many who had not seen me in my healed state.

To join us onstage, we called up Weaver, Clarence, Raul, and Peg, and with the group complete, we bowed again. "We didn't bleed it dry," Peg whispered to me. "We perfected it." She sniffled as we made our last bow.

I squeezed her hand.

"Play something, Dory." The requests began. "Dory, play."

I was no longer known as the Swamp Woman to my countrymen, but as Dory, the piano girl. My fingers twitched with unexpressed happiness.

It was time to play.

Chapter Twenty-Four

The Summer Ball was celebrated in the large courtyard beneath the terrace of the King and the Queen's royal bedchamber. Several varieties of apricot-colored roses were in bloom; they were fragrant and lovely. The guards took turns on duty to enjoy the festivities, while commoners and royalty alike danced to fiddle music.

I stood beside Eunice and watched Wron and Rhoda waltz. In a purple gown, Needa sat happily on Wron's shoulder, holding on to the nape of his cape. Rhoda's round face turned pink when she stepped on Wron's toes, and beet red when she stepped on them a second time.

"It is too bad Needa does not have another color cap," I whispered to Eunice.

"She told me once why she had to wear green." Eunice squinted as she tried to remember. "Some gnome tradition."

Across the courtyard, a lovely young woman also watched Wron. Blonde curls framed her pixie face. She watched him like he was fair game. Wron was attractive and—I smiled to myself—"taken."

"It's a lovely gown you're wearing, Dory." Eunice fluttered an ivory-handled fan in front of her powdered face. "Quite regal."

The gown I wore was dark green and elegant. Interwoven in the rounded bodice was a translucent silver ribbon. "It's one of Princess Alia's old gowns," I said.

"Oh. The commoners will not recognize their Swamp Woman," Eunice said. "I cannot tell from this distance who Wron is speaking with. Can you?"

"He's speaking with a particularly lovely girl," I murmured. "Short blonde hair."

"Oh, it's just Enna."

With a tightness in my rib cage, I watched as he led the pixie girl into the middle of the square.

Someone took my elbow. I turned to see Leeson.

"I did not recognize you." He smiled. "Twice, I looked at you and did not see you."

"You wear a beautiful dress and common shoes," Elza said beside him.

"Yes, I wanted to be barefoot"—I smiled—"but Queen Eunice said that I must wear shoes."

"I am not a good dancer, but would you care to dance with an old man like me?" Leeson held out his hand to me.

"Yes, of course."

He led me to an uncrowded area on the lawn and set his hand to the small of my back. While we waltzed, I returned his heartfelt gaze and was reminded of my sixteenth party, when Father and I had waltzed. God had led me to Leeson and Elza's home for several reasons. They needed me almost as much as I needed them.

While we waltzed, I looked to the center of the courtyard. The lovely pixie was still in Wron's arms, while around them the common folk appeared to be enjoying themselves immensely. I did not share their lightheartedness. I struggled with my feelings. I wanted Wron to ask me to dance at least once. I wanted to know that he loved me before he found out who I really was. I wondered if I wanted too much.

When the music ended, I clapped softly and searched the square for Wron. Across the courtyard our eyes met. I breathed shallowly as his gaze lingered on mine. In the warm summer air, I smelled the subtle fragrance of roses. He looked sad; perhaps he was also miserable amidst the festivities.

Fiddle music filled the air. Wron turned away and took the hand of the nearest maiden. I closed my eyes and told myself that I would remember his long, miserable look all my life.

I strode toward one of the refreshment tables. A gnarly honeysuckle bush rambled overhead along the castle wall. Blossoms floated in the large punch bowl, and I carefully scooped out a few yellow tendrils. I glanced back to the dance, where the lovely pixie girl now stood alone. By her forlorn expression, I knew that my heart was not the only one Wron was breaking tonight.

Cragdon stopped beside me and ladled punch into a glass. "I have finally gathered courage," he said. "Would you like to dance, Dory?"

I smiled at his persistence. Poor Cragdon. Even though I'd climbed out the window at The Bell Tower, he persisted.

"Has Wron told you that I am from a long line of knights?" He set down his glass and, taking my hand, led me through the crowd to the center of the square.

"No, he has not," I replied. Up until now, I'd only danced with Leeson, while Wron had danced with every other wallflower at the ball. I would not feel about guilty dancing with Cragdon.

"You are light on your feet." Cragdon pulled me closer. "In another lifetime, you were a princess."

"You hold me too close, Sir Cragdon."

He swung me out of his arm into the krassant, and to his surprise, I knew how to follow. He pulled me close again, his eyes glistening. "You do not dance like a commoner."

"It is you who does not dance like a commoner," I said, but did not meet his gaze.

"I was to be the future king of Evland before we lost the war."

I stared. His eyes were steel blue and honest.

"What happened?" I'd never heard the other side of the story.

"My father thought we could win." He pursed his mouth. "He'd acquired the new double-barreled guns. For years, he'd planned. He became obsessed with defeating King Ulrich. He didn't know that Yonder had planned for his attack for years."

Spirits heavy, I remembered my father and his incessant pacing. "I'm sorry, Cragdon. Your life has not gone as you would have dreamed."

Briefly, my comrade closed his eyes. "It was kind of King Walter not to behead me. Usually that is what happens in time of war to the entire royal family. I will serve Yonder faithfully all my life because of that."

"Why didn't he?" I was not unfamiliar with the atrocities of war.

Cragdon's chest expanded. "I was born on the same day, in the same year, as his youngest son, Prince Wally. I believe this coincidence is my saving grace."

"I do, too." I nodded.

When the song ended, we parted to clap. "Another dance?" he asked with a fervent smile.

"I'm sorry, I have other commitments."

"I understand." His jaw tightened as he stepped away to follow after a young woman with dark, flowing hair.

Wron and Rhoda waltzed again in the middle of the
square, while Walter and Eunice conversed with guests. At
the dessert table, I set seven berry tartlets upon a plate and
doubted that I'd be missed.

I carried the plate of tarts toward the back entrance to the
kitchen and from there took the hidden route down the prison
stairs. In the corner of his cell, Knot lay half-asleep. Upon
seeing me, he rolled a kink out of his neck, and then he
yawned.

"I brought you a tart." I held the plate against the bars.

"I hear music from above. You are young, beautiful, and
thinking of me." He eyed me curiously before glancing
toward the stairs. "I am surprised that half the king's army
has not followed you." His hand snaked through the bars, and
then he enjoyed his first bite of tart. "You're sad. There is
one fellow that you wish had."

I missed the brief friendship Wron and I had shared when
I became Yonder's royal pianist. Now that I was healed, he
simply avoided me.

"You are brokenhearted about someone or something."
Knot sighed. "I'm much better with political strategy than a
woman's tears."

"I'm not crying." Tears in check, I swallowed.

"You are close." Knot observed me.

I glanced at my old cell. "I know it's wrong of me, Knot,
but I only want to marry for love."

"You are a commoner; you have that privilege." He
chuckled.

I lifted my eyes to his gaze.

"But that is not a commoner's dress." Knot munched on
his second tart.

"It's an old one of Princess Alia's."

"It does not look old." His gray brows gathered. "The
velvet is without blemish."

"Perhaps she merely tired of it."

Knot's eyes flickered with light. "A shocking revelation has occurred to me."

I smiled softly. "I'm sorry, Knot, I'm not in love with you."

"It is not just your broken heart; we are also discussing politics?" He forged ahead.

As I glanced toward the stairs, I unknowingly held the tart plate closer to the bars.

"When will you tell him?" He slid a tart into his pocket.

"Tell whom, what?" I met Knot's gaze.

"That you are Alia."

I dropped my gaze to the four remaining tarts and slowly moved away from Knot's cell toward Stapleton's.

"Dearest Dory . . ." Knot said.

I inhaled deeply and then regarded him over my shoulder.

"By not answering, you have answered." One gray brow lifted higher than the other. "A common girl would have been delighted with such a compliment."

"Thank you, Knot."

He chuckled. "Come here, or I will yell your real name."

Heat filled my face, yet I had no choice but to stand in front of his cell. Knot took another tart from the plate. "From the beginning, everything about you was royalty—the grace with which you move, your voice inflections, your taste in food." He smiled. "Everything, except your pox. Yonder royalty is too close to be judicious."

I wondered what Knot would do with the truth that was now in his possession. Would he use it for harm or for good, this man who'd been adviser to the king? Was I wise to consider him a friend?

ΦΦΦ

One hour before midnight, Leeson, Elza, and I said our good-byes at the gatehouse.

"Preddiest girl ad dee ball," Elza said, while Leeson kissed my forehead.

"Thank you for everything." Arm in arm, the elderly couple walked home across the bridge. The river below was bathed in yellow ochre, and the poignant moment left me feeling uneasy.

"You are like family to me," I called, but the distance was too great, as Leeson did not even raise a hand.

Silhouetted by the full moon, the guards sang the fiddler's song as they stood watch atop the walls. The music serenaded me as I walked back to the festivities.

I stood next to Eunice, Walter beside her, and suppressed a yawn. I thought about politely informing them that it had been a long, wonderful day and I was retiring, but Wron stopped to stand beside his father.

"Where is Dory?" he asked.

"On the other side of your mother," Walter said.

Wron leaned slightly forward and nodded with a faint smile. I nodded in return.

"I have not seen you dance with Dory tonight," Eunice said.

"I do not think it wise, Mother."

"Our people love Dory," Eunice persisted. "They would love to see you dance with her."

"I do not think it wise." Wron shook his head.

I stepped behind Eunice and briefly closed my eyes. I had longed for this opportunity all evening, and now that it had presented itself, I also questioned . . . was it wise? Would his parents be able to read the emotion in my eyes?

Wron stepped in front of his mother and held a hand out toward me. "Dory, would you care to dance?"

He was not taking his own advice. I looked over Eunice's shoulder at him before placing my right hand in his. He led me to the center of the crowded courtyard, placed his hand to the small of my back, and held my other hand in his. Then, quite solemn in expression, he gazed over the top of my head. His steps were extremely precise, as if he was counting in his head to pass the time.

Bored, I stared at his Adam's apple. Though onlookers watched with keen interest, there was nothing for anyone to read into, for we danced like blind strangers. Midsong, he glanced down at me.

"Lovely weather," I said. "I hear there's a drought in the Alps."

His Adam's apple bobbed down, then up. The second time that he peered down at me, his eyes were sparkling. "You will not break me so easily," he whispered.

"May I try?" I suppressed a smile.

He pursed his mouth before nodding.

"For as long as you can remember, you have waited for Alia."

He lowered his head slightly to hear my whisper.

"And she is almost here. Your heart is ready to love her, or perhaps, someone. And while you wait, you continue to fear that you will be a disappointment to each other."

I paused to weigh my words. "I know Princess Alia well, and I can honestly say . . . you will not be a disappointment to her. So now it's narrowed down to your fear. Will she be a disappointment to you?"

Continuing in step, he glanced at my flushed face. "You are too certain of another's feelings."

"Perhaps I speak too much from my own heart." My heart missed a beat as I realized the enormity of my confession.

Wron drew me closer and made two slow turns. His silence was painful. Do not say another word, I told myself.

"I was very fond of you when you were the Swamp Woman." He sighed. "And now that you are healed, I should no longer confide in you. I'm sorry."

"Why?" I breathed.

Like Cragdon, he rolled me away from him into the krassant and rolled me back again into his arms. The music had changed, and we were now into our second dance. He pulled me so close that I wrapped up beneath his chin like a caterpillar in a cocoon. "My parents deem you a counterfeit. They speak of it often in your absence."

I stared at the front of his shirt. "Well, then we have much to talk about tonight."

He continued the monotonous waltz. I glanced up, surprised that he was looking at me. "I have heard . . . that there is an open rose," he said.

"Pardon me?" I could not believe what he'd just voiced.

"I would like to show you the first open rose of summer."

My betrothed loved me.

A thousand shivers made their way to the tips of my toes.

"My parents and my country are watching you blush with great interest in their eyes." He smiled, and I waited for him to spin me away, but instead we kept waltzing.

"I cannot meet your eyes for the emotion that is in mine," I whispered.

His chest inflated. "After the song ends, go stand by my mother. Roger will deliver a message."

The fiddlers paused only briefly between songs. I glanced up into Wron's eyes. He smiled softly and nodded. In full view of his countrymen, he released my hand, and I made my way through the crowded courtyard to the Queen's side.

"Beautiful." Eunice fluttered her ivory-handled fan. "You are both lovely and amusing to watch. My son is very taken with you . . . very. I'm afraid that we may have to send you away soon, my dear. Very soon."

"It's only the full moon," I whispered. For half of a waltz, I suppressed a smile as I remembered being in her son's arms.

As Roger walked behind me, he slid a note into my hand and then grasped the hand of Olivia, the dark-haired beauty that Cragdon had earlier found alluring. I walked to the punch table and, with my back to the dance, unfolded Wron's note.

Face Evland and find the moon; below it you'll see a garden shed. —W. I folded up the note and slid it inside the palm of my white glove.

"Now that you are no longer dancing with a future king . . ." I heard Cragdon's voice behind me and turned to see him flash a tipsy smile. "May I have the next dance?"

"I'm sorry"—I bit my lower lip—"but I again have commitments."

"I will wait for an opening." To my relief, he wandered off into the crowd.

I faced Evland. Was meeting Wron wise? My heart told me that I had no other choice but to meet him and tell him who I really was. Guided by moonlight, I followed the winding garden path to a rustic shed. Through ivy-covered windows, I saw the light of a flickering candle. I pulled the rough-hewn door open and slipped inside. Long-handled implements leaned in one corner.

"I am here," Wron said. From a tucked-away corner, his hands reached out to take mine, and then I stepped into his embrace.

Though I giggled, I felt strangely calm.

"We are playing with fire." At the moment his conscience was playing more havoc than mine.

"I have to tell you that even though I have come to care deeply for you, Dory, I will marry Alia. It would be wrong to let you think any other way."

I looked from his dark, light-filled eyes to our hands. I was the one being dishonest. "There is something I need to tell you, also."

"Not now . . . everything is too quiet. We can't stay here too long." His eyes sparkled with marvelous light, and then my betrothed leaned forward and kissed me for the first time.

Images of Shepherd's Field filled my memory. Multiple shades of vibrant and muted green wove a tapestry. Birds sang sweetly. The sky was that ethereal blue. In a daze, I stepped away only to be pulled back to him.

"You will have to leave, Dory. After I'm married, maybe before, you will have to leave."

I shook my head. "I have much to tell you, tonight." Resting my hands about his neck, I smiled up at him.

The door creaked open. King Walter stepped inside, followed by Roger. I remained in Wron's arms. The time had come.

"Wron, I'm sorry; your mother and I were afraid this might happen." Walter's soft jowls shook as he spoke. "We've arranged for Ivan to accompany Needa and Dory to Evland. While you're there"—he looked at me—"I'd like you to pick a piece of land that you love. We have long held a promise to Blue Sky that Princess Alia will marry our only son. It is a profitable and preferred merger for both countries. It is a promise I do not want broken, no matter how much my son may be in love with you."

"I have a remedy, Your Highness." I smiled, beaming with happiness.

Wron withdrew my hands from around his neck, and, with dull eyes, he looked away. His actions clouded my thinking.

"Young lady, it is you that created this mess. Roger, take her. I want them out of here tonight, before—"

"I need one minute of your time." I held up my index finger. "Well, maybe two."

With a deep sigh of remorse, Walter shook his head. "Cover her mouth, if you must."

The moment had come.

"I am . . ." I said, looking at Walter, "my father's daughter . . ." At the same time, Roger waved something beneath my nose, and all the while, Wron just stared at me as if it were all a terrible dream and he was just waiting to wake up.

Whatever Roger waved smelled strong and odd. *Not like garlic* were my last thoughts before I sank into his arms.

Chapter Twenty-Five

The rattle of wooden wheels bouncing over a rutted road woke me. I was traveling alone in an old carriage drawn by two common mares. Moonlight streamed through the open windows. The countryside was cast in muted grays, and the knit blanket covering my lap was lavender.

Wherever I was going, I need not doubt that Queen Eunice would miss me.

Overhead, I focused on the moon. A full moon often proved to be a fool's moon. It was the moon that had gotten me into trouble. Tears slid down my cheeks as I recalled the Summer Ball and my moonlit walk to the garden shed.

A sniffle escaped me.

"Don't cry, Dory." Across the aisle, Needa climbed out of a sloppily packed handbag. "We're going to Evland. What they think is punishment is really a reward. You want letters, and I want a husband."

The carriage bounced, and Needa's cap slid down over her face. She righted it on her head, looking at me.

"My heart is broken, Needa."

"I don't know what you were thinking—falling in love with Prince Wron." She rolled her eyes. "Now the king is worried that Prince Wron will want to marry you and not the princess. They say you are the best of counterfeits."

"They said that?" I laughed sadly.

"Yes. King Walter said, 'Hers was the best of plans.'" Needa bounced three inches into the air before grabbing the handbag. "They hope to keep us in Evland for ten days or at least until Princess Alia arrives."

"They truly think I'm a counterfeit princess?" I could not help but smile at the irony.

"Queen Eunice said your scheme is brilliant. Now King Walter is afraid that the true princess is wandering the hills. And Prince Wron probably believes every word you ever said."

I gazed blindly at the moon, full and all-seeing.

Several hours later, I awoke to a faint blue sky. The carriage had stopped. Deep in the handbag, Needa had wrapped herself in one of my skirts. A guard, dressed as a farmer, appeared in the open window. He handed me slices of Rhoda's strudel. I set one aside for Needa. The guard remained right outside our window, and together we ate the strudel in silence. He was completely bald on top. Tight white ringlets grew under his earlobes and around the base of his head.

"Thank you," I said.

He nodded before he climbed up into the driver's seat, and the carriage was again in motion.

"Ivan is mute." Needa's green cap slowly emerged from the handbag followed by the round-cheeked, yawning gnome. "He's never been one to gossip. That's why he was assigned to you, well, to us. King Walter wants very little gossip. He wants Yonder to back the coming wedding. An unhappy royal marriage makes for an unhappy Yonder."

"Did Rhoda say that?"

"Yes; she will miss us." Needa reached for the strudel. "When Ivan carried you down to the carriage, Rhoda cried into her apron."

"Where was Prince Wron?" I turned toward the window, hoping to hide my tears.

"I don't know. I don't think he left the garden shed."

ΦΦΦ

Wron lit the candles for the dinner table. The piano in the alcove was a constant reminder of Dory's absence. How quickly they'd all become accustomed to her pleasantries and the richness her music had brought to their home.

Rhoda served from the left instead of the right. "It's too quiet, here," she said. "Even though I banged the kettles extra loud, it is still too quiet." She ground black pepper over Wron's tossed salad and didn't notice when he waved his hand for her to stop.

"Enough, Rhoda, thank you."

"I even miss the sound of Needa sitting on her seesaw cutter. I miss Dory's piano music and her stories of Blue Sky."

"Enough, Rhoda," his father said. "They haven't even been gone twenty-four hours, and you are going on and on."

"Blue Sky?" Wron dabbed at the corner of his mouth with the linen serviette. "What stories?"

"Many stories. Her stories of Princess Alia's sixteenth birthday party, riding the rolling hills, never being allowed to help in the kitchen because of her gifted hands."

"I should have had Dory share more of her stories." Eunice sighed. "I do not know how I will survive for ten days without her."

"You will, Eunice. You will go on just as you did before the piano girl," his father said.

"The air was so empty back then."

"We'll call in some other musicians in her absence." His father patted her hand.

"What a lovely idea, Walter."

"And what do you miss about her, Wron?" his mother asked.

"Me?" he asked, clearing his throat.

His mother took a heaping bite of peas and nodded.

"Everything." He sighed unhappily. "I will miss her presence."

ΦΦΦ

During breakfast the next morning, a young man wearing pointed slippers played the flute. He flitted about the dining room as he played. The music was very disturbing. Wron glanced over at the empty piano bench and recalled the way Dory's music entranced the mind. He wanted to find the flyswatter and swat the flute player.

Rhoda carried a tray to the table, a forlorn look on her large, round face.

"Eight more days, Rhoda, and they'll be back." Wron tried to encourage her.

"Twenty-four meals, Prince Wron." She set the creamer and spoons on the table. "I miss Needa, but I worry about Dory. Will she return?"

"I do not know." He looked to his father, who was hidden behind the weekly paper. "Father told her to pick out a piece of land that she loves. I suppose there's a possibility that only Needa will return."

"You didn't tell me that, Walter!" his mother said.

His father lowered the paper. "I was upset. If the two of them can get along without moonlight in their eyes, the piano girl can stay. Otherwise, yes, she will be sent to Evland for good."

Wron looked toward the piano and sighed. Maybe Evland was best.

ΦΦΦ

At dinner, a young maiden with jet-black hair sat near the fireplace and strummed a painted guitar. Her voice was lovely, but her lyrics were dark reflections of her broken heart. "He's never coming back. He's gone for good. He gave me his love. He gave me his word."

After enduring the dismal song, Wron cleared his throat. "Do you know any happier tunes, fair maiden?"

She nodded. "If I only had a horse, I would have followed him, of course. Over the hills, I would have followed him into the setting sun. But I had none. Now he's gone. Oh! Never love a knight. He only wants to fight. He'll take off in the night and leave your love. Never love a knight."

"Only twenty-two more meals," his father whispered.

The maiden's music put Wron in a sour mood.

He strode onto the terrace and stared at the distant blue hills. Was Dory thinking about him? How he longed to ride after her and find her. But his bride was due any moment. He stilled his mind and tried to think about something, anything, besides Dory. *Perhaps I speak too much from my own heart.* He recalled her sweet confession and knew that eight more days would feel like a lifetime.

ΦΦΦ

During breakfast, Wron's mother hummed the maiden's tune to "Never Love a Knight".

"Tell me, Mother, that we are to enjoy a meal without music," he said, hopeful.

"The harpist is running late."

They were halfway through Rhoda's Giant Cakes when the harpist arrived. Her husband was sick and could not care for the baby. The harpist held the baby in one arm while she played the harp with the other. Though the music was lovely, half the melody was missing.

Wron stared toward the alcove and remembered Dory seated at the piano. With an ache in his chest, he recalled the time that she'd glanced over her shoulder at him while she'd played.

"Wron, not now," his mother hushed. "The harpist is not playing that song."

Unknowingly, he'd been humming the tune to "Waiting."

"Twenty-one more meals," his father said from behind the newspaper.

Chapter Twenty-Six

We reached Evland in two days, not three. Ivan slowed the carriage to a stop in front of a large, hand-carved sign that read: "Evland. Population ~~1,001~~, 281." Ivan climbed down from the driver's seat to prepare lunch.

There is much healing needed in your future kingdom. I recalled Felix's sentiments as I looked around at the scrub and homes that had been burned to the ground.

Needa hopped out of the handbag, and I lifted her up so she could sit in the window for a better view.

"I will find the letters first, and then we will husband hunt," I told her.

"No, Dory." She glanced over at me. "It is the other way around."

"No, I know where the letters are."

"I know where the gnomes are."

Outside our carriage window, Ivan took a dixel from his pocket and showed it to both of us. One side of the coin portrayed King Walter's profile, the other side, Queen Eunice's.

"I call King." Needa crossed her fingers and briefly shook her fists toward heaven.

"Queen." I breathed deeply.

Ivan tossed the coin up into the air, caught it, and slapped it onto the back of his hand. He smiled and showed me Queen Eunice's regal profile.

Needa grumbled for the next hour while I explained the location of the letters to Ivan. "Felix said that his old cottage is six large stones, or blocks, north of the village of Kaye."

"Why do you call your father by his first name?" Needa asked.

I caught my breath. "It is a Blue Sky custom." I slid three fingers out against my knee as I kept track.

After miles of rolling scrub, we entered a small village. Half of the homes lay in ruins, yet small white rock cottages with shutters lined the far end of town. Apron-clad women stood in the doorways of their homes, while small children clutched at their skirts. I waved and recalled Felix's stories of a happier Evland.

Ivan stopped the carriage. I leaned out of the carriage window to see him. He held up six fingers and pointed to a large rock.

"After six rocks, there are three oak trees. They are not close together," I said.

Within one hundred yards, I counted two oaks. Then we traveled for half a mile before counting a third oak tree. Ivan slowed the carriage to point to it.

"We are close now." I opened the carriage door and leaped to the ground. "There will be a white stone cottage." I scanned a rolling meadow. No cottage was in sight.

"It was probably destroyed in the war," Needa said from the carriage. "The rocks were probably used for ammunition."

"I will walk the land and look for white stones. Ivan, please stay here and guard the carriage."

The kind guard nodded.

Without the white cottage to guide me, I didn't know in which direction to walk. "Think. Think clearly." I looked about me.

"I will help you find it," Needa bellowed from the carriage.

I returned to the carriage and placed the wee gnome on my shoulder. "The letters mean more to me than I've explained."

"I know." She ran her small hand reassuringly across the back of my neck. "We will look for white rock."

The grass was tall and the ground rutted. Off in the distance, the land sloped down to a river, which careened through golden hills. As far as the eye could see, there were no neighbors, and to my dismay, neither was there a white stone cottage, though I felt certain we had found the property.

"White rock." Needa pointed off to the right. Fifty paces away lay three rocks. I stopped near the teapot-sized rocks and surveyed the land. The site was as Felix had described, with its view of the river valley.

"West of the cottage, there will be a hillock." I saw a small knoll and counted twenty steps. I now felt certain that the rocks were the old homestead.

For many years, the land had lain undisturbed. Ferns and moss covered the hillside. Large rocks jutted out of the slope. I set Needa on the limb of a nearby plum tree, then gripped the nearest rock and rolled it downhill. I knelt down to examine the ground. It was just dirt. I rolled over three more rocks.

"You don't know which one, do you?" she yelled.

"No." I rested my hands on my hips.

"The large rock looks interesting to me."

A large boulder lay nestled into the hillside. Needa was right; it did look interesting. It also looked heavy.

Rocking it from side to side, I loosened it from the earth, and then I placed my feet behind and rolled it downhill. I knelt in front of the hole and looked inside. There was a tunnel in the dirt, much like a small animal would make. Reaching deep inside, I closed my hand around a metal cylinder. After pulling it out, I stared at Felix's most treasured possession.

"Why did he not take it with him?" Needa asked.

"They planned to return here someday, but neither were able." My voice cracked.

"I'm sorry, Dory."

"I will read it tonight. We will find your husband now, Needa."

ΦΦΦ

In the carriage, Needa returned to my shoulder. "Ivan, do you know Swallow's Glen?" she asked.

Standing outside the window, Ivan shook his head.

"There is a small stream and a red barn. In the curve of the valley, there is a grove of oak trees."

He nodded.

Needa clapped and then clutched at my hair to stay seated.

"When a gnome is born, an acorn is planted. If I can find my birthday tree, I will find other gnomes." Needa clutched at my hair.

I stared sadly out the window and recalled Walter's words, "Find a piece of land that you love." If it came to that, I would pick Felix's old homestead. The land tugged at my heart.

We stopped at a small stream. I set Needa on top of a log. Holding Ivan's gun, I waited, and as in mealtimes past, a bird flew into sight. I pulled the trigger, and a pheasant fell to the ground.

"No wonder Prince Wron wants to take you hunting." Needa clapped.

My heart leaped. "Did he tell you that?"

"He told his mother. He also talked of your sourdough."

"I wish I had the sourdough starter. Rhoda did not think to pack it." But of course, our trip had been very short notice for her.

While I cleaned the bird, I longed for nightfall when I would read Felix's letters by the fire.

"I will bathe in the stream and change into clean clothes. If we find my birthday tree, I will meet my husband tonight." Needa flipped a blonde braid over her shoulder.

I carried her to the stream and washed my hands. While she bathed, I thought of all the possible predators that a six-inch little gnome might have. Needa changed into a lovely, cream-colored dress, and then she topped it off with her green cap.

"For your wedding, we should braid a crown of flowers in your hair," I said.

"No." She shook her head. "A girl gnome wears a green cap until she is married. Then I will wear a brown one."

We returned to the carriage. Needa sighed anxiously. "It is rare that the woman finds the man. Usually it is the male gnome who goes searching for his bride. To find a gnome that is not one's kin can be difficult."

After several miles of traversing over a bumpy dirt road, Ivan found the red barn. Needa stood on my shoulders and scanned the countryside for a grove of oak trees.

"Set me on the ground! No, I am not thinking; carry me to that tree." Needa pointed to an oak that stood amongst many others. I held her on my shoulder while I hiked through knee-high grass toward the canopy of the gnarled oak.

"Not this oak, that oak." Needa pointed to another nearby tree. Leaves crunched underfoot. "Yes, I think it is. Yes, I'm almost positive. Set me down."

In her wedding gown, Needa sprinted to the trunk. She stumbled over a twig and somersaulted. From her seated position, she righted her cap and stared ahead at the runic markings scratched into the side of the trunk.

"This is my birthday tree!" Needa rose to her feet, stretched her arms wide and hugged an expanse of the trunk. "I was eighty-nine when I was captured. Eleven years ago. Get the letters and read here, Dory. Tonight, you will attend my wedding under this tree." She held on to her green cap, and disappeared down a rabbit-sized hole.

I returned to the horses and informed Ivan that Needa had found her birth tree. He smiled and pointed to our gear, indicating that he'd set up camp.

"I will read." I pointed to Needa's tree.

I returned to the oak, shook out the blanket, and sat with my back against the trunk. Before I opened the cylinder, I look heavenward through the tree's gnarled limbs and dark green foliage.

"Thank you, God. Help Needa to find a good husband. Amen."

The writings were in French, my second language. I'd argued with my mother when I was young that I would never have a practical use for French, and now I was grateful for her insistence. As one often does with a second language, I translated the words into English in my mind.

My sweet Claire,

I mourn that I was not there to comfort you in the loss of our child and to hold you both in my arms during the final hours before she died. Though our suffering is great, we will persevere. God willing, we will have another child.

I love you.

Felix

I stared into the branches. Perhaps the letters were too personal for me to read. Too painful. Why had he never told me that he'd lost a daughter? I wiped the tears from my cheeks.

Night had fallen, and with it the day's warmth. I wrapped the blanket round about me. The stars twinkled through the leaves like a million diamonds.

Needa emerged from the rabbit hole, holding the hand of a gnome-sized man. "Dory! Dory! Meet Lehto." The gnome beside her wore a pointed red cap and a long, brown beard.

"Lehto Cauvern." He bowed.

"Cauvern!" Needa frowned, crossing her arms. "I'm your cousin, Needa Tikka." With a lift of her skirt, Needa disappeared into the rabbit hole, a heartbroken Lehto following close behind.

It grew late, and I fell asleep waiting for Needa to return.

Finally, she emerged from the rabbit hole and sat sidesaddle upon my knee. She bobbed a bit to further wake me. I stretched and yawned. Needa waited for my yawn to end and watched me blink until my foggy eyes cleared.

"Do you approve of Lehto?" she asked.

Groggy, I nodded. "He seemed taken with you."

"I am related to everyone here. If they are not my cousin, they are my uncle or brother. There are two eligible cousins, but one will not leave the glen. Lehto said he will follow me to the ends of the earth."

"And what do *you* think about Lehto?" I picked Needa up in my hand to study my wee friend's face.

"He is a gnome"—she held out both hands—"and he is my size."

ΦΦΦ

At midnight under Needa's birthday tree, in front of their family and their friends, Needa and Lehto pledged their eternal love for one another. For the next few days, they honeymooned while Ivan and I stayed in the glen.

After the third day, Ivan pointed to the horses and to his wrist to remind me of the time.

"Yes, Ivan, I agree, it's time to leave."

Needa bawled and Lehto held her as they waved good-bye to loved ones they most likely would never see again.

Across the carriage from me, on top of the handbag, Lehto sat with his arm around Needa. "You will love our little home in the kitchen," Needa said.

"In the kitchen?" Lehto laughed and slapped the patched knee of his trousers. "I will make a new home for us in the root of a tree, where forest gnomes ought to live."

"Once you see our little place, you will change your mind, Lehto." Needa crossed her arms. "And if you don't, I will change it for you."

"We will live in the trunk of a tree," Lehto said firmly.

"I live in a castle within a castle. I will not trade that for a tree!"

"You knew when you married me that I was a forest gnome!"

Their arguing grew louder. I rose and reached my hand out the window and tugged on the back of Ivan's coat. Slowing the horses, he glanced over his shoulder at me.

"They're fighting." I picked Lehto up by the back of his collar and handed him to Ivan. "Absence makes the heart grow fonder," I said.

I looked across the carriage at Needa. "Perhaps your courtship was a bit rushed."

Needa wiped her tears on the sleeve of one of my shirts before crawling deeper inside my handbag. "He wants to live under a tree, and he hasn't even seen my little place."

"Give him time."

Ivan drove well past noon. He was finally forced to stop when the wooden wheel on the carriage made its last turn. It hit a rock just right and turned into a triangle. I tucked Needa into my pocket and stepped out of the carriage.

While Ivan studied the wheel, a ruffed grouse flew out of the brush and took flight. I picked up Ivan's shotgun off of the carriage seat and proceeded to load it. I tapped him on the shoulder. "I will shoot us something for lunch."

"Wait!" a small, muffled voice yelled. Lehto poked his head out of Ivan's coat pocket. "Where's Needa?"

"Tell him," Needa said from within my pocket, "that I feel hurt. He hasn't even seen my beautiful little place."

"Did you hear that, Lehto?" I asked.

He scrunched up his long, pointed nose. "Tell her—"

Ivan pushed the gnome deep into his pocket, crushing his red hat. Using his hands, Ivan motioned that he would release the carriage from the horses. He pointed to himself and then to me, and then he pointed to the horses.

"We will ride home without the carriage?" I asked.

Ivan nodded.

In the curve of the dirt road up ahead, one man walked, while two men rode on horseback behind him. I set the gun on the carriage seat and tossed my hair over my shoulder as I bent down to help Ivan unlatch the carriage hitch. As the men drew nearer, I sensed that one of them was watching me.

I glanced over my shoulder. The man on foot stared at me with narrowed eyes in a gaunt face. "Swamp Woman," he mumbled under his breath.

With angst in my heart, I recognized the uncle of the counterfeit princess. They were the gypsies that King Walter had banished to the mountains. One-one-thousand, two-one-thousand, three-one-thousand. Surely, they had passed. I glanced over my shoulder.

The counterfeit uncle stood in the middle of the road, pointing his gun in our direction. Two shots exploded above our heads, and then both of our horses fell in anguish to the ground. While the madman reloaded his double-barreled gun, his companions rode off. I grabbed the shotgun off the carriage seat.

"You get to walk home like we did." He sneered, pointing his gun at me. Near my hip, I cocked Ivan's gun. Before I had time to lift the barrel, he pulled the trigger. A searing pain struck me below my collarbone, and I was driven backward to the ground.

Little white fluffy clouds dotted the sky. I rolled my chin toward my chest. The madman's gun was now pointed at Ivan.

Though Ivan's gun lay in my hand, I could no longer lift my arm.

Needa slipped out of my coat pocket.

The madman tried to pull the trigger, but the gun jammed. He cocked the gun again. Needa scurried down my leg and lifted the barrel of Ivan's gun onto my knee.

"Bend your knee," she yelled back at me. Wrapping her body around the barrel, Needa clutched the fabric of my skirt. The crosshair was aligned perfectly on the uncle. Deadening my mind to the pain, I pulled the trigger.

Shot in the center of his chest, he fell backward. The shot echoed through the pastoral countryside. Limbs sprawled and lifeless, the man lay in the center of the road.

"Needa!" Lehto climbed down the side of Ivan's pants before dropping to the ground. They scrambled to one another and sobbed in each other's arms.

I propped myself on my left elbow and stared down the road toward Yonder. Blood trickled down my white shirt.

No one knew. No one knew that I, Dory, the piano girl, was their future queen.

I'd die here and be given a peasant's burial, and no one would ever know.

ΦΦΦ

Ivan knelt down and picked me up. He carried me through the brush and up the hillside toward what appeared to be a rock ledge. It was a cave. He tucked me up inside. If it rained, I would not get wet.

"Ivan, in case I die, there's something I must tell you." I searched his sweat-beaded face.

He shook his head.

"I am Princess Alia. I am your future queen." A tear slid out the corner of my eye and dribbled into my ear.

Wide-eyed, he shook his head again. As he hurried down the slope, he picked up Lehto, and then the large man crashed through the brush. Yonder was at least a day and a half by horse, perhaps three days by foot. I might die by the time they reached home.

Needa climbed a nearby alder tree and, scooting out on a spindly branch, landed herself beside me on the ledge. She sat in the folds of my skirt and wept into her hands. The reality that I could die before I married Wron and sealed my country's fate added to my suffering.

"Can you read French?" I whispered.

"No," Needa said.

"Tell me about Lehto and how much you love him." I closed my eyes to the pain that ripped through my right shoulder.

Needa climbed up my other shoulder and sniffled as she smoothed my hair away from my sweat-tinged face. "He is kind. I will let him build a home beneath a tree, if he must. It is the male gnome who presents the female gnome with a home. He had a lovely little home back in Swallow's Glen. It was so tidy and cheerful."

Propped up against the hard rock, I stared at the road below. It began to rain.

Needa plucked a leaf off the nearby alder tree and caught rainwater in its folds. She returned up my good shoulder and poured the water into my mouth, and then she laid the wet leaf on my forehead.

"You have a fever, Dory." Again she caught rainwater with the leaf and poured it into my mouth. Sometime later, Needa lay in the folds of my skirt and slept.

Chapter Twenty-Seven

Before dessert, King Ulrich read the front page of *Yonder Times*. Rhoda plunked a plate of blueberry kuchen between him and the paper.

"It's been a while since you've made your peach pie."

"I will soon make peach pie when Prince Wron marries," Rhoda said. "Oh, that reminds me, we're having problems with Knot."

Walter lowered the paper to look at her. "Knot?"

"Yes, he loves my peach pie," she said, and then, remembering her place, bit her lower lip. "Yesterday Knot threw his dinner plate across the cell and demanded to see Prince Wron or you."

"Why did you not tell me?"

"I walked up the stairs, saw the pile of dishes, and immediately forgot." She grimaced.

"I'll go speak with him." Walter carefully folded the paper. He'd only recently been thinking about granting his old friend his freedom. He missed him.

As he approached Knot's cell, his breath caught in his throat. For decades, Knot had worn a fine uniform, and now his bony shoulders protruded through filthy rags.

"Are you well, Knot?" Walter asked.

"Surviving." Knot's wild hair plumed several inches away from his gaunt face. "You, Walter, have put on weight."

Walter nodded. Even his shoes felt tight.

"Where is Dory? She hasn't visited for over a week."

"She left for Evland to help Needa find a husband. Is something—"

"Why wasn't I told?" Knot gripped the bars.

"The servants were ordered not to speak about it." Walter rocked back and forth. "Rhoda said you wanted to see me."

With his hands behind his head, Knot paced back and forth across his cell. "Those counterfeits you imprisoned last week were from Evland. The gypsies."

A large knot cinched in Walter's chest.

"One of the men was deranged. He was determined to have revenge, not so much on you, but on the Swamp Woman."

"Are you positive they're from Evland?" Walter asked.

"Yes. He was in Dory's old cell." Knot nodded across the corridor. "I'm absolutely positive. How long will it take for the vagabonds to walk out of the mountains?"

"If they are lucky, a week on foot. Give or take a day."

"And when will Dory return?"

"We expect them to return in two, three days."

"Their paths may cross."

Walter breathed uneasily. "Thank you, Knot. You will receive three extra-large meals each day for the duration of your stay. And I want you to start doing push-ups."

Knot's smile filled half of his lean face. "When you have time, bring a hot cup of coffee, and I'll tell you more about the girl."

Walter waved before he hurried toward the stairs.

"Walter, it's very important that you find her. Very."

ΦΦΦ

Prince Wron stood amongst his men. *What is going on?* His father stood atop a whiskey barrel in the midst of a battalion of fifty men and beckoned for silence.

"An unexpected crisis has been brought to my attention. You are to ride through the night toward Evland. You are not to stop or sleep. Once you find Ivan, Dory, and our gnome, Needa, then you may set up camp and rest."

His father paused and found Wron's face amongst the crowd. "I have just been informed that the gypsies whom we abandoned in the mountains are from Evland. One of the gypsies is very intent on revenge, not in regards to me, but toward Dory. She is from Blue Sky and informed us that the gypsies were counterfeits."

No. Wron closed his eyes. "Dear God, keep her safe. Keep Dory safe."

Soldiers talked amongst themselves before his father continued. "I pray that their paths have not and will not cross. I pray that all of you will return safely to us. Now, leave together at once."

As Wron rode, he realized that if Dory was harmed, it was his fault. They had involved her in identifying the counterfeits. The gypsies should have received a harsher punishment, but there were women involved. Women always received a lighter penalty. He cringed. They should have taken Dory aside and asked her opinion in private. She'd become the target of the gypsies blame.

The armed battalion rode hard into the wee hours of the morning. The men were hungry and tired, but Wron commanded them to push on. Midmorning, they dismounted for a short break. They stretched and ate sliced ham on Rhoda's buttered bread.

Wron had one foot in his stirrup, about to remount, when he saw movement up ahead in the distance. An apparently exhausted man was running more with his shoulders than with his feet. The height and breadth of the man resembled Ivan. Wron mounted his horse and rode toward him.

Ivan stopped and panted with his hands to his knees. Wron slid off his horse and stared into the exhausted man's eyes. Time ticked slowly by as he waited for Ivan to motion, to point behind himself, to mumble. Instead, Ivan pulled a gnome out of his hip pocket. The little man had brown hair, a brown beard, a wide belt cinched around his middle, and a red pointed hat.

"Are you Prince Wron?" the gnome asked.

Dry mouthed, Wron nodded.

"I'm Lehto, Needa's husband. They're back there." Lehto pointed in the direction from which they'd run. "Ten, twenty miles. A man shot our horses, and then he shot the woman, Dory. He went to shoot Ivan; but before he could, my Needa raised Dory's gun and Dory pulled the trigger."

"She's alive?" Wron whispered.

Lehto set a hand over his heart. "I don't know."

Wron rallied his men. He got Ivan on another horse to lead the way. Wron rode in shock. Dory's trip to Evland had turned into a nightmare. It was his fault. Somehow, he should have prevented her exile, prevented their separation. *Please, God, let her live.* After many miles, the battle scene came into view. A man lay dead in the middle of the road. Flies buzzed around the horses. Ivan slid off his horse and waved for Wron to follow.

Wron gave orders to his men. "Four of you keep watch while the others set up camp. Prepare a meal and rest." He followed Ivan through the brush and up a rocky embankment. *Is she alive? God, let her be alive!*

Ivan stayed behind as Wron climbed the last ledge. Dory lay asleep with her head propped against the cave wall. Her pale face was moist with sweat. Her shirt was soaked with blood. He gripped her wrist and found a weak pulse. She was alive, for now.

Needa unrolled herself from Dory's skirts, hugged his arm, and began to weep.

"Did the bullet pass through?" he asked.

Needa shook her head.

He turned to Ivan. "Lehto . . ." He waited for the red-capped man to emerge from Ivan's pocket. "Tell my men that we need to get the bullet out."

He took Dory's hand to see if she would awaken. Her eyes opened, and she stared at him with dark, dull eyes. A faint smile ebbed at the corners of her mouth. "You're here."

He nodded, too emotional to speak. "Knot knew you were in trouble."

"An angel," she whispered, closing her eyes.

Did she mean Knot was an angel or . . . He brushed her hair away from her clammy face.

"She saw an angel," Needa whispered. "I can't see him."

Either she was delusional or she was near death.

ΦΦΦ

Roger joined them. He'd sanitized his medical tools in the fire and returned them to his bag.

"Dory." Wron studied her dark eyes. "Roger's going to get the bullet out. It will be painful." He turned to his guard. "Do we have whiskey?"

Roger shook his head. "Brandy."

Wron held the flask to Dory's lips. She didn't like it and turned away. "You must," he said firmly, and was both surprised and concerned when she obeyed.

"What can I do?" Needa held on to the neck of Wron's shirt.

"Pray," Roger said. "Prince Wron, hold down her arms. Needa, pray."

Clutching the back of Wron's shirt, Needa peered over his shoulder. He gripped Dory's shoulders to keep her from thrashing while Roger worked with precision. Dory moaned. Her eyes looked like dark agates as she stared at the rock overhang. The horrific pain of extracting the bullet put her into shock. Finally, she stopped moaning.

"Help her, Lord Jesus. Ease her pain," Needa prayed. "Watch over her, Lord Jesus."

"Thank you, Roger. Take Needa to her husband, and ask the men to pray."

"Owh!" The gnome howled as Roger lifted her by the back of her clothing, placing her on his shoulder.

"Hold on and keep praying, Needa," Roger said. "I'll have one of the men bring up blankets."

Alone with Dory, Wron looked at her pale face. Her skin was now cool to the touch. A guard raced up the hillside, Cragdon delivering a blanket. The fair-haired guard hid no emotion while he stared at Dory.

"May I stay here with you?" he asked Wron.

"No." Wron tried to calm the fire in his belly. "She needs to rest."

"And so do you. Come down and have a meal with the men."

"I will rest here, Cragdon. Leave us."

The young guard's face paled. "I'm sorry, I did not realize." Cragdon ambled down the shale hillside.

Wron took Dory's slim hand in his. "You cannot leave me. I command you, Dory, you cannot leave me."

"If I die . . ." He could barely hear her whisper. "Father..."

"Don't talk like that, Dory." He swallowed. She couldn't, couldn't think like that.

Her eyelashes fluttered against her cheeks as she returned to sleep. Hours later, her voice woke him. "Do you see him?"

Wron looked about the cave. At the far end it was tall enough to stand in. He saw nothing. "No, Dory."

"Why isn't it Felix?" She stared up at Wron with dark eyes.

He felt her forehead and wondered if it was indeed an angel to take her home. Eyes closed, she returned to sleep. Her left hand relaxed, exposing a scrap of paper. He carefully slid it from her palm and unfolded it.

Face Evland and find the moon; below it you'll see a garden shed. —W.

Placing his cheek against her forehead, he wept.

ΦΦΦ

Ivan brought Needa and Wron a sandwich. While he ate, the gnome sat on his shoulder.

"Roger said that if she makes it through the night, she will live," Needa said and patted his neck.

Wron nodded.

"He said we should tell her what is on our hearts in case she doesn't." One of Needa's tears slid down the open collar of his shirt onto his skin.

"When she wakes, you will go first," he said. "Then you will visit Lehto and I will be alone with her."

Needa nodded.

Dory awoke with dark, sunken eyes in a pale face and stared into Needa's round blue ones. Needa stood in Wron's steady hand. "There is much to live for, Dory. Lehto and I will have children, and I will name our first girl . . . Dory, after you." Needa's eyes glossed with tears. "Because of you, I returned home to Evland."

Dory's eyelids fluttered before she returned to sleep.

"I did not get to say what I need to say!" Needa squished her fists into her eyes and sobbed.

"You can try again later. Visit Lehto."

Ivan brought dinner—dried venison jerky, bread, and an apple. Wron ate. He smoothed Dory's hair away from her face; her color was now ashen. She was dying in his arms, and he had not said what he needed to say. He kissed her forehead, and her eyes slowly opened. Usually a warm hazel, her dark eyes urged his words.

"You do not want to live." He wanted to whisper the contents of his heart, but his future was not his own. "But, I do. My life is better with you in it. Even if we are not to be, my life is better . . ." Holding her, he finally slept.

He awoke to a small bird, which twittered from the branches of the nearby alder tree. Dory stirred slightly to look at the bird and then into his eyes. A soft pink tinged her cheeks.

"Are you in pain?" he asked.

She nodded. "I fear that I will live."

"You will have a good, full life, Dory."

"I may have to learn to shoot left-handed."

"Perhaps." He nodded. "I'm sorry, Dory . . . for everything. I'm sorry I wasn't here to protect you."

ΦΦΦ

Without any guards to attend him, Walter felt like the impish boy of his youth as he ambled down the dimly lit passageways to the prison. He carried a tray with a teapot full of coffee, two mugs, and a plate of Rhoda's buttermilk cookies. Knot had always had a sweet tooth.

When he reached the cavernous pit, the cells were empty. The treadmill was in motion. Walter set the tray upon the cot in Knot's cell and, feeling a tad lonely in the dreary surroundings, ambled across the prison toward the treadmill stairwell.

Four men walked the treadmill in unison. He could not see their faces, but their legs were lean, and their clothes were tattered and soiled.

Noting his presence, Duron yelled at the men to stop. Above the roar of the river, the treadmill came to a slow stop. One by one, the haggard men shuffled off.

He recalled Dory's words: *Your present countrymen.*

"What is it, Walter?" Knot asked as he neared him on the stairs.

"I brought us coffee. Thought we'd finally have that talk." They walked together toward Knot's cell. Walter left Knot's door open behind them and glanced over his shoulder at Duron. "Give us some privacy. Knot and I have some catching up to do."

Duron nodded and rolled the long key around his wrist as he stepped away.

"Took you long enough," Knot said.

"What?" Walter grinned as Knot poured coffee.

"You forgot sugar, but I can drink it this way. I said it took you long enough. It's been three meals since we spoke. I thought that I whetted your curiosity enough that you'd return as soon as you could."

"My memory is not as sharp as it used to be." Walter sighed. It felt good to finally share it with someone. "Eunice is weepy. Rhoda is understaffed, and Wron is away."

"You've come here for empathy, not information."

"Both. We need to find someone to help Rhoda in the kitchen."

"Power is a difficult position," Knot said. "You want to employ only those whom you trust, but you find you often cannot trust anyone you employ."

"I trusted you . . . for many years."

"Yes, and I find I still cannot apologize for betraying your trust."

"Because you were right," Walter said. "Had I listened to you, the war would have been shorter. Lives would have been spared."

"Thank you. Your apology has almost made the last three years in this hole worthwhile."

"I would not consider what I said an apology."

"It was, Walter. The only words you left out were *I'm sorry.*"

"Well, I am, Knot; I want you to know that."

"I'm glad to hear it. Now, before we waste any more time, I want to share a theory I've developed." Knot munched thoughtfully on a cookie. "Dory's father did not die in the Giants' Snare before Shepherd's Field."

"What are you saying? Have you seen him?" Walter's brows gathered.

"No." Knot shook his head. "What I'm saying is the man she was with was not her father."

Knot's theories often made his brain hurt.

"I have Dory's stories mapped out on the wall behind me. Raised in Blue Sky. Knows French. Very accomplished. Gifted pianist. Everything's going along smoothly until her father is killed in the Giants' Snare three weeks before Alia's presumed arrival."

"Yes, it all makes perfect sense to me," Walter said. "You see, Dory and her father traveled ahead of the wedding party, because Dory's father wanted to visit Evland—his homeland—before the wedding. You see... she was Blue Sky's royal pianist, and she is to play at the wedding. And, let me tell you, the piano girl is very good."

"Yes, Walter, but you are missing one important insight." Knot dunked the last cookie into his cup of coffee and took a bite. "Being a royal pianist does not make you royalty."

Walter scrunched his forehead and thought about this.

"Everything about Dory is royalty," Knot said. "Even when she had the pox. Dory, you see, is a *counterfeit commoner*."

"I knew the girl was a counterfeit." Walter shook his head. "I knew she was not to be trusted. From the start her story was . . . pianist from Blue Sky arriving three weeks before the wedding, and she looked so much like . . . oh, what is her mother's name?"

"I am convinced that Dory's true father is King Francis, and whoever the man was that she traveled with from Blue Sky was not her father, but a bodyguard," Knot said. "Walter, they traveled as commoners."

"Why?" Walter shook his head.

"The girl will unite two powerful kingdoms. People always fear the unknown. Due to the war, little has been done for peace and restoration. Your people are restless. They want change, and little has been implemented. One of the best things Francis could have done was let his daughter see it firsthand. Not from a carriage."

"But the danger." Walter shook his head.

"How can royalty understand the challenges facing their country when they're cooped up in a castle?"

"Wron listened too much to you as a child."

"Did he?" Knot grinned.

Walter sighed and clapped his hands to his knees. "To think Francis knowingly put his daughter through such a journey."

"It's Francis," Knot whispered.

"I know." Walter patted his knees and rose to his feet. "The infant had a mark, you know?"

"Yes, but only one of us needs to see it to believe."

Walter sighed and, pulling the cell door closed behind him, motioned for Duron.

"The infant also had a middle name," Knot said. "Do you remember it?"

"Vankern. Her mother's maiden name." Walter grinned. Maybe his memory wasn't half bad.

"That is her second middle name. Do you remember her first?"

"You know me; I've never been good with names. My future daughter-in-law is Alia Vankern Wells."

"I'm just going to have to tell you." Knot shook his head.

"Yes, please do." Walter stepped aside as Duron swiveled the key in the lock.

Knot waited until Duron was out of earshot.

"Dory." Knot smiled. "Alia *Dory* Vankern Wells."

Walter swallowed. She'd been such a beautiful little thing in his arms. She'd gripped his finger firmly with those long piano fingers of hers and smiled up at him. "I hope she's okay, Knot."

"We need to ring the bells, Walter, and ask the citizens of Yonder to pray for the safety of their future queen."

"Yes, that's what I will do."

Walter fumbled up the stairs. He'd get the bells tolling immediately throughout the village. The good people of Yonder needed to pray.

ΦΦΦ

When we reached Yonder, half the kingdom lined the streets, awaiting our arrival. Crowds four people deep and half a mile long lined the road to the castle. Our soldiers stopped their horses and waited for Wron to lead the procession.

With one arm around my middle and one hand on the reins, Wron stopped in front of the people. "All is well; Needa found a husband and Dory is alive."

Leeson and Elza were in the crowd; I smiled in their direction.

"She will live." Wron rode another fifty feet and again told the people: "All is well; Needa found a husband and Dory is alive."

Men, women, and children bowed, looking up at us. My injury was cloaked in a blanket. Over and over, Prince Wron delivered this message to the good and noble citizens of Yonder, my future countrymen. After we reached the royal stables, he slid off of his horse and eased me into his arms.

"I can walk," I mumbled.

"I will carry you."

"It's not my legs that are injured."

"You are delirious. I will carry you."

The arguing weakened me. He boosted me to one knee, and felt my forehead.

His mother and father and Rhoda waited outside the postern as he carried me toward them. Eunice began to cry. Walter stood tall and swallowed. Rhoda stared wide-eyed, biting her knuckles.

"She is alive." Wron carried me past them and down the wide corridor. He carried me into Rhoda's room and laid me on my old bed. In silent vigil, everyone gathered around my bed. The blood-stained bandage was visible through the soiled cambric.

"I am no longer dying." I attempted a smile.

"Eunice, send for the doctor," Walter ordered. "Rhoda, get warm, soapy water and towels. Wron, wash up and get something to eat."

After Wron left the room, his father held my hand.

ΦΦΦ

"Dr. Orgel said you need plenty of liquids and toast."

For dinner, Wron delivered Rhoda's cabbage soup and toast. He set the tray on my bedside table, and then propped pillows behind me so I could sit up. My forehead was still hot to his touch. Holding the bowl below my chin, he spoon-fed me several bites before I shook my head.

Exhausted, I lay back against the pillow. "Rhoda's soup does not make me want to live."

He smiled and leaned toward my good shoulder. "Tell me why you want to live. Tell me, Dory, the many reasons you have to live."

Painful memories were behind my lids. I peered at Wron. "Why wasn't the angel Felix?" I murmured.

He shook his head. "Who is Felix?"

In my delirium, I tried to rid my mouth of the cabbage soup taste.

"Look at me, Dory. Why do you want to live?"

"I watched the road for you." I smiled faintly. "I hoped you would come for me. And you did."

"Yes." He nodded. "You must get well." He smoothed my hair away from my face and waited until my eyes closed before he sent a guard to get Dr. Orgel.

ΦΦΦ

Throughout the kingdom, prayer replaced music and song. Three days after my return, Dr. Orgel told me: "You are going to live. You need a bath. You need to start eating real food, and you need to start walking before your muscles soften. Dory, did you hear me?"

"Yes. About my shoulder, how do I strengthen it?" I asked.

"After you take a bath, eat, and walk, you may slowly begin to move it. It will improve, but it will take time."

Rhoda and Needa helped me bathe. All my plain clothes were dirty, and I was tired of them anyway, so I wore another one of my nice gowns—a light blue velvet—from Felix's saddlebag. After drying my hair by the fire, I sat down in a goatskin chair across from Eunice.

"You're too pale, but you are lovely, Dory. Where did you ever find that dress?" She yanked on her lavender-colored ball of yarn.

"All my other clothes are filthy, Your Highness."

"Yes, but what you have on is quite regal."

I did not know what to say; so, instead, I walked from the fireplace to the piano and sat down. My right arm was in a sling. Otherwise, I probably would have pushed it too much in my desire to please Eunice. With my left hand, I moved between bass and treble clefs and played "The Ballad of Blue Sky." Any day my countrymen would be here. After the travels my father had mapped out for me, it was hard to imagine what he'd planned for himself. I prayed for safe travels.

"It is the loveliest music we've heard since you left. We had a one-armed harpist play in your absence, but her music did not move me like yours."

"She was not one-armed," Wron corrected her as he entered the Great Hall. "She held a baby in the other arm, Dory." He smiled and took a seat across from his mother.

"Is Needa about?" I asked loudly, my back to them.

"No, Lehto and Needa are in the garden fighting about which tree he will build their home under." Wron's voice boomed with life.

I played "Tomorrow, Today" with my left hand, and I tried to not worry about today or tomorrow.

ΦΦΦ

Wron stared at Dory's hair. When he'd been alone with her in the cave, he'd wrapped one of her long auburn curls around his fingers. He sighed unknowingly.

"Within four days, Princess Alia will be here, Wron. It is probably too late now to stop her arrival," his mother whispered. "Roger told your father of talk within our kingdom that the people want Dory to be their future queen. They have heard of all that she did. And word among the soldiers is that while you were in Evland, you behaved like a man in love."

His chest tightened. "I feared her dying."

"Even Roger, who knows you well, told your father that you behaved like a man in love."

Wron's memories returned to the night he'd held Dory in the cave and she'd lain in the curve of his arm. The memory now haunted him. "Alia will not be comfortable with Dory as a live-in pianist. When we are married, Dory will return to Evland."

"That is too far away. Perhaps she can live with Leeson and Elza and continue to play at The Bell Tower."

"No, Mother." He shook his head.

"That is too close." His mother nodded sadly. "Dory, dear," she said loudly. "That is enough. I do not wish to tire you. Come, sit down."

In a blue velvet gown that he had not seen before, Dory took a seat in the wingback chair across from him.

"How is your arm, dear?"

"Heavier than I remember." She managed a soft smile and briefly met Wron's gaze. Pink stained her complexion.

"Excuse me," she said, rising to her feet. "I'll help Rhoda."

"You will do no such thing," Eunice said.

"Let her go, Mother."

After Dory disappeared into the kitchen, Wron sighed. "Her presence is difficult for me now."

"Because you are afraid that you acted out of love, not fear?"

"For the last six years, you have told me that I am to marry Alia and . . ."

"No, it was your father who gave you away, not me."

"What are you saying, Mother?"

"I'm saying . . . find Princess Alia another country to marry."

"Life is not so simple." He chuckled sadly.

Chapter Twenty-Eight

Seated at the servants' table, Needa and I enjoyed a midafternoon snack of fresh figs. Rhoda stopped in the doorway and cleared her throat. "Take this bucket, Dory, and get me enough potatoes to fill it." It wasn't her request that surprised me, but more the unnatural, stilted way she spoke. "Here…" She held out a white enamel bucket.

"I will help," Needa said.

"No, Dory can do this one handed," Rhoda bellowed.

She was usually sensitive to my one-armed condition, but perhaps she was finally fed up with feeding a royal family all by herself.

"Put me in the bucket," Needa whispered. "It's dark down there."

I took the bucket from Rhoda, but the giant woman watched me so closely that I couldn't very well return to the table for Needa.

Rhoda escorted me to the rear of the kitchen, where I opened the door to the cellar stairwell. I glanced back at her, and for a moment I was glad that I'd left Needa behind as a witness. The giant woman usually got her own potatoes. Something was up. Carrying both a lantern and the empty bucket in one hand, I made my way down the narrow stone stairwell. I had visited briefly once before and knew the cold, dark storage room could easily inspire nightmares.

I reached the dirt floor. The cool, heavy air was woven with spider webs. Holding the lantern shoulder high, I passed large jars of pickled baby onions, gooseberries, sheeps' eyes . . . I had to suppress my imagination as I focused on the large burlap bags at the far side of the room.

Suddenly, the pale yellow glow of another light source revealed itself.

Though I'd been expecting something, a gasp still escaped me. I froze in place as someone holding a lantern high moved through a row of stacked goods toward the center aisle.

If I screamed, it would be wasted breath. No one in the castle would hear me. Think . . . think! Rhoda had sent me here for *more* than potatoes.

"Dory."

I tried to recognize the voice, but I was too scared.

The form stopped in the center of my aisle, and the light illuminated King Walter's shiny face and thick white hair.

"I asked Rhoda to send you here." He smiled.

My heart sprinted inside my weakened vessel. With furrowed brows, I peered around. Why would the king of Yonder want to meet me *alone* in the storage room?

"Since you survived the Forest Maze alone, and your trip to Evland, I knew that meeting me in the storage room would be a piece of cake." He grinned. "I wanted a private place for our little chat." He swished his hand.

As I followed him, I reminded myself that King Walter was himself a warlord, and whatever the premise for our meeting, there was good reason behind it.

Lantern in hand, he sat down on a large bag of rice. I set my lantern atop a nearby wooden barrel, and then sat down on a sack of beans within an arm's reach of him. Between the two light sources, we could clearly see each other.

"Knot and I recently shared a cup of coffee." There was a profound twinkle in his eyes.

He knew.

Walter leaned toward me and, bending to one knee, inched the lantern closer. He held his palm up just below my chin and motioned upward with his fingers. I knew what he implied, but hesitated. Lowering my chin, I locked eyes with him.

"Lift your chin, Dory." His voice was firm, like Father's when he really wanted something.

Even in this isolated moment, Dixie's words haunted me. *Tell no one. No one will believe you.* I waited for God's whisper of encouragement.

"Alia, lift your chin," Walter ordered.

Suppressing a smile, I tipped back my head until I looked squarely at the rock ceiling.

Walter tilted his head to the side, and I heard an intake of air. Then he returned to sit on the bag of rice. Walter sat mute, one brow raised.

While he took it all in, my memory revisited the garden shed. How deliriously happy I'd been in Wron's arms. So deliriously happy that I'd been a fool. All I'd needed to say was: "I am Princess Alia, and I have proof."

Yet, despite my present injury, good had come out of my banishment to Evland. Needa had found Lehto, and Wron had found me.

Walter began to chuckle. His hearty laughter echoed in the cavernous room. He wiped his eyes and eventually sighed. "Thank God you're alive!" He shook his head. "When will your father arrive?"

"Soon," I breathed. "He plans to be here for the wedding. They left two weeks after Felix and me. But they took the longer route . . . Perhaps three weeks behind me. Any day." I nodded. "He should be here any day."

"Hmm . . ." Walter's jowls hung low, and his face had lost expression. "Why, why... did you do it?"

"What were my choices?" Didn't he remember my pox?

He nodded and rested his hands to his knees, and studied me again. "Tell me your stories of Yonder that you will someday tell my grandchildren."

His words held such reassuring truth.

I told him about etching *DORY—Piano Girl* into the rock in my cell.

King Walter listened, fascination heavy in his eyes.

By the soft glow of lantern light, I sat on a large bag of beans and told my future father-in-law about my days as a common piano girl in the country where I would someday be called Queen.

Chapter Twenty-Nine

While Rhoda made dinner, I insisted that I was well enough to serve. As I walked between the kitchen and dining area with dishes, King Ulrich lifted the newspaper. He was chuckling behind it. *Bless his heart.* He was trying his best to keep my secret.

"Dory, now that you're feeling better, why don't you and Rhoda deliver dessert to the prisoners tonight?" Walter suggested, lowering the paper.

"Walter, don't be silly. She's still recovering!" Eunice said.

"Father . . . just walking down the stairs will tire her." Wron set down his glass.

"I'd love to," I said.

"Good." Walter beamed. He knew how much I cared for the men, especially Knot.

ΦΦΦ

Rhoda dished out pear-and-ginger cobbler and topped each serving with freshly whipped cream. I paid close attention. The decorative swirl wasn't a flick as I had done, but more a smooth rotation of the wrist.

"Oh, Knot would love a glass of milk," Rhoda said. By the time we were through pouring drinks, two trays were full, and to be honest, I was of little help.

"Ask King Walter if he will help us." Rhoda's voice again sounded stilted to me.

When I hesitated, she waved her hand. "When you and Needa were in Evland, he helped me."

Her voice reminded me of my visit to the cellar. "King Walter . . ." I neared the table. He'd just finished his last bite of cobbler. "Would you mind assisting us with the second tray? Rhoda—"

"Certainly." He smiled.

"I could help, Father." Wron pushed back his chair.

"No, sit down," Walter said.

ΦΦΦ

We served Knot first. Duron even unlocked his cell door.

"It is good to see you, Dory." Knot eyed me closely. "You are pale and thin."

"So are you." I handed him a glass of milk.

"And I will add *cheeky* as well. Several days ago, Rhoda informed us that you made it home to us, alive."

"Today is her first day up, Knot," Walter said. "Do not feel left out."

"I want to hear all about it, and so far, I've heard only snippets. You must visit me tomorrow." Knot selected the largest piece of cobbler on the tray and walked toward his cot. "Bring some of Rhoda's peppersniff cookies."

"I'll bring midmorning tea, Knot." I smiled.

"No, she won't be doing either," Walter said, clearing his throat. "As soon as you finish your dessert, Knot, you will return to your old job."

While Knot met Walter's gaze, Rhoda and I glanced at one another.

"An answer to a three-year prayer!" she gushed.

Tears filled my eyes. This was what Walter, the dear, sweet man that he was, wanted me to witness.

"Is my old room still available?" Knot asked.

"Yes." Walter nodded.

"Then tomorrow morning, Dory and I will catch up on her news at the dining table in the Great Hall."

"Dory sits with us in the kitchen." Narrowing her eyes, Rhoda tilted her head.

"Walter, schedule the tailor; none of my old clothes will fit. Rhoda, make some of your peppersniff cookies."

"I've not made them even once since you have been in prison." Rhoda peered at Walter. "I have been on strike."

Weary but elated, I cupped my arm in Walter's and leaned against him. Rhoda's brows gathered for a moment before she retrieved the dishes from Knot's cell.

"I believe you'll need assistance up the stairs," Walter noted.

"Yes, but it was worth it." My first day up was ending on a very good note.

ΦΦΦ

Happy with the world, I sat on the royal couch and stared into the fire. Walter had finally released Knot. My first day up had been both emotionally and physically exhausting. I almost fell asleep.

"I'm almost too tired to get up," I admitted to Eunice.

"Pretend you are asleep." She winked.

I rested my head on the couch arm and, in my pretending, nearly fell asleep again.

"Wron, come here, please," Eunice said, across the Great Hall. He was near the piano studying a wall map.

He drew near. "What is it, Mother?"

"Can you carry Dory to bed? Your father will throw his back."

"Mother!" Wron groaned under his breath. A slight pause was followed by the sound of his knees cracking, and then he carefully picked me up in his arms. With one eye barely opened, I glanced up at him. As he carried me across the hall and down the corridor, he did not look down at me once. In my room, he laid me down on my bed and placed the covers over me.

"Thank you, Ivan," I said as he retreated from my room.

Of course it irked him. He lit the candle near my bedside. With only one eye open, I looked up at him.

"I am not Ivan," he said.

"You're right." I feigned surprise. "Ivan cannot speak. You see, when someone dropped me on my bed and crashed the covers to my head and did not bend to kiss my cheek or whisper *sweet dreams*, I thought of course it must be Ivan. But even Ivan would have been sweeter."

He wanted to shake me, but my shoulder was injured. Instead, he blew out the light and closed the door behind him. A thud followed, as he leaned against it.

In the dark, I found a match and thought of relighting the candle. If my beloved would at least be kind to me, I'd end what had been a wonderful day on a blissful note. The door reopened, and then his knees cracked as he knelt beside my bed. I sat up and struck the wooden match against my metal bed frame before I relit the candle.

In the candlelight, I pretended surprise. "Oh, it's you. I thought it might be Ivan again."

"What I'm going to say is difficult." His chest expanded.

I knew by the tremor in his voice that what he had to tell me was not good news.

"You're about to break my heart?" I bit my lower lip.

"Yes, I'm sorry." He gazed sadly in my eyes. "Princess Alia will arrive within four days and . . ."

"And you don't love me?" I fingered the dark bedcovering.

"I did not say that."

"You love me, but not enough."

He bowed his head. "I was afraid you were dying, and I gave in to my fear—"

I interrupted his heartbreaking confession. "I'm glad you told me the truth, Prince Wron." I inhaled deeply. "Tell your father there is a piece of land I fell in love with when I was in Evland."

"Why did you call your father Felix?" He swallowed.

"When did I do that?" I did not remember.

"When you were delirious, you called him Felix. I have never referred to my father as Walter."

"Perhaps it was due to my delirium." I held the four fingers against my leg. Lie number four.

"I am not certain if you will go away."

His feelings for me were confusing. Did he love me?

He sat on the edge of the mattress and looked across the room toward the arched window. "My parents and many others love you. You can continue to play piano and have a good life."

"I may only be half as good as I used to be."

"My parents' love for you extends beyond your piano playing."

He sounded so sure.

He'd hit a soft spot. I blew out the candle.

"It is not fair, Dory. I have always tried to be honest, and now that she is almost here, you demand my heart." He remained by my side.

"I know. I ask too much . . ." I stopped myself.

Wearily, he rose and exited the room. I stared at the ceiling in the dark. Did he love me? Really love me? Was I asking too much?

ΦΦΦ

In the middle of the night, two people wearing long white nightgowns stood at the foot of my bed. "It's only us," Eunice whispered.

Half-asleep, I sat up against the headboard. The pain of forgetting not to use my shoulder made me wince. It was the first time I'd seen Eunice with her hair down. Her thick white hair nearly reached her waist. Had she not spoken, I might not have recognized her.

"It's only us. Rhoda is an amaz—" Eunice was interrupted by a rumbling snore. "Very loud snorer." She waved a hand for me to follow them. "We're too close to Wron's room." I shrugged on my robe and started after them down the corridor past the entry to the Great Hall and around the maze-like bend.

A fire in the hearth and dark green drapes warmed the spacious room. Walter and Eunice returned to their king-sized bed while I sat upright in a dark green velvet chair, which was unlike any of the other furniture in the castle.

"I take it that Queen Eunice knows." I looked at Walter.

"I'm sorry, Dory . . . Alia. She knows me too well." His cheeks bunched. "When one's own wife is involved, it's much easier to share a secret than to keep one."

"I must tell you, I still cannot believe it! But I think your plot to see if you could love each other is absolutely marvelous." Eunice beamed. "I have always been a romanticist."

Her response warmed my heart, but she was misguided. "I had no plot. If it had not been for the swamp pox, I would have told all of you much sooner."

"He loves you, Dory." Eunice shook her head. "He is torn between his obligations and his love for you."

I closed my eyes to my most recent wound. "He told me tonight how he behaved in Evland was out of fear and guilt."

"He is betrothed to Princess Alia," Walter said. "Both of you have forgotten that two vast kingdoms will become one powerful—"

"You were already allies." Eunice waved a hand.

Tears sprang to my eyes, and for once, I did not hide my pain. "But to just tell him who I am is too simple now."

"I agree. You are a romanticist, like me." Eunice smiled softly at me. "We have much to plan."

"He's a royalist, not a romanticist." Walter shook his head. "He's being responsible, as he should be."

Eunice lifted a finger thoughtfully to her lips. "Too bad we already did the Summer Ball. It would have been perfect."

Chapter Thirty

Upon Knot's request, Rhoda made Giant Cakes for breakfast. I set the glass pie plate down in front of Walter, while Rhoda delivered the others.

"There are land disputes. I'll be back for dinner," Wron said.

While I set the gravy boat filled with maple syrup on the table beside him, he looked straight ahead at his mother. When I brought a bowl of freshly sliced strawberries to the table, he stared at his plate. When I stood beside him and poured him a fresh cup of coffee, he closed his eyes.

"Perhaps Dory could accompany you to town today," Walter said.

Wron chuckled. "It's only her second day up. She should be resting."

"Rhoda, is it too late to request seconds?" Knot interrupted their banter.

"Yes. Eat more fruit!" she bellowed from the kitchen.

"We don't need to call the tailor." Walter chuckled. "You'll be wearing your old clothes in a week."

Knot stuffed another bite of cake in his mouth and nodded.

"What do you think, Dory, about accompanying Wron today?" Walter lowered his chin, looking at me.

Eyes wide, Wron's shoulders dropped. "Look how pale she is—"

"You will need to take the carriage," Eunice said. "She is not ready for horseback."

"I would like that very much. Thank you, Prince Wron." I carried the butter dish around the table to Knot.

"Has everyone gone mad?" Wron asked, and huffed.

ΦΦΦ

Though Wron and I sat on the same side of the carriage, our shoulders touching, so distant was his expression that we might as well have been worlds apart. The carriage bounced over a pothole, and I could not help but wince when my wound contacted the side of the carriage.

"You should not have come." He moved to sit across the aisle from me, so I could move to the center of the seat.

"To Yonder or with you today?" The jostling had opened my scab. Beneath my cloak, my bandage felt moist against my skin.

"You know very well what I meant."

I gazed sadly out the window at the rolling countryside. Perhaps Wron did not love me. Perhaps he'd simply acted out of fear and guilt in Evland.

"Will you please answer me?"

The edge in his voice pierced my heart. "I didn't hear the question, My Lord."

"Why is my father suddenly inclined to team us together?"

Our eyes locked for a moment. "He knows that a day with you will be less strenuous than a day with your mother playing one-handed piano."

Turning toward the window, he suppressed a smile. "I will miss your humor, Dory."

I was so ready to tell my betrothed and beloved that I was his, but the needles of Eunice's romantic imagination had begun their knitting, and our lives were her yarn.

Several miles out of town, in the middle of rolling wheat fields, sat a small sod house. A large-boned woman stood in the doorway.

"There is a land dispute. My men and I will walk the property. You may stay here or . . . ." Wron regarded me.

"I'll visit the woman of the house."

He stepped out of the carriage first, and then, without meeting my gaze, held a hand up to me. On exiting, I held up the left side of my dress, but the right side was too long.

"I'm snagged."

Wron's sour mood turned, and he gently lifted the right side of my gown and assisted me out of the carriage. Afterward, he greeted the waiting farmers. Four of Yonder's guards dismounted to join him, while I walked alone in the direction of the sod house.

The woman standing in the doorway wore the back side of a man's old shirt about her waist as an apron. She wore a headscarf from the same material. "No dea. No coffee." Wide-eyed, she gripped her hands below her chest.

"I know you did not expect company," I said, "but I have an injury and I fear it's reopened." I motioned to my shoulder hidden beneath the cloak.

The woman stepped back and held the door open. The one-room house was sparsely furnished. A crude table and two chairs stood off to one side, a pile of wood lay near the fire, and a baby cradle sat in the far corner. An infant lay sleeping there.

"I am Vreida." Vreida's face was red and splotchy, like she washed her face often with harsh soap.

"I am Dory." I nodded.

"Prince Wron's Dory?" Her dark brows rose.

"Yes."

"Dory, who defended Yonder?" She bent both knees to the dirt floor.

"I am not worthy." My heart felt stretched. "Stand up, Vreida."

Setting her hand to the table, she slowly stood.

"On the way here, my wound opened. Do you have anything I may use as a bandage?"

Vreida turned and opened her only cupboard. She took out a scrap of towel and led me to a basin of water on the table. "Id is freshly pumped," she said. With large, warm hands, she helped me slide the cloak over my head. Blood had soaked through my bandages onto my cambric blouse.

"Shod by a counderfeid. Shod for Yonder," she said under her breath. With gentle hands, she removed the bandage.

"No." I shook my head. "Needa and I did what anyone would have done if they'd been in our shoes."

She shook her head. Like one who had seen much blood in her life and bandaged many a wound, Vreida took care of me.

The door flung open, and Vreida's husband and Wron entered. Vreida rinsed her towel and wrung it out before she carried the basin filled with red water past the men and out the door.

Feeling Wron's concerned gaze, I averted my attention to the wood-planked floor. He'd been right; I should not have come. The baby began to cry. The husband picked up the infant and walking about the room, tried to hush him.

The woman returned with a fresh basin of water. After setting it on the table, she took the infant from her husband's arms and wrapped him in a soft green knit blanket and nuzzled the child against her.

The crying ceased.

"Thank you, Vreida. You have been a kind and generous hostess," I said.

She shook her head. "I'm sorry we do nod have coffee."

ΦΦΦ

Wron assisted me inside the carriage and pulled the door closed behind him. "Why did you not tell me that your wound reopened?" he asked.

"Why did you not tell me that your countrymen live in squalor while you eat Giant Cakes off fine china?" My tongue held back no sharpness.

"Answer me!"

"They have no coffee or tea. Their towels are rags," I said hotly, close to tears.

"You do not understand."

"In Blue Sky, our motto is a middle-class society with no poverty."

"With the war, we acquired a vast amount of land, a vast amount of people. There are many needs and much to be done. A new road to Blue Sky will put many people to work. New towns will develop and thrive. Skilled mapmakers have put much thought into this plan, Dory. With my marriage, the future of Yonder is bright." When he met my gaze, a sheen of tears filled his eyes.

I closed my eyes and turned toward the window. What a wonderful man he was. "Their only possession with any color was the baby blanket that your mother knit them," I whispered.

Silence dwelled between us for a few miles while golden fields of knee-high wheat stretched as far as the eye could see.

"What is next?" I asked.

"I have nothing else planned today."

"What would you have done until dinnertime?"

"I thought of going to The Bell Tower to listen to Long, and then to sit with my men and polish our guns."

"You did not want to be home because of me." He avoided me now as often as he could.

"In less than a week, I will be married." His cheek muscle twitched as he looked out the window.

How I longed to tell Wron that I was his, but his mother had painted a romantic picture in my mind. With careful planning, the picture might make the present pain worthwhile.

"What will we do now?" I tried to caress his cheek with my voice.

"We're going home."

I sighed. "With your permission, may we buy coffee and new towels for Vreida and her family?"

"Yes." He suppressed a smile.

Oh, how I loved him.

ΦΦΦ

After we set five pounds of coffee, sugar, and towels upon the counter, my eyes fell upon an apron. "How much may we spend?" I asked.

"It's not too much." Wron eyed the apron that I fingered.

I selected a checkered fabric for Vreida.

"Her husband will feel left out." Wron placed hand-kerchiefs on the counter and a new pocketknife.

During our return to the farm, I held the bag of coffee beans in my lap. "If it is all right with Vreida, may we stay for coffee?"

"Yes."

Vreida's husband was out front splitting wood when our carriage returned. He paused to wipe his brow with the back of his sleeve. Then he hurried to the house to inform his wife.

Alone, I approached the door, while Wron waited inside the carriage. I held the bag of coffee under my good arm, and used my kneecap to softly pound on the door. Vreida opened it. Her husband stood in the background, holding the infant and patting his back.

"Vreida, we brought you some coffee." Fumbling, I moved the package to my hand and held the burlap bag out to her.

She covered her mouth with one hand and waved with the other, motioning me inside.

"I don'd know whad do say. Almer, Prince Wron's Dory broughd coffee!"

"If it's not inconvenient, may we stay for coffee?"

"You and Prince Wron?" Wide-eyed, Vreida nodded. She turned to find a dusty coffeepot on the lowest shelf.

I returned to the carriage, where Wron stood outside, conversing with his men.

"They are pleased to have us stay for coffee." I beamed.

ΦΦΦ

That afternoon, the Queen requested *knitting* music. I found myself looking out the large picture window while I played. I recalled Wron's conversation two nights before when he'd told me he acted out of fear and guilt, and then I recalled his sheen of tears in the carriage today when he'd told me about his country's bright future. I felt responsible for his confusion and his pain, and tried to focus on the distant hills of Evland.

"Your music is waning," Eunice said. "Just play 'Tomorrow, Today.'"

It was such a sad song. It had always reminded me of Felix, reminded me of losing him and the horrors of my travels. I glanced over my shoulder at Knot, who sat with the men near the fire. If I had the use of both hands, I would play very dreary music that would bludgeon the depths of my soul.

"Your playing is very choppy, Dory, even though it is one-handed," Eunice said, over her lap-sized afghan. "Whatever is the matter?"

"I play by memory. It's hard to play one-handed to the depths of my memories."

"Before you know it, you'll be well." Eunice yanked at her ball of yarn, which rolled off her chair onto the slate floor. She sighed, "And I was so comfy."

I rose to assist her, and set the ball of yarn near her hip. "Are you knitting another blanket?"

"Yes, I am two babies behind." She sighed, looking up at me.

"I treasured your blanket when I was in Evland. It felt like a love letter from you."

She smiled tenderly at me. "Some of our people are very poor. I knit blankets."

"Today when we visited the farmer's regarding the land dispute . . ." I turned from the piano to regard her. "I visited with the farmer's wife. The only fine thing that they had in their home was the light green blanket for their baby."

Above her knitting needles, she sighed. "I knit, Dory, but your brain is different. You will find solutions."

I had not always been that way. My father and Felix had been right in the adventures they'd mapped out for me. Without them, I would not have been a queen who knew her people.

ΦΦΦ

That evening, when Rhoda snored on the other side of the room, I pulled back my mattress, which jutted against the wall, and retrieved Felix's saddlebag. After Father arrived, Princess Alia would finally meet Wron for the first time. I wanted to wear my beautiful light blue gown for the memorable occasion.

I slid back the leather tongue of the bag and fingered the material of the gown I'd worn for my sixteenth party. I pulled the exquisite gown partway out of the bag, and I felt something that didn't belong amidst the organdy. Paper.

Surely it wasn't a letter from Father. For our safety, Felix had burned all correspondence. Mouth dry, I unfolded a cream-colored piece of paper. I was not in the back of a wagon surrounded by chickens, or in the middle of a barren field, but I sensed that what I was about to read would be as defining.

Dory,

I'd stood over Felix's shoulder many an evening when he'd penned his letters to my father. The slanted scrawl was indeed his.

As you've probably determined by now, I will not be joining you in Yonder. At least not yet. When your father and I first mapped out this grand adventure, the swamp pox were not a part of the plan. You were to arrive alone in Yonder, a beautiful young woman who could easily prove who she was due to your birthmark, the horses, and simply who you are.

Though my heart wanted to stop, I had to keep reading.

My orders were explicit. I was to leave you at the Giants' Snare. You would believe I was in battle, while you made your trek alone. The decision was your father's. I had no say in it. No matter how well our journey had gone up until this point, your father wanted you to face Shepherd's Field, the

Forest Maze, and Yonder on your own to strengthen you and teach you valuable lessons for your future role.

From the start, I was very torn over this decision, and even more so after you contracted the pox, as you have become like a daughter to me.

Someone knocked at the door.

Jolted out of my transfixed state, I shoved the saddlebag beneath the blankets. "Come in." I sniffled, wiping my cheeks.

"Sorry, Dory, this will just take a minute." Wron entered and, bending to one knee near Rhoda's bed, turned the giant woman to her side. As he rounded the side of my bed, he glanced my direction. Only the letter in my hand was visible.

His shoulders relaxed, and his gaze narrowed. "Are you reading your father's letters?"

The motion of nodding brought a wave of tears. I bit my lower lip.

"Is it one you haven't read?" He leaned his head to one side, and his brows gathered.

I nodded and, laying the letter against me, covered my mouth with my left hand. I was so close to totally unraveling.

"Is there anything I can do?"

I closed my eyes, shaking my head. "Thank you," I managed.

His footsteps retreated across the hallway, and I waited for the sound of his door closing before I sighed and returned to the letter.

I want to assure you that I will survive the Giants' Snare. I have taken this route multiple times before when they've been awake. The giant women are easily tamed, and many actually look forward to my visits.

I'm sorry that you were led to believe otherwise, yet . . . I believe your father was correct. You would not have traveled alone of your own choosing.

I am sorry to say that I will miss your wedding. I have gone back to collect Greda, my niece, and her daughter, Sadie.

He was related to them. I smiled.

I plan to retire in Evland, so I look forward to seeing you often.

Until then,

Felix

I stared across the room at the stone wall. I remembered Felix and how he'd changed after my swamp pox. He'd been torn over my father's decisions, and yet it was his duty to obey. I saw his love for me so clearly now.

After folding the letter, I tucked it back inside the saddlebag and returned it to its hiding place. I blew out the candle and lay back on my pillow.

I peered into the darkness. I knew what my journey had taught me. While my father—the king, the strategist—had often failed me, my heavenly Father had given me Felix to make up for him.

I closed my eyes. *Nothing is to happen to her. Nothing.* Wren's sweet childlike voice reminded me of what she'd overheard outside Father's study. It was just like Father to be unpredictable like that—to change course, to fool his adversaries. He was brilliant. But I, his own daughter, had been his pawn.

Chapter Thirty-One

I tossed the pillow on the floor so I could lay my head flat on the bed, still my mind raced. Felix was alive and I had his letters. Someday, I'd return them to him. In the dark, I rose and felt through my top dresser drawer for the round cylinder. Only clothes greeted my touch. Could Wron have taken it?

With a blanket wrapped about me, I walked across the dimly lit hallway to his room and softly knocked. After much fumbling about, he opened the door and peered out the six-inch expanse. "Rhoda's no longer snoring."

"I cannot sleep. Do you have the letters?"

"Yeeesss." He fumbled about in the dark shadows of his room, before handing me the metal cylinder. "You do this only to pain me."

"What do you mean?" I didn't understand.

"You read of your father's love . . . because you cannot have mine." His voice broke.

I held the cylinder closer to me. I was still gaping at him when he closed the door between us. Was that his way of telling me he loved me? His pain made mine resurface. *If he never tells me, I'll go to Evland and live on Felix's old homestead. I'll build a white rock cottage and find gnomes for friends.*

I set my pillow against the headboard, lit a candle, slid under the covers, and got completely comfortable before I unrolled the top letter.

Felix's cursive looked different—less slanted. Wrong.

Forgive me, Dory . . . My heart leaped. Wron had written me a letter.

I have not thought about the princess since you left. Before I met you, the waiting was difficult. Now I think only of you... while it is my obligation to marry her. I am sorry. I cannot express it any other way and not cause you pain.

I paused to close my eyes and smile . . . Wron loved me.

In spite of my feelings for you, I will fulfill my duty to my country. I will marry Princess Alia. Yonder and Blue Sky will merge, and our two countries will prosper because of it.

The stars were marvelous in Evland. You will be that one shining moment in my heart that I will often reflect on. We will grant you any piece of land there that you wish, and I will think of you often.

Wron

Wiping tears aside, I found my notebook and ripped a page out of the back to write a response. I dipped a goose quill pen into the bottle of ink on my nightstand. With great difficulty I wrote with my left hand.

Wron,

Forgive me for the lack of title. Thank you for your letter. I will cherish it all of my life. There is purpose to my horrible injury in Evland, in that I may never have known how much you cared.

I understand your obligation and responsibility to your country. As the future king of Yonder, you are a public servant, and you would not be serving Yonder if you did not marry the woman who is best for your country. The same holds true for Alia.

Knowing you love me will make everything easier.

If Princess Alia does not arrive tomorrow, may we meet at the fire? May we share the Yonder stars as I lie in the curve of your arm?

Dory

I walked across the hallway and slid the paper under his door for him to find in the morning.

ΦΦΦ

Dressing one handed was difficult. Buttoning the front of my blouse was painstakingly slow. Someone slid an envelope beneath the door. I stared at the cream-colored paper and smiled. It was from my beloved, the man I'd been betrothed to since shortly after I was born. I sat on the edge of my bed and opened my letter.

Dory,

I will be gone on business today. I will return late this afternoon. After dinner, you and I will slip away without my parents' knowledge. I will think of tonight all day.

Wron

I reread the note two, three times; and then I placed it inside the cylinder for safekeeping.

ΦΦΦ

While I helped Rhoda serve breakfast, I learned that Wron had grabbed an egg sandwich before he'd left.

"What business did Wron have today?" Walter grumbled. "Princess Alia could show up at any minute."

Eunice turned to me.

I had no idea and shrugged.

Rhoda carried a silver tray hosting a coffee decanter, creamer, and Needa. "He's gone to Delfrey to get a wedding present for Lehto and me," Needa said, with glistening eyes.

Rhoda set the tray down beside Walter. He poured himself a large mug of coffee and added cream. "Why today, of all days?"

"Now that I am married, I am the worst person to ask about why a man does what he does." Needa curtsied. She stepped over the lip of the tray to move closer to Walter's plate. "At this moment, Lehto is outside studying the roots of trees. My next home will not be a castle."

"Needa, as wives, we are not to complain about our husbands," Eunice said kindly. "Wron is usually a better communicator than this. I do not like the mystery."

I agreed; the mystery was disconcerting.

"How are things between the two of you?" Eunice eyed me.

"Better."

Eunice's mouth bunched. "Hmmph . . . perhaps we should not delay in telling him."

Needa strode across the table to stand near Eunice's glass of pear juice. "Telling him *what*?"

"Something very telling," Walter said, from behind his morning paper.

"Hmm . . ." Eunice tapped her mouth thoughtfully. "Perhaps *you* should arrive tonight, Dory."

My stomach knotted. I thought of our plans for an evening fire and looking at the stars. I knew of his love now; perhaps it was best that sharing the stars would not be bittersweet.

"We have much to prepare then, don't we?" I finally murmured.

"Yes!" Eunice clapped her hands together. "We must take matters into our own hands."

ΦΦΦ

Walter and Eunice wrote out speeches and practiced them aloud while I sat at the granite table and offered critique and encouragement. The sound of marching in the corridor announced Roger's and two other guards' entry into the Great Hall.

"Your Highness, we have a visitor," Roger said, his posture rigid, his hands at his sides.

"Who now?" Eunice sighed.

A visitor? I thought of Felix's letter. But no, he'd gone to get Sadie.

"Who?" Walter turned to face the men.

"Another gypsy, Your Majesty, but he insists that you will know him."

"Make certain he has no weapons and have five, no, six guards escort him."

Walter returned to his speech writing. It was obvious by the way that he pulled at his hair that he very much disliked the writing and perhaps the presentation of speeches, as well.

A wiry man was ushered into the Great Hall. He was indeed the lowest of peasants. His mud-caked clothes were rags. But I rose from the table, drawn to him in a curious way. It was something about his hair.

"Stay where you are, Dory." Walter stiffly held out his arm.

His hair, though very greasy, was parted on the same side as my father's. His complexion was tinted the color of walnut and coated with a layer of dust and possibly blood.

Despite Walter's warning, I moved toward the peasant.

"Dory, do not get any closer," Walter commanded.

My feet would not obey him. "Father . . ." I whispered.

The gypsy smiled.

"Dory"—Walter set down his quill and rose from the table—"Roger, get between them. It may be a trap."

Still the man smiled at me. Love was in his eyes. Before Roger could reach me, I threw myself against him and felt his chest cave with emotion. There was no doubt in my being that the man I hugged was my father.

He held me and he held me, and like my sweetest memories, he whispered, "Everything is all right. Everything is all right."

ΦΦΦ

My father's tears dripped onto my face, and I knew his travels had been far more complicated than even he'd foreseen.

"Roger, how many men accompanied him?" Walter asked.

"Two. But from the lookout, there appear to be one to two hundred more men on horseback near the Delfrey hills. We believe he left his army behind."

Walter's brows gathered as he drew closer. "You have my permission to speak."

"My my, Wally," Father said. "The years have made you roly poly, and *why* is my daughter's arm in a sling?"

"Because she's a lot like her father." Walter chuckled and slapped my father's shoulder. "You old coot. Did you travel all the way here looking like that?"

"Yes. Word is there's a merger about to take place. A king's head like mine would be a nice trophy at this time."

"Everyone"—Walter held out his hand toward us as he turned to face those in attendance—"I want you to meet King

Francis of Blue Sky, and his daughter, Princess Alia Dory Vankern Wells."

Chapter Thirty-Two

My future country was awaiting my arrival, so the people of Yonder were summoned and gathered into the courtyard. From the balcony of their royal bedchamber, King Walter, with Queen Eunice by his side, made known our plan. Father and I waited in the wing.

"We are fortunate, our good people, to be able to share with you one very fine secret," Walter loudly announced. "My son is away on business today, and in his absence we will prepare the city for Princess Alia's arrival."

"He's in love with your servant, Dory," interrupted a man near the front. I knew the voice; it was Raul's from our reenactments at Peg's.

Demonstrating great patience, Walter waited for the murmurings of the crowd to dim.

"Yes, Prince Wron is in love with our Dory," Walter said. Then he beckoned for me to join them on the balcony. I was still in common clothes, with my hair loose about my shoulders.

"What our son Prince Wron has not yet been made aware of"—Walter cleared his throat—"is that our Dory is his Alia."

A deep hush fell over the crowd as the people stared and then began to bow.

"Princess Alia came to us nearly a month ago . . . covered in swamp pox sores." Walter spoke loudly, employing both hands. "She did not arrive with an entourage of one hundred men like we'd anticipated. Instead, she arrived alone, a commoner covered in swamp pox, and unable to prove who she is. Several of our bordering countries are not in favor of this merger. We pray all of you are, as it will make our countries very strong allies."

A flurry of hats flew into the air and cheers of "Onderyay!" as the people celebrated the news. Walter waited patiently for the crowd noise to dim.

"Why, Princess Alia?" asked Clarence from the mercantile. "Why did you not inform everyone when you first arrived?"

I peered down at the sea of faces. "Because of my pox, I could not prove who I was," I said in as loud a voice as I could rally. "And then, once I was healed, I became afraid that I could still be deemed a counterfeit and abandoned to the hills. I have a birthmark beneath my chin that King Walter knew about, but fear kept me from revealing who I really was." Tears stung the backs of my eyes, and I waited for the emotion to pass.

"Forgive me, my good people, but I would not trade the past few months for anything. My father, King Francis, and Felix, my bodyguard, wanted me to have an adventure that would shape me into a better queen. When I contracted swamp pox, the plan went astray, and I became indeed a commoner amongst commoners. Because of this, I know your struggles and your dreams in a way I never would have or could have . . ." I shook my head, at a loss for words.

I stared about me at the sea of faces, so many that I knew. Long, Leeson, Elza, Clarence, Peg . . . and my heart could not contain the vastness of the moment.

I stepped away from the balcony, and Walter took my place.

"Now . . ." Walter raised his hand. "No one is to say a word to Prince Wron about this. If anyone does, they will be thrown in prison, made to walk the treadmill, and only served drippy porridge for a month." He cleared his throat. "At five o'clock this evening, I want you to line the streets in anticipation of Princess Alia's arrival. Tonight, you'll witness history when Prince Wron meets his future bride."

"But he's already met her," interrupted Peg, who had always been a bit slow regarding matters of the heart.

"Yes." Walter nodded. "But like most of us, Wron still does not know that Dory is Alia."

*Awh*s of understanding rippled through the crowd.

"We have much to prepare," Walter said. "Tonight, when you hear the church bells ring, please gather in the courtyard. And in the meantime, no one is to say a word to Prince Wron. No one."

ΦΦΦ

Midday, Wron arrived home with three packages from Delfrey. No piano music filled the Great Hall. He paused in the kitchen doorway and scanned the room, hoping to find Dory. Jars of peaches lined the island. Rhoda cut butter into a large bowl of flour, and Needa sat nearby on her seesaw cutter chopping fresh herbs.

"Are you making what I think you're making?" Wron suppressed a smile.

"I am," Rhoda said.

"You know that your peach pie is my favorite, and I know that you only make it for very special occasions."

"We are, uh, throwing Needa and . . . Lehto a belated wedding party tonight," Rhoda said stiffly and wiped her forearm across her face.

"Peach is also my favorite," Needa said over her shoulder.

He hoped the party wouldn't last too late into the evening. He wouldn't want anyone to notice when he and Dory stole away to the fire.

"Where is Lehto?" he asked.

"Building. He found a nice rabbit hole underneath the king's elm tree." Needa pushed off her toes as she lifted into the air. "He's always been fond of elm trees."

Bending low, Wron set a silver-wrapped package on the floor near the gnome-sized blue door. "I bought you and Lehto a wedding present. Open it tonight after he's had time to rest."

"Did you get me anything?" Rhoda asked. Flour marked her face and checkered apron.

In the old days Wron had bought chocolate for Rhoda in Delfrey, but it was before he knew about her headaches. "Yes, Rhoda. Can you wait until tonight? Or would you like it now?"

"Neither Rhoda nor I can wait until tonight." Midair, Needa whined. "Tell us. Waiting is very hard for women— both giant and small."

He'd try and remember that. "Both gifts are practical." He knew Needa would pester him until he told. "Needa, yours is a gnome-sized rocking love seat for outside. I thought Lehto and you could enjoy the evenings together."

"Thank you, Prince Wron," she gushed. "You are so thoughtful."

"And Rhoda, I bought you a new hat for church."

"But I love my old one that you got me." Rhoda's large forearm muscles bulged as she worked the pastry blender into the flour.

"Well . . . now you have two." He placed the package on the counter. "You can save it for extra-special occasions."

"Tonight is a very special occasion."

"It is." He smiled at Needa, who was still in her everyday clothes. "I would think you should be getting ready, Mrs. Cauvern."

"I will soon." Needa bounced into the air.

"You don't happen to know where Dory is?"

"No," Rhoda said.

"Maybe she's sleeping," Needa said.

Wron tucked the small remaining present deep into his pocket. He walked into the Great Hall, where his mother sat knitting.

"Do you know where Dory is?" he asked.

"Sleeping." Eunice pulled on her ball of yarn. "With Needa's wedding party tonight, Dory wanted extra rest. She is still not entirely herself."

He nodded. He was still surprised that she'd recovered as quickly as she had. "Where is Father?"

His mother looked around as if she had just noticed his absence. "There is something in town he went for . . ." She nodded. "We don't have a gift for Needa either. I wish you would have let us know before you left for Delfrey. Shopping is so much better there."

Wron walked down the corridor to Dory's room. His father disliked shopping, but he loved Needa. Wron sighed. He had not seen Dory today. He'd glance in on her while she slept. He knocked lightly before entering her room. The bedspread was perfectly smooth. She wasn't anywhere. His heart quickened.

He returned to where his mother was seated in the Great Hall. "Dory is not sleeping, or in her room."

Eunice inhaled deeply and nodded. "I promised I would not tell you," she whispered.

"Tell me what?" His shoulders dropped.

"I can see that you are too worried for me not to tell you."

"I am." He nodded. "Tell me."

"In your father's absence, I gave my approval for Ivan to take Dory hunting. She hoped to shoot a chukar. Something about a midnight snack. It did not make sense to me, but she was unusually persuasive."

Wron chuckled with relief and sank down in a nearby chair. "Who will shoot it, Ivan or Dory left-handed?"

"Dory thinks she will be the one to flush it, did she say?"

"Ivan will shoot it then . . ." He nodded thoughtfully.

"Do take a bath, Wron. Tonight will be a very special party for Needa and Lehto."

"Whose idea is this on such short notice?"

"It was unanimous." His mother focused on her lavender knitting.

ΦΦΦ

While Wron stood in his closet, mulling over which of his uniforms to wear, the church bells rang. With his own birthday only three days away, he felt surprised by his parents' spontaneity in throwing Needa and Lehto a party. He combed through his dark hair and peered sadly into the mirror. One of the largest parties of his life would be soon. He sighed deeply and returned to the Great Hall.

His father had returned from town, wearing one of his finest capes.

"You look grand, Father." He smiled and turned to see his mother enter the room in her peach organdy gown and fine jewels. "You look exquisite, Mother."

She regarded his dark uniform. "That is what I hoped you would wear."

"Is Dory back?" He looked back and forth between his parents.

"No, I don't believe I've seen her." Walter cleared his voice and then strode out onto the terrace.

"She'll be back soon." His mother patted Wron's arm. "Maybe they're having a difficult time flushing chukar."

Wron couldn't help but feel anxious. He strode into the kitchen. Twenty beautiful peach pies cooled on the counter. Rhoda's round cheeks were flushed beneath her new cream-colored hat with its large cluster of purple grapes.

"Rhoda, I command you to relax. You have worked too hard today. Relax with us now and enjoy this joyous occasion."

Rhoda nodded. "Uh . . . Prince Wron, the coffee for your father is ready." She looked down, running a rag over the splattered counter. "Can you deliver it to him?"

"Yes, of course, Rhoda." Carrying the hot cup of coffee by the handle, Wron walked through the Great Hall. His mother pointed toward the terrace, where Wron joined his father.

"Thank you." His father took the cup and set it on a nearby table. "Son . . ." His father peered over the balcony. "Something is happening. There appears to be a great commotion."

Below them, his countrymen gathered in the courtyard, while over the bridge, a legion of white-and-blue uniforms waited outside the castle gates. A large knot tightened in his gut.

Roger entered the Great Hall.

"I believe Francis and Alia have arrived." His father patted him on the back. "The day we've been waiting for has finally arrived."

Roger halted in the doorway. "A large caravan has arrived from the north. Perhaps two hundred men in all."

Wron glanced south toward the aspen trees lining the river, where Dory and Ivan were hunting. *There might not be a fire tonight.*

"Father, I can't help but feel uneasy." He tried to shake the heavy feeling.

"I'm sorry, Wron, this is not a time to dwell on the past. Come, Eunice." His father took his mother's arm. Wron followed. Together the royal family walked through the underground passageway, and then up the stairs leading to a raised reception area. Soldiers lined the fortress walls, overseeing their safety.

Thousands had quickly thronged to line the streets and fill the grounds.

"Our country has gathered," Eunice said with awe.

Wron inhaled deeply. The response of his countrymen was overwhelming.

"They have been waiting as long as you." His mother patted his arm.

"Where are Dory and Ivan?" He searched the sea of faces. "You'd think they'd see the commotion."

"They'll find us." Chin lifted, his mother smiled. "I hope she flushed one."

"Mother!" As the large procession approached, Wron's lungs filled with air. Beautiful dark horses pulled a stately white carriage. If they were counterfeits, they'd invested a lot of money. Over two hundred men on horseback accompanied his future bride. The blue-and-white uniforms of his future countrymen rode into view.

He felt torn, divided. But, now was not the time to think about himself.

"Roger, for our safety, please greet them," his father said.

"Perhaps it's another counterfeit," Wron said. "Where is Dory?" He scanned the crowd. How had the people gathered so quickly?

"Wron, it's only three days until your birthday," his mother said. "Of course it's Princess Alia."

Of all times for Dory to go hunting. He sighed.

Roger strode up the walkway toward them, carrying what appeared to be a white handkerchief. "Ambassadors of Blue Sky have escorted Princess Alia. They are extremely fatigued from their long journey, but the princess desires to meet her future husband." Bowing slightly, Roger presented the folded handkerchief to Wron.

"From your future bride."

On the corner edge, embroidered into the cloth was a gold crown with one blue jewel—the Blue Sky emblem. "Where is Dory?"

"Here, give that to me"—his mother held out her hand—"before you toss it."

"Escort them to the commons. After they have freshened up and eaten, we'll meet them in the Great Hall." Wron nodded to Roger.

"No!" His father overruled him. "I have been waiting for this day for sixteen years. Roger, escort the princess to us now."

"Father!" Wron sighed. "You are too trusting. Where is Dory?"

"Escort the princess." His father's face flushed.

Roger disappeared through the crowd.

Both Blue Sky and Yonder soldiers addressed the people. "You must make way. Make way for the princess."

A red carpet was unrolled from the foot of the carriage. Two Blue Sky soldiers nudged it over one hundred feet before it stopped one foot shy of Wron's polished boots.

"They thought of everything." Again he searched the sea of faces for the woman he knew he did not want to live without. "Where are you, Dory?" he whispered.

The carriage door was opened, and Princess Alia emerged from the carriage. A hush fell over the crowd. Her future countrymen and women bent to their knees and watched as she, with the assistance of a wide-girthed guard, began her descent from the carriage. Her head bobbed down and then up, as if she were stuck.

He chuckled. The counterfeits had found a young woman who could obviously not walk in high heels. Blue Sky soldiers suddenly surrounded the carriage, and for a brief moment, he could not see the princess. Wron instinctively took a step forward.

The soldiers cleared. The princess now gripped the arm of a wiry-built man with gray hair, and they began their walk toward them.

"Oh, they're bowing." His mother's voice broke as she began to cry.

The sight of his countrymen bowing to someone who was most likely a counterfeit greatly saddened him. In his absence, his parents had rushed ahead, ill advised.

He was reminded of the first night Dory had arrived in Yonder. Cragdon had greeted her at her camp. From the glow of her fire, she'd been filthy. Her clothes thickly soiled. But the uniforms of tonight's Blue Sky's soldiers were . . . Shaking his head, he turned to his parents. "Look at their uniforms! They're too clean! They have just traveled for over a month."

"Perhaps they changed in Delfrey." His father, calmly, rocked back and forth heel-toe, heel-toe.

"Father, I will not be fooled. We will wait for Dory's opinion."

"You are jumping to conclusions, Wron. You must trust my intuition this time. Princess Alia has arrived."

Dropping his shoulders, Wron sighed.

Through the sea of blue-and-white uniforms, the princess stepped closer. Princess Alia was dressed in an opulent blue gown, and her auburn hair was spiraled high above her head. Tendril curls framed her face. The young woman carried herself with grace as she and her father moved toward him.

Around them, the crowd hushed, spellbound by her beauty.

Where are you, Dory? He took one last look toward the distant hills.

He reminded himself that Princess Alia's eyes were hazel. He looked about the crowd once more for Ivan's large form, for Dory returning with her shotgun in hand, before his entire attention beheld the princess.

They stopped ten feet away from him, and the man posing as her father kissed her cheek before the beautiful young woman walked the remaining distance toward Wron.

As she stopped before him, he saw that her eyes were indeed hazel. And yes, she and Dory were of the same height. He felt sadly dumbstruck as she held out a white-gloved hand.

Instead of taking it, he bowed slightly. "Our customs are different, Princess Alia" were his first words to her. "In Yonder kingdom, a woman extends her right hand for the greeting kiss, not her left."

The princess smiled softly and nodded. She appeared hesitant, perhaps shy. In the back of his mind, he recalled that Dory had once said, *Alia is not shy.*

"As in Yonder tradition, will you please extend your right hand to me now . . . to show my people that you will soon be one of theirs."

The young woman retracted her hand. She glanced past him, perhaps to his mother or father, before her gaze settled on his.

"I cannot extend my right hand, Prince Wron," she said, and her voice carried the familiar Blue Sky accent. "To do so would prove very painful for me."

He looked about the crowd one last time for Dory before he sadly gave Princess Alia his entire attention. "Why is that?" He shook his head slightly.

"Because, Prince Wron"—she held his gaze and smiled softly—"I, Princess Alia . . . *Dory* Vankern Wells, am also . . . your Dory."

At the mention of Dory's name, he glanced sadly up at the stars before he let his eyes lower to hers. *It couldn't be! It couldn't possibly be.* He let his gaze linger on the beautiful young woman before him before he turned to his parents.

Behind a sheen of tears, his father nodded.

"Yes." His mother nodded. "Alia is our Dory." Gripping her hands tightly beneath her chin, she continued nodding.

He stepped closer and stared into the young woman's hazel eyes and briefly touched the smoothness of her cheek. "There are similarities." Gently, he smoothed back the right sleeve of her gown to see the ugly deep purple-and-brown scab below her collarbone.

She'd almost died.

Gently lifting her chin, he leaned down and glimpsed the heart-shaped mark beneath. "Has it been there all this time?"

"Since the day I was born." Tears shone in her eyes.

"Why didn't you tell me?" He swallowed deep emotion.

Her gaze lowered. "At first there was the pox . . . my father's absence, the fear of being abandoned in the hills. It's a long story, Prince Wron, but I had my reasons."

"It's too much to take in." He sighed and lifted a hand to caress her cheek. Stepping closer, he gently took her into his arms and gazed into her sparkling eyes.

For a long, treasured moment, their countries watched as their future king and queen—two people very much in love—officially met for the first time.

"Onderyay!"

Chapter Thirty-Three

After a piece of Rhoda's delicious peach pie and a family celebration, Wron and I met as planned by the fire. Seated with our backs against a large log, Wron pulled a small box from his pocket. "I've carried this all afternoon." He smiled, looking at me. "I bought you a gift in Delfrey."

He held the velvet box for me while I tugged at the ribbon that bound it. Without another word between us, I lifted the lid and stared at a rare jade ring. A wave of emotion passed over me as I recalled Greda's words.

May your kindness return do you.

Wron pulled the smooth stone ring out for me and held it up to the moonlight. "If you look closely, inside, there are two inscriptions."

"Where did you say you found it?" I sighed, leaning against him.

"At a merchant's in Delfrey. A trader I see every now and again." He glanced down at me. "There are two inscriptions, because I added one."

"Let me guess the first." I looked up at the starlit sky. "It reads A-D-W."

"How did you know?" My beloved stared amazed at me.

"A-D-W stands for Alia Dory Vankern Wells. Vankern is my mother's maiden name, and it is just like my father to leave that initial out." I smiled. "He gave me this ring the morning I turned sixteen, and I in turn gave it to Sadie's mother."

"What?" His brows gathered.

"Sadie's home was Felix's and my first stop on our way here. Their need was far greater than my own. I'll tell you about Sadie someday . . . maybe tomorrow."

Happy with the world, I nuzzled closer in Wron's embrace. "What did you inscribe?"

He kissed my forehead. "My words are simple: 'Forever Dory.' I wanted you to know that though I will marry Princess Alia for my country, I would never forget my memories of you."

Wron slid the ring on my wedding ring finger, and as I gazed into my beloved's eyes, he kissed me for the second time.

The End.

Sign up for new releases on Sherri's website:
www.christianromances.com

In 2016, I hope to release the next book in the *Counterfeit Princess Series*. It will be about Alia's sister, Wren.

Acknowledgements:

My daughter, Cori, has nudged me through the years to get this novel done before she's a full-fledged adult. Thank you, Cori, for all your help and encouragement.

This book took a village. A thank you to my editors: our family friend, Kristi Weber, for catching so many of my commas and grammar issues; and my editor Carolyn Ingermanson, for her expertise and attention to detail.

To my writing group—Randy, Patty, John, Lydia and Traci—you are such a blessing to me.

And, lastly a thank you to Wil Nuygen. He wrote numerous reference books about Gnomes. See the *Gnomes Deluxe Collector's Edition* for a fun read.

See the following pages for
Two of Rhoda's Recipes

Rhoda's Giant Cakes
also known as Dutch Babies

Make sure you proofread the recipe, and have an adult help you with the hot pans. This is an easy recipe, and my children have enjoyed making them for years.

2 Tablespoons butter
4 eggs, well beaten
2/3 cup milk
2/3 cup flour
¼ teaspoon salt

Important: You'll need: two glass 9 or 10-inch pie plates. They have to be glass for the cakes to climb the sides. The cakes will be puffy when you first pull them out of the oven, and then they'll fall a bit.

Preheat the oven to 400' F.

1. Divide the 2 tablespoons of butter into two glass 9-inch pie plates—one tablespoon in each pan—and slide into the oven. (The warm pans help the batter rise more.)

2. In a medium-sized bowl, whisk the eggs until yellow and frothy. Add the rest of the ingredients and whisk until well combined.

3. Keep an eye on the butter in the oven. When it is thoroughly melted, carefully remove the glass pans from the oven using potholders. Swirl the butter around in the pan until it covers the bottom. Pour the batter into the pans and return to the oven for 12-16 minutes. Oven temperatures vary.

The cakes will rise a lot, and the edges will get golden brown while the center stays a glossy yellow. Make sure that the center of the cake has finished cooking. But, don't over-bake, or the edges will taste dry.

Serve with warm maple syrup and your favorite fruit—peaches, strawberries, bananas . . .

Say a prayer and thank the good Lord above that you're not having dribbly porridge.

Note: This recipe also works great for gluten free folks. Substitute your favorite GF flour in place of the wheat flour. The batter doesn't rise, but the finished pancake is still yummy. My oldest daughter is gluten free; and she loves this recipe.

Rhoda's Peach Cream Pie

Read through the recipe first. This is an easy pie to make, if you follow each step. There are three steps to this recipe: the crust, filling and topping. You'll need a good size pie plate to fit all of the ingredients. This pie is amazing with fresh peaches, yet also delicious with canned peaches. This pie is best slightly warm. This recipe is from Marci Kulla, a royal friend.

For the easy Crust:

1 ½ cups flour

½ teaspoon salt

½ cup butter, cold

Preheat oven to 400' F.

Mix the flour and salt together with a whisk. Cut the butter into the flour, using a pastry blender. Press the mixture into the bottom of a 10 inch pie plate and up the sides.

For the Filling:

1 cup sugar

3 Tablespoons flour

¼ teaspoon salt

1 egg

½ teaspoon vanilla

1 cup sour cream

4 cups sliced fresh peaches

In a medium-sized bowl, combine all the ingredients, folding peaches in last. Pour into the crust. **Bake at 400°F. for 15 minutes**, and then **reduce the oven temperature to 350°F. and bake 20 minutes more** <u>before</u> adding the following topping.

For the Topping:
1/3 cup sugar
1 teaspoon cinnamon
1/3 cup flour
¼ cup butter

Whisk together the sugar, cinnamon and flour. Using the pastry blender, cut the butter into the dry ingredients and mix until crumbly. Sprinkle over pie. **Bake for an additional 10 minutes**. The pie should not be jiggly in the center. Using hot-pads, remove the pie from the oven and set on a cooling rack. Wait at least 40 minutes before serving. This pie is delicious served warm with fresh whipped cream or vanilla ice cream.

Afterwards, make sure you tidy up the kitchen, and no food fights! Sorry, it's the mom in me.

Christian Romances by
Sherri Schoenborn Murray:

*Fried Chicken and Gravy – young adult and adult
Sticky Notes - adult*

God bless you!